Dead to Her

ALSO BY SARAH PINBOROUGH

Cross Her Heart

Behind Her Eyes

Dead to Her

A Novel

Sarah Pinborough

HARPER LARGE PRINT
An Imprint of HarperCollinsPublishers

An excerpt from the song "Runs in the Family" taken from the album *Who Killed Amanda Palmer*. Lyrics by Amanda Palmer.

HarperCollins books may be purchased for educational, business, or sales promotional use. For information, please e-mail the Special Markets Department at SPsales@harpercollins.com.

FIRST HARPER LARGE PRINT EDITION

ISBN: 978-0-06-297889-9

Library of Congress Cataloging-in-Publication Data is available upon request.

20 21 22 23 24   LSC   10 9 8 7 6 5 4 3 2 1

For the real Marcie and Jason (and their cat collective . . .)
With much love.

Dead to Her

PART ONE

Hell is empty, and all the devils are here . . .

THE TEMPEST

1.

The candle burns.
   Crisp paper. A pen.
WHAT HAPPENED TO JONNY?
Envelope.
Seal.
Whisper.
Wait.

2.

You can't tame a wild thing.

The thought bubbled up from someplace deep inside Marcie, a ripple in the stagnant water that had become her life. She could feel Eleanor's appraising eyes on the guests, looking down from the gilt-framed portrait that still hung on the staircase wall, overshadowing them all. Dead less than a year. What would she make of this turn of events?

A hubbub of quietly spoken comments from the tight circle of people among whom Marcie stood fluttered in the warm air. Elsewhere, the tension of repressed snickers and sideways glances.

"Well my, will you look at that."

"The old dog."

"Has he lost weight? Sure doesn't look like a man ready to retire."

"I didn't know what I was expecting, but she is something . . . else."

"And so young."

She was young, this newcomer among them, this second Mrs. William Radford IV. What, twenty-two? Younger? Twenty-three at the most. Eleanor had been forty years older than that when she died.

"There's no fool like an old fool." Iris. Ever dry. Eleanor's close friend since they'd been young together a different world ago. It was Iris who'd done her best to keep Eleanor the elegant Savannah belle she'd long been, even when the cancer had ravaged her to skeletal. By the end her makeup was so thick Marcie had thought Eleanor looked like Baby Jane, but what could she say? She'd said the same as everyone else did, My, you're looking so well, Eleanor. Always so lovely. Can I fetch you a sweet tea?

This new wife, though, this black second wife, was ravishing, not ravaged. Her skin shone with health and strength. She was sleek and proud with strong, slim limbs and perfect curves at hip and bust. Hair, straightened and glossy, was pulled back tight. A small belly that promised a steak indulgence rather than a rabbit salad. The kind of belly men loved in women and women hated in themselves.

She came down the sweeping stairway smiling, with her chin held high, eyes alight with pride as if the man on her arm were a handsome movie star, not a sixty-five-year-old with vein-purple cheeks, who may have lost some weight, but on whom years of indulgence had taken their toll. William Radford IV was the epitome of indulged; wasn't that why they were all there after all?

Neither bride nor groom looked toward the painting of the last wife, whose influence lay like a film all over the magnificent house.

Eyes scanned the new wife's gold dress—Versace maybe—figure hugging, but an inch too short for this society crowd. The heels—half an inch too high. The jewelry, thick coils around her neck and hanging from her ears, impressive but attention-seeking. All the women—nearly all over fifty—would be making the same assessment: *she's not one of us.* Marcie knew how that felt.

"Her name's Keisha." Elizabeth bustled over, dragging Marcie's attention away. Staid office wear had been abandoned for the night in favor of a green dress that looked new—although certainly *not* Versace. Elizabeth's short, dark, curly hair, run through with wiry gray, had been fluffed up so she looked like an aging poodle. Did Elizabeth feel it too? This frisson of excitement—of change? Their feathers being ruffled by the sudden arrival of this cuckoo?

"She's just turned twenty-two and is from London," Elizabeth continued, leaning in closer, eyes twinkling with as yet unspilled gossip, happy to have snippets of information to share that might make her feel part of the set. There was a fondness for her, but it was the kind of affection you might give an old dog simply because it always wanted to please you.

Elizabeth might have been Eleanor's assistant forever—and then William's when Eleanor got too sick—but she was still only *staff.* William said she was *family,* but Marcie knew better. *Real* family mattered in this circle of friends. Your blood. How far back your name went. There was pride in history. Elizabeth had no eminent cotton or sugar ancestry and no style. She'd been stillborn into the waters of this society.

"That's where they met: London. Four months ago. A whirlwind romance. William wanted to keep their early return as a surprise, but someone had to get them home and arrange all this." Elizabeth wafted a hand around as if she'd been spending her own money on the occasion. "He swore me to secrecy. But thank the lord for Julian and Pierre. They truly do organize the best parties." She smiled again.

"Here come the happy couple," Emmett muttered—William was always going to bring her to them first, his best friends, the club set—and then it was a flurry of exclamations and smiles and wafts of perfume as each of the women leaned in to air kiss the pair. Marcie, the other second wife, the older second wife, took a few involuntary steps backward as the rest crowded in. Close up, Keisha was even more magnificent. Her skin was a deep rich brown. She glowed. Eleanor had glowed once too.

Marcie watched her friends chirruping their joy—*the queen is dead, long live the queen*—vying to be the happiest at the new union. Iris, birdlike and papery old, but elegantly preserved, and her husband, Noah, the judge, portly, red-faced, and yet somewhat regal, the two of them cornerstones of Savannah society. Virginia, constantly smiling, her body starved to slim but her full face, under her Stepford wife blowout, forever betraying the larger size her God had meant her to be. She was a stalwart of the church, where she was adored almost as much as Jesus himself for the size of her charitable donations. Beside her was her foppish husband, Emmett, slight and short and impeccably dressed. Also somewhere in his midfifties, he brokered various stocks and shares to pretend to himself that he didn't simply while away his life on inherited wealth, using the club as an easy pool for investors.

Sometimes, in the increasingly frequent bad moods that struck when this life threatened to suffocate her, Marcie wondered if she'd reach menopause early just by being around so much middle age. But now, in the wake of poor Eleanor's demise, here was youth among them, a shard of obsidian glistening in the staid, patted-down chalk. Freshness. Excitement.

And *twenty-two*. Four years younger than Marcie had been when she'd met Jason. An affair, a year or so of melodrama, an unpleasant divorce—*goodbye, Jacquie*—and by twenty-nine, *she* had been the young second wife taking careful steps to find her place in this world.

Now she was nearly thirty-five, with Jason coming up on fifty-three, and she was cemented—stuck—into the set. But Jason wasn't like the others in many ways. Not *quite* of the same stock, even though his family had been around for generations. And then there was the business with his father. He'd had to rise above that; no mean feat in this world. He'd crawled back onto the social ladder while married to Jacquie. It was something they had in common, this tenacity to achieve *more*, and Marcie was determined they'd keep climbing. She looked at the chattering, gushing wealth embodied in her friends. How wonderful it must be to be born an Iris or a William, when people hung on your every word, wanted to please you. Royalty. Shame they didn't have anything of note to say, but then they didn't have to.

She glanced toward Jason, wanting to share a quick secret smile at the ridiculousness of all this, but her husband's eyes were on Keisha. Marcie watched as his hand half-stroked the young woman's bare arm when he leaned in to kiss her cheek, as if he couldn't resist touching her.

Unlike the women's, this was no air kiss. Did his lips linger against Keisha's flawless skin a fraction too long? He wasn't smiling, not amusedly dazzled like the others, and she noted his Adam's apple dipping as he swallowed. She knew that look too well. *Lust.* It was the way he'd looked at her in the first heat after they'd met. He hadn't looked at her like that for a while. She felt her stomach constrict, her champagne suddenly sour.

Once a cheat, always a cheat.

"Jason, introduce your wife, where are your manners? Oh, these boys . . ."

"Yes, Marcie, what are you doing back there? Come on in!"

"Marcie?"

For a moment she didn't even recognize her own name, still feeling the sting of that heated expression in Jason's eyes, and then the huddle parted as William's thick fingers touched her arm and she automatically smiled, all worry hidden away.

"Congratulations," she said softly. "I'm so happy for you." She turned to Keisha, tall and glorious in front of her, suddenly feeling old. "And, of course, lovely to meet you."

Their eyes stayed locked for a second or two too long, rich, deep brown on her watery blue, and Marcie knew she was being appraised—judged—in a way the other wives hadn't been. They were in a different age bracket. They weren't competition. But maybe Marcie wasn't so old, after all.

"I feel like I already know you all." Keisha's English accent was hard and clipped; strangely captivating. *You all.* Two words. Even Marcie now automatically drawled them together in that Southern liquid way. "Billy's talked about you so much."

Billy? Eleanor would turn in her grave. William Radford IV was no one's Billy. Or at least he hadn't been. Times were changing. Keisha turned her attention back to Jason. "Especially you. The great Jason Maddox, the brains of the firm and all-round great guy. I hope you don't disappoint." She winked, flirtatious and friendly, at ease with being the center of attention, and then laughed, a surprisingly brash sound, or perhaps just uninhibited, and they all dutifully joined in, a tinkling of politeness. When Jason winked back at the new star in their firmament, Marcie wasn't sure if she wanted to rip this breathtaking woman's eyes out or go and scream in a corner.

"I know this has all been sudden and you may think we're crazy." William took two glasses of champagne from a passing waiter, handing one to his new bride, and then letting his fingers slide down to the curve of her back. "But when you know, you know. Keisha brought life back into my heart. I didn't think that was possible."

"You didn't want to take the other six months as a honeymoon?" Jason asked, at last looking at William. "You were so adamant you were going for a year."

"Plans change, Jason. Plans change. And how could I stay away from my wonderful friends for so long?"

"Well, I know you're retiring but . . ."

"No work tonight." William slapped Jason hard—maybe a little too hard—on the arm. "Now come on, let's go eat. I want Keisha to see what she's been missing out on over there in London." He leaned into Jason. "And I should thank you. If you hadn't told me all the best places to go on my trip, I'd never have found her."

As they walked away, friends following in their wake, Marcie noticed that this time it was William who

Jason was watching. A dark, thoughtful expression. Maybe Keisha was upsetting the apple cart for both of them.

Once the champagne and cocktails had washed away their polite shock and the band had struck up on the terrace, the party turned out to be less of a bore than Marcie had been expecting. The guests kicked off their shoes and danced in the night air, care for expensive dresses forgotten, and even Iris and Noah took a turn on the grass. As they swayed, Marcie thought she caught a glimpse of ghosts of the teenage sweethearts they'd once been.

Marcie watched as Jason chatted loudly to some of the other guests. She couldn't get the look he'd given Keisha out of her head. He'd been pulling away for a few months, but she'd put it down to work—the responsibility of running the partnership while William was away, gearing up to take the next step of buying him out.

Their sex life had dwindled down to occasional drunken screws and she wondered if those were only to fulfill his need for a child, an heir, a social accessory they could send to County Day and expand their affluent network.

Looking at him now, the same questions swirled in

her head as they had for weeks. Had he grown bored with her? Was she a challenge completed? Now, here, in that look that whispered thoughts of betrayal, there had been the first clear fracture in the structure of their marriage. She'd never seen him look at another woman that way. Never.

Keisha had come to join them once or twice, increasingly unsteady on her feet but still trying to twirl and shimmy to the music, head thrown back, laughing that raucous, fascinating sound. She lingered too close to where Jason and Marcie were sharing a lounger later in the evening, and although Jason did snatch the occasional glance her way, if Keisha was looking for further flirtation she was disappointed. But still, that look. William, following constantly in his young wife's shadow, finally led her away and they didn't see her again. Given her state, he probably had Zelda, his housekeeper, put her to bed.

Virginia was all raised eyebrows, even though she wasn't beyond having one or two drinks too many when the mood took her, church or no church, but Iris pointed out that it must be hard to move across the world and be expected to live up to someone like Eleanor when you were so completely different. *Completely different.* What she meant was young, crude, and, the most unspoken word of all, *black*. Anyway, Keisha hadn't seemed awkward, just a drunk girl who didn't care what people thought of her because she'd just won the jackpot. A rich old man. Still, it wasn't a prize Marcie would want to win. The thought of William heaving away on top of her . . . God, no wonder Keisha had been draining the champagne and flirting with *her* husband.

3.

She and Jason finally got home around one, and before they'd even turned on the lights he was kissing her, catching her by surprise.

"You wanna have another go at making a baby?" He grinned, his mouth all lopsided charm, made somehow more attractive by the beer haze in his eyes, and before Marcie could answer he was pulling her up the stairs and tugging at her clothes. She couldn't help laughing. Yes, he was drunk, but she wasn't exactly sober herself and it was good to feel him wanting her again. To be close to him. To be something like they were before. Maybe she was wrong to worry earlier. Keisha was beautiful, but he loved her, his *wife*.

They fell on the bed, only half-naked, a mess of panting urgency. She sought out his eyes in the gloom as he pushed her arms over her head, holding her wrists down with one hand. She tried to nuzzle at his face to get him to look at her, to kiss her. With Marcie's legs gripping his waist, he thrust himself inside her. She gasped—she always did, there had never been a man who could come close to Jason at turning her on—but his face stayed pressed into her shoulder, his breath dampening her skin as it quickened. *He's not with me.* The thought was a cold shower between her thighs. *He's not thinking of me.*

He finished fast and when he flopped over to his side of the bed, Marcie stayed breathless. It was one thing that they rarely fucked anymore, but until now, when they had, she'd always felt he was present. Not this time. Had he been thinking of *her?* It was nothing. It meant nothing. People fantasized all the time. She was overreacting. What was it about Keisha that unsettled her so?

"I love you," Jason said, perfunctorily, his hand reaching across and resting on her thigh.

"I know," she answered, and let out a chuckle she didn't feel. She couldn't make a thing of it. She wouldn't.

"Oh so funny, Mrs. Maddox." He let out a long, contented sigh. Marcie's heart was still racing.

"I think she likes you," she said, the words blurting out. At least she sounded mildly amused, not jealous or insecure. His eyes were no longer shut. He was staring at the ceiling.

"Who?"

"You know who!" Why hadn't she kept her mouth shut? She felt stupid. *Obvious.* "Keisha."

"Ah, *that* she." He stared at the ceiling a moment longer, expression unreadable in the dark, and then he rolled back on top of her, and smiled. "Your old man's still got it. You'd better work harder to keep me." He kissed her, slow and soft, and she kissed him back but she felt hollow. She'd worked hard enough to get him; she didn't want the rest of her life spent working hard to keep him. *Was he even worth it?*

Half an hour later, when he was sprawled out and snoring, Marcie got up and padded into her dressing room beyond the his-and-hers bathrooms. Under the glare of the light, she looked at herself. She remembered how proud the new Mrs. Radford had been coming down those stairs. How beautiful. The way she'd danced, so drunk. She didn't *care,* that was it. She reminded Marcie of someone she herself used to be a long time ago, back before she'd met Jason. Before she had entered this world.

When had she started to feel so small? Was it when the house—much as she adored their new home— got so big? Or was it after the boutique failed and they—Jason—quietly decided that a life in business wasn't for her? *No more expensive hobbies.* When had she stopped being hungry for excitement? When she'd become a good Southern wife? Was Keisha a reminder of all she'd given up for this life and was that why she felt so untethered around her?

Too much time for self-reflection, she decided as she opened her small chest of creams and toiletries.

She'd have to wait and see how it all panned out. No doubt Keisha would be in a nice prim dress and pearls—full submissive wife—before the first whisper of fall and Jason would be back to his normal charming, attentive self, she would make sure of it. Keisha was just a small bump, a momentary distraction. She was determined to get their marriage back on track; after all, wasn't this all she'd ever wanted?

The thought didn't bring her as much comfort as she expected. Was she angry at Jason for getting bored with her because she knew deep down that she, in turn, was growing bored with him? Maybe this *had* been what she wanted, but that was before she'd gotten it. Now her wants had changed. She was tired of being so goddamned dependent. *Grateful.* Even so wealthy, she felt like a second-class citizen. The other wives might tolerate her, but she didn't have any of their *respect,* and these days she wasn't even sure she had Jason's. She'd hoped money would bring that, to finally be a *person of merit,* no longer looked down on, but apparently it wasn't enough.

You wanna have another go at making a baby?

The thought of bringing a child into this made her stomach tense. If they divorced and she was saddled with a kid, then what? No man here would want her with baggage.

She worried at her lip as she looked in the mirror. Making sure the door was locked, she carefully pulled away the inner lining of her vanity case and took out the strip of pills hidden inside. She stared long and hard in the mirror and her eyes hardened as she popped one free.

No, Marcie thought, looking up at the air-conditioning grille on the ceiling as she swallowed the secret contraceptive. *No, I don't want to make a fucking baby.*

4.

Marcie wished they'd had this late lunch at the house rather than on Iris and Noah Cartwright's boat moored at the end of the jetty. Perhaps then she wouldn't be forcing a smile through her nausea from the slight movement of the creek beneath them. Although it was a still day the air was humid and heavy with the endless heat suffocating the city, and even the water was lazy in its wake. Iris knew Marcie got motion sickness, but Noah loved his boat and they always entertained on it in the summer. It was a tradition and it had been clear from the start that they wouldn't change for Marcie.

"You have to get used to it," Jason had said when they'd first gotten married. "Water's in the veins as much as blood here. We grow up on it. But I guess you're all landlubbers back in Boise, Idaho." He'd smiled as he teased her and she'd wanted to point out that they had water in Boise too, but he wouldn't have cared. That was one thing she and Keisha had in common. They were both from *elsewhere*. Boise could be as far away as London. Only the South mattered. In the main, Marcie liked it that way.

At least this would be the last of the boat for a while. Noah and Iris were going away to the Hamptons to visit their beloved daughter, Heather. The only girl out of their four children. She was a few years older and frumpier than Marcie, and had just had their latest grandson, whose name Marcie couldn't remember even though she'd dutifully bought gifts of booties, baby gowns, and bears for him and gushed over photos. Babies all looked the same to her and given Jason's recent thirst to reproduce she was always happier when the subject changed.

She leaned her head against her husband's broad shoulder and breathed slowly as the queasy moment passed. Across the table Keisha clearly wasn't bothered by the movement of the water. She had a half-empty margarita in one hand while biting into a plump king prawn plucked from the platter of iced seafood in the middle of the table. It wasn't her first. She ate with gusto while Marcie, Iris, and Virginia sipped chardonnay and let their stomachs gnaw on their own linings.

Iris occasionally fed Midge, their old black cat, a fishy tidbit as if it made up for her barely eating herself.

"They don't come like this in Tesco," Keisha said, and Virginia, still primly dressed from church, laughed, although she probably didn't know what Tesco was any more than Marcie did. Keisha was wearing a thin summer dress and as she leaned over to kiss William on the cheek with her wet glossy lips, the curves of her breasts were clearly visible. Jason had his aviators on, and when Marcie glanced his way—*was he looking?*—all she could see was her own distorted face reflected back at her.

Keisha showed no signs of a hangover from the previous night's party; if anything, she was still glowing with health, but William looked tired. *Poor old fool.* Marcie heard the words in Eleanor's voice. Always so forgiving of her man.

"More wine, Virginia?" Noah refilled the glasses, wine never in short supply here, and Virginia took it gratefully. She'd had an *exhausting* morning at the church, she'd told them. So much to help with. Charity events to organize. She was alone; Emmett had a prior engagement with some investment client. The number of times he took meetings on Sundays was a clue to everyone bar his wife that he wasn't as keen on prayer as Virginia. Marcie imagined that the endless hours of fund-raising and work at the homeless refuge that filled her hours could grate very quickly.

"I called you this morning, William," Jason said. "Zelda told me you were on the treadmill."

"She didn't mention it."

"It wasn't important. But jogging? I've never known you to do more than stroll around the golf course."

Jason had called William? Marcie hadn't known that. When? Had she been in the shower? Had he hidden himself in one of the many empty rooms in their new house? Why would he need to speak to William on a Sunday morning when he knew they'd be seeing each other later? A thought curled like dark smoke. Had he been hoping Keisha would answer maybe?

"Never too late to get in shape," William said. "My new routine. Up early, down to the treadmill, and then a coconut water to raise my energy. I tell you, I feel twenty years younger."

"Are you sure that's the jogging?" Iris, ever the dry wit, raised an overplucked eyebrow and glanced at Keisha.

"She sure helps," William conceded, and everyone smiled. Marcie tried to imagine him on the running machine. It wasn't a pretty image. The state-of-the-art home gym had been Eleanor's and she'd used it religiously. Fat lot of good it had done her in the end.

"Do you jog too?" Marcie asked. She imagined Keisha in tight gym gear and regretted asking the question immediately. That was not an image she wanted in Jason's mind.

"No, I'm a night owl. Nothing wakes me before ten. Sometimes even midday. But I'm trying to change. I know I've married an early bird."

Marcie couldn't imagine Keisha changing. Conforming. But then *she* had. It was amazing how you could contain yourself—imprison yourself—if you really tried. If you loved someone. She looked down at her sweet summer dress from that new expensive little boutique on Broughton that all the club wives loved so much. Cuff sleeves, buttons down the front, deck shoes on her feet. Six or seven years ago she'd have been wearing cutoff denim shorts that showed the curve of her ass and wouldn't be seen dead in something as *old* as this. Probably why her own store had failed. She hadn't known back then how sedately her customer base dressed. Well, that and all the bad-mouthing from Jason's ex-wife. Marcie should have let the dust settle before trying to do something for herself. Now she was trapped in expensive cotton and reliant on her husband's credit card.

"Although I draw the line at coconut water," Keisha continued. "It's disgusting. Tastes like sperm. No wonder Billy drains the carton in one go." Iris nearly choked on her wine at that. Combined with the appalled look on William's face and the flush on Noah's, Marcie couldn't help but laugh. Jason joined in and then so did Iris.

"I'm so sorry! I have no filter!"

Keisha clapped a hand over her mouth, her eyes suddenly nervous as they glanced at William. For a moment he looked like he might implode and then, seeing that his friends weren't offended, his face relaxed slightly into a taut grin.

"I'll take your word for it on the taste." He squeezed her knee, and looking at his fat white hand on Keisha's young dark skin made Marcie think of that English king, the one with all the wives she'd watched the TV show about. Old and fat and with a beautiful young girl he believed loved him. Didn't end well for the women, if she remembered correctly.

"It's so hot," Keisha said, when the titters stopped. She leaned back in her chair and looked out over the water. "And muggy."

"Welcome to the South," Noah drawled. He'd been virtually dozing for the past hour or so, an old beached walrus splayed on his seat, but now he picked up a piece of corn bread and tore away a corner to eat despite Iris's side eye. Noah could do with losing more than a pound or two himself. "Storms that come in fast and clear away as quick. Heat that clings to you like a needy child."

"You'll learn to move slower," Virginia added, fanning herself with a coaster. "In this weather you don't get a choice."

"Oh, I love it. I can feel my whole body relaxing. But," Keisha said, unfurling from her chair like a languid cat, "I also can't resist the water." She kissed William, chaste on the cheek, and then her shoulders were slipping free of her sundress, which slid to the floor, revealing a string bikini beneath it.

"I'm going in!" She was already pushing the ladder over the edge and climbing over the side, oblivious to the eyes on her body, William calling her back, and the look of disapproval on Virginia's face as she declared, "Oh my!"

Keisha jumped from the boat's edge, arms in the air, a whoop of joy carrying her down into the splash, and by the time the others were on their feet and at the railing she was breaking the surface, treading water, face full of delight.

"Be careful!" Noah called, leaning over the side. "We get 'gators sometimes!"

Keisha ignored him and ducked under the water again, childlike in her joy.

"She's quite the live wire, isn't she?" Iris said, but there was no hint of disapproval. If anything, she sounded surprisingly impressed. What would Eleanor make of her best friend embracing her replacement so quickly?

"She needs to learn to control her urges," William grumbled.

"Oh, she's just young," Iris said. "So much energy. I can see why she caught your eye, William."

Marcie could see why Keisha had caught William's eye written all over Jason's face. He'd pushed his glasses on top of his head and was looking down at the glittering water and the woman in it. Marcie slid her arm through his, the feel of his cotton shirt and the taut arm under it both familiar and exciting, but he didn't respond. It was as if she wasn't even there.

Keisha, squinting in the sun, one arm shading her eyes, was looking up at him. "You guys should come in! I dare you!" No one said a word, and Marcie, hot and queasy, thought how nice it would be to strip to her underwear and jump from the godawful boat, but she wasn't a *novelty* like Keisha, the new pet, the unreal girl in their midst, and Virginia would have it all around the club that Marcie Maddox was basically naked on Judge Cartwright's boat and trying to compete with William Radford's gorgeous new wife.

"Never mind the alligators," Keisha said. "I'm surrounded by chickens!"

William looked around the group, disgruntled and in no shape to strip and swim in the creek. "I've done my exercise for the day. One of you will have to entertain my wife." His eyes fell on Jason, who, as if he needed no more encouragement, pulled his arm free from Marcie's and started to unbutton his shirt.

"What are you doing?"

"What does it look like I'm doing? Someone has to go in."

"This isn't the office," Marcie hissed. "You don't have to do what William says."

"Until he officially retires I do. It's fine. Don't make a deal of it."

Marcie bit her lip. She *wasn't* making a deal of it. She just didn't see why it had to be him. "Maybe I should go in instead."

"Don't be stupid. You hate the creek. And I'm half-undressed now." He was unzipping his pants, kicking them away and leaving just his black Calvin Klein shorts, a trail of dark coarse hair spreading from his flat stomach up across his broad tanned chest. How must he look to Keisha next to William? *Desirable.*

She caught Virginia's sharp eyes registering her displeasure and she quickly turned her frown into the grimace of a smile as they joined the others.

"I'd go in myself," she said, "but I'm not wearing

any panties." No one laughed, all watching Jason as he dived over the side, splashing Keisha and making her squeal. "I'm kidding." Marcie picked up her glass from the table and leaned over the railing. "Of course I'm wearing underwear." She was smarting. If Keisha had said it, they'd all have found it funny. What was so different?

She drank some more wine, large swallows, as they gathered, crows on a wire, observers of the sport below. Jason ducked beneath the surface, invisible for what seemed liked forever as Keisha twisted around looking for him, and then, finally, she shrieked as he pulled at her feet.

"You bastard!"

He popped back up, laughing and coughing as she splashed water into his face. It was like watching teenagers. What was William thinking of this display? Jason was at home in the water in a way that Marcie never could be. She liked to see what was around her. The creek could be murky and that word, *alligator,* was never far from her thoughts. Keisha and the potential alligator merged in her mind, a predator waiting to consume her husband. She drank more wine, her thoughts hardening. Keisha might learn the hard way that Marcie was hardly prey herself.

As it was, Keisha didn't stay in the water much longer and was soon back on deck and wrapped in a robe Iris spirited up from a cabin below, yawning happily. Jason sat beside Keisha—*don't want to get creek water all over you, honey.* "You should have come in," she said to Marcie, all nice as pie. "Jason's like a fish, isn't he?"

Yes, slippery, she wanted to answer. "I prefer poolside to creek water. You never know what you'll catch in there."

"Or what will catch you," Virginia murmured with a smile. She'd been drinking steadily since she'd arrived and was now on the tipsy end of sober, her hamster cheeks shining in the heat. Was that a snipe? Hard to tell. Virginia was Marcie's friend because she and Emmett had known William forever, and so also, by default, Jason, but there were twenty years between the two women. Marcie could fake the church thing for the sake of appearances, showing up once a month or so and helping out at the soup kitchen, but she was never going to buy into God, whatever she put in the plate. Virginia, who could be so patronizing, but who'd never worked a day in her life.

No, maybe they weren't friends. Maybe they just tolerated her for Jason's sake. For all she knew they still spoke to Jacquie regularly. She looked at the beauty opposite her, fighting jet lag, but whose yawns were signaling the end of the afternoon. Keisha had a lot to learn about their set. Suddenly Marcie felt very alone. Out of place.

"Home time, I think," she murmured.

No one disagreed.

5.

It was with relief that Marcie closed the heavy front door behind them and stepped into the cool of their house, her sanctuary. Her head ached with the remnants of her seasickness, too much heat, and this awful fear that she was losing her grip on everything. Plus the wine, she conceded.

Even though it was still early all she wanted was a shower and to go to bed. The car ride had been quiet after she'd closed down any conversation Jason tried to start. His good mood had been bubbling over, his enjoyment of the afternoon in direct opposition to how dark she now felt.

Once a cheat, always a cheat. Thrill seekers seek thrills and that's all there is to it. Just be careful, dear.

The words still stung, said by a near-stranger, one of

Jacquie's friends, in the club's restroom when she and Jason first "came out" as a couple. Not long after the divorce Jacquie had met a retired orthopedic surgeon and moved to Atlanta. She no longer had *cheat* worries though. Her second husband had died of a massive heart attack not long before Eleanor passed away apparently. Jacquie was now off in Florida somewhere on an extended vacation on his insurance. It almost gave Marcie a pang of envy. All that freedom.

"I didn't know you'd called William this morning," she said, kicking off her shoes, the cold tiles delicious on her hot feet.

"Does it matter?"

"You didn't mention it, that's all. Is everything okay?"

"He wasn't due home until after Thanksgiving. I wanted to see if he was going back to work or not."

"Couldn't you have asked him this afternoon?" She got herself a glass of water and swallowed two Advil from the cupboard. This throbbing head wasn't helping her mood, and her stomach was tight, nervy. Did she want a fight? No, she didn't. So why was she pestering him?

"No business when socializing remember? William hates that. Anyway, why does it matter? What's wrong with you today? It was work."

"Like jumping in the creek was work."

There was a long pause after that and her heart raced. Finally, Jason put his beer bottle down on the counter and stared at her. "Why are you acting like this?"

She stared right back at him. "I think you *like* her."

"Don't be ridiculous." He looked so appalled she very nearly believed him, until he uttered the death knell of denial. "She's not my type."

The words were a slap in the face. He *did* want her. And not just in a *yeah, she's hot, I so would* jokey way.

"Really?" The word dripped from her, heavy with sarcasm.

"For God's sake, Marcie, am I never supposed to look at another woman, ever? Is that how you'd like me? Castrated?"

"That's not what I'm saying!" What was she saying? "This seems different, that's all. It makes me feel odd and I don't know why." She suddenly felt teary. She was making it worse.

"I don't want to sleep with her," Jason said, softened by her upset. "I just find her . . . refreshing, I guess."

"Refreshing?"

"You know"—he shrugged—"a bit wild. Young. Different from our friends."

Your friends is what she wanted to snap at him, but

she bit it back. They weren't Marcie's friends, they'd simply absorbed her into them. Scrubbed her up and made her respectable. She hadn't fought it because she loved him. She'd *allowed* it.

"I'm not boring," she said, and he burst out laughing.

"No," he said. "No, you're not. A bit crazy maybe, but not boring." He reached out and pulled her close, kissing the top of her head. A sterile kiss. "She's young, that's all," he breathed hot on her scalp. "Too young for me."

Thought no man ever.

Later that night when she snuck away to take her *no baby, thank you very much* pill and had locked the dressing-room door, she stood on her vanity chair and carefully removed the overhead vent cover. Up on her tiptoes she reached as far as she could and pulled out the small tin sandwich box she kept hidden there. She calmed a little just running her fingers over the surface.

Why was she feeling the need to look inside? *Keisha Keisha Keisha,* that was why. Remembering how Jason had looked at her in the water, how desperately eager he'd been to abandon Marcie and jump in to join her, Marcie wanted to kill him. It was what men never understood. The little disregards hurt the most. The shift from adoration to feeling comfortable. Taken for granted. Disrespected. She had never wanted that. She *didn't* want that. Her blood ran too hot in her veins.

She stared at the box. Her reminder of how far she'd come. Her anchor. Whenever this life she fought so hard for made her feel suffocated, all she needed was to look at the box. Yeah, life wasn't the perfection she'd hoped for, but things could be a lot, lot worse. She didn't need to open it to know that the first item, the one that covered all her other memories, was a photo of her and Jason, her arms around his neck, both laughing. *Free.* Back when they'd first met. When everything was passion and they'd have died for each other. God, how she missed that passion.

Thrill seekers seek thrills and that's all there is to it.

No, she thought, that's not true. People can change. People do change. Everything was going to be fine. Marcie and Jason Maddox were meant to be.

Weren't they?

6.

Keisha couldn't get back to sleep. She wished she could turn off the air-conditioning and feel the night heat, which might help soothe away the ants in her brain that were keeping her awake. The worries. The sense of isolation. The anxiety and dark muddled thinking that had plagued her since she was a child and now were threatening to return.

Her eyes kept glancing to the corner of the room where the shadows stretched longest. When she'd woken she'd been sure she'd seen him there. A ghostly boy emerging from the gloom, as if he'd followed her from her childhood and her dreams to this place so far away from home. She'd shivered, repeating the words that had been her mantra all her life—*there was no boy, there was no ghost*—until her breathing evened out.

Still though, she felt panicky, lying so still and awake in the night. Billy wouldn't sleep with a night-light on. He'd laughed at her when she'd asked him. He laughed at her a lot. Or shouted.

Don't fuck this up, she told herself. Fuck. Billy didn't like it when she swore and she'd tried hard not to speak like she had at home, where cursing was part of the vernacular. Despite the Egyptian cotton sheets, soft against her naked skin, she was consumed with a longing for home. The traffic noise, the dirt, the tiny flat on the tenth floor of a building where the lift mostly didn't work. Where the stairwells stank of piss and the corridors were filled with broken old people trying to hold on to their dignity in a changed, uncaring world, while teenagers tried to sell you crack.

Everything was different here, and not just the way of life and the quiet, still nights. In London, her family and all the other girls at the club had laughed at Billy's pathetic romantic overtures until they realized what he was worth and then it didn't matter that he was old and fat. Then they'd all made sure his pursuit of Keisha was serious. The dollar signs were lit up bright in everyone she knew.

Think of the money, her uncle Yahuba had said, eyes flashing sharp with endless greed. Dolly had said the same, teeth gritting with envy and all the other women nodding along. They were hard girls at the club, no goodness in them, grifters, *graspers*, making hundreds of pounds by night and none of them with the sense to save a penny. Smile, dance, and take the money. Drink your way through it. More fool the men.

But Keisha, Keisha with her odd moods and erratic behavior, had not been like that. The dancing she could do, the feeling of being lost in music under a spotlight, real life forgotten, but *not* the men, and so she'd become a drinks waitress, her tight clothing staying on, no hands allowed to paw at her. She certainly didn't do *afters*, even knowing she could have made so much more, enough to break free of her uncle's control perhaps, to pay her family back what they said she owed them for raising her, and then maybe enough to run somewhere even her awful dreams couldn't find her.

The air-conditioning clicked and started to hum again, the sound enough to keep her awake without the addition of Billy's sleeping pig grunts and snuffles beside her.

Her sleeping prince, her hero, she had hit the jackpot with him. *Her.* Everyone had seen. A rich lonely American widower. She'd have been stupid not to grab at it, and once her uncle and auntie had seen the gifts he'd bought her she'd had no choice. Back then, at the beginning, she hadn't even minded. Billy was kind. He was fragile almost. He was saving her and maybe she could help with his fear of being old. Dying. Rotting away like his first wife. He was a man who had been forced to look in the mirror and realize that time was no longer on his side.

Auntie Ayo had told him there would be no lingering cancer for him, after the long and awkward wedding celebration where Keisha had been forced to take him to Peckham and watch her relatives circling like sharks. They'd both drunk too much to get through it; Auntie Ayo said he wouldn't die in his own shit. People believed her, said she had a gift, a knowing—it shone through— and Billy was no exception, although Keisha could see that Auntie Ayo slightly scared him too.

He'd fallen for Keisha harder after that, seeing himself as her knight in shining armor saving her from her wicked relatives. He'd said she was his lucky charm. She made him feel young, as if there was clean new breath in his lungs, and she'd thought a life with Billy, even with everyone else clamoring for her to clean him out, could be good. An escape.

Her past wouldn't haunt her. Perhaps no more dreams of the boy who was never there, the ghost boy who cursed her. She couldn't wait to get here. But now she was living it, and everything was different.

He'd changed too, now that they were in this hot

alien place that was *his* comfort zone. He was shedding his lonely-widower skin.

"Don't ever embarrass me like that again," he'd said on the way back from the boat this afternoon, his warm smile dissolving as soon as they'd gotten in the car, his whole demeanor suddenly colder than any chill the AC could put out. "This isn't some trashy part of London, and my friends aren't your revolting family. You can't talk like that here." She was so stunned at the sudden shift in his mood—only seconds earlier he'd been holding her hand as they said their farewells—that it took her a moment to realize he'd meant her comment about the coconut water.

"Everyone laughed," she'd answered softly. "It was just a joke."

"You sounded like a whore." His words were bile, raw acid hitting her.

Only after she'd burst into startled tears, full of apologies, did he pat her on the knee, as if reassuring a scolded child, and tell her he loved her. It was a moment of revelation. Now that she'd married him, all the things he'd said wouldn't matter actually did. He was well respected. He had power. He didn't want to be embarrassed, not even by her. Maybe especially not by her. He wanted her to be perfect.

She took a deep breath. She could do this. *He'll be*

dead soon enough, Dolly had said when they'd hugged goodbye. *With you riding him every night.* They'd laughed at that too, but even the sex was harder work than she'd expected.

It went one of two ways. If he was feeling sweet and sentimental and hadn't taken a Viagra he simply labored for hours with his head between her thighs, checking she was happy, while she fantasized until she finally came or faked it like a porn star, her sex chafed from his crude mouth. Either way, she made sure she climaxed noisily. A man like William would never understand a true female orgasm. Quiet. Intense. Private. What validation would there be for him in that?

Then there was the *other* sex. The Viagra sex. Reclaiming his youth. All the things he'd never done with his saintly first wife he wanted to do now. With her. Of course she had to let him while finding the fine line between agreeing and not behaving like a *whore.* He wouldn't like that.

Tonight had been that kind of sex and she felt bruised and hollow. She wished her friends from the club— Dolly, Ange, and Sabena—were here. They'd know how to play this better than her. It had all sounded much easier in London.

She pushed the sheets back and reached for her robe, pulling the thin silk around her strong body.

She was too restless to just lie there, corpselike, as the hours ticked around until dawn. She needed to move, to remind herself of what she'd won, to shake off this feeling that she'd been duped into imprisonment so far from home and that it might break her.

Downstairs, she went to the kitchen first, draining milk straight from the container to settle the acid burning her chest from an afternoon's drinking. She stared at all the stupid individual cartons of coconut water that Billy somehow thought would make him young again. It *did* taste like sperm, however much he may not have liked the comment. She wanted to twist one open and spit in it. She closed the fridge and padded out into the vast hallway.

Eleanor stared down at her in the gloom, her expression unreadable, and Keisha shivered. There was no space for the *boy* here. It was Eleanor's ghost who stalked this house. The dead mother of the dead son. Keisha could feel her. She was on the walls and *in* the walls, her energy the blood that ran through the veins of this mansion. Her clothes were still in the closets of the master bedroom—Billy and Keisha used a different room for now—and her drawers were filled with her trinkets and memories.

Keisha had looked, of course she had. Her need to know about *what came before* had been overwhelming.

Tucked away in a cabinet against one wall were so many framed photos of Lyle, the dead son and heir, that Keisha had been afraid they would tumble out and her nosing around would be discovered. Lyle had died before Eleanor and William had moved into this house—his death and Eleanor's grief the cause of the move—but it was strange to Keisha that all his pictures were hidden away, from kindergarten and with school friends to the proud young man in his military uniform, the uniform he'd die in, serving in Afghanistan, shortly after. Billy had said he'd been killed fifteen years before. If he'd lived he'd be older than Keisha. Would she have liked him more than his father? He had a sweet face, she thought. Shining eyes. No wonder Billy still couldn't bear to talk about it. No wonder they'd hidden their grief away.

On the dresser were more photos, displayed this time, old pictures of Eleanor and her friends or siblings maybe as children, and also of the happy couple—Billy barely recognizable as a young man and Eleanor aloofly elegant—and then in the drawers, hidden amid various items of carefully folded clothes, she found some jewelry and a small box containing far more interesting treasure: a bag of grass and cigarette papers and a sealed packet of syringes alongside a vial of morphine. That was a revelation. Perhaps Eleanor had kept a lot of her pain from Billy and her nurses or Iris and Elizabeth and whoever else looked after her. Maybe there had been more to the saintly Eleanor than met the eye. Everything about this world felt like an act.

Keisha wandered through the house, resisting the urge to go back upstairs and dip further into the dead wife's possessions, instead taking comfort in the endless rooms and fine furniture. *Her* domain now. The demands of her family were an ocean away. Just the one man to take care of. *Keep him happy,* she thought. *He's nearly seventy. He'll be dead soon.* It was a harsh and horrible thought, but she couldn't help it. There had been no prenup. It had all moved too quickly for that, her family pouncing while he'd been intoxicated by her, but he'd made her sign a postnup as soon as they'd landed, maybe the first clue that her knight in shining armor wasn't so soft. She knew, even when he died, that she wouldn't get everything, but she'd get enough. Plenty to get her family off her back and then maybe to flee somewhere wonderful where none of them could find her.

Her stomach fizzed as she passed a wall of photographs, black-tie events at the country club with various politicians or local celebrities. There were a few now familiar faces smiling out from some of the pictures, and as her eyes lingered on one, a hand subconsciously floated up to her neck, teasing the skin there, imagining a touch as her heart raced. This was the bright light in her new life. She thought back to the laughter on the boat. Their eyes meeting. The way she felt in the excitement of a flirtation. Never had Billy seemed so old and ridiculous beside her. She'd felt breathless. Girlish. Giddy. Alive. An overwhelming surge of lust.

She needed to be careful, she knew that. She couldn't put all this at risk with one of her wild emotional obsessions. She had to keep her head straight. To concentrate on Billy—and that meant *not* getting distracted. She took a last glance at one of the photos before turning away. She had to keep those feelings boxed up for private moments. Something to fantasize about while Billy wheezed and slobbered all over her.

She turned the alarm off and went out onto the terrace, the night a wall of heat to penetrate, no hint of a breeze. It calmed her though. She had to think kinder thoughts about Billy. He had rescued her from a life she hated and a family who scared her. This was a beautiful place. She had to find a way to enjoy it until it was *all* hers.

Tiny yellow bulbs twinkled on strings in the trees, leftovers from the party. A light was also still on in the apartment above the garages, where Zelda lived. She must be a night owl too. What time was it? One in the morning? Two? The light went out as she stared up at the window and she smiled. Maybe Zelda had the right idea. It was too late to be awake. She should have taken a pill or something to help her sleep. There was only so long Billy would put up with her sleeping half the morning and the less time she could spend in bed the less chance there was of him pawing at her more.

She took a last look at the glittering trees and then went back into the cool house. Her skin had goose-pimpled as she crept back under the sheets, and for a while she just lay in the dark, lost in her heated thoughts of eyes meeting, before, finally, she fell into a fitful sleep of lustful dreams and family memories she'd rather forget.

7.

It was ten when Keisha woke, the sheets tangled between her thighs like a drained lover, and she squinted against the light that streamed through the large windows. It made her feel good. A fresh start. Today, she would be a good wife. She stretched for a moment before grabbing her robe and heading downstairs. Coffee. She needed coffee. Strong, lovely American coffee.

She filled a mug from the machine in the kitchen and then followed the trail of noise to Billy's office. Her nose crinkled as she passed several large vases filled with pungent flowers, a cacophony of color and scent filling the hallway that gave her a wave of cloying nausea.

"Jesus, Billy," she said, as she drifted into his office

and went to kiss him dutifully on the cheek. "Where did all those awful flowers come from?"

"Morning, honey." He was leaning against his desk, face red from the treadmill, a carton of coconut water in hand. She should be glad he was making an effort, but the sight of him in his sportswear, so pleased with himself, made her want to cringe. Youth was for the young. His was gone. No matter how often he got on the treadmill, he couldn't run from old age and death. He'd be better off making his peace with it.

"Oh, I'm sorry." The voice came from behind her. Elizabeth, sitting demurely on the leather couch, notebook and diary open on the coffee table. "It's habit. I used to get them for Eleanor every few days. She loved all the perfumes. I did it without thinking."

"Oh no, *I'm* sorry," Keisha said, feeling entirely not sorry. There was a brief glint in the secretary's eye that made Keisha wonder if the flowers had been bought to remind her once again that she was simply a poor replacement. "Of course. Eleanor." She spoke the last word softly. The dead wife who wouldn't be laid to rest.

"I'll get Zelda to throw them out." William squeezed her waist and she gave him her sweetest smile.

"Only if that's okay." She leaned in, pressing her body against his. *Think of the money. The big prize. The inheritance.* All those voices in her head, hers only one among those of others she knew, family, friends, lover. "I know it's hard for you."

William took another sip of his drink. "No more flowers unless you've chosen them." He paused. "And I'll have that portrait taken down too. You shouldn't have to look at that every day. This is your home now."

"Thank you." She kissed him again, this time on the lips. Was he having the portrait taken down for her or for him? Did he feel guilty that he'd moved on so quickly? Either way, it didn't matter. She knew men. She'd seen enough at the club. Out of sight was out of mind. Whatever his lingering feelings were for his first wife, they'd vanish with the painting. Maybe that's why all the photos of Lyle were hidden away too. Men weren't very good at *feeling* was what she'd learned in life. It was too hard. Too real. She was the opposite. Sometimes she was sure she would be overwhelmed by real.

"I'll get it put in storage." Elizabeth scribbled herself a note. "And I'll speak to the kitchen designer about that faulty drawer. I have no idea how things are falling down the back into the space there but maybe don't keep your glasses or passport in there anymore."

"Thanks." William turned to Keisha. "Will you be okay if I go into the office for a couple of hours?" William said. "I've got to start your green card paperwork and there's no point paying another lawyer to do it when I have a firm of them."

"Of course, I'll be fine. Take as long as you need."

"I also want to get a new life insurance policy. And make some changes to my will." His eyes shone. Today he was in a good mood, her adoring puppy, not an old dog baring its teeth. "Now, I'd better go shower and change." Elizabeth took that as her cue to disappear and leave them alone.

"You sure you'll be okay?"

Keisha smiled. "I'm a grown-up. I'll be fine. Why don't I meet you somewhere for lunch when you're done?"

"That's a great idea."

"Hey, why don't you ask Jason and Marcie to join us?" The question was light, as if a momentary afterthought. "I should get to know them better."

He held her tight and she didn't flinch from the cooling sweat in the gray hairs of his barrel chest as they rubbed on her skin. *Life insurance. Will.* She luxuriated in those words instead, using them to build a hard shell around herself.

"Good idea." He kissed the top of her head. "I'll speak to Jason and let you know where to meet us."

"It's a plan. Now shower. Go!" She pushed him playfully away. It *was* a plan. Four months of Billy had left her aching for something else, something for her heart, and there was no crime in looking. She waited impatiently for William to dress and leave. A few hours to herself would be blissful. She'd take a Valium, keep the demons in her head quiet, play loud music, and have an hour-long bath to relax.

First though, once he was finally gone, she found herself back in Eleanor's room, carefully picking through the dead woman's jewelry boxes. She wasn't going to take anything, but she wanted to see if the pieces Billy had thus far given her—expensive as they were—were not just trinkets in comparison. How was her worth measuring up?

"Are you looking for something, ma'am?"

Keisha nearly dropped the string of pearls she was examining. "Jesus shit, Zelda, you made me jump!"

"I'm sorry, ma'am. I didn't know that Mr. Radford was happy for people to come in here yet. I must have been wrong."

Keisha looked at the diminutive black woman in the doorway. There had been definite disapproval in her tone. A slight distaste in her expression. Keisha's hackles rose. There were too many people controlling her life. There always had been. She wouldn't take it from a housekeeper. Who was *she* to judge?

"Billy won't mind," Keisha said, breezing out of the

room. "He's—*we're*—only waiting for Iris to get back from vacation, then this will all be sorted and cleared out." She paused and looked down at the housekeeper. Why was she even explaining herself? "And anyway, it's my house now, I can go where I want."

"Yes, ma'am," Zelda said.

"I'd like some tea—English style—and bring it to my bathroom."

She didn't even want any tea. But she *did* want to be respected. No one had respected her at home. That wasn't going to happen here. Zelda was going to have to change her tune, or Billy would be looking for new staff.

She ran the hot water, swallowed a Valium, and tried to shake off her irritation, even managing a thank-you when the drink arrived. Lunch, she thought, as she slid naked into the vast bath, submerging herself in the bubbles. Relax and think about lunch.

8.

In Southside, it always felt ten degrees hotter to Marcie and her hands were slick with sweat in her plastic gloves, but there was no way she was going to take them off. The community center that served as the Mission's soup kitchen stank of stale summer sweat and the thick meaty stench of the paper mills, as if any breeze that passed over the city dragged it here where it could settle away from the polite squares and strollers in Forsyth Park. There were worse smells too, ones that emanated from the warm bodies, and there was no way she was going to touch any of the shuffling line of homeless degenerates lining up for stew and dumplings and a beaker of cherry Kool-Aid.

Unlike the other volunteers, who chatted together,

Marcie kept herself to herself. They were all fully paid-up Baptists and she didn't want to get absorbed into the inner congregation by accident. Another *set*. Savannah was full of sets.

Out among the tables Virginia was in her element, touching shoulders, relishing the gratitude. It was different for Virginia. She'd never been poor. For all the time she spent here, these people weren't real. She didn't see them as whole, good, bad, ugly, or somewhere in between. They were simply *unfortunate*, as if none had ever been part of his or her own downfall. Marcie didn't like being around the homeless, but at least she didn't diminish them.

She glanced down the line to where an old man, Harold, was slowly moving forward. His face was a portrait of etched unpleasantness and although she never acknowledged it, she was aware that his free hand went down to the crotch of his pants whenever he looked at her, a move designed to make her feel uncomfortable, a way to take a little power back.

She slopped the stew over the side of the bowl, spilling some on him.

"Oops, silly me."

"Dumb bitch," he muttered.

It's not me who's going to die on a street corner one day, stinking of my own piss, though, is it? she wanted to hiss back. Instead, she handed him a biscuit, as they glared at each other.

"Over here, Harold," Virginia called. "Lawrence saved a seat for you."

Lawrence and Harold. The most ridiculous names for two old drunks, if those were their names at all. It's not like anyone here checked ID's. Crude and foul though, both of them. The worst of the *clients,* as Virginia insisted the tramps be called.

Jason couldn't understand why she always went back. Whenever she'd come home from helping she would bitch about *Harold this* or *Lawrence that.* How could she explain it to him? She wasn't here just to cozy up to Virginia or fill a few hours with *something* after the embarrassing failure of her boutique; it ran deeper than that. She liked to remind herself of how life could turn on a dime. One bad deal at work, one divorce, a couple too many drinks, and then you're sleeping in a square all day with everything you love in a brown paper bag. Life changed. And it could change fast. It never hurt to remember that.

These raggedy shells of humanity disgusted her on a visceral level, but she *needed* her disgust. Jason would never understand that. Sure, he'd had problems with his father, but he'd never been poor in his bones. He'd come from the right blood and the right blood rallied around and helped pick him back up when Maddox Senior had done the honorable thing in his disgrace and killed himself.

She caught herself. That was blunt, even for her. Everything was setting her on edge. She felt claustrophobic. The plastic gloves on her hands felt too tight, suffocating her skin. The weight of this life, one she'd done so much to secure for herself, had at some point settled around her neck like a noose.

Jason. She was embarrassed by her behavior of the day before. It wasn't like her to either feel so weak or *show* weakness like that. To allow the jealous paranoias of a younger woman. She cringed when she thought about it. Maybe she'd go and surprise him. Yes, that's what she'd do. Take him somewhere lovely for lunch, somewhere decadent and *not* like this. Try and get some of the good of their relationship back.

As soon as her shift was done, she freshened up in the staff-only restrooms and then rushed out to her car, eager for this run-down part of town to evaporate behind her—out of sight, out of mind.

He was her husband. *Hers.* Thoughts of this little bitch weren't going to sour that. She'd make it right. Keisha was no one. Jason might want her physically, but no matter who she was married to, Keisha didn't fit in and she never would. As Marcie put the car in drive, she tried to ignore the quiet voice at the back of her mind that whispered, *But why would she ever want to?*

"He never goes for lunch before two." Marcie frowned, quietly fuming. It was only one thirty and there was no sign of Jason in his office. She'd tried his mobile, but it was going straight to voice mail. So much for her big romantic gesture. Where the hell was he?

"He was with Mr. Radford," Sandy, the partners' assistant, told her. "They left about thirty or forty minutes ago I guess."

"Did he say where they were going?"

"No, just lunch. Did you try his cell?"

"It's been a bit glitchy. I can't get through." How stupid did Sandy think she was? Or was she enjoying seeing Marcie on the back foot? *Damn you, Jason, for embarrassing me.*

"Oh, Elizabeth was here earlier!" Sandy exclaimed. "She probably made the reservation, since I didn't. You could try her?"

Back out in the heat, still annoyed and sweating, Marcie wondered if she should leave them to their boys' day, but after the morning with Virginia immersed in the grime of the city, she *wanted* to see Jason. To settle any choppy water beneath them. To feel like she belonged again, not a cuckoo in the nest like Keisha. And what else was she supposed to do? Go home and drink wine alone? She dialed.

"Hey, Marcie!" Elizabeth's voice crackled, distant, as she answered. Still chirpy though. Ever chirpy, that was Elizabeth. "What can I do you for? You'll have to talk loud, I'm in the car and this hands-free thing doesn't work so good."

Typical Elizabeth. Surely she could afford something better, or get William to pay for it. She probably didn't want to be a bother. Elizabeth survived in this luxury jungle of theirs by not being a bother. "I'm looking for Jason. Wanted to surprise him. But Sandy said he'd already gone for lunch." Why did she feel so ridiculous asking? It's not like she normally knew where Jason was every minute of every day. It hardly screamed *problem in marriage*. In fact, if she *did* know where he was all the time, that would be more of an issue.

"You're not with him?"

"Obviously."

"Sorry, sorry." The irritation in Marcie's voice must have been clear even if the line wasn't. "It's just that I thought you would be. I booked the table for all four of you. The Terrace at Carmello's. For one o'clock? They'll still be there I imagine, if you want to go find them. The food is great but the service is slow, but William said to book somewhere nice to sit out."

Marcie was barely listening and muttered a thank-you before hanging up. She was supposed to be there? So why hadn't Jason called?

All her unease. Her gut feeling that Jason was pulling away, wanted someone who wasn't her. She was right. There was something to it. Heat rose through her. She looked at her watch. It was nearly two. *All four of you.* Jason and Marcie and William and of course Keisha. *Keisha, Keisha, Keisha.* Sandy hadn't mentioned her though, so maybe the men had decided to go on their own? She dithered by her car until the heat got too much.

Perhaps she was overreacting. There was a reasonable excuse. *It's only lunch,* she told herself. *Stop making a deal out of it. Just go.* If the men were on their own she'd be charming for one drink and then leave them to it.

9.

The men weren't on their own.

"Ah, *there* she is. The wife!" That blunt, strange accent.

Marcie's blood chilled, turning her stomach to ice water. Keisha was sitting between William on one side and Jason on the other—a very startled Jason, Marcie noticed as her face flushed pink in a surge of something she couldn't blame on the weather. He quickly leaned back in his chair but a moment too late to hide that he'd been leaning in, hanging on every one of Keisha's words, so much so that he hadn't even noticed his own wife standing by the table. Splinters of her heart broke off and she wanted to stab him with them. Stab both of them.

"I thought I'd surprise you for lunch." She ignored

Keisha and tried to smile at Jason. "Elizabeth told me where you were."

"I thought Marcie couldn't make it?" William said to Jason, who hurriedly got to his feet to pull out her chair. She barely moved as he kissed her on the cheek. *Contain yourself*, she thought. *Don't show weakness. Not where this gloating pig-in-shit stranger in front of you can see it.*

Keisha's brown eyes, perfectly made up of course, darted sharply between Marcie and Jason. Could she pick up on the tension between them? She looked beautiful. A low V neckline in her cream sleeveless pantsuit accentuated her bust and the red sash tied at the waist made her look slimmer than she probably was and Marcie once again felt her own beauty fade in comparison.

"Thank you, darling." She took her seat, as did Jason. His white shirt was open at the top button, showing a slice of his tanned, strong chest. A little but not too much. Why didn't men fade like women? How did they get to retain some allure that wasn't couched in ghosts of a tighter skin and past glory? How come they got to stay sexy or, in fact, for a while, get sexier? Maybe that was the root of her problem. She felt her space in the group being erased. She'd been the youngest for so long. It was what she *had*, that quiet envy of their friends, and now it was being stripped from her by this confident younger usurper.

"Sorry, Marce," he said. "I thought you were at the Mission with Virginia today."

"I was. But I was done so figured I'd find you for lunch. And here you are."

"Well, that's great." William signaled over a waiter who poured Marcie the dregs of a bottle of Chablis before disappearing to fetch another. They were having a good time it seemed.

"The Mission?" Keisha said. "So you're a missionary kind of girl?"

So that's who'd been drinking most of the wine. The barbed innuendo was obviously lost on William, who answered for Marcie. "It's a food kitchen. Free lunches for the poor. Virginia organizes it with the church. You help out there quite a bit, don't you, Marcie?"

"Beats going to church. And probably does more good."

The waiter reappeared and she ordered a small chicken salad as he topped up her glass. Maybe Jason didn't have an ulterior motive. She *did* usually do a later shift at the Mission than she'd done today, so it was natural for him to think she was busy. But still, every fiber in her being screamed that Jason hadn't wanted her here.

"Billy says everyone in this town loves God as much as they love a good time," Keisha said.

"I'm not from here." Marcie was being snippy, she couldn't help herself.

"Bad morning?" Jason asked. She ignored him.

"You're one of us now, Marcie, and no fighting it," William said. "You're family. One of our congregation. And anyway, everyone believes in some version of God. Don't try to tell me otherwise. Nothing wrong with a little churchgoing. It balances the soul."

"I guess," she said.

"But now that you're here, you can help with my dilemma. Keisha's trying to persuade me to go back to work."

"Bored already?" She looked her nemesis in the face for the first time and smiled. They all laughed as if she were joking. Friends together.

"No, of course not." A flash of dark eyes. The sting had hit home. "But you know what they say, driven men die when they retire."

"Thanks, honey!"

"I'm being serious. You read about it all the time. Six weeks out of the office and then dead on the golf course. Anyway, I can't imagine you sitting around doing nothing all day, though I'm sure we could find something to pass the time." Keisha gave William's hand a squeeze, but her eyes darted to Marcie's.

And what will you be doing all day if he goes back to work? Marcie wanted to ask but didn't. That would put her on dangerous ground. Her one attempt at work had turned into a money pit, and Jason had snapped at her over her spending on the new house last week when the interior design quotes came in.

"I like the idea of being a housewife," Keisha continued. "Preparing dinner for when you get home. Sweet tea out on the porch. Dinner parties with y'all. That kind of thing."

"*Y'all* can cook?" asked Marcie, barely hiding the disbelief in her voice and mimicking Keisha's attempts to be cute.

"Ha! We'll make a Southern belle of her yet, won't we?" William said, slapping Jason on the back and ignoring Marcie's barb. He sat up a little straighter, all testosterone now with the thought of an adoring little woman waiting at home for him, and Marcie fought the urge to laugh out loud. Oh, she was good, this gold digger. Make it all about him when it was obvious she wanted him out of her hair as much as possible.

"It's true, I have missed the buzz of work," William said. "Not at first, but recently." He sipped his wine, thoughtful. "I could do a couple of days a week."

"No way you could," Jason said. "Before you know it, you'd be in every day, stressed as all hell and going home late to a pissed wife and a burned dinner and a credit card she's maxed out to punish you."

Marcie stared at him, incredulous. Where had that outburst come from?

Jason laughed, suddenly aware of how sharp he'd sounded. "Unless you're as lucky as me." He wasn't fooling anyone, and Keisha glanced over at Marcie, her look a blend of humor and victory. Marcie forced her whole body to stay relaxed, as if his words had washed over her into nothing.

"It'd take some spending to max out my credit cards, Jason."

"True." Jason gave William a rueful smile. The edge in the atmosphere softened but Marcie had definitely heard some bite there. What was the matter with him?

"But that's a thought for another day," William said. "Right now I'm enjoying being home and settling back in with my lovely new wife."

"We missed you while you were away." Marcie took another sip of her wine. It was going to her head, the small salad she'd ordered yet to arrive. Elizabeth had been right about the service here. Had anyone truly missed William? she wondered. Unlikely. It had all been so miserable in the months before he left. Eleanor slowly dying, elegantly at first and then getting oddly confused about things when it spread to her brain. Crying about Lyle as if he'd only just died rather than over a decade ago. Then that awful day—*my pearls my South Sea pearls where are my pearls*—incessant and endless and so upset, hands fluttering, eyelids twitching, until Jason and Elizabeth finally found the necklace out by the pool house.

Iris would wheel her around the club like some reminder of all their mortality while the men played golf, everyone pretending it was going to be fine when it wasn't. Even William started to shrink away from her toward the end, as if her impending death were contagious, flirting with some waitress at the club to cling to life. Yes, he'd been heartbroken when Eleanor died, but he'd also been relieved, and when he took his grief to Europe for the year, that had been a relief for everyone else. They could get on with living their wonderful lives. Maybe that's why even Iris and Noah had taken to Keisha. No one wanted miserable William back. Although, for Marcie at least, that would have been preferable to him returning with *her.*

"Shall we get another bottle?" Keisha asked. "It's so lovely here."

"Not for me, I've got my car," Marcie said. She'd had too much already.

"Lucky you. I can't drive that big thing Eleanor had. I'm used to something smaller. Something zippy."

"Why don't we go and choose you a car this afternoon?" William took her hand. Marcie snorted quietly behind her own wineglass. Keisha was so blatant and William ridiculous for not seeing through her. How could a clever man be so stupid? They deserved each other.

"I've got a few things I should do back at the office. Or," Jason said, before looking over at Marcie, no hint of the black cloud of moments ago, "I could play hooky and spend the afternoon with my own gorgeous wife." He winked at her. "A little siesta?"

She laughed and her heart melted. Even more so when she caught the downturn in Keisha's mouth. Disgruntled. Heat flushed between her thighs, as much from her small victory as from the idea of an afternoon in bed with her handsome husband.

"We're lucky men, Jason Maddox," William said, holding his glass up to toast this moment of male pride.

"Amen to that." Jason clinked and they both drank. Despite the sudden lift in her mood, Marcie had never felt more like a trophy. Bought and paid for rather than won.

The sex they had that afternoon was wild and urgent. Aggressive and mutually demanding. Nothing was off limits, like in the old days of illicit thrilling meetings in hotel rooms. They were absorbed in each other, the heat and the wine and the late-afternoon decadence bringing out the beasts in their blood as they laughed and panted and bit and wrestled. By the time they had finally finished, she stank of him and he of her, and they were filled with the taste of each other. She ached deep in her muscles, but it was a pleasant pain, a reassurance that her marriage was fine. He wasn't bored. She wasn't bored.

Jason rolled onto his side and up on one elbow, gazing at her for a long moment, not studying her body, but looking her right in the eye.

"What?"

"I need you to be her friend."

Goose bumps prickled across Marcie's skin. "How do you mean?"

"Keisha."

"I know *who* you mean. But why?"

"This business of wanting William to go back to work. Change her mind."

She was fully alert now, all sense of relaxed joy evaporating like the dregs of a glorious dream. Was this what the afternoon together had been leading up to? Sex was a woman's tool—had it just been used against her?

"He was supposed to be gone for a year." His eyes had moved away from her, staring out toward the French windows at the far end of the bedroom, focused on something she couldn't see. The chess board of his mind moving pieces around.

"So?" She needed more information.

"I started making a few changes already. I don't want him coming in and trying to keep us as stagnant as we are. When I buy him out—if he doesn't change his mind on that—I was going to reach out to Bardon and Briggs in Atlanta. See if they still wanted to merge with us. It would be a massive step forward." He paused. "And make us a lot of money."

Her heart pounded in her chest so hard it echoed in her ears and throbbed in her hot feet. Was this why he'd been distant? Just work? Was it why he'd been making such a fuss of Keisha too? To get her on his side? Of course, of course, of course. It all made sense now. She *had* been a fool. It was all Jason, being his ambitious self.

"You never told me any of this."

"It's delicate. Yes, William verbally agreed he'd retire and I'd buy him out, but I know him, he's doubting his decision. If he sees I've started making changes—well, you know how he can be about change. He likes that we've always been a boutique partnership as if it's a hundred years ago and nothing exists outside of the South." He chewed his bottom lip, thinking. "I'm going to work on him from the inside. Maybe take him to Charleston or Atlanta for a late bachelor party. I'll get Elizabeth to find somewhere he'll love. Vegas even. Show him how he could be spending his time. You work on her. Be her friend."

It was Marcie's turn to be thoughtful. "She's using him, you know that, don't you?"

He shrugged.

"You don't care? You're one of his closest friends and she's a gold digger. All that stuff about a car at lunchtime. And the money he's spending on her. She's probably in his will by now. Shouldn't you warn him?"

"She *is* in his will. He drew up the changes this morning with Brody. When they got back, she signed a postnup, in case they divorce, but he's leaving her pretty much everything if he dies. If I try to warn him about her, he's going to turn on me *and* all my work plans will be screwed. No one likes to be told they're being stupid. Let his gorgeous wife be a distraction for now."

"Is that why you've been flirting with her a bit?" Marcie asked.

"I haven't been flirting with her." He bristled and she felt her regained shield of confidence crack again.

He must have seen something in her expression because he relented. "Well, maybe a little, just to keep her on our side."

Too late, babe, Marcie thought. *The denial came first. There's always guilt in denial.*

"Just do it," he said, pushing back the sheet and striding naked to the bathroom. "For me."

10.

Marcie didn't have to reach out to make the first move. Elizabeth had called to say she was going to show Keisha a few of the sights and asked if Marcie wanted to come along. *Want* was a strong word, and it was turning out to be a long, hot morning.

They'd done the Davenport House, where Elizabeth pointed out various supposedly interesting details of history and Keisha and Marcie had trailed behind, listless, both obviously bored by the commentary. It might have made Marcie warm to the young woman if everything she said didn't seem to be related to Jason. *So, how long have you been married? Did you know his first wife? He must work long hours, how do you keep busy? Don't you want children? Does he stay away much? I have to come and see your new house.*

Jason said at lunch that it's amazing. You must be so happy.

"Yes I am," she'd answered. "Blissfully so. We both are." Keisha had faltered at that and changed the subject. God, she was so obvious. And only just married. What was that old saying? Someone who marries for money earns it. Did Keisha really think she could get away with a flirtation on the side?

She was messing with the wrong woman if she thought she could pull the wool over Marcie's eyes with this sugary sweet routine. It might work with the others, but Marcie wasn't filled with that ingrained, unspoken racism born in the blood of their wealthy, classist generation that made them fall over themselves to be nice by way of embarrassed apology. Marcie wasn't like them. She saw Keisha for what she was—a serpent in their midst. But she'd play along for now.

As they strolled through the quiet squares, scented with citrusy, honey-sweet magnolia perfume, pausing en route to gaze up at wrought-iron balconies on beautiful painted houses and the pretty old-fashioned streetlamps under the boughs of Georgia oaks, Elizabeth seemed so enthralled by the quaint charm she may as well have been a tourist rather than a late-middle-aged woman who'd lived here all her life. Savannah sure was a beautiful city, Marcie knew that, but she couldn't help but wonder how it compared with the hustle and bustle of a cold place like London. An alien land no doubt. Keisha didn't strike her as someone who'd traveled beyond Europe a lot. There was too much city grit in her eyes. Marcie's used to have it too.

"What's that stuff?" Keisha was looking up.

"Spanish moss," Marcie said. "It's everywhere in Georgia."

"Beautiful, isn't it?" Elizabeth joined in. "So Gothic against the architecture."

"I guess." Keisha didn't sound convinced. "It gives me the creeps. They're like the kind of cobwebs that would come at the end of the world. Shrouding everything."

"Maybe that's appropriate. After all, this is a city of live oaks and dead people, that's what they say. Which brings us to our next location on the tour," Elizabeth continued breezily, as Marcie groaned internally.

"Colonial Park Cemetery," Elizabeth said as she led them through an arched gateway. "Opened around 1750, so pretty old for the States. There are hundreds of gravestones here but about ten thousand buried bodies, so do the math on that one. Those with the stones are the lucky ones. There's a mass grave for seven hundred yellow fever victims, and we're probably standing on some other residents; in fact, they spread right out under the streets."

Keisha didn't look too impressed as she took in the vast space of tended lawns, paths running through them, and scattered gravestones. The heavy heat had driven sensible people inside, and Marcie could see only a solitary visitor, a large black woman with umber hair sitting on a bench in the distance, her walking stick beside her, under a wall of old grave markers. Keisha's mouth pursed. "Is this where Eleanor is buried?"

"Oh no, there're no new graves here. Eleanor's resting in Bonaventure with Lyle, God rest that boy's soul. Eleanor was born to end up there, if that doesn't sound too strange. It's so full of beauty and grace, just as she was. A lot of the old families have plots and mausoleums, bought up years ago. That's a place you really *should* visit—not Eleanor's grave if it makes you feel too uncomfortable—but the cemetery. This one has historical significance, but Bonaventure has a life of its own, if you'll excuse the pun. So much atmosphere. People come from all over to wander through it. So peaceful. And the monuments and statues are definitely something to see."

"Not for me," Keisha said. "I don't like to spend time with the dead."

"That's a shame. It's quite the wonder. I like to go sometimes and just sit and think. I've seen Zelda there too on occasion. All walks of life are welcome in Bonaventure. Death is a great leveler, isn't it?"

"Does your family have a tomb there too?" Keisha asked and Elizabeth let out a tinkle of amused laughter.

"No dear. My family isn't originally from this part of the South. And we're not really mausoleum people."

Marcie could imagine. Elizabeth still had a mother somewhere—she'd gone visiting her for a while when William was in Europe—but her father's grave was probably in some gaudy cemetery, like those ones that advertise "a whole afterlife package" on late-night TV.

"I don't think I need to see any more gravestones," Keisha said as Elizabeth's phone began to ring. "My auntie Ayo says it's bad luck to disturb a dead man's bones." She smiled, but there was a definite sense of unease in her confidence. A crack in her armor, perhaps.

"Then let's go and wander along River Street and see the *Waving Girl* statue. There'll be more of a breeze there too, and you'll love the cobbled street and all the little stores and restaurants. But oh my, the steps. With those shoes you're wearing we may need to ride the elevator down. Just let me take this—it's William." Elizabeth smiled apologetically, turning away to answer and leaving the two women standing in awkward silence as she talked behind them.

"God, I need a drink," Marcie muttered eventually.

"Hell yes." Keisha flashed a grin at her, and Marcie

was once again struck by her youthful beauty and she ached with envy for that power. She'd been as glorious as Keisha at that age. Before she'd started to fade.

"So sorry," Elizabeth said, tucking her phone back into her sensible purse. "I've got to go run an errand for William that can't wait. Virginia and Emmett are at the house and he's organized a late lunch for y'all, so Marcie, why don't you drive Keisha back and I'll meet you when I'm done? I'm so sorry to cut our tour short. We can pick it up another day."

"Can't wait," Keisha said drolly, and much as Marcie didn't like her, she did almost laugh.

Marcie watched as Elizabeth bustled off, untouched by the humid heat, and then pointed down the street. "My car's about five minutes away." They started to stroll, Keisha's hips rolling confidently with every stride. Even the way she walked made Marcie feel inferior, awkward. *Be her friend,* Jason had said. Like it was that easy. Men knew nothing about the tricky waters of mutual mistrust women swam in. After a few minutes of awkward silence, Marcie forced herself to talk. "I take it you're not a great fan of museums and history?"

"Am I that obvious?" Keisha asked. "I've lived in London since I was five years old and not even made it to the Tower of London. Only seen it from outside." She shrugged. "I guess that must seem pretty ignorant."

"Oh, I'm the same. I'm all about the present and the future, not the past." It was pretty close to the truth, Marcie thought as she led them into Wright Square. "You've moved to the wrong city if you don't care about history though. 'The most haunted city in America' is on the tourist advertising. And apparently this is our most haunted square. Jason brought me down here one night when we first met and we picnicked at midnight. It was very romantic." *Jason. My husband. Never to be yours.* Keisha needed to learn that Marcie wasn't the sort to give up her possessions easily, that she was a force to be reckoned with under her newly acquired demure exterior.

"Why's it haunted?" Keisha asked. "Who by?"

"The first woman executed in the city was hanged here for murdering the farmer who employed her. She was Irish. They left her up there for three days after she was dead." She paused and looked up at the trees. "The story goes that Spanish moss doesn't grow here because it won't grow where innocent blood has been spilled."

"She didn't do it?" Keisha asked.

"Who knows? Probably. Maybe he deserved it. But," she continued, "tourists say they've seen her spirit running through here looking for her baby. But then if you believe everyone who says they've seen a ghost here, there'd be more dead people on the streets than live ones."

"Don't you believe in ghosts?" Keisha asked.

"No," Marcie said. "No, I do not." She paused. "Only the ghosts of our past selves and even they stop breathing when we do." She hadn't meant it to sound so weighty, but she noted Keisha's face tightening. Marcie had put her past in a box where she could control it. It looked like Keisha carried hers inside. What secrets did *she* have?

A deep, throaty chuckle from behind cut between them, the sound like a sudden breeze in the still air, and both women turned. An elderly black woman with umber-orange hair was standing behind a bench to their right, in the leafy shade of the overhanging trees. Laid out across the wooden seat were various trinkets and candles, as well as little charm bags, like Marcie had seen in New Orleans. Marcie stared. The woman was tall, over five eleven, and with the barrel of fat around her stomach she appeared vast and formidable. How had they not seen her as they strolled past? Marcie frowned. She looked like the woman who'd been sitting in Colonial Park Cemetery, but it couldn't be the same person. She couldn't have gotten here so fast and set up her things.

"Ghosts," the woman said, slapping her thigh and laughing harder, wiping her eyes, before looking up at them. "Ghosts indeed. Ghosts you may be, but I see you," she said. She raised one hand and pointed a fat finger. "I see both of you, light and dark and dark and light. All your secrets. I see all to come, and I see what will become of you. I *dreamed* you. Oh my." She laughed again, shaking her head as if in wonder at something. "Ghosts right here. Oh my."

She picked up her cane from where it rested against the bench and gripped it, the handle carved like a snake's head, before banging it against the ground three times. The oddness of the movement made Marcie shiver, and beside her Keisha had stiffened.

"Oh my," the old woman repeated, before turning and starting to stroll in the opposite direction, abandoning her wares and leaving the two women staring after her.

"Well, that was . . . odd," Marcie said, eventually.

Keisha was staring at the items laid out on the bench as if one might leap up and bite her. "She sounded like she knew you. Knew who we were. What was she talking about?"

"I have no idea," Marcie said. "I guess that shit is her sales pitch. Freaks people out and then gets them to part with their money for all this trash."

"It's not trash," Keisha said softly, eyes still scanning the objects.

"Well, if it isn't, why did she walk off and leave it all here? Maybe she's drunk."

"Maybe." Keisha didn't sound convinced, and her eyes darted over to where the woman was strolling away. Was Keisha afraid?

"Do you want any of this?" Marcie looked down at the strange bags and vials and strings of colored beads and small wax carvings laid out on a large patterned scarf. Only now that she was closer could she make out the small chalk markings under the bench, symbols etched in white on the ground. This old woman took herself seriously, or maybe it was all for any passing tourists' benefit.

"No!" Keisha looked shocked. "I wouldn't buy it, let alone steal it. Those charm bags could be for anything."

"It looks like a heap of cheap tourist crap if you ask me. Jason and I brought some like it back from New Orleans a few years ago," Marcie said. She was quite enjoying seeing Keisha so unsettled. "But if she doesn't come back someone *will* steal it."

"Then they'd be a fool. My family are from Nigeria. They call this juju. Do good, get good, do bad, get bad. And bad can get really bad. It's all about karma. These bags and stuff should protect you from it."

Marcie smiled. "She's an old drunk conning tourists out of a few dollars when they stray from their road trips and think they've found some Louisiana voodoo. And if she *is* drunk, then she's ahead of us." The overhanging trees suddenly felt claustrophobic. She was trying to laugh it off, but Keisha was right. The woman had talked like she knew them. This crazy city full of crazy people made crazy by the heat and too much liquor in the sun. "Let's get back to yours and fix that."

11.

Keisha had been stuck between Virginia and Emmett ever since they'd got back and she hadn't gotten to talk to Jason and Marcie at all. Virginia had swooped down on her and that was that. The diamond glinting against her possibly surgically enhanced bosom was a match for the sparkle of gossip in her eyes. She hadn't shut up. First, she'd gone on about her children, one in Paris studying fashion, one graduated from Harvard and living in New York, and the youngest, Richard, still here in Savannah sharing an apartment downtown with three others and setting up an Internet start-up that Virginia laughed about not understanding even though she was paying most of the bills for the venture. After that she was all fawning about how nice it was to see William happy again, asking a few questions about London, but then going on about the sainted Eleanor—whose portrait was still on the wall, Keisha noted—and how tragic it was she'd been lost so relatively young.

Relatively young was right. People in Keisha's tower block back home died young. If it wasn't the teenage gang stabbings, it was drugs or drink or just the weariness of poverty; a government that squeezed the poorer members of society as the rich got richer. Keisha came from society's disposable stock. At least Eleanor had had the best care and a wealthy life. She'd had a family who no doubt treated her like a princess and gave her everything she wanted, before handing her over to William, who then did the same. Eleanor hadn't had to pay anything back. She wasn't held accountable for anyone else's failings like Keisha had been. As if it had been Keisha's fault that her mother drank herself to death when she arrived in England, forcing Auntie Ayo and Uncle Yahuba to have to raise her little girl, now wanting every penny they'd spent on her returned and then some. It was hard to feel sympathy for Eleanor.

"But she knew she was loved and that's important at the end, don't you think?" Virginia was still talking. "Iris kept her beautiful and Elizabeth kept her comfortable. Emmett would play cards with her, and Jason would come and read to her in those last days too. An hour every afternoon. Even when she was so confused and getting herself upset about things." Virginia looked down to the other end of the table. "You were very good to Eleanor, Jason. She knew that, even when she was fading."

At last the conversation had opened up and there was an opportunity for a glance and a secret smile. Something to store away for later. Something *alive*. She'd felt smothered by the dead today, and although they'd made a joke of the mad old woman in the square by the time they'd reached Marcie's car, there was something in her tone, her confidence, that reminded Keisha of Auntie Ayo and her dark secrets. Maybe she'd google later about Louisiana voodoo, or whatever Marcie had called it. Seeing those trinkets had left her feeling on edge. She'd thought that kind of stuff was only in New Orleans. She had hoped to be out of reach of Auntie Ayo's long shadow here, but maybe she hadn't run far enough. Even in the sunshine, it seemed that ghosts fought for breath.

"That's very kind," Jason said. "But I'm sure Keisha doesn't want us talking about Eleanor all the time."

"Jason's right," William said. "It's time to focus on the future. Speaking of which, when do you two leave us? Grand Cayman again, Virginia said?"

"Wednesday morning," Emmett answered. He

smiled, the expression strained. Keisha wondered if he'd had Botox. He must be nearly sixty, and the skin on his small face was unnaturally still, no movement in his forehead or around his eyes, making smiling seem like an effort. "It's only for a couple of weeks. Some work, some pleasure. We may do some island hopping."

"It's such a relaxed way of life," Virginia crooned. Her face was stretched smooth from her full cheeks, but she too, no doubt, had rid herself of any unwelcome wrinkles. It seemed the way of life here. Sure, plenty of girls Keisha knew in the club back home were Botoxing in their twenties, but the look on firm skin was more subtle, less like the preservation of the dead. Even the tissue-thin skin around Iris's eyes spoke of work done in the past when youth had still been close enough to try to grasp.

"So much less hectic than here. I'm always so busy. Between the club, my charity work, Richard's start-up, the church, and the Mission. Well." Virginia shrugged as if her short list explained some kind of exhausting daily routine.

Keisha wondered how she'd cope in London. The pace of life here seemed so luxuriously slow in comparison, each day like a cat's stretch. It would be blissful if it wasn't for Billy. Her irritation with him was heightened by the proximity of Jason and Marcie, she knew that. It bubbled constantly under her skin. Why was desire so hard? Why was the danger so alluring? So self-destructive? She needed to rein in her impetuous heart. Thank fuck for her Valium. She'd take one later. How many did she have left? Fifty maybe? She'd brought as many as she could get her hands on, but at some point she'd have to tell Billy she'd taken them for years to calm her anxieties and needed more, but not yet. They weren't his business.

"Maybe we should have a party here when you're back," William said. "Something for the Fourth of July. Noah and Iris will be home then too. It'll make a change from our usual dinner at the club." He smiled at Keisha. "New wife, new traditions."

"Great idea," Emmett said, raising his glass. "We'll be back before you know it."

"You'll still do Monday and Wednesday lunchtimes at the Mission, won't you, Marcie?" Virginia asked.

Marcie shrugged. "I'll try. But I'm quite busy myself. The house and everything."

"When I bought that house I thought it was pretty perfect." Jason rested his elbows on the table as he leaned in, talking as if Marcie wasn't there. "But apparently it needs a full remodel. Who knew?"

Marcie's perfectly made-up face tightened even as Jason laughed, turning the comment into a joke, and

Keisha's stomach fizzed with intrigue. There was definitely some discord between them. She could almost taste it. She could *use* it. A quiet throb started down between her legs even as she told herself once more not to let her loins fuck this sweet situation up for her. Oh, but she loved the longing. The distraction from the craziness that threatened her head. The itch of lust was almost as good as the act. *Almost.*

"Miss Elizabeth is outside, Mr. Radford, sir." Zelda had silently appeared in the doorway. She didn't glance at Keisha even as she nodded at the other guests, and Keisha tried not to let it sting.

"We'd better go and see what she wants, honey." William heaved himself up out of his chair. His eyes were shining as he came and took her hand, his palm sweaty despite the AC, and she couldn't stop herself suddenly picturing his damp, salty crotch, and the line of wet skin under the overhang of his belly. "Y'all coming?"

They dutifully traipsed out front into the thick heat, designer sunglasses dropping quickly in front of eyes so that any injected skin wouldn't fight back and wrinkle further from squinting in the sun.

"Voilà!" Elizabeth said as they rounded the corner to the drive in front of the garage. She was holding her hands out sideways like a magician's assistant introducing an act. Not that the gift needed pointing out. Keisha's heart leapt as she let out a squeal of delight. *Freedom.*

"A little runaround to tide you over until the Mercedes arrives."

"Oh Billy, it's wonderful!" She kissed him without hesitation, pressing her lips against his red cheek. "Thank you, thank you!"

"It's not new but only one owner. Low mileage. The best I could do at short notice."

Keisha traced her fingers across the hood like she would on a new lover's skin. It was sleek and low, a proper American convertible sports car and the metallic red shone bright and clean. Even second-hand it must have been at least forty grand worth of car, and in a few weeks her delicious $150,000 Mercedes would arrive. The sums added to the tingles in her body. She'd have to make sure all the paperwork was in her name. She couldn't stop smiling, giggling like a child. Dolly would just *die.* Keisha hadn't called her back, ignoring the texts that had come in while she was sleeping. Maybe she should totally ghost her now. Dolly would only find some way to pull all of this down. She was too jealous to be happy for her.

"Well, aren't you the lucky girl," Emmett said. "A little red Corvette."

"It's very showy." Marcie, as ever, loitering at the back as if she didn't want to be seen.

"I like showy." Keisha plastered on a huge smile as she grabbed the keys from Elizabeth and pulled open the driver's door. The seats were low and the perfect leather smelled new. A rich, wealthy scent. *This* is why she had to keep Billy happy. She pushed the seat back to accommodate her long legs and through the windshield she could see the others looking on, expressions unreadable behind their shades. Keisha wasn't fooled. They—well, maybe except one—liked her only because Billy did, but she didn't care. Billy was the bank account. Her shot at freedom. He was all that mattered.

She started the engine, enjoying its throaty purr vibrating through the leather beneath her. "Can I take her out? Just for a minute? Get a feel for her?"

"If someone goes with you. She's got some bite and remember you drive on the wrong side of the road in England."

"Get in then, hubby!" He was the Billy she'd met in London again, kind and generous. The car was glorious. The fact that he'd buy her something like this on a whim just to tide her over was also glorious.

"If I get in that, you'll need to call the fire department to pull me out again."

"I'll go with her." The volunteer had spoken before

Billy had barely finished his sentence. Jason. Of course it was.

William slapped him on the back. "Good work, wingman. Take care of her."

"Come on!" She revved the engine. "And buckle up!" She laughed.

She was still laughing as they pulled away, wheels screeching on the tarmac, one arm waving out the window at those they'd left behind.

12.

*T*he car, the car, the sleek shiny car. That, and the numbing buzz of the half Valium and wine, was enough to keep Keisha pliant while Billy's tongue pressed against hers as he panted into her mouth. His saliva was thick and unpleasant, his lips cold and rubbery—old man mouth—and rather than squirm her head to one side she pushed his head down to her chest and arched her back as if it were desire and not revulsion that made her shiver. His weight shifted as he followed her silent command, his fat fingers kneading her breasts, twisting one nipple while sucking at the other.

That was better. She could get into her zone now, close her eyes, and drift into a fantasy of younger hands and warmer lips pressing her back onto the hood of her

new red sports car. She pushed Billy's head down farther. She'd come fast tonight. She was too full of *heat*.
She hadn't had such a crush in ages. It would keep the
darkness at bay.

She moaned as his tongue worked at her and he
groaned and grunted in reply. She wished he'd stay
silent. She didn't want him shattering her fantasy,
not now, not while she was so close. She concentrated
harder, blocking him out. It didn't take long after that,
and this time there was nothing fake about the orgasm
that shuddered through her, expelling its excess energy
in a loud gasp.

Billy clambered back up the bed and lay beside her,
his chest heaving as if he'd fucked her senseless for an
hour. She rolled onto her side to face him and smiled
despite her inner revulsion, before reaching down to
his semi-erect cock. *The car, the money, the future.*
She tried to think like Dolly. His skin was soft, no hint
of tautness there, and she realized that semi-erect was
a flattering exaggeration. He was pretty much flaccid.

"Is it me?" she asked, wide eyes hinting at insecurity. Like fuck was it her. She could make a man rock
hard from fifty paces when she put her mind to it and
she knew it.

"No, no, don't think that. You have no idea how
much I want to. I didn't take . . . you know . . . the pill.

Thought I could do without it." He couldn't bring himself to look at her. Embarrassed. How strange it must be to be a man. So much of their self-worth wrapped up in that tiny odd-looking appendage. No amount of time on the treadmill or foul coconut water could get the blood pumping to the right place.

"You did just fine without it." She curled up into his chest, happy in his impotence. None of his games tonight. No "trying new things."

"I thought I'd feel younger with you." He stared up at the ceiling, and she knew his thoughts were swirling toward death and decay. Maybe *he* needed the Valium. "But somehow you make me feel twice as old."

"Don't say that," she murmured. "Don't take it all so seriously. You're fine. Who cares if you have to take the pills? That's what they're there for." She sounded calm, but her unease was growing. What if he changed his mind about her? What if she had to go home empty-handed?

"I want you to be happy," he said. There was an edge of disgruntlement, of irritation, in his voice. Embarrassment in a man could be dangerous.

She leaned up so she could look at him. "I *am* happy. You know that. You've made me so happy. And safe. And that's more than anyone else has in my whole life. I couldn't *be* any happier." She was amazed at how earnest she sounded given the enormity of the lies. "And," she continued, "little blue pills or not, you *satisfy* me."

He smiled at her then and she relaxed. Crisis averted. If there was one thing she understood about Billy, it was that he'd never abide any hint of pity.

"Jason's booked us a boys' weekend in Atlanta next weekend," he said. "Delayed bachelor party."

"That's nice." She kept her tone neutral, even though her heart tripped slightly.

"Something's up with him and I can't figure it out," Billy continued. "And if he thinks I don't notice that he can't keep his eyes off you, then he's crazy."

She laughed aloud at that. *If only he knew. If only.* "He's your friend. I think he's just being nice," she said. "And I guess if he's been in charge or whatever while you've been away, it must be a bit weird for him if you're changing your mind."

"That's true. I don't know. Maybe I'm imagining it."

"Go on your boys' trip. You're a smart man. You'll figure it out."

"You're right," he said, pulling her close to kiss her. "You want me to do that again?"

"I don't think I'm ready." She kissed him back, chaste, mouth closed. "That was amazing. How about we just snuggle?"

"Deal," he said, chuckling. He reached over and flicked out the light, plummeting them into darkness. "Damn, it was a lucky day when I met you."

As it was, although William was snoring within ten minutes, Keisha couldn't sleep, not even after the wine and the Valium and the orgasm. It had satisfied her immediate lust momentarily, but the terrible desire for someone *else* was still there. She got up and headed down to the warm night air of the terrace, taking her old UK mobile with her. The cicadas were chattering, echoing the buzz of thoughts in her head. There had to be a way for her to have her cake and eat it too. She couldn't live like this for much longer, with no excitement. It had been only four months with Billy and already she was suffocating. If this went on too much longer all her old anxieties would come back. She was never good when she felt trapped. Never.

When she'd met him, she'd wanted the rich life far away from home so much she hadn't thought long term. The same old man every night. Keeping him happy while waiting endlessly for him to die or until she'd gotten enough hidden away to leave him. How much would be enough? Enough to satisfy Uncle Yahuba and free her from fear of Auntie Ayo. But also enough for *her.* She understood greed, it was a family trait, and greed took people to dark places. She wanted as much as she could get, what was wrong with that? She'd have earned it. And after that she never wanted to be under someone else's control again. All her life she'd felt *owned.* No more.

But still, despite her hard and mean thoughts, she ached. Lust had always been her downfall and always would be. Pretending to love someone day after day was hard, when someone else she was sure she *could* love, who at least made her body hum, was so close at hand. Why couldn't Billy just die?

She looked down at her old cell phone, chewing her bottom lip, before looking up again, hesitant, still thoughtful. She froze. Zelda was at her window, a still figure against a backdrop of light. She didn't move as Keisha stared up at her. What was she doing? Was she spying on her? A strange unsettled feeling, a slight fear, prickled at her skin, as if Zelda had been standing there for hours waiting for her to appear. As if she could see into the darkness of Keisha's thoughts. How did she appear from up there? As guilty as she felt? *Box clever,* she thought. *Don't show how unsettled you are.*

She raised one hand to her forehead as if squinting in sunlight instead of darkness and then flashed a smile and waved. For a long moment Zelda remained so still Keisha began to wonder if the housekeeper had fallen asleep standing upright, and then the figure stepped out of sight before a blind dropped down. She hadn't waved back.

Fuck you, Zelda, Keisha thought, returning her attention to her phone, her fingers flying over the keys. *I'm going to have the last laugh for once, just you wait and see.*

13.

Jason's phone, beside the bed, was on silent but when the text came in the flash of screen light was enough to wake Marcie even without the quiet vibration. If he hadn't moved, she'd probably have fallen straight back to sleep, but as it was, she felt the mattress shift as he rolled over to check it. That wasn't like Jason. He usually slept like the dead. His body tensed and then he very carefully pushed the covers off and got up.

She closed her eyes and kept her breathing slow and steady. First there was only silence, a long pause in which he was probably making sure she was still sleeping, and then came the quiet sound of his tread as he crept, secretive, out into the hallway.

She opened her eyes in the dark, her heart thumping. Why hadn't she just asked him who it was from?

What instinct had kept her quiet? It was probably a work text. *People don't text about work in the middle of the night.* Unless it was an email. Yes, maybe one of the junior partners was working late and wanting advice on something. Not that she knew whether that was likely or not. She wasn't interested in Jason's work, mainly because she didn't understand it. Legal language was *designed* to make people like her not understand it.

But still, that pause. The furtiveness of his movement. Another layer of unease cloaked her. What was so urgent he had to deal with it at—she lit up the screen on her own phone—two in the morning? She sat up in the darkness, wide awake, and looked over at the grainy shadow of the bedroom door that he'd so carefully closed as he left.

Despite the cool whirr of the AC, sweat prickled her hairline as she got up and went after him, and her mouth was dry. Why was she so nervous? So what if he found her looking for him? That's what wives did, wasn't it, if they woke up and their husband wasn't in bed? Checked he was okay?

It wasn't *him* she was afraid of, she knew that. It was whatever secret thing he was doing. What she might find out. More strands of the rope that tied them together fraying in her hands as he pulled away. *Rope like his father hanged himself with.* The creaking, that's what Jason said haunted him most after finding the body. That terrible sound that told him he was only moments too late. The stillness of death hadn't completely settled after the frantic movement of dying. Had Jason now echoed his father and put a noose around their marriage, choking the love out of it?

He was in her dressing room. She could see the light through the crack under the door. Her heart thumped harder and she almost laughed—albeit slightly hysterically—at the irony. The dressing room was where she housed *her* secrets. No. Not exactly secrets. Her private things. Stuff that had never impacted Jason— and never would. Nothing he needed to know about. Reminders of how far she'd come for when she found it all so overwhelming. And, of course, her pills. She felt a twist of guilt. Those did concern him. But right now, as she pressed her ear against the door and heard his voice, almost a whisper, too infuriatingly quiet to make sense of, she was glad she had them. Why lock himself in her dressing room to make a call? Why not just go to his study? This was not a work call. There was too much *urgency* in his tone.

She stayed a moment longer, goose bumps rippling across her skin, and then turned back, resisting the urge to push open the door and demand to know who he was talking to. It would be pointless. He'd lie, they'd fight, and she'd end up feeling bad and paranoid and still be none the wiser. She was smarter than that.

The five or so minutes between rearranging herself into a sleeping position and Jason creeping back into bed felt like forever. As he pulled the sheet back over him she murmured, as if only half-awoken, "You okay, baby?"

"Just needed the bathroom," he said quietly, as he lay with his back to her. "Go back to sleep."

She rolled away slowly to her side of their vast bed, her breath surprisingly slow and steady as she faked sleep, and she could almost feel the tension in his back as he pretended to do the same. She was numb. Shell-shocked. *Just needed the bathroom.* He'd blatantly lied to her. She felt sick. She felt hot. She didn't know what she felt. Betrayed? Lost? Fucking angry?

Her fingers gripped the edge of the pillow, the only outlet for her pounding emotions as they both lay there, in a farce of sleep. Who would want to speak to him at this time of night? Who would he take a call from? Who?

Keisha is a night owl.

The thought had been bubbling since the flash of light had woken her, but finally she gave it voice. Keisha stayed up late and got up late. William would be asleep, just like Jason had thought she was. Her stomach turned to water. Surely she was being paranoid. It was one thing to suspect flirting and maybe a little bit of *want*, but this was affair territory. Did she really think that was what they were doing? How would Keisha have gotten Jason's number anyway? They hadn't— Her stream of thought stopped dead. The car. Jason went with Keisha in her flashy red car. They were gone for what, fifteen, twenty minutes? A lot could be said in that time. Even if they didn't *do* anything, how easy would it have been to find a reason to exchange numbers? Especially if you *wanted* to.

Once a cheat, always a cheat.

Her love was evaporating in the heat of her jealousy and she wanted to turn over and flay him alive with her nails. She forced herself to lie still, trapped under the blanket of night, alone with her dark thoughts. What was Jason thinking on his side of the bed? Quietly planning how he could escape her? Is this how Jacquie, the first wife, had felt? When had her moment come, that second when trust slid into mistrust and love cracked wide, emptying, leaving only the brittle shell?

Jacquie had confronted Jason, and he'd told her it was all in her imagination, stringing her along until he was finally ready to leave. That wouldn't happen to Marcie. She wasn't going to let loose with hysterical accusations. Evidence. She needed evidence. There'd be no gaslighting *her*. She was *way* smarter and tougher than that.

Of course, the caller might not even have been Keisha. Now that Marcie had opened the door of suspicion in her mind, other shadowy suspects emerged onto the stage. Sandy, the secretary? No, surely not. If Jason had wanted to bang her, he'd have done it years ago.

Someone at the club? A waitress from the members only—which meant *men only* given that wives were members by association—games' nights at the club? Everyone knew William had been quite taken with one girl when Eleanor was dying. What was her name? Michelle, wasn't it? Yes, Michelle from Michigan, who was there for only a short while and then went back home to study. It hadn't been a serious thing, an old man cheering himself up, but what if William's actions had given Jason an itch for something new or a little something on the side that was now getting out of hand? He'd been behaving oddly—closed off—for a while.

But her mind returned to Keisha. Beautiful, strong Keisha. A different kind of beauty from hers, just as her own blond delicate look was different from Jacquie's brunette sophisticated one. Jason wanted control of the firm, did he think he could have William's wife too? It was almost too audacious, but Jason was nothing if not ambitious.

Her thoughts whirled around and around until she was sure she'd drive herself into a fever of madness, but instead she exhausted herself into an hour or two of fitful sleep, the past and present colliding in her dreams in which she screamed in frustrated rage at her faithless husband and Keisha and Jacquie and others she thought she'd forgotten, until she woke, breathless and sweating, at first light.

She'd hoped to check his phone when he went to take a shower but her breaking heart sank when he took it with him. Another tick in the guilty box. She wasn't deterred. She'd had plenty of time to think while he dozed before getting up. Jason didn't stay so good-looking without any effort. He was a man who *groomed*. He never spent less than fifteen minutes in the bathroom and fifteen minutes might not be long, but it was better than nothing. As soon as she heard the water start to run, she scrambled out of bed and darted into his study, where his laptop sat on his desk.

The leather seat was cold on her thighs through her thin robe as she quickly flipped open the lid and typed in his password—Atlanta_Braves89—and the home screen came up. She let out her breath, relieved he hadn't changed it. She moved the mouse to the bottom of the screen to find the iMessage icon. He may have taken his cell to the bathroom but all his messages would still show up here. After a quick glance out to the corridor, she clicked on it. She frowned. Nothing. No messages. How could that be? He was always working in here, often having left his phone tossed on the kitchen island or by the bed. He didn't need it. He could make calls and answer texts from his laptop.

He'd disabled it. That was the only answer. His phone was no longer connected to his laptop and he'd deleted all his message threads. Why would he do that? *Secrets.* He was keeping secrets from her. New secrets. Maybe Keisha wasn't the first woman to text him and he only just thought to remove all traces from the laptop. Cleverer men than Jason had been caught out by messages popping up on iPads and computers.

She'd try WhatsApp. Not that Jason ever used it, but maybe Keisha was that kind of girl. A *girl about town* with various groups like the awful tennis set at the club or the self-proclaimed YummyMummies who spent their days at the spa and then in the bar after leaving their precious children at County Day.

She searched his applications folder. No WhatsApp. That was gone completely. Her heart thrummed faster. That didn't mean anything in and of itself. He could have just been cleaning up his computer and decided he didn't need it, but combined with iMessage being empty? An app she knew for a fact he used? The whole thing stank of guilt and secrets.

Shaken, she sat back and looked at the photo that filled the background of the screen. The two of them a few years ago, her arms wrapped around Jason's neck, cheeks pressed together, both grinning for the selfie, determined to capture that perfect moment of happiness. She remembered exactly when he'd taken it. Out on a boat. He'd just proposed. Jacquie was finished. Marcie had won. She was still new to all this then—this fascinating life of expensive clothes, nice cars, eating out whenever you felt like it, never looking at the price of things. She was in love—totally and completely—with Jason and everything he could bring to her life. Safety. Security. Respect. Well, despite her recent longing for financial freedom, she didn't feel very safe or secure anymore and the respect had never been forthcoming. The happy couple in the image, smiling smugly out at her, were like strangers now. What had brought them to this?

She was about to close the lid when she spotted a folder in the corner of the screen. *Untitled Folder.* That wasn't like Jason. He was neat and organized. A lawyer. Everything in place and a place for everything. She double-clicked, and it opened. Her stomach lurched in expectation of being presented with awful images of spread-eagled women smiling up at her husband from some awful motel room bed. Just like she used to. *Stop it, stop it, stop it,* she told herself. *This is a path to madness.*

Her heart slowed and her face flushed as the dullness of the actual document presented itself. It was only a spreadsheet of some kind. A list of numbers allocated to letters that meant nothing to her. Probably some shorthand for something to do with work. She needed to get a grip.

But still, she thought, as she closed the lid and left his study as she'd found it, heading downstairs to put on the coffee, there was still the phone call.

There was still the lie.

14.

Keisha was wide awake and, for once, in a great mood. It was barely eight thirty and she'd had only four hours of sleep, but the phone call before she'd crept back into bed had put a smile on her face and there was a spring in her step as she grabbed the rose gold Mac-Book Billy had bought her and headed downstairs. Why shouldn't she be happy? She just had to be careful, that was all.

"Would you like some breakfast, ma'am?" Zelda was over at the walk-in refrigerator, having somehow already been to the store, unpacking individual cartons of odious coconut water, lining them up on the side shelf in pride of place. "I'm going to make Mr. Radford some eggs and home fries." She was behaving perfectly normally, no hint of how she'd stared down at Keisha the night before. Keisha's skin prickled as she remembered her still shadow. The brazenness with which she'd been watched.

"It's too early for me." She looked at the housekeeper as she meekly emptied the bags. "How did you sleep?"

"Oh, I always sleep like the dead."

"Really?" Keisha poured herself coffee from the machine. "I was sure I saw you last night. At your window. It was late. I went into the garden for some air. Cream, please."

"You must be mistaken, ma'am. I was in bed early." Zelda put the carton of cream on the large island. "Would you like a jug?"

"This is fine." *You lying spying bitch*, Keisha thought, even as she said, "It must have been a trick of the light then." She flashed her best razor smile. What was the woman's problem? She didn't like Keisha? So what? It wasn't her *job* to like her.

How old was Zelda? she wondered. Old. Fifties, at least. Maybe even over sixty. How long had she worked here? Billy probably had told her, but Keisha often found her thoughts drifting away when Billy was talking. She tried to remember. Twenty years? Or was it more? Had she loved Eleanor too? Did she think Keisha was an insult to the first Mrs. Radford's memory? *Eleanor, Eleanor, Eleanor.* The wife who would not be forced from this house, even in a coffin.

But Eleanor was gone and Zelda would get used to it. Now that it was morning and the sun was shining gloriously bright, Keisha was feeling too zesty to let the housekeeper and her nighttime antics bother her, so she took her coffee and her laptop out to the sunroom by the terrace.

She opened up a tab to her Gmail with dread, knowing what she was going to find. There was a message from Dolly sent a couple of days before—"*Hope you're having fun! Is he dead yet?*" followed by a couple of cry-laugh emojis and then "*Miss ya!*" and some kisses. There were three emails from Uncle Yahuba. All wanting money. She had to be a good niece. She knew what she had to do: various levels of implied threat. She sighed and closed them down. How was she supposed to send them money? She had a new credit card, true, but it wasn't as if Billy was filling her bank account with cash. Why couldn't they be patient? *Why couldn't they all just leave her alone?*

They knew how to play her, how to draw on her insecurities and her dark, confused moods. As ever, the echo of Auntie Ayo's words, spoken when Keisha was just six years old, not long after they took her in, when she'd seen the ghostly boy, haunted her. *You got yourself cursed blood, KeKe, it's there in the cards, no good will come of you, KeKe.* Her mother's nickname for her, all she remembered of her really. Keisha Kelani, my KeKe. Auntie Ayo and Uncle Yahuba had even taken that from her, and now it was synonymous with her cursed blood.

Was that true or simply something Auntie Ayo had said to stop her blabbing her mouth off at school about the boy? She didn't want to think about the boy. The boy had never been there. She knew that. They'd told her. The boy was an error of her crazy mind. The boy was the first sign that she was *wrong*, a bad seed, unbalanced. She deleted the emails. Her family were thousands of miles away. She didn't want to think about them today. They could wait. They didn't have a choice.

"Honey?" Billy's voice, that of the master of the house, echoed through to her. "Hey honey?"

"Coming!" she answered, light and frothy. A good wife. *Keep him sweet.* She grabbed her coffee and went to the breakfast room, where she found him still drenched in sweat from the treadmill.

"You're up early," he said, through his mouthful of eggs and fried potato.

"It's such a beautiful day." Keisha took a seat opposite him. "Shame to miss it." Zelda brought her some orange juice and a croissant even though she'd said she didn't want breakfast, and then disappeared again, taking the empty carton of coconut water on the table away. Billy always downed it in one long swallow, Keisha noted. Maybe he didn't much care for the flavor of it either, no matter what he said.

She peeled off the edge of her croissant, not really sure what to do with it as there was no butter or jam on the table, and ate it dry while watching him shovel his food into his mouth. His cheeks were flushed redder than normal, bursting veined beetroots on his face— had he run farther and faster to make up for his inadequacies in the bedroom? Trying to recover his masculinity?

"You're supposed to dip it in your coffee," he said, staring at her as crumbs fell down her top. "Like the French do. That's how Eleanor did it." He returned to his plate for a moment, easing his irritation with another mouthful of eggs. The pastry stuck to the roof of Keisha's mouth, and she cringed once more with her ignorance and the hurt of the open comparison with Eleanor.

"Sorry," she muttered, before tearing off another piece and carefully dipping it into her drink.

"You'll learn. Anyway, we need to think about our Fourth of July party." Billy finally rested his fork. "You want to organize it?" He smiled at her as if this were some great offering of trust in her wifely abilities.

"I can try," she said, eager for his approval. Kind Billy was always preferable to mean Billy. "You'll have to help me with invites. I only know about five people."

"That'll change, honey." He reached for his coffee. "Oh, that reminds me, I've booked you in for some tennis lessons at the club. We can go down to the pro shop and get you fixed up this morning. Maybe try the driving range too? Work on your swing. The girls here love golf and tennis as much as the guys. You'll meet some great people. Soon you'll be running charity galas like it's second nature."

"Sounds wonderful." Her heart sank. Golf and charity galas. He was already trying to shrink her into Eleanor's shape. Who was he trying to kid? Her or himself? She wasn't like Eleanor and never would be. He was displaying her like a piece of art he picked up on his travels. And calling his friends girls and boys was laughable. They were all so *old*.

But, she thought as she ate some more of her croissant, she'd play the game for the time being.

She had no choice.

15.

It had been a bad couple of days. Alone in the house, Marcie stared into her box of private things. She'd tossed the photo of Jason and her over the side, resisting every urge to tear it up and flush it. While she'd tried to keep her suspicions to herself and behave normally, he'd been coming home late, snappy and distracted. He'd rarely had his phone out of his pocket and when it was, he put it facedown. Casually, as if accidentally, but she knew better than that. This wasn't his first rodeo. You'd think he'd have learned not to be so obvious. He hadn't even mentioned trying for a baby or wanting sex, which until *she* turned up had been the only addition to their new house he seemed interested in.

She thumbed through the various pieces of old paper, all folded tightly, reluctant to be examined. Things she wished she could throw away but knew she had to keep. Documents she might need one day. Relics of the past. This ritual of hers was normally a comfort, a reminder of how far she'd come—now she was trying to find her old strength in it. Maybe she'd have to be that person again. Someone who had the power and resolve to start over from nothing. And do it fabulously. But this life had softened her and now she wasn't sure she could. Just the thought of it was exhausting. Maybe she no longer had the balls she'd had in her twenties. A couple of weeks ago she'd been feeling suffocated and quietly longed for some freedom, and now she was terrified of losing this smothering safety. No, she realized. She wasn't afraid of losing it. What she couldn't stand the thought of was someone else daring to try to *take* it from her. She hadn't changed *that* much in the past decade.

She closed the lid and hid the box back in the ceiling before taking a deep breath to pull herself together. She looked in the mirror. There were dark rings under her eyes but nothing that some carefully applied concealer wouldn't hide. She had to keep a cool head. She would *not* become the paranoid wife—at least not visibly. Whatever he was doing, Jason wouldn't divorce her. Certainly not yet. It had taken a long enough time to make him picture a life without Jacquie, and where one divorce could be forgiven in this polite world they inhabited, she wasn't so sure he'd get away with two, however many people might privately gossip that she was getting what she deserved. Not combined with what his father had done. The fine families of the South would start to withdraw. Jason came from good stock, but certainly not the best.

How far back could the Maddox name claim heritage? A century? Longer? Certainly not as far as William's, Noah's, Eleanor's, and Iris's families. They were American blue bloods. Never a shameful moment of history with their ancestors, if the way they told it was to be believed. No doubt anything that might harm their good names had been smoothed away with cold hard cash. Maybe that was the shackle that bound them. All that virtuous goodness constantly on show. Not like her own tribe.

She started to brush brown shadow onto her eyelids, highlighting her blue eyes. There had been no virtue in her family. Scrabbling for dollars. Living on welfare. Looked down on by everyone. Resenting every new accidental mouth to feed as if it were the baby's fault rather than that no one had thought to stick a rubber on his dick or get some birth control. Never enough money to go around. She imagined William's blood to be a rich red wine. Hers would stink of rust. Name had never counted for anything good in the trailer park in Boise.

As each layer of makeup went on, she felt better. At least she'd taken a small revenge yesterday while Jason had been at work. She'd ordered three new divine pieces of furniture for the second dining room out at the back of the house. They were one-offs and hand-made to order. Eye-wateringly expensive for a room they'd probably never use and which Jason had been insistent they didn't need to furnish right away. Her stomach clenched at the thought of the argument to come when he got the bill, but she reminded herself he deserved it. He'd lied. He was lying, constantly, about something. Or *someone*.

She dressed in a slim-fitting pantsuit, consumed by the memory of that lie.

Just needed the bathroom.

The few words that had forced the widening cracks in her marriage to finally shatter. It hadn't helped that over the past day or so she'd come to the lonely conclusion that she didn't even have a friend she could call and confide in. Someone to reassure her and calm her down. Iris was away, and although she could be snooty, she was sage. There was no one else Marcie could trust to listen sympathetically without then blabbing to all and sundry that Marcie Maddox thought her husband had fallen out of love with her. People might be endlessly polite face-to-face here, but one thing she'd learned was, good lord, this city loved to gossip.

Shopping, she decided. She'd go shopping. Buy herself some new clothes. Revamp her look. Something less middle-aged. Something cool like the stuff the kids wore at the club. The *kids*. They were only a year or two younger than Keisha, most of them. Shopping always made her feel better—adding to her possessions so she didn't have to face how lonely she was. Jason had brought her into this world, and all she had now was him. She didn't share the years of friendship the others had. She didn't have coworkers to laugh with. She really had nothing of her own anymore except Jason, and now they were broken.

She wanted to wear her vintage Hermès scarf tied around her throat like a sixties movie star. She loved that scarf. It made her feel bold rather than a pale ghost of a beauty who once was. Where had she put it?

She groaned. The last place she'd worn it had been to the Mission. Her heart sank. *And* it was Wednesday today. If she went to pick it up the other volunteers would all side-eye guilt her into staying for her two-hour shift, the one she'd promised Virginia she'd try to do.

Just needed the bathroom.

Maybe it wasn't such a bad idea to go and do the

hours. There could come a time when she'd need these friends on her side and as much as there was something snide about Virginia, she'd make a better ally than an enemy if Jason was doing the dirty. Women tended to rally in those situations in a *there but for the grace of God go I* kind of way.

The Mission then, she thought, leaving her glorious new house that now felt like a paper castle, and then she'd shop. Build a protective wall of expensive clothing around her damaged heart.

16.

"Hey, Marcie!"

She was about to replace the empty tray of mashed potatoes with a fresh one from the kitchen when the voice cut across the room, and she froze, knuckles whitening against the steel.

Keisha.

Her accent was immediately recognizable. Marcie's veins burned as she handed the tray to Frannie, one of the least irritating of the church volunteers, mumbling an apology before turning to face her glamorous rival.

"What are you doing here?" Marcie couldn't peel her serving apron off fast enough, as somewhere in the room someone let out a low, appreciative wolf whistle. It wasn't for her.

"There's an emergency," Keisha said. "Nothing

to worry about. Just need you to come with me." She looked over Marcie's shoulder to the other volunteers. "A water leak. Sorry!" And with that, she'd taken Marcie's arm and was dragging her outside. "Thank me later," she whispered. Marcie's jaw clenched. Thank her for what? Embarrassing her in front of all those good Savannah women? There had been no sense of emergency in Keisha's tone, only mischief, and they'd see through it. So much for keeping Virginia on her side. This would get reported back in no time at all. Maybe that was the point.

"What are you doing here?" Marcie repeated, pulling her arm free. She looked back. "I need to get my purse. My things."

"Then go get them. Let's get out of here." Keisha leaned over the side of the gleaming red convertible and plucked a bottle from a grocery store bag in the back seat. "I bought tequila. And a load of snacks. We can chill by the pool back at my place and get drunk."

"I've got my car."

"So what? Follow me to mine and then get Jason to pick you up later."

Jason. Of course. An elaborate ruse so Keisha could get to see Jason again.

"I've got errands to run."

"Yeah, right. Of course you do."

The words stung, amused and dismissive. Who was Keisha to judge her? And what did she actually want? She clenched her jaw. There was only one way to find out, and maybe spending a few hours alone with this young pretender to her throne would allow Marcie to do some digging of her own.

All the way to the house Marcie tried to figure Keisha out, her eyes fixed on the little red Corvette ahead. It was one thing screwing around with someone's husband, but it was taking things to a whole other level trying to be friends with his wife while you did it. What was she playing at? Maybe it hadn't been Keisha on the phone the other night? But Jason's furtive behavior. The way he was around Keisha. Even if they weren't *doing* anything yet, had they formed a secret friendship? The sort that came before anyone wants to mention sex, but is just as intimate a betrayal as that act? Or was she going mad and the phone call was nothing to do with Keisha at all?

The outside clouds burned away in the heat of her racing thoughts and by the time she parked behind Keisha the sun was brilliant against a clear blue sky.

Keisha thrust a bag of groceries into her arms. "I can't get enough of all this American shit. The sugar helps with the lack of sleep."

"Jet lag?" Marcie asked, following her up the drive.

"I'm better in the mornings, but I still can't drop off until about three A.M."

Three. The text that got Jason running for her dressing room had come in at two.

"Let's get started on the margaritas then." She smiled, trying hard to sound relaxed. "If those don't knock you out later, nothing will." If Keisha *was* behind the mysterious call, then how would Jason react to having to collect Marcie and finding them drunk together? He wouldn't be happy. She remembered when she'd tried Facebook stalking Jacquie and he found out. He'd hated that. He liked things in his control. Keisha could definitely be marking her card with this move.

"Don't be so sure." Keisha winked at her as she opened the front door. "I can drink like a sailor."

The morals of one too, Marcie thought, following her inside and ignoring her own dubious past.

17.

Within half an hour they were out by the pool, a jug of margaritas on the table between them alongside a family-size bag of chips and a sack of dough-nuts. Marcie had drunk her first cocktail fast, Dutch courage against her unsettled mood, and although their loungers were in the shade of a vast umbrella, as she sipped her second, the liquor was going straight to her head in the heat. Keisha had made it strong.

She looked down at the modest blue two-piece she was wearing. It was the best of a bad bunch of guest swimwear—no doubt picked out by Eleanor years ago—but couldn't compare with Keisha's red swim-suit, which plunged in a deep V down to her belly. A scrap of thread linked it to the super-high-cut legs and thong by a gold hoop that somehow held the whole thing together, and every piece of skin on show was firm and taut.

"I had a tennis lesson at the club yesterday," Keisha said, stretched out, luxuriating in the heat. "I hate tennis. I only went because Billy had already booked it and I didn't really have any choice. Those people at Billy's club are never going to like me. I'll never fit in there."

It was a surprisingly open admission. Keisha clearly hadn't learned yet that no one in this town, certainly not at this social level, ever showed weakness. It was a shark pool, and the women were the worst. Bored and half-drunk most of the time. What else was there to do but bitch, judge, and gossip about one another between charity events?

"You get used to it." Had she herself ever gotten used to it? Really? "Underneath all that money some of them are nice. But it's like school, you know? Different groups. Everyone worried about what people are saying about them and who they have to stay friends with for their husband's promotions or to get invited to the right parties. It's harder for you. Eleanor was born and bred local royalty. She and William and Iris and Noah. Blue bloods. But people forget fast. This will be the new normal in a couple of months."

Keisha sat up and refilled their glasses, waving away

Marcie's slight protest. "Must have been hard for you as well. Given the circumstances," she said. "Was Jacquie popular?"

The circumstances. So, Keisha knew they'd had an affair. Marcie's skin prickled. And she knew Jason's first wife's name. She'd been a busy little bee. Who had she been talking to? Just William? Or the women at the club too? They'd love to spill some dirt on Marcie Maddox she was sure. She took another long swallow of margarita.

"She was popular, yes. But the difference between her and Eleanor is that Jacquie didn't die. She very quickly remarried—a retired orthopedic surgeon who died just before Eleanor as it happens—and moved to Atlanta." She paused. "Which may be worse now I think about it."

Keisha burst into a throaty laugh. "So"—she grabbed a handful of chips—"what's your story? You're the only other person I've met who doesn't come from Georgia."

"No story to tell, really."

"Everyone has a story. Where are you from?"

What was it with this woman and questions? In Marcie's experience most people just wanted to talk about themselves and she liked it that way. "Boise, Idaho," she said, in a bored drawl, hoping to cut the conversation short. "And if you'd ever lived there, you'd know why I left." That wasn't even a lie. No doubt she *would* know. Word choices could make the truth malleable and it was always better to stick close to the truth. "I figured if I didn't get out when I was young, I never would."

"Have you got any family?"

"None that I want to stay in touch with. We were never close. My dad died. My mom remarried. Had a new family. I was surplus to requirements." It sounded so much more sanitary than it was. An old and ordinary tale of young girl grows up and leaves town. The rest of it belonged to her alone, packaged up in the box in the ceiling. "You?" she asked.

"My mum was . . . well, not very stable, I guess. She died a long time ago. After we came to London from Nigeria. I was raised by my aunt and uncle. A long and boring story. They stay in touch but I'm not planning on inviting them over for holidays. I'm kind of hoping they'll just fade away, you know?"

She did know. Maybe she and Keisha were quite similar. Maybe that's what Jason liked. Keisha was how Marcie used to be, even though he was the one who'd changed her. The same way that William was no doubt trying to change Keisha now, squeezing everything they'd liked in the first place into a whole new shape.

"But how did you end up here?" Keisha continued. She was like a dog chewing over a bone for the soft marrow inside. "In Savannah?"

The sun was bright overhead and Marcie stared at it before smiling, privately amused, as she looked over. "I liked the name."

"And then you met Jason, it was love at first sight, and you lived happily ever after."

Jason again.

"Well," Marcie said, "it wasn't quite that straightforward, but yes."

"How did you meet? Billy's never really told me I don't think. Just that you worked locally."

Marcie sat up, drained her margarita, and poured another. If Keisha wanted to do this, so be it. They'd do it. She was tired of being something she wasn't. Her head buzzed. Tequila made her wilder. It also made her want more tequila. So what if Keisha told people? It would embarrass Jason and he deserved some embarrassment.

"They're all such social snobs," she said, even though she'd kill to have the respect that Iris and Virginia had from the rest of the town's society. "Jason still tells new people that I was working as a receptionist at a client's office just outside of town. He's said it so often even I've started to believe it."

Keisha peered over her sunglasses. "Not true?"

Marcie shrugged and shook her head. "I was a broke waitress in a diner and living in a motel out by Hunter. Jason used to come in for breakfast when he had meetings that way. He liked my smile apparently." She paused. "Funny, he didn't mind me being a waitress *then*. In fact, he thought it was kind of cute. Obviously cute wasn't enough when it came to being the wife." She was surprised by her sudden bitterness. She resented her relationship with Jason more than she'd realized.

There was a long pause and then Keisha laughed, deep, throaty, and coarse. Marcie stiffened. "Are you laughing at me?" She sounded prissy and felt stupid. Of course Keisha was laughing at her. She was *constantly* laughing at her behind this faux-friendly exterior.

"No, no. Fuck no." Keisha held one hand up and shook her head as she got herself under control. "I'm not laughing at you. It's just it's so funny."

"What's so funny?"

"All of it. *Them.* Billy tells everyone that I worked in a travel agency. Apparently I was helping to plan the next leg of his European trip for him."

It was Marcie's turn to peer above her oversized, overpriced sunglasses. "That's what he told us. Said he hadn't wanted to interrupt Elizabeth's visit with her mother so he took care of it himself."

"Yeah, right. Like Billy would think like that. He's used to everything being done by someone else. Of course Elizabeth took care of it."

"How *did* you meet then?" Maybe this afternoon would turn out to be worthwhile after all.

Keisha pushed her glasses onto her head and sat up, taking a long swallow of her drink and then a deep breath before she started to speak.

"You can't tell anyone." Her eyes gleamed, mischievous. The tequila had hit her too.

"Of course I won't," Marcie said. An age-old lie. The first rule of big secrets, Marcie had learned, was that you kept them to yourself. The second rule of big secrets, she'd also learned, was that most people found it impossible not to break the first rule. She was not most people, but it appeared Keisha was.

"I was a waitress too. I worked in a club. Not like your country club. This was the kind with sticky carpets and cheap champagne and where girls dance for lonely old men or brash city boys out for the night. Billy came in one evening and we got talking. He came back the next day and the day after that, and one thing led to another and here we are."

"You worked in a strip club? Did you dance?" Marcie couldn't believe what she'd just heard. Why on earth would Keisha be so stupid as to share something like that? With *her*? The whole day had brightened. William Radford IV, king of the hill, had gone off and married a waitress from a strip club, maybe even a stripper.

"No! No, I couldn't do that. Not that I judge my friends who do it, but it wasn't for me. Anyway, it wasn't a strip place but table dancing. Close enough, though. Didn't bother *him* at the time either."

"Wow." Marcie snorted out a giggle and found she couldn't stop. Keisha was right. It was funny. These two preening men so concerned with what everyone else thought. Slaves to it despite their success and wealth. And what *would* everyone think if they found out? Eleanor would die all over again. Jacquie had been enraged at being replaced by a "trashy waitress," but this was something else. And she only had Keisha's word that she'd been a cocktail server. For all Marcie knew the English girl had actually been a stripper.

"I didn't know he had it in him to go to a place like that," she said, and laughed some more, and then Keisha was laughing too and within minutes their eyes were streaming and they were clutching their sides and they weren't even sure what was so funny anymore. It felt good, though, to properly belly laugh. She hadn't in such a long time. Why was that? When had she and

Jason stopped laughing like this? Maybe Keisha made him laugh like this too, she thought, and her giggles dried up. Perhaps that's what she had.

The sun was melting into the blue of the afternoon, slipping like oil streaks down the sky. She should probably text Jason in case he finished work early and wondered where she was. *Drinking tequila with the stripper you're hot for.* How would that go down?

"Anyway, now you know my big secret, maybe you'll take that stick out of your arse and start to relax a bit," Keisha said once they'd both got their breath back. "Please don't tell the others, though. I see how they look at me already. Like Billy not only went crazy and married some young girl, but chose a young *black* girl on top of it."

Marcie started to protest, but Keisha hushed her. "I may be ignorant on a lot of this, but I know when people are looking down on me. Everyone does here. Even Billy."

Keisha sounded so forlorn, Marcie didn't know quite what to say, but then Keisha whispered, "You want to get high?"

"What?"

"Weed. I found some. In Saint Eleanor's room."

"You're kidding."

"Nope. Come on. It'll be fun. I already had a Valium this morning, so if it's not going to kill me, it won't kill you."

"Oh, I really shouldn't . . ." Booze and drugs. This was turning out to be quite the afternoon. A treasure trove of information.

"We've got a couple of hours before Billy gets back. Let's be *young*. Play some music. Have a laugh. Please, Marcie?"

What was it with this woman? She didn't need Marcie's help. Keisha was hell-bent on wrecking her new life all by herself.

"Put some clothes on. I'll see you inside." Keisha grabbed the jug and glasses. "Let's get mashed."

She couldn't be serious. "What will Zelda think? And what will she tell William?"

"I'm tired of caring what people think. And she won't tell him anything, because she's about to get the rest of the day off."

Marcie stared after Keisha as she turned and headed for the terrace. Get high? No she was *not* going to get high. She was done with this weird day of game playing. She'd get dressed, go inside, call a cab, and go home. There was no way she was staying. No way.

18.

By six, Marcie was truly baked. Her ears buzzed and the R & B playing in the background, some English artist she'd never heard of, was now in time with the slow thump of her heart.

"This is really trippy weed," Keisha murmured and then coughed out a small laugh.

She was right. Marcie was at once floating on air and at the same time her limbs were heavy against the soft cushions. Everything was amusing and she cared about nothing. Where had Eleanor gotten this shit? Had she used it as pain relief when she was dying? Probably. But still, kudos to the old girl. Whoever her dealer had been they were good. But then Eleanor always *did* have the best of everything. At least her leftover grass wasn't going to waste.

They were out on the deck, sprawled on the double lounger, watching the sun sinking languidly toward the horizon, the doughnuts eaten, passing a joint between them. At some point Marcie had texted Jason to tell him where she was and that he'd have to pick her up, but she hadn't looked to see if he'd answered. Screw him, with his lies and his moodiness and his making her feel like shit. All that belonged in a world outside this bubble. She deserved to have some fun.

How strange that she was having fun with *this* woman though. The snake in their grass. She lay on her side and watched Keisha as she exhaled smoke from her perfect cupid's bow mouth. The knot in Marcie's guts, ropes of jealousy, insecurity, and paranoia tangling together tight, had gone. It was the smoke, she knew that, but she felt completely relaxed, observing her own life from the outside, fascinated by this creature who was possibly flirting with, or even screwing, her husband while pretending to be her friend.

"What?" Keisha said. "Why are you staring at me?"

Marcie shrugged. "I'm trying to figure you out."

"What do you want to know?"

"Nothing I think you'd tell me." She let out a half-laugh. She wasn't sure why. It wasn't funny and yet it was. She was being played at her own game. In fact, she was being outplayed at her own game.

"Try me." Keisha shrugged, childlike in her openness. Underneath the veneer of confidence she wore, Marcie was starting to see how young Keisha really was.

Marcie took a careful toke on the joint, without the hint of a cough this time. This was not how she'd seen this lunch date panning out. She'd planned to keep her cool and draw information from Keisha without giving away any of her own. Now she was about to blurt out exactly what she thought.

Keisha rolled onto her side, so that they lay facing each other. "Go on, what is it? I won't be offended."

That made Marcie want to laugh again. Her, offended? Wow, she was good. She sighed the laugh away. "There's only one thing I want to know."

"God, you're stoned. Spit it out."

"Okay." Screw it. She was too high and too tired of worrying to care about games anymore. She looked Keisha in the eye and rose up on one elbow. "Why are you pretending to be my friend when you obviously want to sleep with my husband?"

She spat the words out hard like poison darts, and Keisha looked stung.

"You think I want to fuck *Jason*?"

"Oh, come on! You're always wanting to be near him. Trying to get between us. Flirting and laughing.

Asking questions. Jason this and Jason that. I'm not stupid."

There was a long pause before Keisha burst into a fit of giggles, waving one perfectly manicured hand in front of her face. "Oh, that's too funny," she gasped between bouts of snorting laughter.

It was Marcie's turn to feel stung. How dare she? How dare she laugh? Why did what this woman think of her hurt so much? "Yeah, I guess it must be." She got unsteadily to her feet, trying to stay dignified. "How *stupid* of me to try to talk about it like adults." She wanted to get away. Everything was a mess and she'd made it worse. Getting drunk and stoned like a teenager. Speaking her mind. Making herself look like an idiot. The world spun slightly as she stumbled toward the patio doors, hoping the freezing AC inside might straighten her up.

"Marcie, wait!" Keisha, following her, grabbed her arm and spun her around. "Oh, for God's sake. I don't want to sleep with Jason." She stared at her. "Don't you get it? Of course I don't want Jason. I want *you.*" Her grip softened and she let go, slightly embarrassed. "You. It's all you," Keisha continued.

Marcie's world suddenly stilled. It didn't make any sense. "No, but I saw . . ." What *had* she seen? The way Keisha had looked up at Jason from the creek when they were on the boat? Marcie had been standing next to him and Keisha had been squinting. It wasn't Jason she'd been calling to come into the water at all. It was Marcie. She hadn't stayed in long after because the wrong person had joined her. Another memory flashed vividly. Marcie going to surprise Jason at lunch, and Keisha's greeting—*Ah, there she is. The wife.* She'd been waiting for *her.* And all the questions about their relationship. They hadn't been about whether Jason was unhappy, but about whether Marcie was. Could Marcie have been reading the whole thing wrong? It was crazy.

"But what about the phone call in the middle of the night?"

Keisha paused—*was that a flash of something?*—and then frowned. "Not me."

"So, you don't want to screw Jason?" Marcie was still struggling to absorb this new information. Hazy as she was on weed and tequila, it was like a fever dream.

Keisha shook her head. "I already have one husband and that's enough for anyone. It was supposed to be enough for me. I was going to be a good wife. But when I saw you that first time it was like lightning. I couldn't—can't—stop thinking about you."

"Me?" Marcie's face flushed. Could that be true? Had she gotten it so badly wrong? But she was here getting drunk and stoned, not Jason. And why would Keisha lie about something like this?

"I'm sorry. I shouldn't have said anything. I don't want you to feel weird around me. You're the only good thing in this place."

Marcie almost laughed. The thought of Jason preening, all male arrogance, launching himself at Keisha whenever he could, not knowing what a fool he was making of himself. Oh God, it was glorious. There was something so comically brilliant about it. For once, it wasn't all about Jason Maddox.

"And I know you're married," Keisha said. "I get it. So am I, after all."

"I love Jason," Marcie said, softly. Did she mean it? If the middle-of-the-night phone call hadn't been Keisha, it was still somebody. He'd still lied. He'd still been distant for months, so much so that she'd immediately thought he'd been trying to screw Keisha from a few looks. But what else was she supposed to think when he only wanted to fuck when he was drunk. She still felt she was walking on shifting sand in her marriage. Like she should be grateful for any crumb of affection. "He *was* flirting with you though, wasn't he? I didn't imagine that."

Keisha shrugged again, that helpless charming gesture. "Probably harmless."

The music was still playing and as the tune drifted through the patio doors, Marcie wanted to let it take her. "When did life get so complicated? I want to be nineteen, dancing in a field somewhere, in cutoff denims and a crop top," Marcie said, raising her hands above her head, finding the rhythm. It was a slow groove with a steady beat and it made her uninhibited in her movement. The sun had lost its midday rage, but the air was thick and warm, and a slight breeze caressed her as she moved; a tentative lover's touch. She let her hips tilt side to side as her head rolled, her hair falling into her face. What was happening here? Why did she feel so good? So *free*?

She pushed all thoughts aside. She was tired of thinking. Of worrying. She was just going to *be* for once, a reed in a river, carried on a current. She spun around, smiling. She liked the way Keisha was looking at her. As if she was *everything*. It was decadent, illicit, *wrong*. It made her feel alive. It was turning her on.

"You want a blow back?" Keisha asked.

Marcie nodded. It was good to be high. It felt so *dangerous*. All of it. A loose thread that could unravel a carefully wrought tapestry. This was not what *Marcie Maddox* did. Screw Marcie Maddox. Tonight, she was someone else. Keisha carefully relit the joint, barely a stub left. "Don't put it in backward," Marcie murmured. "You'll burn your mouth."

"It's the last draw I think," Keisha said, coming close until they were face-to-face. "You ready?"

Keisha sucked in hard, the paper crackling as seeds inside popped. Her nose furrowed, cute, making Marcie smile as she opened her mouth. Keisha slowly blew, and the secondhand smoke was sweet and cool as Marcie breathed the stream in, her lips barely an inch from Keisha's. *I'm breathing her in*, she thought, randomly. Air from her lungs. She shivered and closed her eyes momentarily, before quietly sighing the smoke from her own body. She stood, still, as the tingle ran from her toes to her scalp.

"You are so beautiful," Keisha whispered, eyes wide with awe. Keisha looked up to her. *Respected* her. It made Marcie tremble with delight.

"No," Marcie said. "*You* are beautiful." She reached up and cupped the other woman's face, pulling her gently closer until there were soft lips brushing hers and they were kissing. She should stop, she knew she should, but she couldn't. Her whole body was suddenly on fire. She traced her fingers down Keisha's sleek, elegant neck, and the other woman sighed into her mouth, her tongue darting forward, delicate and sweet. Electricity coursed through Marcie's veins.

She was drunk. She was high. And she was kissing a woman. She was kissing Keisha.

"Honey? You and Marcie here?"

The voice was barely audible over the music, but it cut like frozen steel through the moment and even as Marcie startled, Keisha had pulled away. They both gasped, kids nearly caught out, and Keisha turned the music down as she called, "Out here!" Looking around as she quickly smoothed her hair, Marcie expected to see evidence of their debauchery laid bare in an afternoon's worth of food and drink debris, but the solitary margarita jug—even empty as it was—two glasses and bag of chips that were on the table looked almost respectable. The dancing, the weed, the confessions, and the kiss all felt as if they belonged to a dream Marcie had been suddenly woken from.

William and Jason appeared in the doorway, both in polo shirts and pressed pants, straight from the golf course. The party was over. The men were back.

19.

Marcie had managed to appear passably sober until they left, but as soon as Jason started driving the motion of the car sent her head spinning and stomach lurching. She turned the AC up high and took deep breaths as she focused on keeping the contents of her guts where they were supposed to be. She hadn't felt this bad since . . . when? She could barely remember. A different life.

"Not so fast on the corners," she muttered as her throat constricted with nausea. A cold sweat broke out across her chest. This was not going to end well.

"How much did you drink? You're a mess."

She looked over at him, at the irritated frown furrowing his forehead. She shrugged and pointed at herself. "This much?" Her giggle turned into a groan. "I'm going to puke."

"Jesus, Marcie. Can you wait till we get home?"

As it turned out, she couldn't, and even as, hanging out of the open car door, she retched up chunks of doughnut and the acid tang of tequila and lime, she could feel his disapproval coming from the driver's seat. Finally, when she was getting her breath back and the world had settled slightly back onto an even keel, he dug a tissue out of the glove compartment for her to wipe her mouth.

"Better?"

"A bit." She flopped back against the leather seat. "I just want to lie down."

"You normally handle your liquor better than this." Jason's eyes narrowed. "Were you smoking?"

The tone of his voice was really starting to irritate her. How many times had she looked after him when he'd rolled home drunk after a boys' night out? Okay, not so many times in the past couple of years, but she *had.*

"Don't be so uptight. It wasn't cigarettes." No, he'd made sure she quit those as part of her transformation from hot waitress to high society wife. "Just a bit of weed."

"Weed?" He twisted around in his seat to face her. "Where the hell did you get that from? Don't tell me you bought it from one of those tramps you feed? Who knows what could be in—"

"Calm down, it wasn't mine. Keisha found it." She let out a half-laugh. "You'll never guess where. In Eleanor's stuff. Hidden in with her underwear apparently. There was morphine and needles there too." She raised an eyebrow at him. "So be glad I didn't try *that*."

"Jesus."

"Anyway, you're the one who wanted me to be friends with her."

"Yeah, but I didn't mean turn into some kind of college dropout and embarrass yourself."

"Oh, screw you, Jason." Her patience snapped. He wasn't her father. "It's not a big deal. You're going away for a whole weekend tomorrow and you're pissed that I had some fun?" *Some fun.* She'd kissed a girl. She'd actually kissed a girl.

"Yep." Jason pulled back onto the road, faster than he needed to. "Puking out of the car sure looks like fun."

They sat in silence while her stomach roiled once more. She swallowed hard, pretty sure she was going to be sick again.

"William will lose his shit if he finds out she looked through Eleanor's things."

"I wasn't planning on telling him," Marcie said. "And you'd better not either. Can we let it go now? Or I'll hurl again all over your legs." She gave him a grimace of a smile and he begrudgingly smiled back.

"Sometimes I forget you're still pretty young."

Yeah, she thought. *Sometimes I do too.*

It was dark when she woke, head throbbing and mouth acid dry. Her stomach muscles ached as she carefully sat up and drained the glass of water Jason had put there for her before she'd passed out. As she lay back down she didn't reach for him as he slept beside her, one arm stretched out under his pillow.

She was going to feel awful tomorrow. Was it the weed or the tequila or the combination that had wrecked her? Probably all of it. The grass had been strong. Stronger than anything she'd ever smoked and she was very much out of practice. Had Keisha been sick too? Probably not.

Keisha. God, what an afternoon. Marcie still couldn't get her head around it. Everything felt upside down, all that hatred gone. They were alike, there was no denying it. Both from tough backgrounds, both a lot younger than their husbands, both being forced into a mold that wasn't their shape. Both alone. There were differences too, though. Marcie hadn't married Jason for his money. Yes, it had been attractive to have a man who could look after her, but she'd loved him when they got together. She still *did* love him.

Didn't she? A worm of doubt wriggled through her veins. All the money she was spending on the house— that was boredom. The social climbing. How much did it actually matter to *her*? The way he'd been so quick to close down her business rather than help find ways to make it work. None of it made her want to have his baby. To tie herself to him forever.

He'd swept her off her feet at the start, that was for sure, but how did she really feel about him *now*? His secrets. The way he looked at Keisha. *Just needed the bathroom.* If it wasn't Keisha on the phone, who was it? Was a lot of how she felt built on resentment?

Keisha. Her thoughts came back to Keisha, as they had ever since she'd turned up on William's arm. Now sober, with all the angst of her hangover kicking in, she burned with embarrassment at the kiss. What if Keisha told William? No, she wouldn't. Or would she? There was something unpredictable about Keisha. How easily she'd opened up about her past. Keisha was a sharer. A dangerous thing. What if she got drunk around Iris or Virginia and told them? The dancing. The kiss. The weed. They all thought Marcie was second rate already, this would make her a joke. Oh God, what had they been thinking?

Marcie rolled onto her side and curled up in a ball. There was no point in worrying about it now. If Keisha brought it up, Marcie'd blame it on the cocktails, laugh about it, and hopefully they'd both forget it ever happened. She closed her heavy eyelids, sleep coming to take her again. She'd kissed a woman. It wasn't that weird.

No. The thought slipped in as she drifted for once too deep into the darkness to even hear the quiet buzz of Jason's phone as a text came in. *What was weird was how much she'd liked it.*

20.

Steam billowed out from the sliding door as Keisha stepped under the shower jet. She'd turned the water up as hot as she could stand, wanting to burn herself free of him, free of everything. She'd feigned sleep while Billy got up to go and use his stupid treadmill, but the truth was that she'd barely dozed for more than half an hour or so all night. Even the call she'd crept downstairs to make hadn't lifted her mood, and she'd kept her eyes on her feet as she went, sure that if she looked up in the night there'd be ghostly boys coming from every corner to drag her into the darkness. Maybe the Valium wasn't going to be enough this time. It was hard to stay shining and bright and confident when in so many ways she felt trapped and afraid. After what had happened with Marcie, she should feel good. More than good. Everything was going better than she could have hoped for. But then there was Billy with his Jekyll and Hyde ways.

She let the hot water pummel her shoulders, but where the spray from the jets cut across her buttocks, she winced. He had not been sweet and gentle and pathetic Billy last night. He'd taken two Viagras, eager to enjoy her loose mood and maybe punish her for it too. Perhaps she'd shone too much when he got home. Maybe he wanted that all for himself. Whichever, when they'd gone to bed he'd wanted to experiment. Play out some fantasy, he said. She cringed inside, remembering it. The spanking she could cope with, but this time he'd taken it up a level, using his belt. At first it was just teasing, light and playful, but that didn't last long. Seemed it had to get harder to make *him* harder. The less he could fuck easily, the meaner his sex got.

She scrubbed her skin, trying to focus on the good things. The future. The reassuring words on the phone. The sex had probably lasted only an hour or so before he fell asleep, but it had felt like an age. She'd wanted to cry. Especially when he went in *there*. She could just about cope with a fat old man when he was gentle, but not when he was grunting obscenities while hurting her. She wasn't made for this. She couldn't switch off and just do it, no matter how hard she tried.

The fact that she'd been so stoned had made it worse. It made her emotional. That grass had been good but weird, leaving her head heavy and fuzzy, as if it were something stronger. *Trippy* had been the wrong word. It had been *dreamy.* But she knew only too well how dreams could turn quickly to nightmares—*the ghostly boy, the boy, the boy who wasn't there*—and after the dream of her evening, the hour of sex had become a nightmare.

How could she have seen Billy as such an adoring puppy when they were in London? Harmless. Impotent. Sweet. Maybe sweetness belonged to those in the middle, not the poor or the rich. She knew she wasn't sweet. She wasn't a good person, she knew that. *Cursed.* Why had she presumed *he* would be? Maybe wicked recognized its own.

What was he going to be like today? Snappy with her? She wasn't entirely sure that, after it was done, Billy overly liked himself when they'd had *that* kind of sex, and she figured it was easier for him to blame his urges on her than on himself. To say she brought it out in him. She was going to have to be extra nice to him today and make him feel better about it. Just the thought weighed her down in her bones.

She turned toward the water and tilted her face into it. She'd feel better when her hangover and comedown were over.

"Got room for me in there?" Through the steam Billy's naked body appeared as he pulled open the door. "I'll soap your back if you soap mine."

She laughed and smiled as her heart sank. She didn't want him near her. Not when she'd just gotten clean. She had to toughen up. Everything was going well. Her mind drifted back to the double dose of Viagra Billy had taken last night and, as she closed her eyes and let the water soothe her, ignoring his hands on her, she thought how much easier everything would be if it had given him a stroke.

21.

"So sorry I'm a little late," Elizabeth said. "I forgot I'd offered to go check on Emmett and Virginia's place to sort their mail, and that took longer than expected, and then I had to go to the bank and there was such a long line. After that, I went to feed Midge for Iris, which should only have taken thirty minutes or so, but I couldn't find him anywhere." She wiped away an imagined hair from her forehead, her natural dark curls tight and short in the humid air. Marcie had never seen Elizabeth look so flustered. "He hasn't eaten yesterday's food either. I'll go back and search properly later but I've told the pool boy and gardener to check anywhere outside he may have gotten stuck before they finish up."

"He'll be back," Marcie said. "Cats like to wander. He's too old to have gotten too far."

They were at the club, in the luncheon pavilion, Marcie having had a blissful morning lying out by the pool, the sun glittering diamonds on the surface, freshly squeezed orange juice by her side, and a terrible trashy novel to half-read while Jason, her deceptive handsome husband, had been at work. Now he was here by her side, looking relaxed for once. William had joined them after a round of golf. Maybe that's why Jason looked happier. He hadn't had William trying to take back the reins at work.

"I'm sure you're right, and yes, he's old and sick, but Iris just adores that cat. If anything happens to him, she'll be devastated. Anyway," Elizabeth continued. "Sorry I missed you at the office. Here's your travel details." She handed an envelope to Jason. "Flight leaves this afternoon at four thirty and a driver will be waiting to take you to the hotel. I've emailed it to you as well."

"You want to stay for some lunch?" William asked.

"Oh no, I've got a million things to do today. You know how it is. And Zelda has some family coming in by bus for her weekend off. I'm going to give them a ride. But thank you. Oh." She squinted in the sunlight. "Here's Keisha. My, she suits those tennis whites."

The comment sat somewhere in tone between an honest compliment and a snide snub, and Marcie wasn't sure which Elizabeth intended. Her stomach knotted and she automatically reached for her wine, thankful she had her shades to hide behind. What was it she was feeling anyway? Cringing embarrassment? Yes, but not just that. A hint of nerves too. Excitement maybe. Jesus, she needed to get a grip. It was just a woman, not Tom fucking Hardy. There was no reason to be so flustered. Keisha obviously hadn't said anything to William, because Marcie would have heard by now. It had been nothing. A stupid drunken moment. No reason to feel so odd. Still, sweat prickled on the backs of her thighs and her position in her chair suddenly felt awkward.

Keisha, on the other hand, looked totally relaxed, pausing at the pool area gate, chatting her goodbyes to May and Charlene. God, poor Keisha, sharing her tennis lesson with them. Never had two duller Yummy-Mummies walked the planet. They were both older than Marcie, forty at least, under the Botox and fillers, and, as she recalled, had loathed each other until bonding over IVF and their subsequent miracle babies, Joshua and Megan. Spoiled and whiny, both of them. But then so were their mothers.

"She does, doesn't she?" William said, as Keisha strolled toward them, a big smile on her face as her hips rolled in that confident, sexy, tilted-forward walk. Marcie could see Jason watching her, taking it all in, and it still rankled, the way she became invisible when

Keisha was around, as if she were nothing. Jason wasn't
the only one studying Keisha. Behind the expensive
tinted glasses, all eyes in the pavilion were watching her, filled with mischief and gossip, eager to get a
glimpse of the young black gold digger who'd replaced
the saintly Eleanor Radford. Women leaned in closer
to one another to comment with wry smiles, William
no doubt the butt of the jokes. Keisha didn't notice as
she sauntered by. Marcie had always noticed when they
were whispering about her. Felt each glance like a knife.
Keisha was either oblivious or used to it. Maybe women
always looked at her like that, as if she were a threat
who had to be dealt with. At least Marcie had had the
good grace to be meek when she'd slid in among them.

"I've passed your number to Keisha, by the way,"
William said. "Thought you could help her with some
ideas for the party, seeing as you two are getting along."

"No problem." Marcie's heart was pounding as Keisha
finally reached them, leaning forward to kiss William—a
nice display for the crowds—and she tingled as she remembered the feel of those soft, painted lips on hers.

"So," Keisha said, as she sat down, one hand holding
William's. "They're abandoning us for the weekend,
Marcie. What will we do while they're gone?"

"Whatever you do, not so much tequila," Jason
cut in, answering for Marcie, which was a good thing

because her throat had inexplicably tightened a little, and the joke let her laugh it out without looking like a giggling idiot. "God no," she finally said. "I think I actually died for a while yesterday."

"We should do something though," Keisha said. "While the cat's away and everything . . ."

"We're going to be having a sedate weekend of golf and early nights," William said. "So perhaps you two should have dinner here. I can make you a reservation. Save your energy for when I'm back, honey."

Marcie wanted to laugh. What did William sound like? *Save your energy.* It was pathetic, really, this need in older men to impress younger women. Maybe they were the only women some men *could* impress. "I'll call Julian and Pierre. We could have them over to your place for brunch and see what they can do for your Fourth of July party. But it's not that far away, they may be booked up."

"They'll do it," William said. "Julian used to be like family." His mouth tightened at the same time as a solitary wisp of cloud drifted across the parched sky, and Marcie couldn't tell if the shadows were from that or a slight darkening of his mood. Maybe he didn't overly like the boys. Maybe Julian had been a favorite of Eleanor's. She'd have thought the couple would have been *too pansy* for old-fashioned William.

"Hey!" Keisha suddenly exclaimed. "I almost forgot. Guess who Charlene says she was sure she saw at the mall yesterday?"

They all looked at her.

"Jacquie. Charlene said she called after her but she couldn't have heard. She was too far away to catch up with."

"Jason's Jacquie?" William said.

"Can't have been Jacquie." Jason's voice was cold. "She wouldn't come back here. Must have been someone who looked like her."

Marcie barely noticed as the waiter brought her salad. Jacquie? Sneaking back into town? After she'd raged and cursed at Jason, even as she walked away with a lot more than Jason *had* to give her in the divorce, yelling, *I'd rather die than come back to this snake-infested place and I'm not talking about the wildlife!*

No, it couldn't have been Jacquie. If it was, she'd have breezed into the club for lunch with one of her old friends to rub Marcie's nose in it.

"I guess not then," Keisha said, drawing her chair up closer to her oozing burger. "Anyway, I'm starving. Let's eat."

But if it was Jacquie, Marcie wondered as she picked up her fork, what could have brought her back here?

22.

It had been a long time since Marcie had slept naked, but after a shower she'd stretched out on the bed, the open shutters to the Juliet balcony letting the evening breeze in, enjoying the air on her skin. She'd felt such a surprising rush of freedom she hadn't even bothered to put any underwear on.

It was odd being in the house alone. It was far too big for two people, let alone one, and without Jason there it felt enormous. A beautiful Italianate seven-bedroom mansion that somehow felt like a mausoleum. For what though? Her marriage perhaps. Jason with his bad moods and secret phone calls—*if it wasn't Keisha then who was it?*—and eyes for other women. She hadn't heard from him since they'd landed and she wasn't surprised. Distracted didn't cover Jason at the moment.

And now, on top of everything, maybe Jacquie was back. Was that bothering him? Did he already know? Jason liked to be in control, she knew that, but maybe he was learning that women often only gave the illusion of submission.

God, she was bored with thinking about Jason, and now she had her own distraction. It wasn't thinking of Jason that had her sleepless in the night. She looked at her phone again. Keisha had texted almost immediately after William had left for the airport. *Let's do something this weekend. Kx.* Marcie hadn't answered, not right away. She wasn't sure why. The quiet drumming in the pit of her stomach that screamed both danger and excitement. Was it the memory of that kiss?

No, not even that. It was the reminder of who she'd once been. Free. Wild. Mad, bad, and dangerous to know. If she went back to that, who knew where all this would end? Running away in the grip of a scandal and working in a diner after screwing up her life? A person could only do that once with any sense of energy and she'd used up her shot. It wasn't worth the risk simply to have the thrill of something illicit. In the end she'd set up Sunday brunch with Julian and Pierre and sent a formal text back to Keisha saying she'd see her then. There had been a pause and then, *Okay thx. I'm about all weekend so if u get bored before then let me know.*

Still though, Marcie couldn't sleep. It was one thing to tell yourself not to do something, but it was quite another to stop thinking about it. Her mind was turning over and over, her body tingling, while her head went places she never ever thought she'd go about someone she actually knew. *Hot* places, as if now that she was no longer worried that Keisha would tell William, something had been unlocked inside. Doing the kind of things she'd only seen in porn. It was ridiculous, and yet she couldn't stop.

She stared at the ceiling. Keisha had said that when she'd seen Marcie it had been like a lightning strike. Is that how it had been for her too? She could still vividly see Keisha coming down the stairs on William's arm, wearing that too short Versace dress, so glorious it had almost hurt to look at her. Had her envy and fascination actually been attraction on some subliminal level and she hadn't realized? God, it was all so confusing. But she couldn't stop herself fizzing with fantasies of what might have happened if the men hadn't come home so soon.

She stared at her phone again. Still nothing from Jason, and all she felt was irritation rather than hurt. Even when he'd gone to Europe last year for some client or other, and she'd been stuck at home with an awful stomach bug in their cozy old house, he'd at the very least texted her every evening before bed. How times had changed. Maybe they'd been changing then.

She opened her message thread to Keisha again, her heartbeat getting faster. Screw it, she decided. There was only one way to find out what she was really feeling. She typed quickly, before she could change her mind. *Let's go out tomorrow if you like. Get some late drinks or something. I'll let you know where in the morning. Sorry if this woke you!*

It had barely been sent before a reply pinged back. *Wild! See you then. X*

Wild. God. Her stomach knotted. No going back now. She stretched out on the bed, her legs slightly parted. It felt good. She felt sexy. She slid her hand down under the sheets. There was no crime in fantasizing after all. Maybe she just needed to get it out of her system. She closed her eyes and remembered the kiss.

She woke later, startled, and sat up, her body on sudden alert, instinctually aware that something wasn't quite right. A noise. Was it someone in the house? She listened, heart thumping in the hum of silence, for soft footfalls or a creak of wood. There was nothing. Not in the house. Outside. An engine running. That was all.

She got up and went to the balcony doors and shutters to close them, the breeze having dropped and the night air now thick hot tar filling the house. The car engine still thrummed and she frowned. This wasn't the kind of neighborhood where people came and went at all hours of the night, loitering outside houses while saying good night to a beau. It was wealthy and sedate. Alarm systems turned on and residents in bed by midnight, barely even the chirp of cicadas on the neatly tended lawns to disturb the peace.

She peered out, mildly curious. The car wasn't moving, just sitting there on the street opposite the house, headlights turned off, engine purring. It was a sedan, maybe blue but it was hard to tell, stopped as it was away from the gentle beam of the streetlamps. Who was inside? And who were they watching? On impulse, she stamped on the switch for the tall floor lamp by the dresser, filling the room with light, and then peered back out again, hidden from view. A brief moment later, the car pulled away, going a hundred yards or so before turning the headlights back on.

Her breath caught. *Her.* They'd been watching her. Or Jason. Or studying their new house. She stared into the silent darkness a little longer, until she was sure the car had gone. Who would want to watch their house? *Jacquie.* Maybe Jason's ex-wife really was back in town.

She turned the light out and the AC on and got back into bed. Could it have been Jacquie texting Jason in the middle of the night? Surely not. The divorce had been so bitter, there was no way she'd want him back now that she was single again. That love had long ago turned to dislike, if not outright hate.

Marcie closed her thoughts down. It was two in the morning and she'd long ago stopped losing sleep over Jacquie. Screw it. Tomorrow she'd go and buy something new to wear and then she had a night on the town to look forward to. A night with Keisha.

23.

Keisha was on a high and not only from the joint they were smoking in the dumpster alley behind the bar on River Street, heels wobbling on the cobbles. The air was filled with jazz and live band music, combined with the scent of seafood cooking, all spilling out from the lively bars and restaurants looking out over the water. This was Keisha's kind of place, and the night was going great. Better than great. Marcie was wearing a shoestring-strap black glitter minidress that looked new, bare freshly tanned legs on show and hair loose around her shoulders, scrunched scruffy sexy. And she'd been there before Keisha arrived. The sight of her made Keisha's heart thump too fast. She was curious, Keisha just knew it. For all that they'd laughed it off as a drunken moment over the first drink, their kiss had opened a door inside that they were both tempted to go through. Maybe they would. The night was still young and it felt good to be out in it, surrounded by people her own age, where she could breathe, away from the oppressive atmosphere of the staid luxury she now lived in. Away from all the ghosts, those who belonged in this city and the ones—*there was no boy*—she'd brought with her in her own fragile mind.

"I can't believe we're doing this again," Marcie said, with the snort of an almost teenage giggle as she took a long hit on the reefer Keisha had brought with her. "I've only just recovered from last time."

"It's fine. I'll hold your hair when you throw up."

"Ah, true love." Marcie laughed again and handed the joint back. Her eyes shone and Keisha laughed. She felt good tonight. Her head was clear. She liked these moods, they were way better than when the pendulum swung the other way and left her feeling needy and out of control.

"You not much of a smoker, Marcie?" One of their new friends, Daria, took a long hit before passing it on to Jade, her companion. There had been a drinks collision in the busy bar and they'd all gotten talking. The two girls were at Savannah State University, staying in the Tiger Court residence, their whole lives ahead of them. Daria did shifts as a waitress to make extra money for her tuition and Jade was thinking of dropping out and traveling for a year, working her way around beach resorts in Goa and Thailand. They were *normal*. No trust funds, no little Mercedes from Daddy. They were almost like some of the girls Keisha had known back home.

"Marcie's been married too long," Keisha teased. "She's forgotten how to have fun."

Marcie pulled a face at her. "You laugh but give it another five years with William and your joint days will be long over. Joint pain management is how you'll be spending your time as you push his wheelchair."

"Five years? I was kind of hoping he'd be buried by then." They all laughed, Keisha the loudest. Maybe her mood *was* slightly manic, the excitement in danger of tipping her over the edge. Breathtaking highs, or terrible lows, those were the landscapes of her emotions. An inheritance from her dead mother. *Cursed.* She pushed the word away.

"And they say romance is dead." Jade glanced at the time on her cell. "Anyway, great meeting you, but we've got to split." She tugged Daria's jacket. "Come on, I told Laz we'd be there by eleven thirty. He won't wait and then we'll never find him."

"Hey, you two should come with us!" Daria said. "Gonna be wild! A kind of underground club night in the woods down by the Truman Parkway. Music, drink, food. All kinds of tents set up and stuff given away free. Happens every year. Goes on till dawn for those who have the energy."

"What do you think?" Keisha asked Marcie after a pause. "Could be fun?"

"I don't think so. I'm not really a staying-up-till-dawn-partying kind of girl," Marcie said.

"We don't have to. Just stay for an hour or so."

"Okay, let's go."

"Wow, quick turnaround. I didn't realize you were so easily led. That's good to know . . ."

Marcie rolled her eyes at Keisha's teasing, but a blush had crept across her cheeks and Keisha thought she looked beautiful.

"So, you guys coming?" Jade said, fingers flicking over her iPhone. "I'm getting an Uber."

"Sure." Keisha flicked the roach to the ground. "We love a party."

"Oh, you're going to really love this one." Daria's eyes gleamed. "Craziest night of the year for those in the know."

24.

M arcie held her breath as they hurried past the pile of garbage sacks that acted as a border between normal life and the homeless town that existed under the parkway. The mountain of uncollected waste stank and she dreaded thinking how much vermin was probably living in it.

"Nearly there," Daria said.

"We don't have to go through that do we?" Keisha nodded toward the camp of battered tents and beaten people living under a concrete sky. Here and there, faces stared out at them, impassive. Not overly threatening but definitely unsettling, huddled by fires that crackled in oil drums under graffitti-daubed pillars. The underbelly of the city that no one wanted to see.

"Don't worry," Jade said. "We're going into the woods. We'll be fine."

"Glad you sound so sure."

"Like I said, it's a special night."

Marcie wasn't convinced. What on earth was she doing out here following two women she'd only just met to some no doubt illegal party? For all she knew they were about to get robbed. Or worse. This was the sort of impulsive shit she'd done as a kid, but not *now*. She was here only because Keisha had obviously wanted to come. Keisha. As Jade led them up a narrow path into the woods, Marcie reached for the other woman's hand and gave it a reassuring squeeze. There was no going back now. She may as well try to relax and enjoy it. It was a few minutes' walk in the dark, only cell-phone lights to guide them—thankfully also showing full signal—and then Marcie heard the first hints of sound, a thrum of life somewhere up ahead. The path reached a peak and then as they ducked under some branches, it dipped down sharply to a surprise large clearing, half the size of a football field.

"Wow," Keisha said, as Marcie looked around, wide-eyed. Okay, so they weren't going to get robbed. Lights were strung in trees at the edges, and there were tents and stalls set up here and there, a large unlit bonfire down at the other end, candles burning, food cooking, and a lot—maybe a hundred or so—of people dancing and laughing. Music hummed in the air, a sensual rhythm, heavy on the drums, as if it pulsed through the earth itself.

"St. John's Eve, baby!" Jade leapt into the arms of the shaven-headed black man waiting for them, her legs wrapping tightly around his waist. He was so tall he made her look like a child.

"Hey, Laz. We brought a couple of friends," Daria said. "And we all need a drink."

The man, Laz, extracted himself from Jade, and then led them to a small table, where a middle-aged hippie woman was filling paper cups from a punch bowl.

"Welcome to the party," he said as he handed them each a cup. "Drink, eat, dance, and be merry. Tonight our wishes come true."

"What is it?" Marcie asked, peering inside.

"Tafia. Homemade rum."

She watched as the others, including Laz, drank theirs, her instinctual paranoia about her drink being spiked causing a brief knot in her stomach, but the rum had to be safe, it had all come out of the same bowl. She glanced over at Keisha, who winked at her. "Bottoms up." Marcie stared into the cup for a moment, took a deep breath, and then drank.

After that, the world swirled and time stretched like molasses as they moved through the thick hot mess of nature and people. They'd lost Daria and Jade to Laz, but Marcie wasn't bothered. She didn't feel drunk exactly, but somewhere close. The tafia burned her throat but relaxed her body and as she and Keisha wandered through the crowds it felt perfectly natural to have their hands linked and to feel Keisha rest her head on her shoulder when they paused at this stall or that to look at what was cooking or what was being sold.

Heat. That's what Marcie felt as Keisha led her farther into the steadily growing throng of people. Somewhere up ahead, the bonfire had been lit and as it blazed, the air was becoming an acrid mist hanging low. A passing man with short bleached hair and wide trippy eyes lined with black kohl that was harsh against his white skin grinned as he refilled their cups, shouting, "Drink to old John Bayou! Tonight is his night!"

An elbow dug into Marcie's back as dancers jostled for space, and she tugged at Keisha, nodding her forward to where there was more space. Yes, it was near the bonfire so they'd be hot, but at least they'd be able to breathe. The music had gotten louder and more energetic and the dancers, sweaty faced and slick backed, were happily keeping up. Thank God Keisha didn't look like she wanted to join in either. In fact, she was frowning slightly, peering off to her right.

"You okay?" Marcie leaned in and shouted.

Keisha nodded. "I just thought I saw . . ." She paused and then shook her head, her face smoothing out. "Nothing. Just all this smoke getting in my eyes."

Marcie took the lead and pulled her out of the heaving crowd to a small space at the edge of the clearing. She was happy to see a proper tarmacked path leading out of it on this side, and the trees didn't look as dense farther up that way. At least they could get out of here easily enough when they wanted to.

They'd gotten off the improvised dance floor at the right time. A fresh tune was playing and it had brought everyone onto the grass. Marcie didn't recognize the heavy beat, but as several of the party-goers jumped up and down shouting *"Dansé Calinda!"* along with the chorus, it was hard not to be swept along by the energy, the freedom of it. Faces loomed out of the smoke, smiling and damp, as they bounced and twisted in the air.

"This is crazy!" Marcie said.

"Yeah, like some awful rave. But kind of fun. We just need some pills."

It was different for Keisha. She'd probably had heaps of nights like this back in London. Wild parties.

Nightclubs. Marcie hadn't been to a club in what felt like forever. Definitely not since she'd been with Jason. It felt a little overwhelming. She wasn't sure she belonged here. She wasn't sure where she belonged anymore. She drank back half her cup and then coughed at the burn.

"Take it easy," Keisha said, laughing. "I don't want you throwing up all night again." Her face was radiant in the firelight and Marcie couldn't stop looking at her. Her blood fizzed and her face flushed, warmth flooding through her. What was it about this woman that fascinated her so much? What was she being drawn into?

"What do you want me doing all night instead?" she murmured. She trembled slightly and the noise around her dimmed as if she were underwater, only Keisha there with her.

"You know what I want," Keisha said, the fragility breaking the surface of her glorious confidence for a moment. For a moment they simply gazed at each other, eyes locked, unable to break away. It was intense. Too intense. Part of Marcie wanted to run like a frightened rabbit, back to safety, back to her dull life with her middle-aged husband. Her husband who lied and made middle-of-the-night secret calls and who was always in a bad mood in their big house with their rich friends. No, she would not run. Not tonight. Not in this night that made her feel as if anything was possible. She reached for Keisha's face, once again pulling her close.

The heat of the fire was nothing next to the heat of the kiss, burning slow and soft and deliberate. Keisha let out a moan, pressing her body into Marcie's, and Marcie was sure she was melting. Everything was too hot. There were too many people around. But she couldn't stop herself. After a second, Keisha pulled back, her eyes as glazed as Marcie's own must have been, and glanced around. Was she worried about being seen by someone too? "Maybe we should—"

Suddenly the music stopped and instantly everyone around them stilled, the sudden silence almost deafening.

"What the fuck?" Keisha muttered. Briefly, there was nothing, not even a breath, and then a slow drumbeat started. First a solitary thud, before more joined in, the sound coming from all around them, drummers hidden in the woods, as if the forest itself were letting its heart be heard. The frozen dancers were staring at the bonfire, eyes wide with expectation.

"Look," Keisha breathed beside her. Marcie did. There must have been a platform of some kind behind the blazing fire, because three figures emerged, looking as if they were rising up behind the flames and hovering there. Marcie frowned, her eyes trying to focus. It couldn't be. The central figure stepped forward and as she came into view, the drums stopped. The whole crowd gasped as two men threw dust on the pyre, sending searing multicolored sparks high into the air, fireworks bright, and Marcie flinched, momentarily blinded, spots in her vision. But still she was sure she was right. It was. It was *her*.

25.

Keisha stared, her mouth slightly open, even Marcie forgotten. It couldn't be a coincidence, could it? *No.* Auntie Ayo's voice was bell clear in her head. *It's in your blood. It will always find you, KeKe, for good or bad.*

"It's her," Marcie murmured beside her, and all Keisha could do was nod. The tall, fat, ancient woman, framed by the sparkling flames, took another step and the bright umber of her hair made it look as if she were atop a pyre and burning alive in the night.

The woman from the square. The crazy lady with the stall. It was her. Marcie was right. Keisha understood then what this was. Not a rave. Not a party. A *celebration.* Of the power. Of what was called many names and what ran strong through Auntie Ayo and what Keisha had always run from. She ran and ran and always it found her. Even now across the ocean.

Above them, the old lady smiled, benevolent, at the crowd and then raised her cane, bringing it down three times, the drums in the forest matching her timing, *boom boom boom!* The crowd immediately dropped to the ground and banged their fists against it three times, an echo of a reply.

Behind the old woman were two figures, one to her left and one to her right, veils over their heads and shoulders. On the last beat, they raised their arms high.

"Are those live snakes?" Keisha glanced at Marcie. Her pale face reflected the flames as she watched, part horrified, part fascinated, the large serpents weaving themselves around the women's arms. "Is that . . . ?" Marcie's voice drifted away, smoke in the night, her face momentarily confused by something.

"Tonight we dance!" the old woman bellowed, the rich voice that defied her age commanding Keisha's attention back. "We call on them to dance with us! The spirits! The ghosts! The great Doctor John, old John Bayou!" A cheer went up, a sea of arms rising above heads, bare feet stamping on grass. "The queen, the mother Laveau, and her daughters! Let the ghosts weave among us!" She banged her cane again three times, and the crowd once again echoed her, this time chanting as they did so, *"Faith! Hope! Charity! Li Grand Zombi!"*

Keisha felt the hum of it in her soul, this earthy religion they were practicing, part what Auntie Ayo believed, part something old and Southern, and part something all its own, and she gazed at the woman on the stage. She was not like Auntie Ayo. She was not hiding in secret, practicing dark, forbidden magic. This woman, this priestess, was worshipped. Adored. There was love here. Keisha could feel it. Perhaps this was the yin to Auntie Ayo's yang. Good goes to good, and bad goes to bad. That made her shiver in the heat. Could this woman sense Keisha was wrong? Cursed? Damaged? An outsider, even in this crowd.

For a moment, as the crone scanned the congregation from on high, her ancient dark eyes, embedded in those fat cheeks, met Keisha's own, and fire seared her veins. She was seeing her. Really seeing her.

The old woman laughed, throaty and amused, just as she had in the square when they had thought her mad, and then she lifted her arms, the cane held as high as the snakes behind her, the carved serpent handle gleaming bright, and called out, "Tonight he grants your hearts' desires! Now *Dansé Calinda*! Badoum! Badoum! Bring the spirits joy!"

With that, the flames burst magnesium white, rushing skyward, and when they faded, she and the two women behind her were gone, as if they had been ghosts themselves. The music roared back to life, no drums this time but instead bursting from speakers, and Keisha felt a surge of energy.

There had been more in the punch than just rum, and from the slight rushing tingles on her skin and the smooth joy that filled her, she'd guess a dash of liquid MDMA. It should have bothered her that it had been spiked but it didn't. Everyone had shared. It was communion wine. She felt blissful. At one with everything.

"What *was* that?" Marcie was startled, disconcerted, if a little hazy from the drink taking hold. "Voodoo shit? That woman from the square again." She was looking around the bonfire as if willing the woman to appear. Those women with the snakes . . . I was sure that . . ." She frowned, confused, and drank some more.

"Stop thinking," Keisha said, pulling her close and swaying to the music. This time she reached for Marcie, kissing her again, her heart alive. *He grants your hearts' desires!* It was a sign. Everything was going to go just how she wanted. Billy would be dead soon and she'd be free and rich and have love. Maybe Auntie Ayo was wrong. Maybe she wasn't cursed. Maybe she was blessed. She could feel it.

"Oh my God," Marcie said. "Look at everybody."

Keisha turned. Bathed in firelight, the revelers were still dancing, but they were also entwining, hands touching and pulling at clothes as mouths met, a hand on one person, lips on another, clothes peeling off and being abandoned as bodies became joined. Keisha's mouth dried slightly, the heat she suddenly felt nothing to do with the fire or the night air.

"Aren't you going to join in?" The voice made her jump, and she turned to see Daria, hand held in Jade's as Laz drew them into the mass of people. She kissed him, and as his hand slid under her T-shirt, Jade's joined it, pushing the thin fabric up, exposing her pale breasts. Daria broke away from the kiss to pull Jade in closer, one last grin at Keisha and Marcie, and then the three of them were on the ground, lost in their own moment, absorbed into the sea of flesh.

"Maybe we should go," Marcie said. Her words were breathy and her eyes were fixed on the seething mass of bodies licking and sucking and sighing and fucking in front of them, lost in their own worlds, filled with sensory, heady pleasure, simply *being* and enjoying one another. If there was a God or the spirits, surely this was what they wanted from people. This joy?

Keisha gently kissed Marcie's neck, tracing her tongue along her skin, breathing heat onto her until she groaned, her head tilting backward, eyes closed, lips slightly parted. Keisha's fingers slipped under the straps of the delicate glittering dress and slid them down Marcie's arms. "Maybe we should stay," she whispered, as Marcie's skin goose-pimpled under her touch. As they dropped to the ground, hands exploring each other, Marcie didn't argue.

PART TWO

I walk on gilded splinters,
I want to see what they can do!

<small>Translation of an old Creole song</small>

26.

Marcie's limbs ached from being out all night, falling asleep in the grass amid strangers' bodies, waking up cold and barely dressed before smoking their last joint and grabbing an Uber home at dawn. But now as she slowly woke a few hours later from the sleep of the dead in her own bed, even the aches were blissful. She luxuriated in Keisha's touch, shivering as the other woman slid down under the sheets, hands on the insides of Marcie's thighs, opening her up. As her mouth made contact, Marcie gasped.

It was all so different. Sex in a mirror, not up against one. Reflection, not objectification. Soft skin on soft skin, no rough stubble chafing her, no demand for noise and validation. They understood each other's bodies. Inexperienced in this kind of sex as Marcie was, she'd still known how to please Keisha. How to find the right spot. How fast or slow to move. Just how hard to bite down on her nipples. How to tease her. This was sex among equals. This was not a battle, even when biting skin or tugging on hair.

One hand went to her own breast as Keisha's mouth and fingers worked at her until bright stars moved across the backdrop of her closed eyes and her whole body shuddered. She sighed and let out a half-laugh as Keisha returned to her arms, breast against breast as they relaxed into each other. How strange this was. Ridiculous. Crazy. It couldn't continue, of course, and would have to be simply a weekend of madness, but at the same time it was so glorious she didn't want it to end. She felt so free.

Her eyes were bleary and she pressed her face into Keisha's shoulder to keep out the sunlight before giggling again. Keisha was in Jason's bed. This was so far from how he'd probably imagined it, but still, she thought, amused, *Be careful what you wish for, Jason Maddox.*

"What's so funny?" Keisha asked.

"Nothing. Everything."

"Isn't it strange"—Keisha rolled onto her back, looking up at the ceiling—"how people find each other? Like you and me? There was a girl back home—Dolly—but I didn't love her. Not really. She was hard as nails. Too many sharp edges to her heart. But with you, with you I just knew that if I—if we—got a chance to get together, it would be amazing."

"Let's not forget that we're both married," Marcie said.

"Minor detail. We could always leave them. Take a settlement and run." Keisha said it lightly, but Marcie's stomach constricted.

"Ha, I can imagine that. Both of us working in some club or diner, too poor to party, too tired to screw. Resenting each other."

"That's what I like best about you, Marcie, your positive outlook on life."

They both smiled and then lay in comfortable silence for a while, Marcie tempted to doze some more. It had been forever since she'd had a lazy, decadent day of sex and laughter in bed.

"When Billy dies, I'll be a rich widow," Keisha said. "You'll want me then."

"All the girls will want you then." Marcie rolled over, grinning. "The boys too. I'll have to fight them off to get to you. Or you'll take all his money and run back to London and the bright lights of the big city."

"No." Keisha's face clouded. "I'll never go back there." She glanced sideways at Marcie. "Did you make a wish last night?"

"What are you talking about?"

"At the thing. What the old woman said. Dr. John will grant your heart's desire." She said the last in an exaggerated dramatic voice, but she didn't look like she'd found it funny.

"Don't tell me you believe all that?" It was quite sweet to see this side of Keisha more and more. A little fragile. Childlike. Not so confident as she appeared.

"My family do."

Marcie sat up. "Really? Voodoo? In London?"

Keisha shrugged, awkward. "Something similar. It's all from African heritage after all. Ours was darker maybe. I guess seeing that woman like that last night, and everyone celebrating and so happy, it kind of spoke to me. Showed me the light side. So joyful. Magical. I'd never seen that before. But still . . . it scares the shit out of me." She tucked a strand of hair behind one ear, an endearing gesture, and as the sun cut through the shutters she looked breathtakingly beautiful.

For once, Marcie's awe wasn't tinged with jealousy, only pure fascination. The novel strangeness of her situation. She couldn't imagine having sex with any other woman—sex with women, faceless strangers, had only ever been a rare fantasy, nothing she'd ever wanted to actually *do* with anyone—but with Keisha she felt electrified and insatiable. She wanted to explore and explore and explore. Make the most of it before the inevitable end. This was something she had entirely for herself. A new secret.

When had she last felt like this? Jason, the early days. She'd even had the same thought. To get as much of him as she could before it was all over. But she'd fallen in love with Jason. He'd been her promise of a good future. Money. Comfort. Security. And maybe finally in her life, some respect. Could she now be falling in love with Keisha? What did she promise? Decadent freedom? Rebellion against them all and their constant quiet rejection of her in their inner circle?

"I saw a ghost when I was little," Keisha said, staring into the distance, her voice soft. "In my auntie's house. A boy. A boy who wasn't there."

"There's no such thing as ghosts," Marcie said.

"Uncle Yahuba beat me when I said I'd seen him. Auntie Ayo said it was a sign I was cursed. Crazy like my mother. They told me never to think of it again. They put me on Valium when I was about thirteen. Been on it ever since. It helps."

Marcie leaned forward and kissed her again. "There's no such thing as ghosts," she repeated. "Only tricks of the light and memory. Now let's make the most of our morning, and no more crazy talk."

Keisha smiled, shaking her thoughts away, and suddenly she was bright and happy again, her mouth on Marcie's as her back arched with desire. Mercurial, that's what her moods were, Marcie decided. Light and dark and back again in an instant. Jason had been right. She *was* refreshing. The ring of Marcie's cell phone cut through the moment, and she groaned as she looked at the screen. "It's Elizabeth. What the hell can she want?"

"A threeway?" Keisha raised an eyebrow and Marcie snorted a half-laugh. "Come on, don't answer it." Keisha brushed her mouth over Marcie's exposed nipple. "Ignore her."

Despite the tingle of pleasure, Marcie couldn't. Elizabeth calling was a dark cloud against the sunshine—a reminder of the real world. She hit the answer button.

"Hey, Elizabeth. What's up?"

"Sorry to bother you, but I tried Keisha's cell and it's going straight to voice mail. Is she with you?"

"Uh, yeah, we went out last night and she stayed over." Marcie's skin burned as if she sounded as guilty as she felt. It was ridiculous. Women had sleepovers all the time when their husbands were away, there was nothing suspicious about it, but still she felt so transparent. "I guess she ran out of battery." She looked at Keisha, who retrieved her phone from where it had been tossed somewhere on the floor with her clothes, checked it, and nodded.

"Oh, I see," Elizabeth continued. "It's just that Julian and Pierre are here. When they got no answer at the main door, they buzzed Zelda, who let them in and then called me. We were all a bit worried! Aren't you supposed to be having a brunch with them today? To plan the party?"

"Oh God, yes!" Julian and Pierre. How could she have forgotten? Another rope of control slipping through her fingers. She needed to get a grip. "What time is it?"

"One thirty."

"I'm so so sorry. Can you ask Zelda to get them some drinks? We'll be there as fast as we can."

"I'll take care of it. Zelda's got family here and I don't want to disturb her any more. It's her weekend off."

Was that a reproach? They probably deserved it, to be fair. "I'm so sorry, Elizabeth," she repeated.

"Don't worry, I wasn't busy. I'll rustle something up or order in and see you when you get here."

"Thank you, thank you. And please apologize to Zelda for me." She hung up. "Shit. Shit, shit, shit."

"What?" Keisha said.

"Come on, get dressed. We've got to go." Her heart thumped hard. Marcie Maddox did not miss brunches. She was always on time. Under control. Aware that any slipup was simply a validation that she didn't truly belong here. She couldn't let everything unravel because of this Englishwoman. Yet still she ached between her thighs, irritated at the interruption to their languid day. "Now!" she said, as Keisha didn't move. "We're supposed to be party planning." If it was already nearly two, Jason and William would be back before long. Early evening, she was sure he'd said they were landing. God, she probably wouldn't even have time to change the sheets.

She yanked a dress from her closet and pulled it on before quickly making the bed. Would it smell of sex? Perfume? She thought of spraying deodorant on it and decided not to. It was men who caused the stink of sex anyway. Like dogs having to make their mark.

"Oh fuck, I totally forgot," Keisha said, tugging her party dress over her head and down to her knees. "There was something weird last night."

Looking at her, Marcie wanted to moan again and this time it was nothing to do with pleasure. There was dirt on it from where they'd screwed in the clearing. And she was pretty sure she could see a small tear in the fabric. This was not going to look good. She'd lend Keisha something if her clothes would have fit, but she was at least three inches taller than Marcie and there was no way her glorious tits were going to fit into any of Marcie's tops.

"There was plenty weird last night," she said, only half-listening. "What specifically?" She hadn't realized how hungover she was until she'd stood up. Not hungover exactly, but something similar. What exactly had been in that stupid rum punch?

"Zelda. You know, I'd forgotten till just now, but I thought I saw her last night for a second. It was someone I kind of recognized anyway. At the rave. A familiarity about them. Can't remember properly now. It's all a bit hazy."

A vague memory scratched the surface of Marcie's consciousness. Hadn't she thought she'd recognized someone for a moment too? One of the women holding a snake. Could that have been Zelda? Last night? Marcie's guts turned to ice water. Oh God, if Zelda *had* been there, what did she see? Suddenly freedom didn't seem such a great idea. "You're shitting me."

"Don't look so worried!" Keisha said. "I was high. It could have been anyone. I didn't even see her face, it was just the way she moved that reminded me of someone, that's all."

"Yeah, of course." Marcie forced a bright smile on her face. "Let's go." She steadied her breathing. It wouldn't have been Zelda. She knew that. It was coincidence enough that they'd ended up at the same place as the crazy woman from Wright Square, there was no way Zelda could have been there too. And all the stuff that went on—the drinking, the sex—that wasn't exactly the kind of party you'd take relatives who were visiting to.

But still, pulling her shades on to protect her thumping head from the bright day, just the thought of someone they knew being there had shaken her. This whole thing was madness, she told herself for the thousandth time. It had to stop. Under the lust and the craziness, she was filled with a sense of foreboding. If this didn't end soon it would wreck everything. Her marriage, Jason's job, everything she'd worked so hard to have. If this came out it would humiliate William. He would never stand for that and it would be Marcie who took the brunt of the punishment. She'd signed a prenup before marrying Jason—she hadn't wanted to, but she'd had no choice—and she might not be broke if they divorced but she sure wouldn't have the fancy life she had now.

She took a deep breath as they slid into the car. It would be fine. She'd talk to Keisha about it later and she'd understand it had to end. She wasn't going to want to lose everything either. Her phone buzzed, a text coming in as she started the engine. "Okay Elizabeth," she muttered, irritated. "We're coming."

"Well, we would have been if she hadn't called," Keisha said, with a laugh. Marcie didn't join in as she stared at her phone. It wasn't Elizabeth. It was Jason. *All good here, but missing you and looking forward to being home. Sorry I've been so moody. J xx*

Why did he have to send that *now*? It was time to get her life back under control. She had to break whatever spell Keisha had cast on her. She had to. She *had* to.

27

"Well, looks like someone already had the party," Pierre purred as Keisha raced up the stairs to get into fresh clothes. Marcie poked him in the ribs, keeping her smile bright.

"She fell over on our way back to the house. We weren't even drunk. It was a relatively sedate night if you must know. But that is why I don't wear four-inch heels anymore."

"I can barely manage two-inch heels these days," Elizabeth said. Marcie had hoped Keisha would have managed to change before the assistant saw them but as soon as the front door had opened, she and Pierre had appeared.

"Where's Julian?"

"Stirring the eggs," Elizabeth said. "I should have

known he'd take over. That boy always did like to cook."

"He's hell on my waistline," Pierre added, razor thin as he was.

"You're a lucky man." Elizabeth was dressed down for the weekend: high-waisted, sensibly cut jeans with a comfortable blouse tucked in around her thick middle. "And you know it!"

"Oh, I do, I do. Just don't tell him that."

Elizabeth's affection for the men reminded Marcie of what William had said at the club—that Julian had been like family once. It still jarred. Julian and Pierre were so flamboyant she couldn't imagine William really ever wanting them around.

"If y'all are set now, I'm going to head home." Elizabeth grabbed her purse from the hall table and swung it over her shoulder. "I've got a pot roast on at home and I don't want it burning."

"Of course, of course." Marcie felt a flood of relief. She was in no mood for Elizabeth to be clucking around them like a mother hen. Elizabeth probably didn't want to be here when William and Jason got back because she would no doubt then suddenly have a few more tasks to complete before bed, despite its being a weekend.

There'd been no mention of Zelda, who must have been back in her apartment or out with her family. It couldn't have been Zelda whom Keisha had seen the previous night. If it had been, surely she'd be here to gloat or extort money from them or *something*. Plus, wasn't she a bit old to be at that type of thing, whatever that thing had been? On the remote chance Zelda *had* been there, surely she wouldn't want that known by anyone either?

"Relatively sedate night," Pierre said quietly as Elizabeth waved goodbye and left, ". . . my perfectly toned ass."

"Okay, okay. Maybe we drank a little more than we should have. But no need for anyone else to know that."

"Girl, you don't have to apologize for partying to a party planner. Speaking of which, while we're waiting for the *new* queen to join us, let's go and see that other queen in the kitchen."

They were seated at the kitchen island when Keisha reappeared, looking slightly flustered but at least showered and fresh in a summer dress. She'd been upstairs only ten minutes but looked perfect, leaving Marcie all the more aware of the night's grime still clinging to her own skin.

"I'm so sorry!" Keisha said. "I honestly didn't mean to be late. I'm embarrassed. And William will be so angry." She was doing a good job of looking like she meant it. Marcie could see how William would have fallen for the little-girl-lost act if it was anything like the one Keisha was putting on now.

"We'll keep it just between us," Pierre said, leaning in and squeezing her hand. "Isn't that right, Julian?"

"Secret's safe with me." Julian was putting the finishing touches to scrambled eggs, smoked salmon, French toast, and home fries. "It's not the most elegant brunch, but something tells me you two ladies need this before we start planning your extravaganza."

"We've only just met, but I think I love you." Keisha stared hungrily at the food as she pulled up a chair as if she were a guest in her own kitchen while Julian found plates and cutlery and condiments.

"Sorry girl, but you haven't got the right equipment to love him."

"Pierre stop it," Julian said, serving up. "Let's eat and then talk about what we can do for you."

"I'm amazed you were free," Marcie said. "I was sure you'd be booked up this week."

"It's fine, we had a cancellation." Julian slid a plate toward her. Where Pierre was full camp, Julian turned it on and off when it suited him. Today was a toned-down day. Maybe that was why Pierre was full throttle.

"*Cancellation,*" Pierre snorted. A look flashed between the two men.

"What?" Keisha asked. "God, I hope I haven't caused a problem asking you to plan for us."

"Not you, honey." Pierre squeezed her hand again. "I'll do anything for a sister and you are too fabulous to refuse."

"It's honestly not a problem. We just moved a few things around, that's all."

"Which of course we don't mind," Pierre cut across his boyfriend. "Because, I'm not going to lie, this is going to be far more fun than our original booking, but if you could remind your new husband that the money his late wife gave us was a *gift*, not a loan that we have to work to pay off, that would be delightful."

Marcie's fork stopped halfway to her mouth. That was quite the irritated reveal.

"Enough, P," Julian snapped, and then forced a smile. "Ignore him, he's just being a bitch. Now, come on, eat before it gets cold."

"Don't worry," Keisha said. "You'll get paid. I want this to be fun for all of us. Aside from anything," she added shyly, "I think you two are people I could really be friends with."

"Why, aren't you quite the doll! And Julian's right, don't pay any attention to me. I think I got out of bed on the wrong side today. But this looks delicious." He raised his fork over a tiny portion of smoked salmon and salad, no eggs or French toast. "And I'm famished."

"If I ate like that, I'd have your figure," Keisha said, tucking into her full plate.

Marcie let their banter flow over her as she watched Julian, questions buzzing in her brain. Eleanor had given them money? Had that been to start the business? When had Julian and Pierre burst onto the scene anyway? They'd just sort of appeared and she'd never given any thought to who they were or where they came from. Were they accepted simply because they'd been introduced by Eleanor and so were immediately acceptable? They were smart too—quiet homosexuality might still be silently disapproved of here, but Pierre and Julian made such a *show* of it, being every stereotype expected from a pair of gay party planners, that they had become an objet d'art to be admired.

"Are your parents French, Pierre?" she asked eventually, once she'd pushed enough food into her mouth to stop her stomach growling and drunk half her fresh orange juice. Pierre laughed. "Oh, how I wish they were. I'm a Louisiana boy, born and raised. My mama was a nurse. My dad the school janitor." He glanced at Julian. "No silver spoon private education for me."

"I got financial aid," Julian cut in.

"You must have French heritage though? With a name like Pierre?"

This time both men laughed.

"What?"

For a second, Pierre's theatrical persona slid away. Even the way he sat changed, more upright, broader across the chest, a flash of a handsome, serious young man. "You try being a gay black man in Hicksville, Louisiana," he said. "I was born Peter. I *became* Pierre."

"A reinvention." Marcie smiled. "I get that."

"We all have to be whatever it takes to survive," Keisha said quietly.

"And they will always try to screw us over," Pierre added, before flourishing a hand. "My glamour is my armor."

"And what fabulous armor it is."

The mood lifted again as Pierre and Keisha continued their bonding. Jacquie had flown the two men to Atlanta to help organize her second wedding, and so Marcie had never used their services for any soirees of her own on principle. She hadn't disliked them, but she'd taken them at face value; now she felt a quiet kinship with these three people around her. All who struggled in life. All trying to be something else in order to get ahead in the world and leave the muck behind. Maybe not Julian so much—sounded like he'd gone to County Day. One of Lyle's classmates perhaps? She couldn't see that going down well with William. A gay kid on financial aid hanging around the house. But Eleanor had obviously liked him. How much money had she given him?

It was so odd, Marcie thought. You arrive in people's lives and forget that so much went *before*. She couldn't imagine Eleanor and William young. Or even with a child. Lyle was barely a ghost of a whisper spoken. Jason rarely mentioned him. No one did. "Too painful" was always the explanation. She'd never questioned it—she'd never really cared enough—but thinking about it now it was odd. He'd died a while back. Didn't most people *like* to talk about those they'd lost after a while? Wasn't that the natural way?

"A masked ball!" Keisha clapped her hands together, an excited child. "Let's make everyone *else* hide who they really are for once!"

"Isn't that a little *Shades of Grey*?" Julian said.

"We're short on time to organize something like that," Marcie said. A masked ball. It was like the fantasy of a teenager. "And remember, most people will already have plans that weekend. Maybe think smaller?"

"Are you crazy?" Pierre said. "The great William Radford the Fourth holding a masked ball with his indecently young new English wife? I don't care what people had planned, if they're invited, they'll come. We'll invite enough to make it sensational and leave off enough to create an envious buzz. The perfect way to organize a party." He glared at Julian. "And there will be nothing *Fifty Shades* about it."

"Well, we can't speak for what happens after the party," Julian said, with a wink.

"Did Eleanor ever host something like this?" Keisha asked.

"No," Julian said. "Or if she did, it was longer ago than I remember."

"Good." Keisha sat back, satisfied. "If people are going to compare me to her all the time, let's give them something to really *see*. A night to remember. Fire eaters, contortionists, mimes, all dotted around the garden. Give it a theme. I know! The beautiful and the damned! I went to a club night with that theme in London last year. It was crazy! Let's make it *sexy*. What do you think, Marcie?" A loaded glance.

"Sounds amazing." Marcie nodded, indulgently amused, even though her stomach was knotted again. Keisha was wild and there was no caging that. If she could just be a little more contained, then perhaps this delicious thing between them could continue for a while, but how could Keisha be trusted not to let it *show*? To understand the danger?

"We'll be the belles of this ball." Keisha leaned forward and whispered loudly, "Let them see what second wives can do!"

Even Marcie had to laugh at that. "Okay, where do we start?"

"We start with a Bloody Mary," Pierre said, pulling his iPad Pro and notebook and pen out of his sleek Dolce & Gabbana bag. "And then we make the magic happen."

"What he means is," Julian cut in while collecting plates, "we'll look at my spreadsheet of who's currently in and who's out."

"But first, handsome man, you make the drinks." Pierre shuffled closer to Keisha. "Now, my English slash African Queen, let's talk color schemes. We want something bold, right?"

They were still talking when William got back at four, and when he swept through the room all smiles and kisses, Marcie took it as her cue to leave. Jason would be home and she didn't want him to get pissed at her when he'd sounded in such a good mood in his text. Seemed like the men had had fun. Probably not as much fun as the girls, she thought wryly, but fun all the same.

"We'll be right behind you," Julian said as she

gathered her stuff to leave. "Give the honeymooners some space."

Marcie wasn't surprised. For all the gushing welcomes and William pawing all over Keisha on his return, there had definitely been tension between him and the two party planners, and even though they'd been polite there was no sense that Julian had once been anything like family. Still, why did she care? This wasn't her circus.

"I'll see you out." Keisha slid from her bar stool and followed. When they reached the front door, she leaned in and kissed Marcie chastely on each cheek, but there was nothing chaste about the hazy look in her eyes or, in fact, the sudden warmth between Marcie's thighs. "I'll text you tomorrow," Keisha said with a mischievous grin. "I think I'm going to need your help with this party. Hands-on help."

"I'll do my best to oblige," Marcie replied. It was so tempting. This desire. This passion. Maybe they *could* do this if they were careful. Just once more. She was trembling with anticipation already.

28.

"What's the matter?" Keisha asked eventually. How could Billy's moods change so fast? He'd been fine when he'd gotten home, but since coming downstairs from his shower he'd been in a shitty mood and didn't seem at all interested in or impressed by her party plans. He was the one who'd wanted her to do all this stuff—he could at least pretend to care. An hour ago, he'd been all over her with kisses, his hand grabbing at her ass, but now she was walking on eggshells as they picked at the pasta she'd made.

"Is my cooking so bad? I thought you'd like it. I made it from scratch." She'd actually been quite proud. A proper Italian carbonara from a recipe, not a cheap sauce from a packet like she'd use back in London.

"The food's great," he answered, with little enthusiasm.

"Well, something's not."

He put his fork down and looked at her and for the briefest moment she thought he'd seen into her soul and knew she wished he'd just hurry up and die.

"Your dress was on the floor in the bathroom and I went to hang it up so it wouldn't get wet or damaged. Seems I was too late. From the state of it, I'd say you had quite a night."

"I fell over." Keisha's skin was getting hotter and hotter. It sounded so lame. "I was with Marcie."

"Who else?"

"No one! We went to a bar, had some food and drinks, danced a bit. I just fell over, that's all."

He stared at her, his granite eyes cold. She knew that look too well. It was Uncle Yahuba's expression when she'd held money back for herself, a look that wouldn't be argued with, not without consequences. She'd never expected to see it on Billy's face. Had she run full circle? Still, her story didn't add up and she knew it. The dress was filthy and had mud in places it shouldn't. And it was torn, as if she'd been running from someone or something through a forest.

She bristled. Attack was always the best form of defense. "So what are you suggesting? That I went out with your friend's wife and rolled around in the dirt with some random guy I met in a bar? What was Marcie doing at the time? Watching? Taking a piss?" She glared at him. "Or are *you* taking the piss?"

He flinched as if her crudeness were a bullet. "Keisha, don't talk like that."

"Well, if you're going to speak to me like I'm a tramp, I may as well talk like one."

"I don't think you were out screwing other men, and if you don't want to tell me how your dress got in that state that's your business, but don't expect me to be overjoyed about it. Maybe you were too drunk to remember. Maybe you both were. It's not as if Marcie's an angel, however she likes to dress herself up now. Jacquie was the one with class. I knew everything I needed to know about Marcie when she set up that godawful tacky boutique that ended up costing Jason upward of a quarter of a million. It's good that you've made a friend, and sure, for now, she'll do. But there are better friends to have. The tennis girls. The other club wives. Jason's a good man, but he was a slave to his dick when he married Marcie."

Keisha listened, stunned, to his rant. This was a revelation, this meanness. At least Marcie had *tried* to work, which seemed more than most of the other women she'd encountered. Maybe their men were all like Billy.

Maybe they wanted them to simply stay at home and make sure they looked pretty. No job, no escape route. All this wealth, both inherited and earned. What did it do to people? Entitled, judgmental, devious. Is that what they were behind the smiles and laughter? In that moment she hated him and all of them, but she needed to placate him. To think like Dolly or her family and look out for herself whatever it took. Billy was the key to her future, and she wasn't losing that.

"I made an effort to be friends with her because she's Jason's wife." Smooth, charming, handsome Jason. Did Billy love him as much as he professed or was there too much competitive edge for that? "I thought you'd be pleased." She paused. "But you're right. There were more drinks than there should have been. I don't know if we were trying to impress each other or feel more relaxed or whatever but we definitely drank too much and ate too little. I tripped in the garden at her house by the sprinklers, that's why there's grass and mud on my dress. I was so embarrassed I didn't want to tell you."

The relief flooded his face. Whatever he'd said about not thinking she'd been fucking someone else, the need for those little blue pills hung heavy over him, and there was no kind of paranoid jealousy like an old rich man's. Rich men didn't like to share their things.

"I feel like I'm always messing up," she continued. "Everything here is so different. I'm not used to worrying about what people think of me."

"Maybe I'm overreacting," he said. "Eleanor understood privilege. How to behave and what was expected of her. It was in her heritage. She didn't have to learn it all. I forget what a big change you're having to go through. I'm not an idiot, I know all about your life in London." He paused to sip his wine. "Even the bits you tried to hide from me."

Keisha's skin prickled. Was that a veiled threat? What did he know about? Dolly? Her family's scams? Her chest tightened with horror. *The boy?* No, he couldn't know about that. The boy was a ghost. No one knew about the boy, her made-up boy, the boy who was never there, but always there, the vanishing boy. The cause of her curse.

"Did you think I wouldn't get you checked out? Trust me, I know there's grime on you but grime can be washed away. You're my Cinderella. I wanted to save you from all that."

"You did save me." Her voice was small, diminished in her body as she was in this enormous house. He'd had someone dig around in her life? Her skin crawled, violated. When? While he'd been romancing her, all puppy-dog eyes and expensive gifts?

"You just need to forget that life now. How you were then. That's not you, I can see it. You're better than that. You're not Cinderella anymore, you're the princess."

He saw this as a fairy tale. He'd just told her he spied on her and now he was trying to make it romantic? Did he really see himself as Prince Charming? A mockery of one maybe. She was tired and her mood was spiraling downward, dipping toward the darkness she feared one day falling into forever. Tears stung her eyes. This was so much harder than she'd thought it would be back at the start, way back at the beginning in London. A lifetime ago now. That snakelike voice in her ear. *Marry him, then get rid of him.*

"Hey, don't cry," he said, suddenly tender, the tree of his moods swaying once more.

"It's so lovely." She hiccuped a laugh. "No one's ever called me their princess before. I'm so sorry I disappoint you."

"No, no you don't." He heaved himself out of his chair and came around to her side of the table, sitting down and taking her hand in his. "And I've got some good news myself."

What now?

"I'm definitely retiring. I discussed it with Jason this weekend and he's right. Life is too short. I mean, look what happened to Eleanor. I want to spend my time with *you*."

She threw her arms around his neck so he couldn't see her disappointment. "When?" *Not now, not yet,* she thought. How would she cope with him breathing down her neck and on her neck all the time?

"Jason's going to buy me out. I need to speak to some people, put some actions in place, but I'm pretty much all yours from now on. If I want to work, I can always consult or do after-dinner speaking." He pulled back to look at her. "We can travel—I can show you some of the States. Host some charity events. Relax at the club."

Every word was like a pillow pressed against her face, but he didn't notice. He grinned, his teeth yellow against his purple lips. Each day that passed she found him harder to like. Especially after last night. After everything. "That's great," she managed. Too bright? Not bright enough?

"It's made me feel younger already." His eyes glittered as they dipped to her cleavage. She smiled even as her skin crawled. There wasn't even time to take a Valium.

29.

He'd fucked her over the dining table, huffing and puffing at her back, and even bracing herself, her hips had bruised against the edge. With each thrust she'd dutifully moaned as he grunted, her eyes stinging as she focused on the pushed-aside congealed leftovers on their dinner plates. It wasn't painful and he wasn't mean, but even as he strained to fill her up, she felt empty. Once he was finished, they'd gone to bed, and before long he wanted to do it again, but this time she got away with a blow job. Revolting as she found it, she couldn't bear to have the weight of him on her again. She didn't ask and he didn't say, but she knew he'd taken a Viagra. Maybe even before he'd gotten home—snuck it in on the way from the airport, eager to impress her with his manliness. He'd fallen asleep fast after that, and, as full as her mind was, her exhaustion took over, and she'd sunk into the sleep of the dead.

She woke abruptly, her survival instinct tearing her from dreams of black icy water filling her lungs, driving her to the surface. Her eyes opened, but any relief was lost as weight crushed her chest. She couldn't breathe, she couldn't breathe, she couldn't . . .

Billy. He must have rolled half onto her in his sleep, maybe the dregs of the pill working even as he snored, and now he was slumped, a beached whale, one leg and arm over her, his heavy head pressing on her breasts. His skin was corpse-pale in the gloom and she carefully rolled him away. He shuffled back to his side of the bed without even waking, no doubt a whole first marriage of practice, and his breathing fell silent again.

She was still tired and could have fallen straight back to sleep, but despite the fear of ghosts huddled in the shadows watching her, she relished the peace of the night. For a little while the world was hers alone, and once she was awake enough to realize she was both thirsty and needed the bathroom, she got up, grabbed her phone, and went downstairs for orange juice.

She ached in her bones. Was she getting too old for partying like that? The weekend felt like a dream now; the dancing, the sex, her mouth between Marcie's legs, the *ease* with which they'd given themselves up to each other, both of them rebelling against their constraints. What would Jason make of it? she wondered. Would he smell Keisha in their bed? On his wife?

She stared out the window to the shadows beyond. It was a tangled web she was weaving and she had to be careful. Keep it together. Be tougher. There was no room for her doubts and darkness and worries. Everything she wanted was in her grasp. Money, freedom, love—she just had to be patient. Patience. It had never been her thing. She wasn't calculated like the rest of her family, but then she did wish Billy dead daily, so maybe it was in her blood after all.

Across the ocean of lawn, Zelda's apartment was invisible, drowned, no lights on tonight. It wasn't that late, just coming up on one, maybe. Had her family gone? Keisha hadn't heard anything, but then the house was so big she never knew when cars were coming or going outside.

The lack of light was unsettling her as much as if Zelda had been standing in the window again. *Zelda* unsettled her. Always watching. Maybe watching now in the dark, for all Keisha knew. A snake of concern rattled its tail in her belly. Could it have been Zelda she'd seen in the crowd the previous night? No, not her, but the posture of the woman's back . . . it had been someone familiar, she was sure of it. But what if it *had* been Zelda? What would she want for her silence?

Keisha turned away from the window. There was no point in *what ifs*. There was nothing she could do about it, except wait and see. *Be tougher,* she reminded herself as she crept back up the stairs, Billy's snoring getting louder as she grew closer, as if the house itself were rumbling in the night. She paused, not wanting to slide back into that bed just yet. Ahead, the door to Eleanor's rooms—her mausoleum—was open a crack, tempting Keisha to go and snoop around some more, and she couldn't resist. She slid inside.

It was only her imagination but the air felt cooler and unnaturally still in the vast room filled with elegant possessions that waited in vain, abandoned, for a time when their owner would need them again. Keisha found herself breathing shallowly, as if she might wake Eleanor's ghost more readily than Billy's snoring, sadly very much alive, body. She traced a finger across the dressing table. The hairbrush, comb, vanity mirror, carefully laid out. Why were the dead so fascinating? Why did they feel more present than the living sometimes? Maybe it was just her. Always surrounded by shadows, that's what Auntie Ayo had said to her.

You got yourself cursed blood, KeKe, it's there in the cards, no good will come of you.

She shivered slightly as she remembered her wish at the festival that weekend. *Billy gone, gone, gone.*

There had been nothing good in that. She might not be cursed, but she knew she was wicked. His death was what she wanted, even more so now with her body aching from the weight of him and the echo of his sex present inside her.

She flicked her phone open and idly googled *"How many Viagra would it take to kill someone?"* Billy was that very male combination of arrogant and insecure enough to maybe take too many one night. The results weren't encouraging. Billy was vain but not stupid. He'd never take *that* many, not even if she pretended she wanted him to have sex with her twenty times in a row.

She flopped down on Eleanor's bed for a moment, imagining her predecessor and Billy fucking in it. Had Eleanor loved Billy? Or had their marriage been one of convenience, both pushed together by their parents wanting to keep the elite with the elite? Inbreeding. What was it Billy had said at dinner? Eleanor knew *how to behave and what was expected of her.* Had Eleanor sometimes screamed silent frustrated rage into her pillow at night? Not just this pillow, but all of them, from childhood. Dress this way, walk that way, speak this way, be a good girl. Is that how it had been for her entire life? Keisha had been left to run wild and then there had been Auntie Ayo and Uncle Yahuba and all the shittiness and fear and wrong education *that* entailed, but maybe Eleanor's youth hadn't been that much better. More luxurious, yes, but just as imprisoned.

For the first time she felt a nugget of sympathy for the dead woman. She turned the small table lamp on, checking the door was still pushed to, and got up to look at the photos on the dresser. The glass across the surfaces shone. Zelda must still come in and polish them. They were flashbacks through time. Did Eleanor look happy in them as she stood beside Billy at various stages of their marriage? Smiling yes, but happy? Keisha didn't think so. Certainly not in the later ones. There was a coolness in her eyes and a stiffness in her back. Was this after Lyle's death?

Keisha looked closer, comparing two, taken at some kind of function but maybe ten years apart. Billy had his arm around Eleanor's waist in both but in the more recent image there was definitely a wider gap between them as they stood, as if maybe Eleanor didn't want her husband pawing at her, proprietorial. She looked elegant, yes, and was smiling politely, but something was missing. There was another—this time Jason was in it, looking much as he did now, with a woman who must have been Jacquie, dark and slender with a birdlike brittle beauty. Her hand was firmly gripping Jason's, making the gap between Eleanor and Billy seem more pronounced. As if Eleanor was maybe trying to pull away and Jacquie was trying to cling on. Was Jason already seeing Marcie when this was taken? So many stories, so much history.

Keisha looked at the pictures in the rows behind, some from when Eleanor had been a child. Most were posed family shots where she'd been taught how to sit prettily and tilt her head this way or that, her parents standing behind her, occasionally with a hand resting on her shoulder, presumably meant to look affectionate but somehow seeming as if she was being held in place.

Only in one did she look like a normal joyful girl. The old black-and-white photo was crumpled in its frame and there was nothing staged about it. Eleanor, recognizable by her blond mid-length curls, was laughing on a swing at the bottom of a vast garden. A boy in knee-length shorts leaned against the frame, and a smaller girl was sitting cross-legged on the grass looking up at her. There were remnants of a picnic on the grass. Who'd taken the photo? Keisha wondered. Someone who didn't mind kids being kids.

She tracked Eleanor's life through the pictures, each year older a little more contained and mannered as each year Billy got a little fatter and more red-faced. How ironic that it was Eleanor who was now gone, who'd rotted and died in this very room while her overindulgent husband got to marry again, a fresh young woman to mold. A wolf in sheep's clothing, that's what she'd married, and she'd been an idiot to fall for his puppy-dog routine. He revolted her. He scared her. He made her dislike herself. No matter how many cars or pieces of jewelry he bought her, she was always going to be impatient for him to be *gone.*

She browsed through Eleanor's drawers again, and this time her eyes lingered on the hidden needles and vial of morphine, wondering how it would feel, before she slid the drawer quietly closed and turned off the lamp, ready to go back to bed. Only when she got to the door did she pause and turn back. From within the dresser she took out a hidden framed picture of Eleanor with Lyle as a child, her eyes shining bright in this one, and placed it in front of the others, out in the open, angled toward the bed.

"Good night, Eleanor," she whispered into the empty gloom. "I hope that helps you sleep better." Then she clicked the door shut behind her, leaving the dead and the dark to their own company.

30.

They'd had sex twice the previous night, once when Jason had joined Marcie in the decadently huge walk-in shower that took up most of her bathroom, and then again later, in bed. If there had been any lingering scent of Keisha on the sheets, Jason hadn't noticed. His good mood had left her as breathless as the sex. He'd been grinning like a cream-filled cat when she'd gotten back from the Radfords' house, holding a beautiful gold bracelet he'd picked up for her while he was away, and there was also Chinese takeout on the breakfast bar that ended up growing cold because he was hungrier for her than for any food.

It had been strange, the contrast of his thick chest with the mat of tangled coarse hair that stretched out toward his shoulders with Keisha's dark, soft, and smooth skin. The way Jason kissed was different. His tongue was rougher, filled with a need to prove himself, perhaps. The comparisons were exhilarating, she couldn't deny it. Thinking about what she'd done with Keisha only the night before in their marital bed turned her on, and when she came she was so lost in her thoughts she wasn't entirely sure who she was with, him or her. It was Keisha's face she saw as she came on his mouth, even still when Jason clambered back up the bed to pump himself into her, pinning her down and panting expletives into her face as she gripped his sweaty back and moaned some more, pretending she still wanted his cock until he climaxed.

She hadn't had to do that with Keisha, she'd thought, afterward, when he brought the lukewarm noodles and ice-cold Chablis upstairs to bed. There was no pandering involved. No pretense for the sake of ego or machismo. Maybe her mother had been right all those years ago, trying to drunk-talk her way through some attempt at advice.

Men are fucking babies their whole lives. You spend all your time trying to make them feel better about themselves. For what? For fucking nothing. Take take take, that's all they do. They never fucking grow up. Even that pissy boy of yours you're so sure you love. If you marry him, then you're as stupid a bitch as me.

As maternal pep talks went, on reflection, it had probably been one of Mama's best, but then her mama had been flipped between men like a worn-out pinball all her miserable life and probably still was, for all Marcie knew. Mama had been right in *that* moment, but even a stopped clock told the time correctly twice a day, and Marcie had only made *one* mistake in her choice of men, which given that she was Mama's daughter was no mean feat.

Jason had been a good choice. A *great* choice. So what if she had to fake it sometimes to keep him sweet? She had a beautiful house, a charmed life, and she lived in luxury with a handsome man easily stolen from his wife. Admittedly, that last didn't make her sound so good, she'd decided as she let Jason feed her a forkful of greasy chow mein. Maybe the apple didn't fall so far from the tree after all.

But when the lights were out and he was sleeping beside her, the Chinese food sat uncomfortably in her belly as guilt took hold. She'd cheated on her husband. And what had Jason done that was so terrible? Nothing. All she *really* knew he'd done was lie about a phone call—yes, he'd been moody, and yes, he'd been slightly dazzled by Keisha, but she didn't have any evidence that he'd betrayed her. But she had definitely betrayed him. She was the cheat. She was the one putting all her security at risk.

Once a cheat, always a cheat.

Looking over at Jason now, while he drove, the top of the car down, tanned hands on the steering wheel, his hair mussed up from a day at the beach, it felt for a moment like time had looped back to when they'd been courting. *Courting,* such a sweet Southern word. Courting was probably what Iris and Noah, or William and Eleanor, had done all those years ago. Now it was the word Jason used to politely refer to their affair, as if somehow that would make people forget the whole drama of his divorce.

She didn't want to think about that right now. They'd had a great day, she couldn't deny that, and even though her phone had buzzed quietly in her purse several times, she'd almost managed to put Keisha out of her head. Jason had driven them out to Tybee Island, where they'd wandered on the beach, enjoying the sea breeze and collecting shells, before stopping for a seafood lunch at a cheap crab place. So very different from the crisp, white-tablecloth restaurants of their marriage. It had all made her feel young again. She hadn't spoken much, letting him bubble over with his obvious excitement at the reality of buying William out and becoming senior partner.

"We'll be on the map, baby," he'd said more than once. "Not in anyone's shadow anymore."

"Are we going to be the new Eleanor and William?" she had asked, avoiding mentioning Keisha. It was a tongue-in-cheek question. They could never be like Noah and Iris or William—they weren't *bred in* enough.

"Younger and better looking," he'd answered. He'd been laughing about how William had behaved in Atlanta. Getting up early and going to the hotel gym regardless of how much they'd drunk the night before, *cleansing* with his coconut water, glugging it down, even as he ordered eggs and bacon and biscuits and gravy. All to impress some English girl he'd bought and paid for already and who was only after him for his money. He'd laughed and Marcie had joined in. As they snickered, smug, she'd wondered if maybe terrible people were drawn to terrible people. She was pretty sure neither she nor the man she'd married was very nice.

"Why don't we grab a cocktail at Sacchi's before home?" Jason asked.

Marcie flipped down the visor to check the mirror. "I look awful," she said. It wasn't true. She was windswept and decidedly dressed down, but awful? No. If anything she looked fresh and young.

"You look beautiful," Jason said. She looked at herself again. There *was* something about her today. Is this what a woman's touch could give you? This glow? Maybe it was the heat of having a delicious secret. A slight revenge on her husband for his middle-of-the-night lies and outrageous flirting.

The occasional buzzes from her purse had unsettled her though, and as soon as they handed the car to the valet, she excused herself to the restrooms and checked her texts. All from Keisha. While there was nothing particularly incriminating about them, which was a relief, there was definitely a sense of neediness in her bitching about William's retirement. *I won't be able to breathe. How am I going to get time for doing my own thing? How will I be able to hang out with you so much?;-)* The smiley face emoji was loaded with subtext and it made Marcie cringe slightly. Yes, there was that draw that Keisha had, the magic pull on her she found so hard to resist, but she was also a childlike liability. She read farther down the messages. *Please tell me you guys haven't been in bed all day!* That was followed by a puking emoji. *Answer my texts and save me from boredom! Up for some party planning stuff next week? I need you!!!*

It was like having a bouncing puppy pawing at her legs, and now that she had Jason home and in such high spirits, even with her suspicions about his recent behavior, she wasn't ready to wreck it all by having

Keisha causing trouble. Out of Keisha's orbit, Marcie's sanity was returning. She had been longing for her freedom and youth, that was true, but she wasn't going to lose everything she'd worked for because of some crazy infatuation, and definitely not because the person she was infatuated with couldn't keep her mouth shut. Especially now that everything was going so well for Jason. When they were about to join the true *elite*. The women of the city would be turning to *her* for their lead on charity events and luncheons. No one would look down on the second wife anymore. Not when her husband had access to all their private financial and legal affairs.

Her fingers flew across the keyboard. *Having a day out with Jason! Sorry!* she replied. *But yes, will text tomorrow about party planning. See you in the week!* Not unfriendly, but not intimate. She tucked her phone away again, satisfied. She would take control of this. Control was something she was good at.

She swept through Sacchi's, nodding at familiar faces here and there, enjoying how casual her beaten-soft white jeans and blue and white cotton shirt looked compared to the carefully coutured outfits on display in the old-fashioned leather wingback chairs that filled the gloomy interior. Sacchi's was a home away from home for most of the club crowd, somewhere central and yet familiar in decor and ambience, servers dressed impeccably as they delivered perfectly mixed cocktails before whispering away across thick pile carpet.

When in the cool, softly lit bar, it was hard to remember that it was eighty degrees and humid outside, but thankfully the courtyard in back was a more relaxed affair and Marcie was pleased they'd gotten a table outside. She was enjoying the freedom of the sunshine today, and she didn't care if it meant her back would be slick with sweat under her shirt before too long.

She froze as she stepped outside into the bright light, a stage set before her, as her brain tried to process what she was seeing. Jason had his back to her at the table, but even from several feet away she could see how stiff his spine was. Marcie's own was suddenly a bolt of lead through her core, even as her hands trembled. A dark-haired woman was standing beside the table, leaning forward. All the catlike angles of her face seemed sharper in the bright sunshine, her expression hard as she whispered into Jason's ear.

Jacquie.

Marcie no longer felt the heavy afternoon heat. Instead, a chill prickled over her skin as if she were still inside the fiercely air-conditioned bar. Keisha had been right. Jacquie *was* back. Those feline eyes looked up, as if their owner shared that animal's nine lives and sense of danger, and they glittered as the face pulled into an angular smile and Jacquie straightened up and waved.

Marcie forced herself to smile back, sauntering over to the table on unsteady legs, determined not to put on a show for any beady eyes that might be watching for entertainment. Jacquie was elegant in a powder-blue fitted dress, hips impossibly narrow to still have a waist, slim feet in elegant open-toed sandals, and Marcie felt like a waitress all over again, dressed down as she was. Jacquie had never failed to make her feel like a child. And a dumb one at that. It was something in her eyes and it was stronger now that the heartbreak had left them. Pure disdain with a veneer of polite grace. Jacquie might be all smiles now, but Marcie could see that Jason was pale and angry. What was going on here?

"You're looking well, Marcie," Jacquie said. "Those extra pounds suit you."

Marcie grinned, ignoring the insult. "Bless your heart, thank you. We've had a day date at the beach." She hated how she sounded. Kind of passive-aggressive defensive. A day date? Who ever said that? And why did it matter to her that Jacquie should think everything was rosy in their marriage? Jacquie was history. But what had she been saying to Jason with such intensity? Had Jason known she'd be here? Unlikely. Sacchi's had always been a favorite of Jacquie's. If she was back in town, of course she'd drink here.

"How lovely." Drips from an ice block.

"Oh, I meant to say," Marcie ignored the other woman's cool and kept her own sting sweet. "I'm so sorry for your loss. It must be hard to be on your own at your age."

"Thank you. Yes, it was very sad." Jacquie glanced down at Jason and then back at Marcie. "Of course, some losses turn out to be gains. And who knows what the future holds for any of us."

"God willing, only good things."

Jacquie tossed her hair carefully over one shoulder. "Anyway, I'll leave you two to your afternoon. Annabelle is waiting inside. I only stopped to apologize to Jason for missing his call a couple of days ago. I was at the spa. I meant to call back, but you know how it is, you get started doing something else and then forget." She smiled, razor thin and just as sharp. "I guess that might be my age too." And then she was gone, breezing past Marcie and leaving only a waft of expensive and heavily floral perfume in her wake. It nauseated Marcie. Maybe that was the point.

Jason had called Jacquie. The thought was so absurd Marcie couldn't quite absorb it. It sat like oil on the surface water of her mind as she took the chair opposite her husband. "What did—" she started. *What did Jacquie mean she missed your call?* was the embarrassingly passive-aggressive question she was going to ask, but then Jason's phone started ringing.

"William," he said, cutting her off as he picked up the phone, leaving all her confusion and anger caught in her throat. *Why the hell did you call Jacquie?* Maybe that was the approach she should take. No, that was how she *wanted* to confront him, but this was Jason. Aggression would get her nowhere. When he finished talking to William she'd ask him casually, as if she didn't care. Not that he'd believe that, but politeness was the Southern way, and she'd have half a chance of getting some truth out of him that way.

She looked over at her husband. His face had already been like thunder and nothing William was saying was cheering him up. His jaw had tightened and his knuckles were white on the cell. She listened to his side of the conversation. *Who? When? Of course, absolutely. Looking forward to getting it done.* His upbeat tone of voice was so at odds with his expression that it made Marcie shiver.

The waiter came by and she murmured an order of two margaritas, even though Jacquie's unwelcome presence had killed her enthusiasm for an hour at Sacchi's, and no doubt Jason's too, but why should they give her the satisfaction of driving them out as if they should still be ashamed? Jacquie was the past. Forgotten. And Marcie had never been ashamed anyway. All was fair in love and war. All was fair in *life* if it got you what you wanted.

Finally, Jason hung up. "What is it?" she asked. "He hasn't changed his mind?"

"No, nothing like that. Nothing important. He's getting an audit done before the sale. Figures it's due diligence, which I guess it is."

"What's the problem with that?"

"There isn't one. But they won't start until after the holiday. It'll delay everything by a month or so." He flashed her a smile. "Guess I'm impatient."

"The time'll go fast enough." Their drinks appeared and Marcie forced herself to take a sip, even though an alcohol haze was the last thing she wanted now and the sharpness just tasted sour. "How come you called Jacquie?"

"Why do you think?" He was still staring at his phone. "Because Keisha said she was back. I just wondered why. You know how she can be. I didn't want any trouble."

"She must be done with all that by now, surely?"

"She's still a bitch." His jaw tightened again.

"What did she say to you? You looked totally pissed."

"Nothing. The usual. How shitty I was." He looked up, irritated, and sipped his drink. "Can we forget about Jacquie? We're having this great day, how about we don't ruin it?"

It was already ruined, Marcie wanted to say, but didn't, not wanting a fight, especially not here. Instead, they sat in an awkward silence, Jason's mind elsewhere, their time occasionally marked out by Marcie's asking an innocuous question about a TV show or a friend, answered in monosyllables. Jason was angry about something, she knew that, but who had annoyed him? Jacquie or William? Or was it a combination of both? The way he had looked while on the phone had been so strange; Jason's voice had been upbeat, yet it seemed to come from a robotic or *dead* body. So disconnected.

They finished their drinks and left, Marcie claiming to be tired from a day of sea breezes and fresh air, but in reality wanting to get out of the goldfish bowl of Sacchi's. Jason didn't argue, and when they got home he went straight for a long shower before making supper, which they ate with the TV drowning out the stilted atmosphere between them. When they went to bed, he didn't try to touch her and she found she didn't much care. Once again, she felt filled with mistrust of her husband. What was he holding back? Why wouldn't he share with her?

She finally fell into a fitful sleep, and this time, she felt no surprise when she woke in the dark to an empty bed and no sign of Jason's phone on the nightstand. Another late-night call. Spiders of suspicion emerged, scuttering from the corners of her mind, forming webs to ensnare dark thoughts: If it wasn't Keisha, then who *was* he talking to? Jacquie maybe? Was it whatever she'd been whispering that had soured his mood? Marcie hated to admit it, but Jacquie had looked good. Could Jason be secretly in touch with her again? Was it Jacquie who'd been sitting in her car outside their house when Jason was away? Had she hoped he'd sneak out and talk to her? Maybe now that the surgeon was dead and Jason was heading to the highest rungs of their social ladder, he wanted an old-school Southern wife again. Maybe Jacquie was toying with her, wanting her to feel as bad as she had when Marcie was in the process of stealing her life from her. *All's fair in love and war.*

Marcie closed her eyes and waited for his guilty tread and the feel of him as his body weight sank back onto the mattress. After a moment, she risked opening her eyes slightly. Jason didn't notice. He was staring at the ceiling, his face as cold and impassive as it had been when he'd been on his cell with William. What was happening in that mind? Did she even know him at all? Secrets. Their marriage foundations had been secrets, an affair, and lies. It had been exciting then. It wasn't so much fun now. Not when he was keeping secrets from *her* and she was cheating on him. But still—if he had his secrets, what was so wrong with her having hers? Why shouldn't she have something for herself?

31.

Marcie had been here before. She had shivered with this sense of an imminent and terrible unraveling that she was central to, that she was causing, but that she just couldn't stop. There were so many echoes of her affair with Jason. Even this position, straddling Keisha in the car, her skirt hitched up around her waist, was how she and Jason had fucked the first few times. Then it had been about making *him* come, keeping *him* happy, but now all her thoughts and focus were on her own pleasure and what the other woman was doing with her fingers. Marcie had said *we can't keep doing this* every time they'd met since the weekend, and her resolve had gotten weaker each time. That was the problem with affairs. Once you started them they were so very hard to stop. Addictive.

Exciting. Especially when Jason's moods were still so unpredictable and she was starting to actively dislike him, and there was something flattering, if dangerous, in Keisha's neediness for her. It was so opposite to how Jason had become. It was nice to feel wanted and special and to have her own secret—*screw you, Jason*—even if there was a slightly worrying edge to how hard and fast Keisha had fallen for her.

"You're so beautiful," Keisha murmured. "I could watch you come all day." Marcie pressed herself down onto those long, beautiful fingers as she shuddered to a climax. "I could let you," she whispered, smiling. It was strange how Keisha was so fragile in the emotional side of the relationship and yet so confident in the sex. Marcie liked it. Despite Marcie's constant proclamations to the contrary, the Englishwoman had wormed her way inside her head, and when she wasn't wondering what duplicity Jason was up to, she was thinking about Keisha's soft skin and dirty laugh, which no longer seemed crude and coarse but joyful and fascinating. She leaned forward to kiss her, hair falling across both their faces. "You're so good at that. Do you want me to . . ."

"No, I'm okay. Making you happy makes me happy. Anyway, they'll be waiting for us at the club." Keisha rolled her eyes. "I swear to fuck the only way I get through him touching me is thinking about you."

Another thing Marcie liked about Keisha was the way she cursed. It reminded her of her own youth when life was grittier and her lungs felt raw with every breath just from the power of surviving. "Don't start on that again," she said, sliding back over to the driver's seat. "What are you going to do? Leave him? You're kidding yourself. And I keep telling you, I'm happy with Jason. Things are good for us. I'm not going back to having nothing and being nothing. You need to understand that."

"You're not happy with him," Keisha said. "I can tell. The man's an arse."

"Happiness is relative," Marcie said, adjusting her underwear. Sex with a woman in the underground garage on Whitaker Street. It made her want to both laugh and also slap herself around the face for the stupidity. She was in that moment of postsex clarity, a window of sanity before all her desires resurfaced and lust took over once more. Maybe the sex would wear off and they'd get bored with each other. That would be the best outcome.

"We're not like you and William. Jason doesn't revolt me. And maybe I'm not as in love with him as I used to be, but I *did* love him."

"What does that mean?" Keisha looked stung.

"You know what that means." Marcie softened, leaning over and kissing her cheek. "I don't think badly of you for it, because I totally get why you did it, *but* if you marry a man for his money, sweetheart, you will always end up earning it."

"We could be happy poor?" Keisha was like a hopeful puppy.

"No, we couldn't. I couldn't. And you want money as much as I do, otherwise you'd have left him by now, postnup or no postnup. So forget about it. Please."

"I thought getting married to Billy was everything I wanted. But it's everything everyone else wanted." Keisha's eyes were clouded with hurt and anger. "And he's not who I thought he was."

"No one ever is," Marcie said softly. "Now come on. Go get in that little red Corvette and let's go tell those dull men of ours all about how decadent this party is going to be."

"It is, isn't it?" Keisha smiled then, suddenly all light and life again. She was so childlike. Marcie had seen it again when Julian and Pierre had talked them through the various food options for the night. Keisha had found that boring, Marcie could tell by the way she'd backed off and let Elizabeth, who'd joined them at the start to discuss various food intolerances of some of the guests, take over.

Only once Elizabeth had left and they'd started looking at the various red and black satins and velvets to be draped across marble plinths and decorated with gold snakes wound around them, glittering lights sparkling from open-fanged mouths, had Keisha lit up again, clapping her hands together with delight. They hadn't chosen their dresses yet, but Julian had promised to show them a selection that would make the rest of the partygoers "simply die" with envy. For the first time, Marcie was actually looking forward to one of William's parties. "Now, shoo. I'll go ahead."

Keisha leaned over and kissed Marcie, her tongue sliding between her lips, and despite having just come Marcie tingled all over again.

"I'm so smitten with you, Marcie," Keisha said. "I really am."

"I think you're crazy," Marcie answered, but smiled. "Put some lipstick on, otherwise William will wonder what you've been doing."

Keisha groaned and got out of the car. "God, I wish he'd just *die*," she said, and not for the first time. "Why can't he just die?"

She closed the door and Marcie watched her saunter across the lot, all firm curves, proud and strong. One day she'd have to tell her that life didn't work like that. Men like William got to go on forever. Real life didn't touch them, and Keisha would be best off making her peace with that.

It was funny how life turned in circles, she thought, as she kissed Jason on the cheek, joining him and William in the clubhouse restaurant. Her panties were still wet from Keisha's work, and yet here she was, breezing in all smiles for her husband. Is this how it had been for him, when he'd been married to Jacquie? This shifting between situations?

"Where's Keisha?" William asked.

"Following behind. Got caught at the lights I think." At least Jason hadn't had to manage having Marcie across the luncheon table when he was still with Jacquie. "You're going to be amazed by how well she's organizing this event. She has a natural flair for it."

William looked pleased, as if she'd complimented a pet on performing a trick well. How much did wives mean to someone like William? Did he understand love, or was it all about tradition and ego? How quickly he'd gotten over Eleanor. Perhaps even before she'd died he was already wondering what would come after. That flirting with waitresses he did. Eleanor had been a dead weight before she'd died. Was Jason like that too, underneath it all? Did he understand love or just possessions and social placement? All this politeness and refinement had been sucking the life out of Marcie, a slow puncture she hadn't noticed. She may not want to leave Jason, but neither could she bring herself to give up this passion. Not yet. Men got to have their cake and eat it all the time. Why couldn't she? "Have you ordered?" she asked. "I'm starving. I think I'll have a steak."

Jason looked at her, surprised. "I ordered you a salad. You always have a salad."

"Not today." How ridiculous it was. All these women, nibbling on air, when they could afford the finest mouth-watering dishes. They weren't staying thin for themselves, that was for sure. They were starving their bodies and plumping their faces to fend off the secretaries and the second wives. Marcie used to look at the larger women dotted around the lounges and bars with disdain, but maybe she'd gotten it all wrong. Maybe they were the happy ones. Their marriages weren't based on image or a financial power imbalance. Those were the kinds of women the rest of them—herself included—probably should aspire to be.

"So I guess you'd better change the order," she finished. She was in a fiery mood, ready to spit and crackle at anyone, Jason included. Great sex did that to her. And Keisha might be a little crazy, but she *was* great sex. And suddenly there she was again and Marcie's heart tripped.

"I'll have a steak too." Keisha slid in beside William after kissing the top of his balding head, her lips barely touching his liver-spotted skin. "Looking at all those canapé options this morning has left me starving." She grinned. "But then, I'm always starving. I have a large appetite."

"Marcie says you're doing a great job with the party," William said, and Marcie saw one fat hand slide under the table, where it was probably squeezing Keisha's knee. Poor Keisha. No wonder she was so desperate to get out.

"It's not going to be like any other around here, that's for sure," Keisha said proudly, but Marcie noticed William's face darkening slightly. Worry? Not wanting anything *too* different? Too young or too wild? Nothing that might embarrass him with its gaudiness? "When we get home I'll talk you through our ideas. Then we can change anything you don't like."

William relaxed. The king was appeased.

"I've said it before and I'll say it again," Jason said. "You're a lucky man, William."

Marcie looked at her husband. His eyes glittered, wolflike, as he looked at Keisha for a moment too long before turning his smile to William. It still rankled Marcie, this obvious lust he had for the second Mrs. Radford IV. It also annoyed her that he was so stupid as to let it show to William, when they were so close to getting everything he wanted.

"Oh, I almost forgot. This light came on in my car on my way here." Keisha pulled out her phone. "I took a picture of it so you men can tell me what it means." She clicked through to the image and held it out.

"Oh, that's the coolant," William said, getting up. "Excuse me while I go to the restroom."

"Coolant?" Keisha barely noticed as her husband waddled away.

"I think they call it antifreeze in England," Jason said. "Don't worry about it. I can top that up for you. Check that it's not leaking. Can you pick some up at the store, Marcie, if we don't have any?"

"Since when are you a mechanic?" Marcie said.

"I'm pretty good with cars, actually." Jason flashed her a disgruntled look before smiling once again at Keisha. "Don't worry, I'll get under your hood, Keisha, and get it running again. Can't have you overheating."

"I think we're out," Marcie muttered, staring down at the menu as her husband overplayed his crude innuendos. Her fingers felt sticky and her stomach turned. Suddenly, she wasn't hungry anymore.

32.

The skin on Marcie's thighs prickled and itched with sweat under her skirt from where she'd been sitting, so bored, for the best part of an hour, and it was a relief when the sermon was finally over. It was the hottest day of the year so far, and the pastor had been embarrassed and apologetic about the broken AC, which apparently engineers were working on, but Marcie had seen no sign of them as she'd sat and politely perspired alongside the great and the good of Savannah society. Sunday before the Fourth of July; everyone went to church, she'd noticed over the years—even Jason insisted they show up. As if God were one of them and Jesus wore a cap that said *Make America Great Again* instead of a crown of thorns.

The doors had been left open, but the air was so

stagnant they would have been better closed. Keisha had gone outside, looking slightly off-color, ten minutes before the end, and as they all rose to file out, Marcie noted William didn't look at all pleased about that. Virginia, tanned and glowing from her trip away, happy to be back in the bosom of her church, had whispered, "Maybe she's pregnant," into Marcie's ear, and half-asleep as she'd been in the stifling heat while the pastor droned on, Marcie hadn't missed the snickering tone. She knew why too. William Radford was a blue blood of society. He may have married a black woman, but would he want his only surviving child and heir to be mixed race? She doubted it. Old prejudices ran deep in the subconscious.

She pulled her sunglasses out of her bag and followed Virginia into the bright light, where she murmured her thank-you to the pastor and then scanned the parking lot and sprinklered lawns for Jason. Virginia droned on about how much she'd relaxed in Grand Cayman, how attentive the staff at each of the resorts had been, and how Marcie would absolutely love it there and should persuade Jason to take her. It was so smug. The sticky heat was irritating Marcie's mood as much as her skin, and it didn't help that her sleep had been punctured over and over by anxiety dreams of the past. How wonderful life must be for someone like Virginia. All that

252 • SARAH PINBOROUGH

money of her own. Never having to ask permission to do anything. No nightmares. No memories crammed into small locked boxes.

Perhaps it was simply the heat, but Virginia seemed to be the only one in their group in good spirits, Marcie mused, as her eyes drifted across to where William had found Keisha, leaning against a tree over in the leafy grove that disguised the busy road beyond. Whatever he was saying to her, it didn't look too comforting, even though Keisha *did* look a little unwell. Maybe he'd rather she'd passed out or puked in the pews instead of embarrassing him by leaving before the collection plate had even come around. Keisha, Keisha. Marcie's nerves twitched in irrepressible sexual excitement. It was dangerous, she knew it, but that was a turn-on in itself.

She half-expected to see Jason over with Keisha too—offering comfort or water or a good hard fuck— but instead he was by the far wall, beyond the cars, talking to Emmett. It was rare for Emmett to even show up at church, despite his wife's passion for it, and Marcie was pretty sure he'd dozed off at one point, but if he'd been sleeping then, he was wide awake now as Jason leaned in close, gesticulating while they talked in the shimmering air. Marcie frowned, unable to make out any words from this distance. Jason looked very intense, even as Emmett shrugged and smiled with all his natural ease and foppish charm.

"How about brunch at mine?"

Marcie jumped slightly, startled, as William's question broke her musing. "Sure," she murmured. She glanced back at her husband. Whatever he and Emmett had been talking about, it was done now and they were strolling back to their wives as if they didn't have a care in the world.

"Jason's going to top up Keisha's coolant," William continued. "I told him Elizabeth would take it into the shop, but he says he can do it."

"Oh yes!" Virginia piped up. "He used to have a little old racing car, didn't he? Put it together himself. Back when he was first with Jacquie. My." She sighed. "Where does the time go?"

Virginia, ever the bitch, all misty-eyed for Jason's first marriage.

"Jacquie's back in town," Marcie said. "If you hadn't heard already." It was always better to own information that could be used against you, that was Marcie's policy.

Virginia's eyes widened and there was a hint of glee in the sparkle. Her mouth opened, no doubt to say something spiteful couched in concern, but Marcie didn't give her the chance, turning and heading to the car.

Only William Radford would have air-conditioning in his garage, but thank God for it, Marcie thought, as she leaned back against the passenger door of their own car while Jason pulled the Prestone from the trunk.

"You should go inside with the others, honey," Jason said. "No point in all of us being out here. Can't exactly see you as the type who likes to get covered in motor grease."

Marcie hadn't been entirely sure *why* she'd stayed in the garage. Her heart was thrumming in her chest despite her outward calm and she felt slightly sick, but now that Jason was trying to get rid of her, she was damned sure she wasn't moving.

"I may learn something, *honey.*" She emphasized the last word with a sweet smile, and saw his jaw tighten at her barb. Did she sound jealous, knowing he wanted some alone time with Keisha? Did she even care what he thought?

"Okay then." He opened the hood on the Corvette, propping it open and peering inside. "Yeah, you're definitely low on coolant."

"I think the light on the dash already told her that," Marcie said, and Jason glared at her.

"No one likes a smart-ass." Jason ran his hands

along the hoses. "This one's a bit loose." He held his damp fingers up. "It's been leaking out of here." He leaned in and twisted something, almost grunting as he did it. Marcie wanted to laugh. How macho was he trying to be?

"But that should take care of it. Now to refill her." He picked up the coolant and took it over to the sink. "Just need to mix it in something. I hope you're watching, ladies."

"I'm all eyes," Keisha said, dropping him a wink. She flirted like breathing, Marcie decided, she couldn't help herself, and Marcie watched Jason puffing up under Keisha's gaze as he looked around the vast space. She'd never thought Jason to be a fool before, but maybe all men were when it came to women. There was something slightly hysterical about it. An hour ago Keisha had been near fainting in the church and now she was flirting, all coquettish smiles and thrusting hips, almost a parody of herself. Was she trying to make Marcie jealous? Did she even know what she was doing? For all she laughed about Jason with Marcie, Keisha was flirting back. Something was definitely off with her today.

Jason found a funnel high up on a shelf and an old empty water drum under a workbench, which he half-filled with water. He wrenched the cap off the coolant and Marcie's stomach twisted as he spilled a great glug of brightly colored liquid onto his shirt and over his hands.

"Shit."

"So much for watch and learn," Keisha said, folding her arms across her chest, amused. "Maybe you'd better take that shirt off. That's how real mechanics work, isn't it? Sweaty chests naked in the heat? Or is that just in porn films?"

Jason laughed, shocked, even as his eyes reappraised Keisha. Evaluated this new snippet of information. A woman who watched porn. Why had Keisha said that? Did she like Jason too? Maybe she was screwing them both. Some great sick fantasy. Marcie squashed the thought—it was stupid. Keisha was simply playing with him, but still, this whole situation was setting her nerves on edge.

"Wash your hands," Marcie muttered as Jason stripped to the waist. "Don't get any in your mouth. That stuff is poisonous."

"Yes, *Mom*," Jason said, and she fought the urge to punch him in his stupid, smug, handsome face. Laughing at her to impress Keisha. She wanted to take the coolant and pour it down his lying throat. Even Keisha giggled, tinged with some strange energy that Jason didn't seem to notice but added to Marcie's claustrophobic unsettled feeling. The coolant wasn't the only toxic thing in the garage. They were all poison one way or another, and maybe she was the only one honest enough to see it.

Marcie felt better once they were back in the main house filled with bright, natural light, and no stink of chemicals or gasoline, even if it did mean more dull conversation with Virginia and Emmett, who were still talking William through how *divine* and *much-needed* their vacation had been, as if their lives here were full of woe. Keisha became the doting wife, reassuring everyone that she'd only felt faint for a moment at church and it was nothing serious, and Zelda took Jason's shirt to wash it while he went upstairs to clean up and borrow a polo shirt of William's before they ate. He must have taken a shower, because by the time he came downstairs, tucking the comically too big shirt into his pants under his sports jacket, Marcie was on her second glass of wine, and when he came over and kissed her, asking if he smelled better, she could almost forgive him his pathetic show of flirting earlier.

It was strange how they all fell back into their roles. Sitting next to Jason as they ate, his arm draped casually over the back of her chair, it was hard to remember the passion of screwing Keisha in her car. The freedom of that animalistic desire. It was like a dream now that the status quo was restored. The only pieces not locked into place were Iris and Noah, and they'd be back in the next few days. There was a safety in this boring life, she knew that, and even as she sipped her wine and then coffee, and let Jason take her hand as they left to head home, in that moment, she wanted to cling to it for a while.

She looked back at the open garage door as they drove away, the little red Corvette sitting proudly in the gloom beyond and her skin trembled and her mouth tasted sour.

Later, that night, when the city was asleep and for once Jason wasn't creeping around the house taking phone calls, Marcie locked her dressing room door and stared into the contents of the box. A rare twist of guilt curled like burning paper in her guts.

Whatever secrets Jason was keeping from her, she had the feeling that the ones she was keeping from him were worse.

33.

Nothing good. Nothing good will ever come of you, KeKe, not if you don't change, don't behave, don't stop talking about boys who were never here. You're cursed, baby girl, you know it and I feel it. You got to work harder at being good. At closing your eyes.

Keisha had never forgotten about the boy. She *couldn't* forget about the boy, no matter how much she'd tried, even when she'd stopped entirely believing he was real, and now she knew Auntie Ayo had been right, she was cursed and she couldn't run from that. Nothing was good. Everything was rotten, and she was the black core of it. She'd been stupid to think she could be happy, to think she could have everything, to have believed in the joy she'd felt dancing in the field with Marcie. *Dansé Calinda!*

Yesterday it had all come back to haunt her. It was Sunday morning before church and she'd felt good. Looking back, she'd felt *too* good, even with William breathing down her neck. She'd gone outside into the glorious heat. Gardeners were working hard, pickups coming in and out as they pruned and watered and weeded the already perfect lawns and flower beds. The pool was also being cleaned. There was a delightful joy in the hubbub of others while she had nothing to do. It appeared that maybe here Sunday was only a day of rest for the rich, that's what she remembered thinking as she strolled barefoot on the grass while William showered.

She found it under the big oak tree toward the back of the gardens. A tin plate of rice, peas, and beans, flies buzzing lazily across the congealed surface laying their slick white eggs. Coins glittered in a circle around it, grabbing her attention. She knew immediately what it was, similar but different, like so much in this country compared to home. An offering. A sacrifice. A curse. A warning. It was magic, and no good could come of it.

No good will come of you, KeKe.

She'd run inside, her legs shaking beneath her, calling for Billy, her words a jumble of fear until he came with her outside to see what all the fuss was about.

"It's bad juju," she said breathlessly, as he stared at her discovery.

"It's just someone horsing around," William said. "Maybe Zelda's grandkids made it during the weekend."

He bent over and picked up the plate, nose curling with revulsion, before calling over one of the gardeners. "Throw that in the trash, will you?" The man took it and disappeared as Billy reached forward for the coins, those six silver teardrops among the flowers.

"Don't touch them!" Keisha's voice had been almost a shriek, as she clawed at his arm, trying to pull him away.

"For God's sake, woman!" he'd snapped. "It's only a few dollars! What is wrong with you?" His voice dropped and Keisha was suddenly aware that all eyes in the gardens were on them. "You're embarrassing me," Billy muttered under his breath, his eyes narrow.

Chastised, Keisha had dropped her hand and simply stood and watched as he picked up the coins that glinted in the sunshine, winking their wickedness at her. "Waste not, want not," William had said as he pocketed them, before striding inside again, smiling at his staff and leaving her to her silent fear.

She'd felt sick all the way to church and the air had been so hot and the waist of her skirt so tight from days and days of rich food, she'd been sure she was going to puke right there in her seat. When William whispered he was going to put the dollars in the collection plate, she'd retched with the wrongness of it all and fled outside. It was then that she'd seen her. As if she'd been waiting.

The old woman had been standing under a tree, her body almost as thick and tall as the trunk itself, chuckling to herself in the shade, her dry, frizzy orange hair ready to burst into flames in the heat. While one hand leaned her formidable weight on her walking stick, the other flipped a silver coin, a dollar no doubt, catching it between her fat fingers without even looking.

She winked at Keisha. "I see you," she said, nodding as the coin danced in the air once more. "Light and dark and dark and light, I see all to come. The dead don't stay sleeping, not when Mama Laveau and her daughters come to call. Ghosts got them own needs." She smiled at Keisha, the fat in her face squashing outward. "We all got our own needs. We all got our wishes. Ain't that the truth?"

"I don't want . . ." Keisha had started, panicked, before the words fizzled out. What didn't she want? To be free of William? That *had* been her wish. To be free of it all was always her wish.

"We can't help what we want, honey," the old woman said, turning and shuffling away, back out to the street. "We all got our wishes." She paused before banging her cane three times hard on the pavement, chuckling and shaking her head, amused at something and everything, before going on her way again.

Keisha had said nothing more after that. She'd sat on the low wall by the parking lot and taken the second Valium she'd brought in her purse and waited until the drugs worked their own magic and soothed her trembling soul. She needed distractions from the darkness. She needed to be wild. To be free. She needed not to *care*. To be numb to it, the wickedness that followed her. She'd tapped at the side of her head, trying to knock her hysteria away. She couldn't break now. She couldn't.

And she hadn't. Not yesterday. She'd flirted with Jason in the garage, she'd laughed with dull Virginia in the house, she'd ignored Marcie as best she could, she'd drunk too much wine, and then she'd fucked William like the whore he probably thought she was.

But today, today was a different story. Today, Valium and wine or not, her mind was breaking. Spiders ran amok in her thoughts, scattering her rationale.

The coins were one thing. The conjure ball was something else.

Auntie Ayo had made a conjure ball once. Keisha had seen it. When Auntie Ayo's best friend, Winnie, was left broken-hearted and with her bank account emptied by her cheating husband, Frank, Auntie Ayo had shut the doors to her special room, melting wax and earth and blood and whispering the darkest of words, and not come out for two days. Keisha had seen, through the crack of her bedroom door, when her aunt had come out and shown a lumpen black sphere to Uncle Yahuba, who'd muttered with a contained displeasure that he didn't have the balls to ever really release.

Keisha hadn't known what it was then, the conjure ball, but she heard Auntie Ayo, drunk on rum, tell the story later, after the funeral. She'd slipped it, weighty with dark wishes, into Frank's jacket pocket, and a month later he found the first lump in his unfaithful testicles. It was, of course, too late. He went downhill fast. Too fast to divorce Winnie for his floozy, and Winnie got the house he'd never actually put in her name and the money stashed in accounts he'd never told her about.

Auntie Ayo hadn't done too badly out of it either, but Winnie didn't come around so much after that, not after she'd brought the envelope of money—*a gift of thanks*—not asked for but definitely expected. Winnie sold the house and moved north somewhere, and she dutifully sent cards, but she never visited again. Maybe Winnie had still loved Frank a little at the end. Or maybe she'd never realized the depths of Auntie Ayo's power before. What kind of woman Auntie Ayo was. Maybe Winnie had gotten a little scared that what she'd wished for in a moment of bitter heartache could come true so easily.

And now there was another conjure ball.

She'd been in the hallway at the bottom of the stairs, calling out for William. There was an army of cleaners in the house scrubbing and polishing every already spotless surface to be decorated for the party that weekend, and she'd been sitting out by the pool for an hour to escape the hum and noise while her Valium took hold. She'd also secretly finished off half a bottle of wine to help settle her nerves before being able to face her husband. *Husband.* The word was like the clank of chains on her ankle. It was better in a haze. Nothing mattered in a haze. When she was stoned, the world lost the sharp edges so determined to slice her up whichever way she turned.

Once the mellow began flooding her veins, warming her in places the sun couldn't reach, she'd felt bad for hiding from William. For leaving him inside to run and sweat and shower and eat breakfast alone, and no doubt get more annoyed at her, his less-than-perfect wife. Maybe they should go to the club and get an early brunch. She'd flatter him and laugh at his jokes and he'd be her sweet William from London once again, the ghost who had never been real.

She'd gone inside, giggling as the cool air-conditioning tickled her tingling sensitive skin, and leaned against the banister calling his name, singsongy like a child. Everything would be okay. The Valium would brush away the darkness, sending the dust into sunshine. She was not *cursed KeKe with the damaged mind* but Mrs. William Radford IV, beautiful, young, perfect, and with the world in the palm of her hand.

William hadn't answered her, but instead, amid the distant sounds of vacuuming and activity filling the house, there had been a jarring, heavy thump from overhead. The tread of the dead, clumsy and with too much weight. *Thud. Thud. Thud.* Keisha had stared, her foggy brain trying to make sense of the fear tightening her gut, as the beat sped up, the heavy ball gaining momentum, just as Keisha's heartbeat pounded faster when she finally realized what was rolling down the wide polished stairs.

No, no, no, no . . . She'd thought the words were silent in her head as she flew up the stairs to get away from it before it landed, missing one completely as if the ball might defy the laws of gravity and leap at her, that ball with her blackened soul's desires tied up inside with string, until William came running along the corridor in his robe, fat body still wet from the shower, slick footsteps on the marble, and she wondered if he'd fall right there and then, tumble down, echoing the conjure ball, and smash his head open like a watermelon all over the freshly buffed hallway, just like she wished he would.

"What the hell is the matter?" He didn't fall, but grabbed her arms as she reached the top banister, pulling her toward him. His face was concerned but his grip was hurting her arm.

"Down there," she muttered, looking back. "It came down the stairs. I can't . . . I can't . . ." What couldn't she do? She couldn't look at it. She couldn't touch it. She could barely breathe. She wished she could *stop* breathing. *Cursed girl, cursed girl.*

"What?" William peered down as Zelda and Elizabeth and various cleaning staff trickled out of rooms to see what the fuss was about. Zelda. Her dark eyes were dancing, amused. Keisha pressed her head into William's shoulder, but he didn't hug her or hold her or tell her it was okay. His spine was stiff. He wasn't going to reassure his wife as one would a child. He wanted her elegant and possessed. She wanted to laugh, a hysterical condemned laugh, Anne Boleyn in the Tower of London practicing on the block. *Possessed.* Maybe she was.

"Here, take her. She smells like she's been drinking." The words were muttered as he passed her into softer hands, and then Elizabeth wrapped her arm around one shoulder.

"Let's go and sit down."

"Mrs. Radford's room is empty," Zelda said, shooing the cleaners back to their tasks. "You can go in there, Miss Elizabeth."

Mrs. Radford's room. *She* was Mrs. Radford, wasn't she? It was as if Keisha were the ghost and the dead wife still lived.

34.

Jason had left early for work, and Marcie had gone to the gym to work up a sweat and clear her head of Keisha, the unwelcome reminder of her past that had reared its head yesterday. By the time she got home, having picked up a delicious superfoods green salad from Fernando's on the way, she was in a better mood. She knew she still had good muscle tone, but it didn't hurt to make sure everything stayed perky and where it should be. A touch of Botox could take care of the occasional wrinkle, but her body was all down to the effort she put in. And more than that, she liked to feel strong. Keisha was strong rather than skinny, and her body was beautiful.

Keisha. Just thinking about her body—about the things they'd *done* together—made Marcie's tired body tingle. It was fine her brain telling her she had to stop, but her body had other ideas. Marcie picked up the mail and took it into the kitchen, throwing it onto the counter and hungrily opening her salad box. She wasn't even going to sort through it—the only mail that ever came for her was marketing junk from various stores she'd been stupid enough to give her details to—but then as she went to fetch a fork from the cutlery drawer she noticed the start of her name on an expensive white envelope. She pulled it free and stared for a moment.

The paper felt almost like fabric under her touch and her name had been written in lilac ink in beautiful cursive. It was a Savannah postmark. A wedding invitation perhaps, she thought, but couldn't think of any of their friends who had children who'd recently gotten engaged. She slid a knife into the corner and carefully opened it, oddly both curious and excited. Letters were a thing of the past, gone even as she grew up. Communication was all online or by cell phone. The only mail her mom had ever gotten had been demands for money.

It *was* an invitation, she realized, as she pulled the thick card free and gasped. Not to a wedding, but to something *so* much better. She stared at the words on the first line, all thought of how hungry she was forgotten.

Dear Marcie, we would like to invite you to the next luncheon meeting of the Magnolias.

The Magnolias. Of all the ladies' lunch clubs and organizations in Savannah, the Magnolias were the most prestigious. Iris was in the Magnolias. Eleanor had been. Marcie wasn't even sure that Virginia was. The Magnolias was for the wives of the movers and shakers of Savannah. The powerful men who, each in his own professional way, were the blood of the city. Word that Jason was buying William out must have been spreading, and now Marcie was becoming someone the ladies of the city wanted to keep close. To be friends with. To allow into the inner circle.

Her heart was racing. No one would look down on her again if she was a Magnolia. As much as she bitched and moaned about the Savannah *sets*, the Magnolias were more of an *organization*. There were maybe fifty Magnolias. Too many to be a clique but still aloof, private, and powerful. *Respected.*

She sat down at the breakfast island, placing the card carefully in front of her where nothing would get spilled on it. At last, after a lifetime of being looked down on or laughed at or judged, this girl from Tommy's Riverbank mobile home park whose mama drank too much and slept around and could barely pay the bills or rent on their crappy trailer was now going to be one of the most respected women in Savannah.

She had to make this marriage work. She *had* to. It was time to grow up. And more than anything, she had to stop this crazy situation with Keisha.

35.

Elizabeth had gotten her a glass of water and put a cool compress on her forehead, the two women sitting side by side on the dead wife's bed. "Are you all right?" Elizabeth asked. "You look pale. I hear you nearly fainted at church too?"

Keisha still couldn't speak but sat trembling as the damp cloth and the icy air-conditioning fought the heat that raged in her.

"Are you maybe . . . ?" Elizabeth smiled and then looked down at Keisha's stomach. "You know."

Keisha tried to laugh but it was close to a sob. "No, I don't think so." *She smells like she's been drinking.* "I wouldn't drink if I was pregnant." Would she? Maybe she would. Maybe she didn't deserve a child of her own. Would the child be cursed too? She broke things, that's what she did. She was selfish. She was KeKe and always would be, not Mrs. William Radford IV.

The conjure ball.

She shivered again. She'd wished harm on William—more than wished it—and now the bad juju had come for her, the cursed girl. She'd die here, she knew she would.

William appeared in the doorway, brow furrowed and cheeks redder than normal. His expression screamed, *I don't need this shit, not in front of all these people.* "It was nothing. Just some ball of mud. They've thrown it out."

Mud. Dirt. Graves. Keisha was sure she could taste rot in her mouth.

"A ball of mud?" Elizabeth frowned. "Who would have brought that into the house?" She wasn't as dismissive as William. It gave Keisha a thread of sanity to cling to. Something to stop her from drifting into the terrifying darkness. The ball wasn't normal. It wasn't an accident. Someone had brought it in here on purpose.

"Zelda says two of the maids had their children with them today. They were playing outside earlier. I guess they made it." He paused. "They won't be working here again." He looked at Keisha but didn't come any closer. "You feeling better?"

She nodded. What else could she do?

"Good. I'm going to get dressed, then decide what to do while all this chaos reigns. This party had better be worth it!" It sounded like a threat rather than a joke. "Come find me in ten minutes."

It was a command, as if she were the assistant, not Elizabeth. Maybe they were all bought and paid for. Interchangeable. Robots with different function settings. He paused, his eyes catching on something to his right, and then he frowned. More than frowned. If an expression could growl, that's what William's face was doing. His skin paled, leaving only two red blotches high on his cheeks.

"Did you do that?" Each word was a quiet hissing drop of acid. It took a moment before Keisha realized what he was talking about. She followed his eyes and her mouth dropped open. The photo. The one she'd taken out of the dresser. Eleanor looking happy with her arms wrapped around Lyle, when he was just a smiling boy thinking he had decades of the world ahead of him.

Her mouth moved, unable to form an adequate excuse as William glared, hate and rage and embarrassment at himself for marrying her all fighting for supremacy. She was about to force out some breath of begging apology when Elizabeth cut in.

"Oh, silly me, I'm so sorry. One of Eleanor's charities wanted a less formal photo for a fund-raiser in her name. I was looking for one and must have left that one out." She shrugged, almost helpless. "I'm so sorry, William, I know how you don't like to be reminded of Lyle's death, how painful it is for you. I'll put it back."

But what about Lyle's life? Keisha wanted to ask. *Surely that was something to treasure. Surely that was worth a little pain.* Another boy who was no longer there, like the ghost she saw. Did Lyle exist only in dreams now? That place where no one can hide from themselves, where the doors to all hidden worries and fears swing open at night?

William didn't look convinced, but he nodded curtly, before turning his back on them. "Ten minutes," he called back to Keisha, no warmth in his voice, only irritation. She didn't answer. She wanted to cry. There was a long pause after he left, the two women sitting in quiet before Keisha looked at Elizabeth.

"Thank you. You didn't have to do that."

"I take it that *was* you?" Elizabeth tilted her head, a curious bird. She had deep crinkles around her dark eyes and they looked like laughter lines and Keisha thought it might be nice to one day be old and have skin that creased in confession to a happy life. "Why?"

Keisha sighed. "I don't really know. I don't know

why I do half of what I do. I just thought . . . You'll think I'm stupid. I just thought, well, if there is such a thing as ghosts, and I feel like she is still here, then it might help her rest more easily. All that love and loss shouldn't be hidden away like it never happened."

Elizabeth smiled. "That was very sweet, Keisha. I think you're a very sweet girl."

"I'm not," she said, afraid she might cry. "I've never been good."

"Well, I think you are. I'm sure you're no saint, don't get me wrong, but goodness is something else. And I see it in you. Maybe it's hidden away because it's had to be, but it's there." She took the cold cloth and carefully folded it, even though it was no doubt going straight into the laundry, before getting up and putting the photo back out of sight.

"Why are the photos all hidden away?" Keisha asked, wanting to think of anything but the sickening thud of the conjure ball on the stairs. "I could kind of understand if Lyle had died recently, but it was years ago, right? Didn't they want to remember him? To see him around the house, even if it was just in pictures?"

"Oh, Eleanor would have had them everywhere, especially in this house, where there were no memories of raising him. It nearly broke her when he died. She didn't want him to join the military but you know how boys are.

Lyle wanted to impress his father and he thought that would work. Of course, almost immediately the conflict in Afghanistan started. That was just poor Lyle's luck. He died very quickly. One of the first U.S. casualties."

"Oh God," Keisha said. "That's awful."

"It nearly killed Eleanor as well. I've never seen someone in so much pain. But she was strong. She got through it."

"And William?"

It was Elizabeth's turn to let out a deep sigh. "Men are different. They're like children. He was hiding from his guilt as much as his pain. Guilt for forcing Lyle to do something that was out of character. William couldn't face that any more than Eleanor could face her grief at first."

"Out of sight, out of mind," Keisha said softly. If only she could feel that way about the conjure ball. The strange old woman. The silver coins.

Elizabeth smiled gently at her. "Something like that."

It had been a day that shimmered, like looking through melting glass. Everything was too bright and she couldn't focus. By midafternoon Keisha's head was pounding, each painful thump the conjure ball falling one step closer to her, an endless tread on a stairway to hell. They'd gone for a silent lunch, during which William spent most of the time checking emails on his phone while she drank her wine, and then he snapped at her when she tried to kiss him across the table, saying she was drunk and causing a scene.

She'd cried then, *really* causing a scene, emotional exhaustion brought on by her Valium comedown, too much alcohol, and too much fear. Where was it coming from? She hadn't been this bad since she'd been a teenager, and now her moods were spiraling out of control. She felt sick all the time. She needed an anchor to keep her tied to this world, and if it had to be William for now then she had to try harder. She wanted to be forgiven for things she'd done and not yet done. She wanted it all to go away. She'd try to love him. She'd try to be good.

She'd gone to the restroom, queasy once more, and sent various texts to various people, cries for help wrapped in laughter, but no one had answered. When they'd gotten home, she'd napped for an hour, the house finally mercifully silent and pristine, and when she came downstairs, her head calmer and less noisy, too tired for fear, she found William asleep in his study. The day had exhausted him too.

Zelda was absent; maybe William had given her the evening off, not wanting any more histrionics in front of the staff, and so Keisha made dinner, mashing the potatoes rich with cream and butter and frying some steak and large shrimp with a token gesture of a side salad. Food to break a heart, just as he liked it.

When it was ready, she woke him and even though they ate in relative silence, she thought perhaps he was calming down. "I'm sorry about this morning," she said. "I know I overreacted. It was that ball of mud or whatever, something about it reminded me of Auntie Ayo. I never told you but she's into some—"

"Your aunt isn't here." William cut her off. "And it was nothing to do with her."

He reached into his pants pocket and pulled out the tightly bound plastic bag of pills that had been hidden away upstairs in her Tampax box, where she thought he'd never find them. He placed it carefully on the dining table between them. "I knew you were taking something. I'm not a fool."

She grabbed for the bag, but he was too fast, repocketing it. "It stops now."

"You don't understand," she started softly, scared and desperate. "I've always . . . I have some problems. I need . . . It's not to get high . . . It's . . ."

"I won't be married to a pill-popping lush," he said. "You have to straighten up. No more day drinking unless you're with me and then only two glasses.

I'll get you some therapy. Whatever you need. But no more pills. No more incidents like this morning." He stared at her and it dawned on her that he meant the look to be affectionate, but all she could see was *control*. Irritation. A man who'd decided he was in love and was determined to stick to it. "London is gone," he continued. "None of that exists here. I want you to be happy, Keisha. You've come from nothing and I've given you everything. Don't let me down."

His sentences were guillotine blows and the bottom fell out of her world. Happy? How could she explain what it would take to make her happy? How could she explain that she *needed* those pills? She couldn't control herself without them. Anything could happen. She could *do* anything and that terrified her.

"Eat your food," he said, nodding at her plate. "It will make you feel better. And let's say no more about it."

Say no more about it. Out of sight, out of mind. Maybe that worked when you were the one calling the shots. The one who'd been born with so much money the world was presented as a play toy. She scooped a forkful of potato into her mouth and tried to ignore the way it clung to her dry throat. Maybe he'd give them back to her later. Maybe he'd ration them when he realized she needed them. She could cut down on the drinking, she could do that, but she couldn't do without the pills. Another wave of nausea washed over her, leaving her unsteady.

She was meek and humble as best she could be but he still flushed the pills down the toilet and still the sex was rough—purposefully rough, as if he was making a point rather than losing himself in the moment—and it went on and on, becoming a wearing trial for the both of them, slaves to his Viagra.

Afterward, while he snored, exhausted and lying in his sweat-soaked sheets, she wondered again how much hate there was in this new marriage. She hated him, that was for sure. She could barely hide that now, how would she cope without chemical help? She snuck out into the gloom as had become her habit, the night her only friend, the safety of it worth her nervousness about what spirits might emerge from the shadows, and poured herself a large brandy from his cabinet, sure that he'd have checked the level on the half-full wine bottle left from dinner. The ants in her head were starting to emerge from where they'd been sleeping in their nests and soon they'd be pouring free.

She made a call but there was no answer. No answers to any of her earlier texts either. Alone. She was entirely alone. It was a dizzying feeling, as if she were already dead and forgotten. She poured another drink and headed out to the garden, unable to breathe in the house that stank of William and cloying cut flowers and where all she could hear was the ghostly thud of the conjure ball on the stairs, Eleanor watching it fall from her place on the wall where she hung frozen in time.

Outside, at least the air was fresh, if still, and she could walk on the grass and pretend she had the strength to run far, far away from all of this and be free. This situation could not continue. Something had to break and she was afraid it was going to be her, snapped in half by her own greed. The shell she'd built around her crazy mind was cracking. They'd all see her for who she was soon enough—cursed. A wife to be kept in the attic not out on display.

Up in Zelda's apartment a candle burned in the window, only darkness beyond. The flame flickered yellow and orange and white and Keisha's heart burned as angry as that flame. This was Zelda's doing, she knew it. The conjure ball. The silver coins. Even the old lady, this was all down to Zelda. Maybe she *had* seen her at the crazy rave. What had been in that drink, other than probably some MDMA? Had all this started then with a potion slipped inside her? Zelda wanted Keisha gone. She wanted her *destroyed*.

She stood beneath the window, her glass in hand, swaying in the darkness as a black rage gripped her.

"I know what you're doing!" she shouted up. "I know how this works!" She laughed then, a surprise even to her, a burst of energy fused from fear and exhaustion. "You can't curse a cursed girl though, so more fool you, Zelda!" Tears pricked the back of her eyes. "More fool you," she repeated, more quietly.

The window didn't open and no one shouted at her to shut up. Instead, after a few long moments, the candle went out. No shadow of movement, no hint of a figure leaning forward to blow the fire cold, it just went out.

As if someone had willed it.

36.

Despite Marcie's determination to get her life back on track with Jason—to turn a blind eye to his lies and secrets for the sake of her own fabulous future position in the world—she was finding it hard. She was walking on eggshells around him again, but at least this time she knew it wasn't anything to do with her, or Jacquie, or whoever was at the other end of those nighttime calls. All the computers at work had crashed spectacularly, losing all sorts of client information and files, and it was a *clusterfuck*, which was the closest to an actual explanation she could get out of him. A server meltdown or something. Whatever it was, it sounded serious and could slow down the audit, which in turn would slow down the buyout and the Maddoxes' rise up the social ladder.

The unwelcome accidental reminder of her past on Sunday, and then the invitation to the Magnolia lunch yesterday, had made her take stock. She didn't really want her freedom. It had just been excitement that was missing, and as far as she could tell, Jason taking over the partnership and her new role in the city would give her that, even if their love had soured. His return to moodiness with this computer business wasn't helping. It was hard to like him when he was being this way.

At least he was barely home. He'd been at the office until late last night, and this morning he was up and gone before seven, leaving her alone in their vast bed. He hadn't even tried to have sex with her, although she'd found she didn't mind that so much anymore. Maybe polite separate lives was the way forward for now, even if it did feel empty. With Keisha, it had been so different.

Keisha, Keisha, Keisha. Always somewhere in her head despite Marcie's resolve to banish her. She waited for the coffee machine to finish its gurgles and hisses and then poured a large cup. *Keisha.* Marcie hadn't answered any of her recent texts. There was a neediness in them that unnerved her. Her moods changed too fast, and although Marcie was concerned about her, she also knew Keisha was unreliable. It was best for both of them to end it. It might level Keisha out too. Most important in Marcie's thinking, however, was that Keisha couldn't be trusted not to screw everything up, and after the whole coolant situation, all Marcie wanted to do was cocoon up with Jason—her flawed and secretive husband—and then emerge as a beautiful and brilliant social butterfly when the buyout was done. Keisha had been a reminder of how she herself had once been, wild, crazy, and fearless, but that girl was no more. She had no place here.

Maybe they wouldn't even see the Radfords so much once William retired. That would be better. That would definitely make things easier. She was feeling strong. She could live without love if she had to, for the sake of wealth and power. Marcie hated seeing the young woman so fragile, and she knew that it was partly her fault, but wasn't this cruel-to-be-kind approach the best way to move her forward fast?

The doorbell cut through the quiet and made her jump, the noise as oversized as the house, and tightening her robe around her waist she padded out to the hallway, irritated at being disturbed at the ungodly hour of eight thirty in the morning. No one called on anyone before at least ten unless prearranged, that was the rule of polite society. She pulled open the door ready to snootily send whoever it was away, but her breath caught in her chest.

Keisha. Keisha was here on her doorstep. Like Marcie's thoughts had summoned her.

"You look like shit." It was the truth. Keisha looked awful. What the hell was going on with her *now*?

"I can't think straight. I can't sleep." She had no makeup on and she twitched as she picked at the skin of her bottom lip. Marcie had seen this kind of twitching before, back when she was a kid, and sometimes down at the Mission, but never around here. Not in this perfect part of town.

"My brain won't work without Valium," Keisha said. "I don't know what to do." She looked up, desperate. "Have you got some? Can you get me some?"

Marcie stared at her, this beautiful, childlike, damaged woman on her doorstep, this moth that lived hidden beneath the dazzling painted-on butterfly colors. This fascinating wreck of a human being. "You'd better come in." What else could she say? She needed this *thing* between them to end but she had to manage her. Keisha in this state could say anything to anyone. And the last thing she needed was the new neighbors seeing this display on her doorstep. "Like, now."

"Do you think someone can be cursed?" Keisha's eyes darted around the kitchen as Marcie put a cup of coffee beside her on the breakfast table. "Properly cursed? Like black magic cursed?" Coffee was probably the last thing Keisha needed, Marcie thought as the young woman pulled her knees up under her chin and tugged at a loose strand of hair, a nervous tic. "There was a boy once," Keisha continued, softly muttering. "And then there wasn't. I should never have seen the boy. Maybe he was never there. The next time I saw him he was gone."

"Is this that ghost business again?" Marcie said. "I told you Keisha, there are no ghosts."

"Cursed KeKe, that's what my auntie called me. They said I was crazy. They said he'd never been there. A ghost boy. But I couldn't unsee him."

"You're scaring me Keisha," Marcie said, and it was true.

"I scare *me*," Keisha whispered back, holding her hand. "You can't run from a curse. It always finds you, that's what Auntie Ayo says. It's found me and I don't know what to do." She leaned forward. "I'm wicked, Marcie. In my blood."

"Okay, enough of this." Marcie took both of Keisha's hands and hauled her to her feet. "There's no such thing as curses, and I know what wicked is, and you're not it. We do, though, need to get you straightened out. Come on. Upstairs. I think there's some Xanax somewhere Jason uses when he has to fly. You can have that."

"Is it as good as Valium?"

"It'll be better than going cold turkey like this." Keisha's hand was corpse-cold in hers. "I don't know what William was thinking."

"He hates me."

"No he doesn't. He loves you." Love might be way too strong a word for whatever William felt toward his second wife, Marcie thought as she gave Keisha a tablet to dry swallow and started the shower, but he did *own* her.

"I could just tell him. About us." Keisha looked at her, hopeful. "Pull the Band-Aid off fast or whatever. I bet he'd still give me some money just to take my scandal and disappear. It would probably be enough to have a nice life. Away from all *this*."

Marcie stared at her. "I like all *this*," she said, colder. Fear would always suffocate love or lust and Marcie was filled with dread that Keisha was going to open her big junkie mouth and wreck everything just as she was on the cusp of being respected, of having some social power of her own. "I love my husband. I told you. And there's nothing to tell. I'd deny it all."

"Yeah, 'cause Jason's such a catch."

"He may not be perfect but he's ambitious. And safe."

"Nothing's safe, Marcie." Keisha sounded exhausted.

"Wealth buys safety. You need to learn that. I won't be poor again, Keisha, not even for you, and if you're not careful you'll end up back in the gutter and it'll be a lot harder to climb out a second time. Get in the shower. I'll make you some eggs. You'll feel better when the Xanax kicks in."

"Don't you love me at all?" Keisha asked, peeling off her T-shirt. Marcie stared at her, throat already drying at the sight of that smooth bare skin. What was it she felt? Lust? Definitely. Obsession, maybe. Was it love? What was love anyway? A passing madness? Not worth wrecking her future for. And how could she explain the irrational, nauseating fear she'd felt in the garage on Sunday? Jason was hiding secrets from her, but that didn't justify her secrets from him. That whole situation was a reminder of her old life—her secrets—that she needed to pour icy water over all her newfound childish wildness.

"You know I care about you," she answered from the doorway. "But we have to stop. I mean it. Especially while you're like this. I'll be your friend, Keisha, but from now on, that's it."

"I don't believe you," Keisha said. "You love me. I know you do. I see the way you look at me."

"You sound like a cliché."

By the time she got downstairs Marcie's whole body was trembling. Maybe she did love Keisha a little, but she was on the brink of a breakdown. How could Marcie explain that love wasn't enough? Life wasn't the movies. Love never lasted forever.

37.

Keisha had left without eating any food and without so much as a goodbye, letting herself out before Marcie could even get to the door, but she'd taken the packet of Xanax, which was better than nothing. But when Keisha hadn't answered any of her texts by three in the afternoon, Marcie was worried. She'd tried calling and it had rung out, unanswered. What if she had done something stupid? Gone and got blind drunk somewhere downtown? Or even hurt herself? She wasn't thinking straight, so strung out with withdrawal, and anything could have happened.

What had all that crazy talk been about? Curses and boys who weren't there? Had Keisha had a baby once? Was that it? And it had been given away or something? Maybe an abortion—that could screw some people over. But it could be anything. Who knew what was really going on inside that pretty, unhinged head?

Still, she thought as she poured herself a large gin and tonic, her concern was turning into annoyance. How hard would it be to answer a text or call? She'd given her the Xanax, hadn't she? She may have been hard on Keisha's emotions, but she'd helped her.

It wasn't only the Englishwoman who was getting her pissed. Jason was notably absent today too. She'd called and texted him and the only answer she'd had was a solitary "busy at the office, speak when home," but if she was honest she'd half-expected that. Jason had always been self-absorbed. Keisha wasn't. Keisha had never shown this much control when it came to Marcie. Was she not answering to punish Marcie? That was a downside of getting involved with a woman— there was no hiding from the games they were capable of playing. But she just wanted to know Keisha was okay. Was that too much to ask?

Her day had drifted away in irritation and quiet internal rants at one or another of the people in her life, so when the doorbell rang again at a quarter after three she was so sure that it was Keisha that she was very nearly spitting out an expletive while yanking the door open before she realized it wasn't her.

William. This time it was William and he looked

pissed. Oh God, had Keisha told him? For a moment it seemed as if the vast house around her turned to ash in a breeze.

"Jason's not here," she mumbled, trying to catch her breath. "He's at the office, I think."

"No, he's not. No idea where he's been today either, but that's not my immediate concern."

"Either?" She held the door open to let him inside. Where the hell was Jason if he wasn't at work? With Jacquie? An eel slithered in her stomach. Lies and more lies. William came into the hallway but no farther. His shirt was slick against him, stained with patches of sweat, which was odd given that he'd have gone from an air-conditioned house to an air-conditioned car and then just a few steps to the door. Stress? Anger? Could those things seep through his skin? The way he was huffing and puffing, she figured so. If he wasn't careful he'd have a heart attack right where he stood. "What's the matter?" she asked.

"Have you seen my wife?" *My wife.*

"Keisha?" *She has a name,* she wanted to add, but frowned instead, delicately puzzled. "No, I haven't. I mean, she popped by this morning saying she was off to sort out the final catering or something for the party and asked if I wanted to go with her." She was going to have to send Keisha another text when William was gone to make sure their stories matched. Lies begat lies. "But I had an awful heat headache so she went on her own." She smiled and shrugged. "She probably lost track of time. You know how she is." She didn't ask him if he'd tried calling her. He was gripping his cell tightly in one fat hand. It wasn't only Marcie's calls Keisha hadn't been answering.

"I know how she is," he growled, red cheeks flushing purple.

"Should we call the police?" Marcie asked. "If you're worried?" William wasn't worried. He was annoyed. He was out of sorts. He was a man filled with feelings he didn't understand about a woman he couldn't control.

"No," he said. "Not yet. What kind of man would I seem calling the police because my wife's been out all day? I know what they'd think. She's running around on him already."

"Oh no," Marcie said. "No one would think that. It's great that you're concerned about her. All women want to feel protected." It was such bullshit. He wasn't protecting Keisha. He was safe-guarding his own reputation. "Do you want a drink? I've just made a gin and tonic." She was suddenly aware that it was only midafternoon and she was drinking alone at home.

William shook his head. "No. I shouldn't have

bothered you. I know how I must sound, worrying over nothing, but she's been a little under the weather lately and I don't know what to do about it. I don't know how to manage it for the best."

Marcie said nothing as his frustration and anger seeped into a quiet despair. It was quite a thing seeing the great William Radford IV in this state and opening up to her, Marcie Maddox, the slightly trashy second wife.

"Everything changed when I went to Europe, didn't it?" He sounded exhausted.

"Life's all about change."

"That's easy to say at your age. I want things back to normal. I'm too old for all this." His eyes narrowed. "You heard from Jason today?"

She shrugged. "I tend not to bother him when he's working." It was a blatant lie. Right from day one she'd often disturb him at work to go for lunch or to just say hi, especially back then when they wanted to inhale each other 24/7. How times had changed.

"Working." William grunted. "I'll take your word for it."

"He'll be in a meeting somewhere for sure," she said. "Do you want me to get him to call you?"

He shook his head. "No. And if Keisha shows up here, don't tell her I was looking for her. I'm sure it's like you said, she's just got caught up somewhere."

"I won't say a word, but remember it's a big party to plan for her and it's the Fourth tomorrow and no one's really going back to work before this weekend, so she knows everything needs to be ready today." Marcie smiled. "I know she's been nervous about it, so she's probably with Julian and Pierre. I think the masks she chose were coming today or tomorrow?"

For a moment a flash of something close to guilt passed across William's face as if he had realized that perhaps he'd been hard on his new, young, foreign wife. It didn't last long though. Nothing was ever William Radford IV's fault.

Clouds hung heavy and damp over the late afternoon and the humidity crept into the house through the narrow gaps around doors and windows, clinging to Marcie's skin like her dark mood. Jason got home at dusk, tired and uncommunicative.

"How was your day?" she asked perfunctorily.

"Tiring." He grabbed a beer from the fridge, one silent, judging eye on her gin glass. "Been sorting shit out at the office all day making sure everything is on track to be back online. Most are taking a half-week vacation from tomorrow."

Sorting shit out at the office. Her blood boiled. She was trying so hard to make it work between them and still he was lying. "William came by," she said coolly. "He told me you hadn't been in the office. All day."

"What?"

"You weren't in the office, Jason." Her heart raced as her face burned. She couldn't make this marriage work all by herself. "So where the fuck were you?"

"Don't curse at me, Marcie." He headed for the sitting room, and she followed. This time she wasn't letting him off the hook. She'd given up Keisha for their future.

"And don't walk away from me, Jason. Where were you?"

"What did William want?"

"Why won't you answer my question?"

He spun around. "Get off my back, Marcie! Sorting shit out at work doesn't necessarily mean being in the office. I meant *for* the office, not *in* the office. Jesus, what are you turning into now, some kind of nagging paranoid housewife? I've had a hard enough day without coming home to whatever this is!"

Marcie shrunk slightly against the wall as he shouted but her anger didn't fade. *Nagging paranoid housewife.* Screw him.

"So do I need to call William?" Jason asked her. "Was he looking for me?"

"No," she said quietly. "He was looking for Keisha." She turned and headed for the stairs. "I'm getting in the shower. If you want dinner, you'll have to figure it out yourself."

A long day sorting shit out at the office. That's what he'd said. Not out at meetings or at the club or wherever else he schmoozed clients. At the office. He'd lied to her and if he thought she was stupid enough to buy that explanation, then he didn't know her at all.

Later, in bed, Marcie stared into the gloom, trying to make sense of the thoughts knotting in her head as her anger bubbled under the surface. William's face when he'd asked if Marcie had heard from Jason. The suspicion there. Keisha had been out all day in a terrible state, God only knew where and with who. Jason had been out of contact apart from one text and he'd lied about where he'd been. Maybe Keisha had gone to Jason after her? Had Jason been the manly shoulder to cry on? Or, of course, maybe Jason had been with Jacquie?

Outside, thunder rumbled but no rain fell. A storm was brewing somewhere, perhaps slowly moving toward the city, but for now there was no respite in the crackling tension, either in the house or beyond. She looked over at Jason's back and for the first time since she'd known him, despite her own ambitions, despite how she needed him, she felt a small shiver of revulsion in her own spine.

38.

The storm hadn't broken and the tension in the air was almost unbearable. The sky over the city was the color of a dust cloud, a grainy yellow-gray filter that made you squint even though there was no hint of a bright sun, and as evening fell into a hot gloom there was no relief.

Marcie didn't envy those who'd spent the afternoon at the Magnolia Park parade or the various other outdoor celebrations to mark the Fourth of July holiday. At least here, at Iris and Noah's place, there was the slight breeze from the creek even if the proximity of the water also made her a feast for the midges and mosquitoes that seemed to favor her out-of-state blood.

"We should be able to see the Tybee Island fireworks from here, even with these awful clouds," Iris said and everyone nodded and feigned excitement. The atmosphere in the room was as palpable as the humidity outside, even as they smiled and chinked glasses of perfectly chilled wine and nibbled at their meals. It was a strange reunion and Marcie wondered if their hosts, Iris and Noah, could sense the shifts that had occurred while they'd been away. Maybe. Iris hadn't mentioned the Magnolia invite to Marcie. Perhaps she didn't know yet. That gave Marcie some unease. Would Iris speak against her to the group? No. Iris wasn't like that. She'd give her a chance at least.

Marcie swallowed the last of her wine, for once glad her glass hadn't been refilled. The room was a forest fire of hidden resentments waiting to flare up and it would take only one spark in a comment to get it started and she didn't have the energy for a fight tonight. Instead, she sat back as the coffee arrived, stirred in some cream and sugar, and tried for once to be invisible, an observer of their staid circle rather than trapped within it.

Jason was doing a fine impersonation of joviality now that the systems at work were apparently mended again, but Marcie knew that in truth his mood was as sour as it had been before. He was starting to drain her. Maybe she'd wait until the takeover was all done and dusted in a year's time, and she was firmly in the bosom of a group of well-connected women, and then file for divorce. *See how he liked them apples.* It was an empty threat and she knew it. She wouldn't give him or any of the rest of *them* the satisfaction of their marriage not working and the prenup would limit what she walked away with. If he wanted to leave her, he'd have to do it himself.

She glanced over at Keisha, the cause of all Marcie's discomfort. She was surprisingly together, if demure, sitting beside William and holding his hand as he talked with Noah. Looking at her made Marcie's heart race and her stomach knot.

Marcie had followed her to the bathroom earlier and told her she'd get her a Valium prescription, but the younger woman hadn't wanted it. Said she was fine without even meeting Marcie's eyes. She'd stiffened when Marcie had touched her arm, in a way that screamed heartache, and it made Marcie feel bad. It had made her want to push the crazy Englishwoman up against the wall and kiss her, but she hadn't. Instead, she'd muttered, "Have it your way," and gone back to her seat next to her husband, where she belonged, and told herself it was for the best. As much as she wanted to, she couldn't have her cake and eat it too. Not with someone as unstable as Keisha.

"Isn't it, Marcie?"

"Marcie?"

Dragged from her private thoughts back into the circle, Marcie brought her attention back to Virginia, who'd said something she hadn't been listening to. "I'm sorry, what was that?"

"It's so sad to see so many homeless coming for the Fourth lunch. I was there this morning. I only wish we could feed them all."

"I'm pretty sure some of them have homes," Marcie said, rolling the fine stem of her crystal wineglass between her fingers. As she spun it, her own face distorted in the reflection, creating a monster she barely recognized. "Some simply want free food. They take advantage of you."

She needn't have said anything—she shouldn't have said anything—but Virginia's holier-than-thou routine combined with her smugness was wearing Marcie down. Also, Virginia could totally feed every tramp in town if she wanted to. From Nouvelle's, if she so chose, and that place had two fancy Michelin stars. "Bless your heart, you're too naïve," she finished. It was a sugar-coated barb.

Virginia's shoulders stiffened as she smarted. "The good lord doesn't turn anyone away."

Marcie sipped her coffee. "You must read a different Bible than I do, because as far as I can tell, the good lord is mighty picky about who gets to be on his team."

"Marcie, stop it." Jason reached across and squeezed her hand just a little too tight. "This weather," he smiled at Virginia. "I swear it's making her crazy."

She gritted her teeth to stop from replying *or maybe it's my lying husband who's making me crazy*, but took some pleasure from the secret sly smile that crossed Emmett's face at her words. Her own husband might find her behavior rude, but Virginia's at least was finding her mildly entertaining.

"Just saying it like it is." Marcie's accent slipped slightly, the words drawling in the wrong places. You could take the girl out of Boise, but you couldn't take Boise out of the girl.

"I have to ask." Iris leaned forward, her straight thin back drawing a line across the snippy conversation as she smiled at Keisha. "What have you brought in those bags? I'm simply dying of curiosity."

"Yes, so am I," Noah added.

Marcie almost laughed at the desperation in the swift change of subject. Like Noah gave a shit about Keisha's gifts. Anything to avoid harsh words at a dinner table.

"They're for Saturday's party," Keisha said. "I wanted to give you each something to thank you for making me feel so welcome." She reached down and picked up the first box. "It took me ages to choose them, but I think I've got them right. Here." She passed one across to Iris. "That's yours. Don't open it until everyone's got theirs though, please."

"I think you'll be impressed." William beamed, proud, but Marcie saw the slight flinch in Keisha's arm as he squeezed her hand. Keisha needed to be careful—it was always the small things that would give someone away.

"Okay, you can open them!" Keisha clapped her hands together when each person finally had a box in front of them, her eyes darting at last to Marcie.

There was nothing false about the exclamations from around the table as the lids came off, and even Marcie was left breathless. Venetian masquerade mask, beautifully designed and unique for each wearer. The men's were relatively plain, Jason's ebony black and cut straight across the eyes and nose, a devilish Zorro, and Emmett's was almost Puck-esque—burnished silver with an arched impish expression across the eyebrows and an overlong gilt nose that Marcie thought suited his foppish inquisitive mannerisms perfectly. Noah's was black and gold, understated but at the same time regal and clearly expensive. Whatever Keisha had chosen for William must have still been at home with her own, held back as a surprise, but if the other women's masks were anything to go by they were all going to dazzle on Saturday night.

"Oh my." Iris held hers up to her face. It was a beautiful half mask with filigree, held on a stick rather than tied, and although not brightly colored or ornate, like Noah's, it oozed sophisticated elegance. Although Iris, always charming and polite, must have privately thought the idea of a masked ball a tad vulgar, her smile now was genuine. "It's quite stunning, dear. You have exquisite taste."

"She sure does," Virginia chimed in as she examined her own—a blue-and-gold bird mask with feathers at either side and a small golden beak over the nose—and Marcie wanted to laugh as William said it suited her features. What it suited was the way Virginia was always peck-pecking at people with her superior attitudes.

Marcie took hers out of its box, and there was a fresh gasp from around the table.

"I wanted to thank you for being such a good friend to me," Keisha said. The barb was slight, just there enough for Marcie to pick up on it while it passed the rest by. Heartache always defended itself by attacking. Marcie only hoped that these little remarks would be the worst of it. Still, she ached with regret as she took in the beauty of the mask. It looked pure, for want of a better word. Jason had never bought her anything like this, so perfect for her.

She held it up against her face and knew even without the reassurance of a mirror that she looked magnificent. It was crafted in white gold, burnished, and hued with candy floss pink as it turned in the light. That should have made it look saccharine and babyish but instead it was aloofly ethereal against her ice-blond hair. Where the metal edge around one eye curved up catlike, around the other a butterfly wing emerged, glittering, inlaid with what Marcie was sure were hundreds of tiny sparkling diamonds. It was magical. There was no other word for it. Even the ribbons that went to tie it at the back of her head had glittering stones in them. "And I thought it would suit you," Keisha finished.

Marcie said nothing, still staring in delight at the mask.

"She hasn't been that good a friend," Jason said, his smile as thin as his joke.

"Well, I for one can't wait for this Saturday's extravaganza!" Emmett said, raising his brandy. "It's going to be a night to remember!"

39.

Marcie didn't want to go to the party. She wanted to curl up in bed, pull the covers over her head, and stay there until she died. She wanted to be sick. She wanted to cry. She wanted to be anywhere but here. But once it was all over, the story told, Jason had said nothing for a long time and then growled at her that they were leaving in twenty. He had to see William. They couldn't miss the party. He was insistent, and she was pretty sure that if she'd protested he would have wrapped his hands around her throat and let all that pent-up anger out until her tongue was thick and blue and her eyes bulged lifeless from her head.

She glanced over as they approached the drive, and his handsome face was once again cold, like that of a stranger, but this time it was *her* fault. What was he thinking? What was he going to do?

Fire lamps glittered along the road, dramatically lighting the route, and Marcie's hands shook as she tied the ornate ribbons of her mask behind her head. Thank God for the mask. No one would be able to see how pale and broken and afraid she was.

Her secrets had unraveled.

The thick white envelope had come addressed to Jason, his name printed large and in capitals. No stamp. Hand delivered to the mailbox. She vaguely remembered him bringing it in with the rest of the letters, his face already like thunder. *Bad day at the office, dear?* she'd wanted to snip at him as he poured a whiskey and then disappeared into his office, but decided against it. She was in a good mood despite him, despite his working on a Saturday, enjoying getting ready for the Radfords' party. Her hair was styled in a glamorous updo and her makeup had been set and she knew she looked beautiful already, even without her silver dress and masquerade mask on. As music quietly played on her iPod, she looked this way and that at herself in the mirror, enamored. Her mind had drifted to what Keisha would think when she saw her and then what Keisha would be wearing, and whether they'd speak, and then to Iris and the Magnolias and whether they'd be happy to have her glamour added to their number.

"Marcie! Come in here now!" Even then, when he'd called for her to join him, she'd been so wrapped up in her own thoughts she didn't hear the edge in his voice—the quiet, terrible suspicion.

At first, when she'd breezed into his study, annoyed at being distracted from her preparations, she didn't really *see* what he was showing her. That battered old yearbook. Then she saw the note with that one printed sentence on it—*What happened to Jonny?*—and, in an instant, the book made sense and her world crumbled.

She'd had to tell him everything. She had no choice. How hard her life had been. Her mom. The trailer park. How she found Jonny. The scandal of it all. How she'd had to get away after. To run somewhere she could start over. As his questions came like bullets, she'd had to *show* him everything, bring down her box of secrets—her old driver's license, birth certificate, photos—hidden away in the dressing room ceiling and empty it in front of him as her perfect makeup ran in tracks down her cheeks and her voice choked on snot.

He'd said nothing when she'd finished, but sat in silence as her heart pounded, the guillotine above her life hanging by a fraying thread. Eventually he'd stood up and said he was getting in the shower and she should tidy herself up. They had to leave in twenty minutes. And that was that.

Now here they were, hidden behind their masks, to all the world a beautiful, successful couple with nothing to hide, and as Jason handed their keys to the valet, Marcie felt tears sting her eyes again. What would she do if he divorced her? Where would she go?

"I'll see you at eleven," Jason said. In the dark she could barely see his eyes beyond the ebony of his mask. "Back here."

"But shouldn't we . . ." *go in together?* She didn't get to finish the sentence. He was striding away already. She stared after him, to where two Pierrots were signaling in overblown mime that guests should go around to the back of the house.

"Jason!" she called out. He didn't even look back, and after a moment, she had no choice but to head in the same direction. The Pierrots pretended to cry as she passed, mocking her upset, and then flourished hands with a smile to direct her, as if she didn't already know the way.

There were so many guests. It was as if the whole of the city had been invited, and Marcie felt lost as she walked into the multicolored kaleidoscope of light and music and bodies. Podiums had been placed around the candlelit gardens and contortionists and fire-eaters dazzled the onlookers who sipped their chilled Cristal. The vibe was richly decadent and the mood seemed to have spread through the guests, who laughed too loudly for polite company and touched and flirted around her. Marcie shivered despite the terrible heat. It was dangerous. It was too much. It was very Keisha.

She grabbed a drink from a passing waiter, who, like his coworkers, was dressed in black from head to toe, as if simply a faceless shadow or a ghost, a devilish sprite, and forced her way toward the house.

A few people turned and looked her way as she passed them by, nods of appreciation from the men, circumspect appraisal from the women, but with everyone's face hidden to one extent or another, Marcie could barely tell who was who even when she did know them. The tennis club set were gathered by the lit-up champagne fountain and canapé counter, heads thrown back in overloud laughter as their men talked among themselves elsewhere.

She couldn't see Jason anywhere, nor could she see any of their set. But as more people arrived, the garden was getting crowded. There were way more guests than William's usual hundred or so *closest friends* who were normally invited onto this hallowed ground. Three hundred perhaps. Too many. Marcie's head started to spin. It was crazy that she and Jason were here after what had just happened at home. Was Jason telling William about it right now? Talking to Noah? Discussing how best to get rid of her?

She drained her champagne and reached for another glass on a passing tray. Mint julep. Eleanor's drink. Not to Marcie's taste but she drank it anyway. She needed something to calm her down. It wasn't just that Jason now knew—awful as that was—it was that someone else did. The person who'd sent that envelope. But who was it? Someone here? Were they watching her now? Her breath caught as she turned on the spot, searching the people around her. It felt as if they were looming at her out of the night, laughing at her, faces distorted and monstrous rather than beautiful.

Her own mask was tight against her skin, pressing at her temples and eyes, and for a moment she was sure she would faint. She needed to get inside to the cool air-conditioning, away from the crowd. The terrace doors were pinned open behind the band that played old-style jazz born in a time of prohibition, and Marcie slipped gratefully inside.

She was headed to one of the downstairs bathrooms when an arm grabbed her, long fingernails tight on her skin, so suddenly that she almost shrieked.

"Marcie."

The creature before her was a blazing phoenix. The

red and gold of the ruby-encrusted flamboyant mask was an extension of the dress that swirled bright and tight around Keisha's magnificent body. At a quick glance she was alight and beautiful and powerful, but her eyes, trapped in all that glamour, were bloodshot and fearful.

"I have to speak to you. It's all awful. He hates me. He's going to get rid of me, I can feel it." She gripped Marcie's arm tighter. "Can't we run away? You don't love Jason, I know you don't. I can take some jewelry, we'll have money . . ."

Marcie yanked her arm free. She didn't need this. Not now. "I've got my own shit going on, Keisha. I can't deal with you and your crap." Keisha thought *she* had problems. How could Marcie explain to her what Jason now knew? How her own life, just when it had become filled with so much promise, was rapidly going down the tubes and she had to rescue it somehow? She stared at the younger woman, exasperated. "I've told you before. I can't be poor again. I won't. Where could we run with nothing? Nowhere."

"But you don't understand. I can't go on like this! I can't," Keisha said. "And today he got a—"

"I can't deal with this." Marcie cut her off. "Not now. Take care of your own shit."

She turned away and moved quickly, not so much as glancing back until she was safely locked in the bathroom, finally alone. She ripped the claustrophobic mask from her face and pressed her head against the cool tiles.

She wanted to cry, self-pity welling up inside her. Maybe running away with Keisha was going to be her best option after all, but how would that work? She was used to the finer things in life now, and was on the cusp of being *respected*. They'd be a joke, the talk of the town forever, and torn apart by expensive divorce lawyers, no doubt left with nothing, not even their dignity. They'd end up in some trailer somewhere, where still people would sneer at them as outcasts. It would be worse than it had been before.

Her stomach tightened and she took a few shaky deep breaths to stop herself from throwing up. *Pull yourself together*, she told herself. *It's not over yet.* Jason wasn't going to come at her with a divorce right away. He'd want to think his options through. Plus, this was high society, where appearances were everything; wasn't that why they were at the party? Things between them would probably never be the same, but surely he'd want to paper over the cracks? He didn't need another divorce and it wouldn't do him any good at all if anyone else found out about her past. Mud would stick. He'd already had one scandal with his father; he didn't need another one with his second wife.

She stood up straighter and dabbed at her face with a

paper towel. Anyway, he was keeping his own secrets, wasn't he? Those calls. The lies. Was it Jacquie he'd been talking to? Maybe she was even here, at the party. It was impossible to tell with everyone so overdressed and disguised, and there were so many people. Could it have been Jacquie who'd been doing the digging, who'd unearthed this stinking dirt on her? Did she now want her old life back and was going to any length to get it? Maybe she'd heard that the second Mrs. Maddox was on the rise and wanted to stop it. *That bitch.*

Her overheating panic was subsiding and a chill descended onto her skin. This was a mess that she needed to figure out. But what was she going to do? One thing was for sure, she couldn't stay here, at this party. Keisha was unstable and Jason wasn't talking to her. She'd feign a headache and go home, where she could think.

She retied her mask and took comfort in her reflection for a moment, soothed by her own beauty, and unlocked the door. She knew what she had to do. Find William and make her excuses. If Jason had told him, it would be obvious by his reaction to her. She'd know then how much she needed to plan.

The party outside sounded like it was from another universe, one of carefree laughter and music and noise, a place that was entirely alien to her. She was about to head back toward the patio to try to find their host in the madness of it all when she saw Noah and Iris standing just inside the French doors, for once alone, not surrounded by sycophants. They were locked in a private conversation, their heads turned inward, Iris's face lined and serious, her filigree mask held down by her side. Marcie's heart thumped hard. Were they talking about her? *Did they know?* Maybe Jason wasn't the only one to have gotten an envelope delivered about her. Her stomach tightened again. That didn't bear thinking about. She needed to deal with the problem in hand rather than inventing more. She retreated farther into the house, not wanting to face them, whether they knew or not. Her head was pounding and her body exhausted.

At least it was cool inside, and with Julian and Pierre operating from their glitzy catering truck, the house was blissfully quiet and dark, thick walls protecting it from the decadence that raged in the heat of the gardens. It was creepy though, devoid of life, and Marcie couldn't help but think of Eleanor wheeling herself around as she slowly faded, her body eating her up while her mind stayed sharp, and now there was Keisha, beautifully powerful and healthy, but with her mind collapsing. A cursed house. A cursed girl. Maybe they were all cursed in one way or another.

She shivered. Maybe she wouldn't try to find William. She could sneak away unnoticed without saying her goodbyes. Would Jason care? Had anyone even asked him where she was?

"A mistake? That's all you can say?"

In the silence the voice made her catch her breath—a sharp retort, bullets in the night. Was that William? She froze in the corridor, stilled by his tone. He sounded impatient. Angry. But who with? Keisha? Marcie crept forward, past the sweeping stairs of the main house, following the words like bread crumbs, until she drew closer to William's study. Had he called Keisha in there like a headmaster would a naughty schoolgirl to reprimand her for some misdemeanor? His voice dropped as she drew closer, as if aware that someone somewhere might hear him shouting and that would never do.

"For God's sake, you should be able to explain it."

"It was the system crash—"

Jason. That was Jason, not Keisha. What were William and Jason fighting about?

"To hell with the system. The system couldn't do this. The audit starts Monday, Jason, and if this isn't made good by then—"

"It will be. It's an error, that's all. A transfer gone wrong somewhere. This stuff happens. You're worrying over nothing."

"Are you all right?"

The hand on her shoulder was like a cobweb brushing against bare skin and Marcie almost shrieked as she spun around toward the worried face. Elizabeth. It was just Elizabeth. "Marcie? Are you okay?"

Elizabeth had a mask painted on, quite a delicate design of flowers and birds, expertly done, but it was already starting to run at the edges, where her full cheeks crushed the skin around her eyes whenever she smiled. She was in danger of becoming clownlike. Poor Elizabeth. She didn't belong here either.

"No, I'm not, I'm afraid," Marcie said. "I've got an awful headache. I was looking for Jason to tell him I'm thinking of getting a taxi home." She glanced toward the office door, thinking fast. She'd been caught eavesdropping, so there was no point in pretending otherwise. "But it sounds like he and William are having words. I was too nervous to interrupt."

"Men always do sound so angry, don't they?" Elizabeth said. "I don't know why they need to half the time. Sensible conversation is so much more productive . . ."

The office door opened and both men came out, silencing Elizabeth, and for an instant Marcie didn't recognize either of them, their expressions demonic half-shadows behind their masks. Then they saw the two women a few feet away and light smoothed the darkness as if it had been simply a figment of her imagination rather than an insight into who perhaps they really were.

"What are you doing here?" Jason was looking at her with such disgust, such *irritation*, that she couldn't find any words.

"I . . . I . . ."

"Marcie isn't feeling well," Elizabeth said. "I'm going to run her home."

"I just need to lie down for a while in some quiet," Marcie muttered.

Marcie wasn't sure if she was sad or relieved when Jason didn't offer to come home with her, but instead just nodded. "If you're sure. I won't be home late."

"I've got a headache." William sounded as snippy with Elizabeth as Jason had been with her. "Have you got any Advil in your purse?" Whatever it was they'd been talking about, it was far from resolved. Elizabeth flushed slightly and shook her head.

"No. I'm sorry. Surely you have some in the bathroom?"

William glared at her as if the effort of the stairs was too much.

"Why don't you go get a coconut water?" she said. "They always rehydrate you. I'll stop at the drugstore on the way back. Can't have you not enjoying your own party." She smiled, trying to lift the moment.

"Enjoy the party?" William grunted. "I didn't want this party." He hadn't even looked at Marcie. "We'll pick this up later, Jason, and it had better turn out to be like you said."

He walked away toward the kitchen, and Jason stared after him.

"Is everything okay?" Marcie rested her hand on Jason's shirtsleeve. Through the fabric she could feel the strength in his arms that used to turn her on so much and she'd thought would protect her forever.

"Go home, Marcie." He shook his arm free, not hard enough to make a statement but with enough force to make her feel quietly abandoned. "I'll see you later."

Screw you, Jason, she thought, tears stinging the backs of her eyes. *Maybe I'll tell the world myself just what you think your second wife is. Maybe I'll take the power back rather than leave you with it like a sword hanging over me.* But the words that actually came from her lips betrayed her and made her feel smaller. "Okay. Have a good time. I love you."

"Come on," Elizabeth said, when Jason didn't return Marcie's sentiment. "Let's get you home."

Elizabeth was parked in front of the garage and it was a relief not to have to walk through the throng of partygoers to reach the car, instead slipping out the side door of the house.

"Thank you for this," Marcie said. "You're very kind."

"No problem at all. I needed a break from all the people, if I'm honest. I'm not much of a party person, as you probably already know, but I'm so used to doing whatever William asks it's almost second nature to show up to everything."

Their host had come out front and was standing on the steps, drinking from a carton. He didn't look at them as they drove past, and Marcie was about to turn her attention back to Elizabeth, when her mouth fell half-open as she stared out the window. *It couldn't be.* A fresh gaggle of guests were arriving at the house, climbing out of limousines in five-inch heels and expensive dresses, laughing and chattering as they made their way toward the gardens.

One figure was hanging back, a tight black dress hugging her narrow frame, dark hair thickened by extensions and piled up in curls on her head, eyes sharp as she watched Elizabeth's car leaving. Her face was half covered with a glittering black mask, but Marcie would recognize that slash of a bitter smile anywhere. Jacquie. Jacquie was at the party. As they pulled out into the street, Elizabeth was still droning on, but Marcie felt as if she were listening underwater. Jacquie.

Maybe she needed to go back.

40.

Keisha had floated like an unwelcome ghost through her own party, at times sure she was entirely invisible. In so many ways, she had been. An object, a delight, a curio. And then, of course, by the end of the night, damaged goods. A mockery. But not a person. Not a breathing thing of her own. A hum of unsympathetic whispers as she'd drunkenly taken flight, ushered out by Iris and Elizabeth and Virginia.

Even here, in the quiet dark gloom of Eleanor's bedroom, it felt as if the first wife had more energy in the house than Keisha had, her own dark skin absorbed by the grainy night, leaving her almost incorporeal. There would always be earth and grime under her shaped and polished nails. She shivered and beat her fist at the side of her skull. Who could she talk to? Who would listen?

Could she even make any sense of her jumbled, cotton-wool thoughts?

What time was it? Two? Three? Probably later. Everything had become a haze, the past forty-eight hours a jumbled kaleidoscope of images and memories. *She should have taken the Valium script Marcie offered, always proud KeKe, your pride is your downfall, like you could ever have quit when you'd finished what you'd gotten—who were you kidding, always kidding yourself, a lie to a fool, yes yes Auntie Ayo please shut up in my head I know there was no boy please leave me alone.* The tension with William as she'd quietly climbed the walls when the Xanax ran out, and then this evening, as she'd dressed and preened and pretended makeup and clothes and money could make everything better—*a mask behind a mask, always hiding, always hidden, concentrate, focus, everything is crumbling, drowning, cut to pieces*—the shouting as he held the photo out at her—*head thrown back, laughing, peeling her top off as she danced, breasts out in the night air, whole body wild and full of dark magic like how Auntie Ayo used to be behind her locked door*—slamming the door on Julian and Pierre as their heads turned as one toward the noise as they glided across the marble beyond.

The memories wouldn't stop stabbing her. William's face so red. Spitting at her, hot and wet as he raged, his words just noise as she'd wished he'd die right there on the spot, that throbbing vein in his skull that taunted her when he was angry and when he was huffing and puffing and fucking her. The loathing in his eyes, so obvious even with her junkie itching skin and thoughts so confused no wine could ease them. *"I'll deal with you later. I've got bigger problems than a drunk, slutty wife. And to think I believed I could make something of you."* Make something of her. Reshape her. Break her. He was worse than her family back home.

He didn't cancel the party. How could he? The show had to go on; appearances were everything. She'd tried to be witty and charming and elegant, she really had, but her brain was on fire, and once she'd seen William talking to Noah, eyes darting her way, no doubt discussing cutting her out of his life like a cancer, she'd become too loud and too bright, like one of the circus acts she'd hired rather than a woman of substance, spinning and whirling from one group of people to another, welcomed by none without her rich husband by her side. Then there was Marcie—*Take care of your own shit*—who wouldn't even listen to her and then had vanished.

She'd drifted then. Drifted and drank. Flashes of the night came to her. Emmett and Jason around the side of the house, away from the crowd. Jason shouting, gesticulating. Emmett shrugging and walking away, leaving the handsome man to beat on the wall. Jason hadn't even wanted to speak to her, instead barging past to go inside. Julian and Pierre exchanging a look, darkly entertained, Keisha not the only one watching the party from the outside. Emmett and Virginia dancing, Emmett with his eyes on William as he talked to Iris. Everyone smiling and laughing and pretending to have fun, but all the while simply vipers in a nest, watching and waiting to strike or be struck. That's how she'd felt. She'd wanted to cry and laugh and dance all at the same time, and that's when she'd seen her.

Zelda. Just standing there on the grass, watching. A spider in her web. Who else would have taken that picture and sent it? Who else wanted Keisha gone so badly? Keisha couldn't remember much of what she'd said or how she'd said it, but she stormed through the party and raged at the housekeeper. Noise came out of her, coarse, crude words, angry, upset, accusing, and then there were Iris's dry, cool hands—*Good lord dear, what on earth has upset you, what's the matter*—Virginia's arm wrapped around her, surprisingly strong, so much floral perfume on her skin.

They pulled her away inside, sending Elizabeth running to get a glass of water in the kitchen, where she collided with Jason coming the other way, and then Elizabeth sent him to help get Keisha into a quiet room as if she were an invalid like the last wife. It was like some poor farce. She couldn't remember if he helped. She couldn't remember much before being left alone upstairs while the party emptied out, Iris and Virginia smoothing everything over with a wave of their hands, guests melting into the night as the music stopped, Julian and Pierre left to survey the desolation that had been their great pièce de résistance, before even they were ushered out.

Keisha had waited like a frightened, chastised child until finally she and her husband were the only ones left. William hadn't spoken to her. He hadn't even come to their bedroom but instead had gone straight to a guest suite. She'd been relieved and panicked at the same time. She didn't have to have him near her and she didn't have to face his wrath, but it was also obvious that their farce of a marriage was over and they'd made a laughingstock of each other. He would not forgive that. He would want to destroy her for it. Maybe if he'd let her have the pills she'd needed then none of this would have happened. If he'd been a kinder husband. *If, if, if.* Now he was going to take everything and leave her back where she started. Worse than where she started. Back in the gutter, stripped of her Versace and dressed only in stinking humiliation. Her breath caught in her chest. It had all crumbled so fast.

She got to unsteady feet, one hand still gripping the bottle of champagne she'd brought up from the party wreckage downstairs and drained to try, in vain, to help her sleep. What would happen tomorrow? A small suitcase? A plane ticket?

Flies buzzed in her head, scratching at her skull, making it hard to process anything. She should have gotten that prescription. She'd maybe have been able to think on her feet like she used to, found a way to explain that photo, make him feel sorry for her all over again. But still. That was done. It was all done.

She went to the window and stared out. How many nights had Eleanor gazed out from here while she was dying, too afraid to sleep? Looking down at the wonderful gardens and thinking how bittersweet their beauty was, how soon she'd be nothing, like her boy had become, and they'd all still be here and so would her husband and her friends and there would be a new, cheaper, younger woman sliding into her place. Would it have given the sainted Eleanor a last laugh to see how it was turning out for Keisha?

The sky had cleared and the stars twinkled, fairy lights in the night, and for a moment, in the shadows under the trees, she was sure she saw the flicker of a silver dollar being tossed in the night, and her soul calmed. She wouldn't give all this up. Not yet. There were many dark hours before morning. Anything could change by then. Anything.

She'd always thought that when a body was found, screaming would wake the whole house. It turned out not to be true. No one screamed when William was found and it was at least fifteen minutes before anyone thought to wake Keisha, and by the time she was up, bleary, dazed, and confused, the ambulance was there and people were shouting commands and asking questions that she didn't understand.

It was only later that she thought, as the police came to question her, that perhaps no one screamed because you only scream to try to wake the dead. And William wasn't dead.

PART THREE

All day I've been wondering what is inside of me?
Who can I blame for it?
I say it runs in the family . . .

"Runs in the Family" by Amanda Palmer

41.

"They think it was some sort of stroke. Or heart attack. Something awful like that. He'd been on the treadmill. I guess that must have brought it on."

"Zelda found him just after ten. She'd let Elizabeth in to coordinate the party cleanup."

"As he collapsed, he hit his head on the corner of the desk. There was blood everywhere. Shocking."

"He was so cold Zelda thought he was dead. Must have been lying there at least an hour or two. Thankfully, Elizabeth found a pulse, didn't you, dear?"

"I was just lucky, but dear lord my own heart nearly stopped. He looked deathly."

"Where was he?"

"In his study. Straight to work, you know William."

"It's so shocking. I can't believe it."

Marcie wasn't sure that an overweight old man with a wild young wife having a heart attack was all that surprising, but she didn't say anything, hanging back as Jason quizzed Virginia, Emmett, and Elizabeth. She didn't have the energy. She had problems of her own. Jason hadn't come home until late, after one A.M., muttering something about Keisha having a meltdown, and when Marcie had asked if he wanted to talk, he'd simply gotten up and gone to sleep in one of the guest bedrooms, leaving her lying awake and worrying. Jacquie had been at the party. Is that what had kept Jason there? Some illicit rendezvous in plain sight of everyone? He'd always liked taking risks. He'd taken them with her, why would he be any different now? No one changes.

She'd finally fallen asleep at around five and the next thing she'd known Jason had been shaking her awake, telling her to get dressed, and that they had to get to the hospital. Seems like Jason hadn't gone to sleep till dawn either, because they'd missed several calls and slept through various texts, and now here they were at four in the afternoon, surrounded by their friends and catching up on the horror of this Sunday morning's excitement. Even Jason had come alive as he'd questioned the others. There was a spark in his eyes again. Wolf-like. She wasn't sure she liked it.

"Where's Noah?" he asked.

"At William's house," Emmett said. "He arrived at the same time as the paramedics apparently. William had asked him to come for a brunch meeting." He raised an eyebrow. "What kind of person has a breakfast meeting the morning after a fabulous party?" He paused momentarily before answering his own question. "I suppose the kind of man who has a heart attack after jogging too early in the morning after a fabulous party." He smiled, louche, and shrugged. "Anyway, he stayed behind while Elizabeth came here. Making phone calls, I imagine. Taking charge."

"Something was bothering him," Elizabeth said.

"Yes, his old friend nearly dead on his study floor, I should imagine," Virginia cut in sharply, and Elizabeth said no more.

Marcie was glad of the quiet. For her part, she'd had enough excitement. She wanted life to go back to how it was *before* Keisha. Her safe, dull existence where she was the beautiful second wife. Keisha. She looked around and frowned.

"Where's Keisha?" she asked softly.

"With Iris," Virginia said. "Over there around the corner. She's a little . . . unsteady."

Marcie ignored the gossipy tone and drifted away from the group to the smaller section of the relatives' room tucked around the corner from the counter, where the coffee machine and cookies were. They were seated against the far wall, Iris holding Keisha's hand in one of hers, two cups of coffee untouched on the table in front of them.

"You okay?" Marcie said, taking the seat on the other side. "I'm so sorry. It must be such a shock."

"It's my fault," Keisha whispered. Her body twitched occasionally, and her eyes, no makeup lining them, were bloodshot and teary. "It's all my fault." She didn't look at Marcie, lost in her own world. Marcie wasn't even sure Keisha knew Iris and she were there. "I found the doll in my drawer this morning when I was getting dressed," she continued. "It's my fault. I wished it, don't you see? It's what I wanted." She started to cry, a soft keening sound filled with fear. She stared into space. "There was a boy who was never there and now I'm cursed. It's all my fault."

"Hush now, sweet girl." Iris rubbed Keisha's hands between her palms. "Take deep breaths. Try to relax." She looked across her at Marcie. "Do you know if she normally takes any medications? She wasn't herself last night and she certainly isn't today."

Marcie wasn't sure what to say, how much she should admit to knowing, but there was no denying that Keisha was twitching. "I gave her some Xanax the other day because she was struggling. She normally has a Valium prescription but she hadn't told William. When he found out he threw her tablets away. Said she couldn't have any more."

"Well, that's ridiculous," Iris tutted. "And dangerous. And so typical of that man. No wonder the poor girl is all over the place. You stay with her, Marcie. I'm going to find a doctor and get her something. She has enough to cope with at the moment without withdrawal on top of it."

Marcie simply nodded; her surprise was too great to speak. Was this really Iris talking? Iris with the perfect life who spent it gazing down at them all from the dizzy heights of the top of the social tree? Since when was Iris sympathetic to addicts? As the birdlike aged beauty strode purposefully out of the room—good luck to any doctor who thought about refusing her—a man and a woman stepped inside. Their clothes—both wearing smart trousers and shirts under casual jackets—were not expensive enough for this waiting room. Neither were their haircuts. Marcie's skin prickled. They looked around the room, the woman's cool eyes lingering on Keisha for a moment before scanning the others. The woman moved out of sight and her sidekick followed.

"Keisha, I need you to listen to me." Marcie's stomach was in knots as she took the other woman's hand. Her voice was quiet but firm, hiding her own panic. "Look at me, Keisha." Keisha did, reluctantly bringing herself back to the present from whatever hell her imagination was creating for her.

"Whatever happens, you can't say anything about us, okay?"

"I love you, Marcie. You know that don't you?"

"Yes, I do. And I love you too. But you can't say anything about us to anyone. They'll use it against you. Do you understand? You can't say anything. We were friends, that's all. You got that?"

"Friends." Keisha nodded. She frowned as Marcie's words sank in. "Who will use it against me?"

The two strangers came back around the corner and this time Noah was with them. Plainclothes detectives. She'd recognize them anywhere. Noah couldn't look at her. Whatever had been bothering him, she was at the center of it.

42.

"**I**s he dead?"

The noise in Keisha's head had finally deadened, but she felt hazy now under the meds. It seemed like a lifetime and only moments since the hospital. She'd been feeling sick, waves of nausea not helping her confusion. Marcie had been sitting beside her—*you can't say anything about us*—and then this woman, this Detective Anderson, had said they needed to talk to her. Not at the hospital. They had questions about the accident. And then she'd been crying and Iris had been there with some medication, trying to get the detective to take it with her, while Marcie shrank back into her seat and she was sure that Jason had almost laughed as they took her away, and Keisha had been left to wonder how Iris was suddenly her only friend.

She'd gone into a full meltdown then, hating the feel of their hands on her as they took her into the station. She remembered hysterically crying. Wanting to go home, wherever home was. A doctor came and gave her *something* to calm her and then the world had faded and she'd spent the night cocooned in her nightmares in a strange unnatural sleep.

A different doctor came back in the morning and gave her a pill that she presumed was some sort of Valium. She didn't recognize the name and she didn't much care.

Now she was in an interview room and she had a stranger beside her who'd told her he was here for her and that Iris had arranged it. She didn't say much to him either. No one had ever really *been there* for her, so why should she believe this man now?

She was so tired. She wanted to sleep. And yet, even as the sedative calmed her body, soothed the itch, her mind twisted and turned. Had she done it, this terrible thing they were asking her about? It was all a haze, after her rage at Zelda. Even that was just noise. She remembered her anger. She remembered drinking. When had she finally fallen asleep? Could she have done something awful? By accident? Because she was drunk?

Dan Temple, her appointed defense counsel, leaned toward her ear and once again told her to talk only to answer questions when he said it was okay. He was frustrated, she could tell. When he'd arrived she'd been muttering about Auntie Ayo and the boy and everything that had gone *before* and she'd seen in his face that he'd thought Keisha was crazy.

"Is he dead?" She asked the question again, her heart racing. Detective Kate Anderson, short, squat, and with sandy hair scraped back in an unforgiving bun, and her hulking sidekick, John Washington, hadn't said a word about William yet and she couldn't bear the not knowing.

"No," Anderson answered eventually. "Not yet. Your husband, however, does have severe liver and kidney failure, has lost his sight, and is in a coma. Needless to say, the prognosis isn't good."

All that from a heart attack? A stroke? Or was it the fall? Keisha's hands picked at the skin around her nails as tears threatened her again. *Cursed.* That's what she was. And now the curse had taken Billy. It was what she'd wished for.

"He's lucky to be alive at all," Washington added. His accent was pure deep South and in other circumstances Keisha would have found it warm and comforting. A voice for bedtime stories. "If Judge Noah Cartwright hadn't called us yesterday and told us about William Radford wanting to take you out of his will and divorce you, and that perhaps his fall and subsequent injury could be the result of a physical fight rather than an accident, we would never have gone back to search the house yesterday evening. Our forensics team wouldn't have seen the yellow mark on the carpet and he'd be dead by now."

"What yellow mark?" She ignored her lawyer's signal to be quiet. While Iris had been comforting her, Noah had been calling the police. "What happened to him?"

"You tell me."

Keisha's eyes stung with frustrated tears as the lawyer spoke for her. "My client has already told you she doesn't know how Mr. Radford came to be ill."

"Shall I tell you what *we* know?" Detective Anderson leaned forward. "Would that make this move along quicker, Keisha? Save us all this 'my client isn't able to answer that question at this time' from your attorney while we play cat and mouse? We've had a long night of talking to people and we're all tired. I know I am."

Keisha nodded. What could they know? There was nothing to know.

"For the purpose of the tape, Keisha Radford is nodding," Washington said before Anderson took the lead again.

"We know that the victim was the only person in

the house who drank the cartons of coconut water kept in the kitchen refrigerator, and it's been confirmed by his housekeeper, his friends, and his personal assistant that he always drained a carton after running on the treadmill in the mornings. That was his routine and he stuck to it. Furthermore, we know that the night of the seventh of July, your husband spoke to Judge Noah Cartwright about changing his will to remove you from it. They were meeting yesterday morning to discuss it further. Given that you signed a postnup, this would leave you with nothing even in the event of your husband's death. It's also been confirmed by several sources that during the course of the evening of July seventh your behavior was erratic and you screamed at the victim's housekeeper, Zelda Williams, in full view of your guests, blaming her for your husband's displeasure and saying that she was trying to get rid of you, with such force that the party was ended early. All good so far?"

Keisha glanced at the lawyer beside her before muttering, "Yes." If they said it was right, it must be right.

"We found an empty bottle of champagne in a bedroom in the victim's house—the room that had been occupied by the previous Mrs. Radford, now deceased. We're testing the rim for your DNA."

"I couldn't sleep," Keisha said. "It's calm in there. I

took the champagne with me." She did remember that. Hiding in Eleanor's room, trying to get the haze in her crazy head to settle.

"You couldn't sleep because of the argument."

"Partly. A lot of things." Within the panicked confusion of her brain, a solitary thought punched to the surface. Why hadn't they mentioned the photograph yet? Why hadn't they asked about that? That's what Billy had been so angry about. So why weren't they talking about it?

"Eleanor Radford had a vial of morphine and a packet of syringes and needles in her bedroom drawers that you knew about. You'd found some marijuana in the same place and smoked it with Marcie Maddox, am I correct?" She smiled at the lawyer. "Don't worry, I can't charge your client for that."

"Where are you going with this, Detective?"

"When we found the yellow stain on the study carpet close to the empty coconut water carton, we took samples of both the stain and the carton to check that the stain was in fact from spillage when your husband collapsed."

"I don't understand," Keisha muttered.

"One of the syringes from Eleanor's drawer is missing. Ethylene glycol, better known as coolant—coolant bought solely for your car—had been injected into Mr.

Radford's coconut water at some point last night. There was a needle hole in the top of the carton. The yellow trace from the liquid splattered on the carpet when Mr. Radford threw it into his study trash can."

Keisha's thoughts swirled in kaleidoscope colors. Coolant in his coconut water?

"Your husband was poisoned," the detective finished.

Poisoned? Keisha could barely breathe.

"You were almost very lucky," Washington said, resting his thick arms on the table. "Mr. Radford *did* suffer a heart attack, either as a result of the injury sustained in his fall or as a side effect of the coolant entering, and starting to affect, his system. Ethylene glycol is broken down in the body relatively quickly. Given Mr. Radford's head injury and heart attack, without the staining it's unlikely that traces of coolant would have been found by the medical team before it had vanished. They wouldn't have been looking for it. You could have gone home, gotten rid of the evidence, and then even if others had raised concerns it would be too late."

"Mr. Radford was a powerful man. Powerful men have enemies," her lawyer responded, leaning forward. "There were over a hundred people at Mr. Radford's party. Any one of them could have done it. Do you have this syringe?"

"I'm sure we'll find it." Anderson this time, the two officers tag-teaming their attack. "We're searching very thoroughly. Mr. Radford *is* a powerful man—and he has powerful friends. Trust me, this investigation is not going to be short on resources. And none of those two hundred and forty-eight, at last count, invited guests were about to be cut out of their husband's will in preparation for divorce."

Detective Anderson looked across at Keisha. "And then there's the matter of the emails you've had from your relatives in England asking you when you're going to be getting money for them. They were deleted, but you didn't empty the trash on your laptop. I refer you to these two in particular." She slid two sheets of paper across the table. "For the tape, I'm showing Mrs. Radford exhibits 11a and 11b. The first one is from your uncle Yahuba. That line, 'you know what you have to do.' And also this, from a Dolly Parker: 'Hope you're having fun! Is he dead yet? Love ya!' Could you explain the meaning of those to me? Or is it as obvious as it seems?"

Keisha's breath caught in her throat. *No, no, no.* "She was just—it was just—"

"I need some time to talk to my client," the lawyer cut in, silencing her.

Cursed KeKe. It was all coming home to roost.

43.

The group had a late dinner at the club, perhaps the least intrusive place for them all given that William and Keisha were all over the news, but still everyone stared. Many of the other diners had been at the party, of course, and that added to the frisson of excitement in the air as they chattered about how awful it was, all said with a certain glee. William Radford's life wasn't turning out to be so charmed after all.

They'd only ordered salads, but Marcie couldn't even pretend to eat hers as Noah filled them in with what the police had reported back. Things were not looking good for Keisha, and when he'd told them how William had been poisoned, Marcie's eyes fixated on her plate as the world pounded in her ears until she was certain she'd have an aneurysm. She wanted to go home, take a pill, sleep, and then find when she woke up that this had all been some kind of nightmare. None of it made sense. *That* envelope arriving for Jason and then this happening to William?

"I can't believe it," Iris said. The tension between her and Noah was palpable. Iris had made sure that Keisha had good legal representation—Dan Temple was considered one of the best—even as Noah had been leveling accusations at her. "That girl may have problems, but I don't see her doing something like this."

"As Marcie told us, she has a Valium addiction and William made her stop taking it suddenly," Virginia said. "Lord knows I've seen the effects of drugs with my work at the Mission. People can do just about anything when they're in that sort of withdrawal, and bless her heart, she always seemed a bit *heady* to me. You know, a little too wild, too free? Damaged perhaps?"

"Well then, perhaps she was not in her right mind." Iris flashed a glare at her husband. "I should speak to Dan about getting a full evaluation done. Even if she's innocent, it won't hurt to have one done."

"You don't think she did it?" Marcie asked. She'd expected Iris and Virginia—especially Virginia—to tear Keisha apart once the police had her. *Common. Coarse. Money grubber. Whore. Not one of us.* But no, if anything, they were rallying around. Was this a little rebellion on Iris's part against her husband? Did any of them have good marriages at all?

"Do you?" Iris raised an eyebrow. "You were her friend, Marcie. Does this strike you as her sort of behavior? And if she *did* do it, I doubt it was in sound mind."

"No, not at all," Marcie muttered, wanting no black marks against her potential Magnolia membership if they survived this scandal. Maybe she didn't quite believe that Keisha would poison William, but what could she do to help her? It was like Jason had said in the car. If the police didn't go after Keisha for it, then they'd have to start looking elsewhere, and it wouldn't be long before they turned Marcie's way.

"Well, you ladies are at odds with the evidence," Noah said. "Which seems pretty darned conclusive. They're going to hold her for the full seventy-two hours, but I'm sure they'll be charging her with attempted murder before then."

"What's this?" Jason asked, returning from the bathroom and retaking his seat. Emmett was moments behind him.

"Keisha. Noah thinks they're going to charge her." Marcie's throat tightened. For all they knew, William could die at any moment. It would be a murder charge then. The death penalty probably. Her head spun.

Keisha couldn't have done it. She couldn't, could she? But there were those times, so many times, she'd whispered, *Why can't he just die?* with such longing. Had it all gotten too much? But this method—poisoning—was too cold, too clinical, for her. If Keisha was going to kill someone then it would be in the heat of a moment. She'd stab him or hit him with something. She was all passion, not planning.

"They want a quick result, that's all." Iris shot her husband an irritated glance. "You better than most know how often that happens. If she'd been smart enough to plan this, she'd have been smart enough to get up and clean up after herself and then go back to bed before he was found. Any fool would."

"Do you know what was in her Internet search history on her cell phone?" Noah growled. He didn't wait for an answer. "How many Viagra it would take to kill a man."

There was a long pause. Iris drew herself up tall. "There's a lot of water between thinking about killing someone and actually doing it." She looked at Noah again. "Trust me on that."

"Maybe she was just worried he was taking too many," Marcie said quietly.

Virginia let out a short nervous laugh, which went some way to breaking the tension, but Noah had made his point. There was an overwhelming amount of evidence against Keisha. Why would the police think to look anywhere else?

Marcie's head was throbbing by the time they got home and it was late—nearly midnight—and she felt like she hadn't slept in days. All she wanted was her bed, but her stomach was in knots about Jason and the envelope. What was he going to *do*? To say? They'd barely had a moment to themselves in all this, between their friends and the police and fielding phone calls from the nosy and curious disguising their craving for inside information with Southern care and concern.

"Maybe I shouldn't have told the police about the grass Keisha found," she said, kicking off her shoes and trying to sound normal. "But I didn't know they were fishing about the needles. They just asked if Keisha had ever taken anything from Eleanor's things." That wasn't entirely true. It had been clear they'd been digging for something and she gave it to them, but only for her own survival.

"Sure," Jason sneered. "Because you care so much. Would you rather they were coming for you?"

"I didn't poison William!" she snapped, tears stinging her eyes.

"So you keep saying. But someone did. We just have

to hope that whoever knows about you—whoever sent that yearbook—keeps their mouth shut for now, otherwise it could be Keisha out here and you in that cell. We have to keep our heads down, Marcie. Be William's good friends. Stay in the background."

Marcie's stomach flipped again. He was right. Someone out there was watching them, watching *her.* "But who would have sent it?" she asked. "And why? Why now? And that accusatory note . . . Why didn't they say what they wanted?"

"How the hell would I know?" Jason filled the coffee machine. "And to be honest, I don't even care. I've thrown it all away. I don't want to look at it. And I sure as shit don't have the energy to think about it right now."

"You're making coffee?" Marcie stared. "Now?"

"I've got work to do. I need to cancel the audit, for one thing. That's supposed to have started this morning but I'm keeping the office closed for a few days until we know how—well, how likely it is that William could recover."

Was it her imagination or did he sound as if that wasn't the preferred outcome? William was his best friend and yet he hadn't shed a tear for him either yesterday or today. Maybe it was shock. Maybe she was being harsh.

"I'm senior partner in his absence so the buyout can wait for now," he continued. "Until things have calmed down."

"Don't you want to talk?" she asked. "Tell me how you're feeling. About us. About me. We can't—"

"Not now, Marcie." He looked at her. "I love you. I do. But I need time to process it. To figure out the best way to protect you, and I don't have that right now. And until we know what they want we'll be going around in circles anyway."

"Do you think maybe Jacquie . . ."

"Don't be so ridiculous," he snapped. "And I said not now."

She said no more and went to take solace in a hot shower, the only place she had space to think. He wouldn't even countenance that Jacquie might have done it, and what kind of man defended his first wife to his second anyway? Marcie's reasoning wasn't exactly a leap of imagination. Jacquie had always been a complete bitch, and she obviously wanted to break them up now that she was back in town.

There were also Jason's secrets. He was all holier than thou at the moment, but he wasn't being honest. What about his fight with William that night? He hadn't mentioned that to the police, had he? He hadn't even mentioned it to *her*. Did he think she hadn't heard? Well, she had, and Elizabeth had heard too, at least a little bit of it. Maybe she should throw that at her darling husband. Send a little worry his way and see how he liked it.

She moisturized and powdered and then crawled into her soft, vast bed. She thought of Keisha on a narrow cot, the mattress so thin the springs would be poking through, the blanket rough against her soft skin. The noise of strangers in the night. Catcalls. Abuse being shouted by the drunk and the damned. Would she get any sleep at all?

Marcie wrapped the cool, expensive Egyptian cotton sheets tighter around her own body. She did have feelings for Keisha, she knew she did. But how could she help her? She couldn't. Not without drawing attention to herself, and there was no way she was going to do that.

She lay awake, tossing and turning, her hairline crinkling with sweat even as the AC cranked cool air around the house. She couldn't relax. Nothing made sense. Yes, Jacquie could have sent the yearbook, but what about what had happened to William? What motivation would she have had for that? Games were being played and she felt like a pawn on someone else's board. It couldn't be coincidental that someone would raise her past and the very next day William was poisoned. She didn't believe in coincidences.

Finally, her brain and nerves exhausted but with her heart still racing, she drifted into a restless sleep, and she dreamed of Jonny, her sleep choking in silent screams.

44.

When Marcie woke, tired and sweating, it was to the tread of Jason's feet as he came along the corridor and stopped outside the bedroom door. The dark night had been replaced with the gray gloom of the hour before dawn, and she held her breath until, after a moment, he retreated once again. Jonny was forgotten, all thoughts back on her current husband. So, he wasn't going to sleep with her again tonight. Was this how their marriage was going to be from now on? A quiet punishment? Separate rooms and smiles for the sake of appearances until he met someone else or had climbed so high up the social ladder they could finally slip into a polite second divorce? Or was he waiting for all this to settle down and then he'd screw her over to be with Jacquie again?

She lay there for a long thirty minutes and then pushed the covers away. What had he been doing all night? More late-night phone calls? Probably. He'd have his phone with him so she couldn't check that—but what else? She crept through to his study and turned his computer on, relieved to discover the password hadn't changed. She went to his sent emails and this time she read them all, not just looking for something that might hint at an affair.

He'd certainly been busy. A raft of messages sent to clients explaining that William was gravely ill and that given that they were a boutique firm, there might be a knock-on effect at the partnership for the next week or so and asking for client patience but he would be doing his best to make sure everything was running as smoothly as possible and to email him directly with any queries about their accounts. Next there were two to the auditors putting the audit on hold indefinitely and in no uncertain terms.

Then there was one to Emmett—sent first, at just after midnight—telling him to pick up his phone. She sat back in the leather chair and stared at it until the words blurred. Why would he want to speak to Emmett in the middle of the night? Jason and Emmett weren't even that close. Were they? She closed down his email and stared at the home page, her mind whirring. All those late-night calls. Could they have been Emmett? But why at night? When she was asleep? Because Virginia was asleep too? What had they been discussing?

Money.

Investments.

That's what Emmett did. Had Jason invested money with Emmett? She looked at the screen again and then she noticed. The untitled folder—the one containing the spreadsheet of numbers—had vanished. The only one on his screen to have been deleted. Jason had been tidying up.

The computers at the office all crashing.

The argument with William. What had he said? *The audit starts Monday, Jason, and if this isn't made good by then . . .* How had Jason explained it? *A transfer gone wrong.*

She couldn't breathe, the rush of information to her brain like pure oxygen, leaving her dizzy. That trouble with his father years ago that left his name tarnished and Jason having to claw his way back. Had Jason become like his father? Had he been embezzling from the company?

Money. Not a woman. His foul moods, the late-night calls, all down to money trouble, not a woman. Not Keisha. Not Jacquie. Not some cheap scheming

waitress looking for a rich husband, but Jason covering his tracks. The fights over her expensive furniture
and remodeling choices. This house. How had he paid
for it? Other people's money? And here he was judging
her for her secrets, when he was on the cusp of ruining
them both.

The fucking bastard.

She woke him with breakfast in bed: scrambled eggs,
bacon, and home fries and a pot of fresh, strong coffee. There was even a flower in a small vase on the
tray like he used to bring her when they first got together. She put the tray beside the guest-room bed, as
he blinked, confused at the noise waking him.

"What are you doing, Marcie?" He glanced at the
tray as if it were as dangerous to his health as William's
coconut water had been to his. "I'm not hungry."

She pulled the drapes wide, letting bright sunlight
stream in.

"Jesus . . ."

She turned to face him. "We need to talk."

He groaned, one arm blindfolding him. "I need another hour's sleep and then I should go see how William is doing. Show my face at the hospital."

She poured two cups of coffee and sat on the side
of the bed. Since shutting down his computer, she'd

veered between laughing and crying and now she just needed to know the extent of the shit they were in. It was his turn to squirm a little.

"Don't you worry?" she asked thoughtfully, before pausing and sipping her coffee. Their best china for a morning like this.

"Worry about what?" he snapped.

"That whoever found out about my past also knows about you."

For the briefest second his whole body froze, and then he rubbed his face as if impatient with her. "Know what about me, Marcie? I'm too tired for this."

"The money, Jason." A long pause. "All the company money."

There it was. That strange expression, as if someone she didn't know had slipped inside Jason's skin. "How did it start?" she continued. "The occasional borrow from a client account? Then heavier dipping and having to move funds around? Borrowing from Peter to pay Paul? Did it all get out of hand? Did you invest some client funds with Emmett, hoping to make enough to replace what you'd taken and still buy William out of the firm?" She felt sick as she voiced her suspicions. When had things gotten so bad?

"You're crazy," he said coldly. "You've been crazy for a while now."

"Me? Really? You've been moody as hell for the best part of a year. And don't tell me it's all in my head. That bullshit won't wash with me. Just tell me if I'm right. I need to know the truth, Jason."

He pushed the sheets off and got out on the other side of the bed. "I need to shower. And so do you. We have to go to the hospital."

"You're really going to ignore me?" She found she wasn't surprised. Handsome and charming he might be, but Jason had never been good with confrontation. He closed down. Refused to discuss. He'd done the same with Jacquie when he'd divorced her. At the time Marcie had been young and stupid and thought he was being strong, but she'd been entirely wrong. He'd simply been too weak to face the woman he was leaving.

"No wonder you're so happy the police have taken Keisha. All that evidence they have against her stops them looking at *both* of us, doesn't it? Not just me, but you too, you sanctimonious prick." The cussing tasted good in her mouth. He'd earned it. "Keisha wasn't the only one with something to gain by William's death. This is all working out quite well for you too, isn't it?"

Jason paused in the doorway, spots of color blotched on his suddenly pale face. "What are you imply-ing?" He looked aghast. "Are you asking if I poisoned

William? Of course I didn't. And for what it's worth, I don't think you did either, so forgive me for being slightly relieved for both our sakes that it looks pretty obvious that Keisha did."

Marcie stared at him. "So you *did* steal the money."

"I didn't steal it. I . . . I borrowed it." There was a long pause, and then his spine crumpled, his shoulders rolling forward as he sighed. "It got out of hand. I was in the process of putting it all back, I promise you. But there's been a delay and I could only cover so much. I wasn't expecting William to organize the audit. Not so quickly."

"But why?" she asked. "Why do it in the first place?" Having her suspicions confirmed had knocked the anger out of her, and now she was confused and afraid. Was there anything real in their marriage at all? If this was to come out, they'd be ruined. Imprisoned. Who'd believe that she hadn't known?

"I could see the way you looked at them," he said, shrugging helplessly. "William and Eleanor. Iris and Noah. Even Virginia and Emmett. I wasn't stupid. I knew we were the poor relations of our friendship group."

"You've never been poor, Jason. Far from it."

"Everything is relative. Happiness. Health. Wealth. You envied them."

"So did you. We had that in common."

"I did. But mainly I wanted to make you happy. First your store didn't work out and then you were so insistent about having this house—"

"You stop right there, Jason Maddox." Marcie couldn't believe what she was hearing. What kind of bullshit was this? "Are you really trying to put this on me? I didn't make you steal anything. You did that all by yourself." She wouldn't have been so stupid to have risked their whole lives just for a bigger house. Why the hell had he? "We could have stayed in our old house," she said, quieter this time. "I wouldn't have minded. If you'd explained that money was tight." Was that true? If she was honest, she preferred their old house. It was *warmer*. But this house—this was impressive, it commanded respect, and that counted for something, didn't it?

"No, it's not your fault. Of course not. I'm just trying to explain." Jason was so pathetic, his voice almost whining. "When we met, you looked at me as if I could conquer the world and that made me believe I could. You never put me down like Jacquie had. I wanted to keep that feeling. But it changed. The more you saw of this life, the more you wanted it. And I couldn't— can't—blame you for that."

He looked up at her, his eyes full of despair. "I'm so,

so sorry. I wanted you to be happy. In a week or so all the money will be back where it should be. I promise you. I'll never do anything like it again. It's been killing me, it really has. So much deception. I couldn't look at you or William, I felt so bad." He took her hand. "But I didn't hurt William. I swear to God I didn't. I love you, Marcie. I really do."

Marcie was at a loss for words, instead wanting to pummel all her feelings out against his face. Did he really think she was going to believe that pile of horseshit? That he'd done it for *her*? She looked at him again, his face so earnest, and realized that yes, he did think she'd go for it—maybe he was even convinced of it. It was easier than taking the blame himself. She gritted her teeth. Did she want to have this fight now, or was it safer all around to just let it ride?

"I love you too," she murmured in the end, squeezing his hand back. "But what a mess." Despite her conciliatory words, her heart thumped with no small amount of anger. So she wasn't the only one with a secret to protect in this marriage. Her beloved Jason wasn't so pure himself. *Beloved.* Did she love him anymore? she wondered, as he leaned in and kissed her, his mouth hot and stale from lack of sleep, his tongue probing for comfort and forgiveness from hers. She let him move her back on the bed. Of course they were going to have sex. An affirmation of their union. A reminder that they were in this together, for better or for worse.

What she normally took for passion felt needy as he gripped her neck and hair and pulled her close, panting and pushing himself into her. She let her body move in rhythm with his, and even as her nerves tingled, responding, she felt somewhat detached. He'd been horrible to her for months and then made her feel like it was her fault. He'd gaslighted her and now she was supposed to forgive him, just like that? At least her secrets hadn't affected him. Not until now. They'd stayed hers. Private. Irrelevant.

She ran her hands over the familiar firmness of his chest around to his back, lingering in the curve of his spine before teasing the line down to his ass, trailing a finger along the crevice of his butt, knowing how the hint of the illicit excited him. She wanted him to come and quickly. She wasn't ready to have sex with him. She wasn't sure she even wanted to ever again. She was angry with him. She pitied him. It was all so different from how sex was with Keisha. How *everything* was with Keisha. But Keisha was in jail and Jason was here and they all had bigger problems to deal with than who she preferred fucking.

Thankfully, he came fast.

45.

Keisha hadn't slept all night. Not because of the unfamiliar bleak surroundings and the unforgiving excuse for a bed—in fact the bare cell had been almost comforting; it was almost a relief to find herself back in the gutter where she belonged—but because she could no longer trust her own memory. Her mind had never been her friend, but now that her head was clearer thanks to some proper medication, the thick dark storm clouds had evaporated and left her facing a sea of doubts. What was real and what wasn't?

The past few days were a haze. A terrible dream made up of disjointed moments. Yesterday the police had spent so much time talking to her about what they thought she'd done, they'd half-convinced her that she *had* poisoned William. She'd wanted him dead, yes. She

had *wished* him dead. She could see the bottle of coolant in her mind's eye, the syringe, the coconut water,
her hands at work. But that wasn't real, it was just her
crazy brain making truth out of the detectives' fiction,
her mind trusting them more than it trusted itself. No,
she hadn't tried to kill William in any *normal* way, but
she had wished for his death, surrendered her desire to
Old John Bayou, and in that she was guilty. Who knew
what she'd caused by bringing that bad juju on them?
She could barely look at the items on the desk in case
they sang of her guilt.

Say nothing, her attorney had repeated when he'd
arrived early again this morning. He needn't have
worried. She'd never felt less like talking. She stared
at the two items on the desk that the detectives had
just referenced for the tape and swallowed hard. The
two dolls, one male and one female, were coarsely
hewn and small, but the female one was weighty all
the same. Detective Anderson might not feel that, but
Keisha did. The dolls were made from her clothes and
William's, she knew that, but the weight in hers was
what disturbed her. What was *inside* it? The other detective, Washington, he kept looking too. Perhaps he
had some grit in his soul, a history of night and earth,
maybe some relative somewhere in the city still practicing the old ways.

Maybe she *had* tried to kill William, she thought, staring at the ugly charms. But if she had, then she'd been hexed into it, and if she hadn't, then she'd been hexed into taking the blame.

"You say you found one of these dolls in your drawer on the morning of July eighth, is that correct?"

Keisha looked at her attorney, who nodded. "Yes," she said quietly. "When Elizabeth woke me up and said Billy had had a stroke or something. I rushed to get dressed and found it on top of my underwear."

"Did you react?"

"I didn't want to touch it. I wanted . . ." She bit her lip. She couldn't finish what she'd been about to say. *I wanted Marcie to come and make it better. I still want Marcie to come and make it better.* She couldn't mention Marcie. She'd promised her. That memory wasn't jumbled.

"Because you recognized it as a voodoo doll?"

"Something like that."

"The second doll—the male doll—we found with the victim, on the desk in your husband's study. Where he collapsed. Did you see that one?"

Keisha shook her head. "No. I was too worried about Billy."

"Did you tell anyone about the doll you found?"

"I'm not sure. I think so. Iris maybe. It freaked me out. It wasn't the first thing like that . . ."

"Ah yes. There was a ball of some kind in the house, is that right? Made of mud. You found it on the stairs and caused a bit of a scene."

"Billy said it was made of mud. But it was a conjure ball. They're made of blood and grave dirt." She flinched slightly remembering it. The thud on the steps.

"We've been speaking to the police in London about your family," Detective Anderson said.

"Are they coming here? My aunt and uncle?" Keisha asked. She couldn't deal with that on top of all this. Their *disappointment*.

"They can't get visas," Washington answered. "They both have criminal records."

"And they were neither very forthcoming about your family relationship nor very concerned about your predicament. The English police, however," Anderson continued, "have been very helpful." She paused and leaned back in her chair. "You had a difficult start in life, didn't you? Your mother killed herself when you were five, is that right?"

"Yes." She could barely remember her mother. A ghost. Always ghosts.

"She had a history of mental health issues and alcoholism, and after her death you went to live with your uncle and aunt."

"Yes," she said again.

"Your uncle is a scam artist, isn't he? Advertises his services as a witch doctor and promises to solve people's problems for cash. A lot of cash. Some of which clients are coerced into paying against their will for fear of repercussions."

"I don't know what my uncle does."

"Oh, come on." Anderson smiled. Her front teeth were crooked, but the expression suddenly made her pretty. "You wrote text for his website."

"I know he provides a service. I don't know about any scams."

"My colleagues in London tell me their house— your old home—has lots of these kinds of items in it. Voodoo or some equivalent. Books. Charms. It must have been very unusual growing up there."

"It was normal to me."

"So you saw these items on a regular basis?"

"My aunt is a believer."

"Is it possible, that after realizing it would be difficult to cause your husband's death by overdosing him with Viagra, you considered trying to scare him to death? This is the South, after all. We may not be in New Orleans, but there's still a lot of superstition in our souls. You had all the tricks of the trade you'd learned back in England. Were you hoping to induce a heart attack, perhaps? Mr. Radford was an older, overweight man trying to keep up with a young, new wife. A heart attack wouldn't be suspicious."

"I was the one who was afraid. Not Billy."

"So you said." Detective Anderson leaned back in her chair and tapped a pen against the desk, and all Keisha could hear in her head was the thud of the conjure ball on the stairs again.

"Were you in it with your family?" Anderson asked. "Did they send you here with the dolls and tell you what to do? Judging from their emails they were certainly keen for Mr. Radford's money to start coming their way."

"No," Keisha said. "No, no, no. Auntie Ayo would never share her gifts with me. Never."

It was Washington who leaned forward this time, his thick, gym-heavy arms resting on the desk, his eyes narrowing. He could sense what Anderson couldn't. Keisha's *belief.* "And why is that?" he asked.

Keisha looked him straight in the eye. "She says I'm cursed. That I'm mad. Because of the boy. The ghost boy." She swallowed hard. "The boy who wasn't there."

"What boy?" the two detectives asked in unison.

46.

She wasn't sure quite what the sex was supposed to have cured, but judging by the way Jason kept flashing her his best lopsided sexy grin as they drove to the hospital, telling her that they were a team, the Indestructible Maddoxes, and that within a week there'd be nothing to worry about, somehow by letting him screw her she'd agreed that their secrets had canceled each other out. He was acting as if she'd caught him covering up a red wine spill on a favorite expensive couch rather than risking both their lives by stealing money.

"Let's hope so," she said curtly, as he pulled into the parking lot, and for a second his new good humor slipped.

"Jesus, Marcie, can you at least try to be positive?"

"Oh, I'm sorry, honey." Her blood fired hot. "For

a minute there I thought I'd just found out that this entire year has been a web of lies on your part and that we're lucky your partner has been poisoned, otherwise you'd be in prison and I would at the very least be left homeless."

She stepped out of the car and closed the door, watching him as he did the same on the other side and noticing the two young nurses who passed both giving him an appreciative glance. She didn't blame them. He was still butter-wouldn't-melt, charming, handsome Jason Maddox. Still full of confidence. Still full of shit. "So forgive me if it's going to take me a day or so to *process* this."

"Now you know how I feel," he muttered. "You lied first, Marcie. And you lied for longer."

By the time they reached the exclusive private rooms on the top floor, free of the visiting rules and regulations of the lower levels, they were holding hands, for all intents and purposes the perfect concerned couple, worried about one of their closest friends. As Marcie signed their names in the register, Jason spoke in hushed tones to the nurse, who then led them down a silent corridor decorated with bright modern art and vases of crisp fresh flowers that made Marcie believe even more that William wasn't going to make it. The whole place stank of somewhere that the rich came to politely die.

They didn't need the nurse to point out which of the vast rooms was William's—there was only one door with a plainclothes officer sipping a cup of coffee outside.

She'd half-expected to see the rest of their set already in the room, but there was only Elizabeth, looking tired and older than usual, wrapped in a cardigan, a far cry from her usual staidly smart self, sitting in a reclining armchair by the bed. It was hard to recognize William, his formidable form suddenly *diminished,* now simply a fleshy pale hub for the wires that snaked out of him to various machines humming in the background. Looking at him made her think of the yearbook sent to Jason and she felt haunted all over again, once more a pawn in a game she didn't understand.

"Have you been here all night?" Marcie asked as Elizabeth stood to greet them.

"Most of it." Her eyes were bloodshot. "I couldn't sleep at home, so I came back in. The doctor said he still has his hearing so I thought I'd talk to him for a while in case he's afraid in there. Did some reading when I ran out of things to say." She nodded over at the bedside table, where a battered paperback lay. "*Moby-Dick*. I've always wanted to read it, so I figured I'd do so out loud."

"Is he going to get better?" Jason asked. He sounded hopeful and Marcie wondered what answer he was hoping for. Life would certainly be easier for Jason if William at least took his time getting back on his feet. Elizabeth shrugged, her eyes filling up, and signaled them to a corner, glancing over her shoulder as if William would be straining to eavesdrop. Marcie figured William was too busy straining to stay alive.

"It's so awful. Who would have thought coolant could do such terrible, agonizing things to a human body? His kidneys are failing. His liver is very damaged and the specialists are running tests to see how much. He's lost his sight and is in a coma. There may even be brain damage. An ounce more in that drink and he'd have been dead or a deaf-blind vegetable for sure. But still, the next twenty-four hours are crucial." Her face trembled as she fought back more tears. "But even if he lives, he will never be himself again. Not fully recovered."

"Did the doctors say that?" Jason asked.

"Not in so many words. Not yet. But they did say that if he made it through the next few hours then they'll have to evaluate the extent of the long-term damage. He may need constant care, even if he can be discharged."

"That's so awful," Marcie muttered. Why had she come here? These were details she didn't need. "I can't help but think he'd rather be dead."

"That decision is in the lord's hands. If he lives, even if he lives like this, the lord must have a purpose for him."

"I guess so," Marcie said. "Do you want me to go get you some coffee or breakfast?" Anything to get out of the room. The sight of William, so ruined, was making her skin crawl.

"I'm fine," Elizabeth said. "Really. The nurses have gotten me so much coffee this morning I'll probably never sleep again. I'm still in shock I guess, like everyone else. I can't believe that something like this could have happened."

"The police are preparing to charge Keisha," Jason said. "That's what Noah told us last night."

"I heard. That's shocking too. I don't understand why she'd have done something so obvious. Maybe she panicked when he said he was ending it. The postnup stopped her getting his money in a divorce but she stood to inherit plenty if he died. And I mean *a lot*."

"From what the police say, she nearly got away with it," Jason said. Marcie didn't like the gossipy tone in either of their voices as they talked, so she left them chatting and went to the restroom, where she could breathe freely without thinking she was sucking in William's poisoned air. She took far longer than she needed washing and drying her hands, scrubbing herself clean until her skin was pink and raw, and when she finally returned, Jason was thankfully making their excuses to leave.

"I'm heading home myself in thirty minutes or so, after I've seen the doctors again," Elizabeth said. "I'll get some rest and take a shower. I have to check how things are at the house too. The police . . . I expect they're still looking for the syringe she used. I dread to think what kind of mess they're making. Zelda will be going quietly crazy. You know she likes to keep that place spotless."

"We'll come see William again soon," Marcie said, leaning in to give the dumpy woman a polite half-hug, hoping that Jason didn't drag her back too quickly. This room, with William in it, felt as if it had absorbed all the rot of her past and Jason's present. It was hellish and too warm and cloying. It was trying to suffocate her. She'd be happy to never come back ever again. She would, of course. Appearances had to be maintained.

It was only when she went to sign them out on the visitors' register that Marcie idly scanned down the other names as she waited for Jason to come back from the men's room. She saw it halfway down. A visitor for William Radford at 3 A.M. Jacqueline Marshall.

Jacquie.

47.

It was amazing how such a big house could still feel claustrophobic with only two people in it if the atmosphere was right, or perhaps more accurately, wrong. Marcie had tried to sleep while Jason retreated to his study to carry on doing whatever it took to right the mess he had put them in. As the day ticked around to evening, she'd offered to go pick up some Chinese takeout. Anything for some fresh air. To be out. Away from him and his *I'll make it up to you, it will be a fresh start for both of us* bullshit.

She drove slowly around the city, not heading straight to the restaurant, instead giving herself some time alone with her thoughts. She wished she could speak to Keisha and find out exactly what had happened. In so many ways, Marcie hoped it *was* all true. That Keisha had tried to kill William. It would make everything a whole lot smoother. If William died and Keisha was guilty, then Jason would automatically be senior partner and take over running the firm, probably without the hassle of a buyout, and then there would be a new king and queen in town. A new Magnolia.

It would also be easier to try to get back on an even keel with Jason if Keisha wasn't around. If Marcie didn't have to *see* her, then maybe the spell Keisha seemed to have her under would finally break. She thought about her too much. The feel of her. The touch. Even in the midst of all this madness, there was an animal hunger at her core that Jason's touch couldn't satisfy, especially now that Keisha was so definitely out of reach.

Jason. What was she going to do about him? She burned with resentment and anger at his lies and deceit, but she needed to be nicer to him, at least until they were past this immediate crisis. And after that? Would she divorce him? Would he divorce her? Was he simply being nice to her because she knew? Or maybe he was right—maybe now that they'd stripped down to their bare secrets in front of each other things would be better. She wasn't sure it worked that way somehow. That's why secrets normally stayed secret. Secrets broke things. For now though, she'd play the game. Whatever the hell the game was.

Games. Once again, her thoughts turned to Jacquie. Jason hadn't been concerned when Marcie told him that his ex-wife had gone to the hospital in the middle of the night. He said she was an insomniac and always up and at the gym while the world was sleeping. It used to drive him crazy. Plus, she'd known William for a long time before she moved. It was hardly a surprise that she'd go visit him. Marcie had told him that Jacquie had been at the party too, casually trying to find out if Jason had spoken to her. Apparently not. He claimed not to have seen her; he had shrugged and said that now Jacquie was back, however much they tried to avoid her it was likely she'd end up moving in the same circles as them. He'd then closed the conversation down by saying they had bigger problems right now than being jealous of Jacquie.

Jealous of Jacquie. She'd wanted to punch him for that. What if Jacquie *was* their problem? There was still an odd edge to Jason when he spoke of her. Was that simply the awkwardness of discussing an ex-wife with a current one? Or something else? Jason had proven himself a slippery eel when it came to the truth. Was he keeping more from her? What had Jacquie been talking to him about that afternoon at Sacchi's? Jason had *called* her. Marcie couldn't forget that. Jason, who was so bad at confrontation, had called his bitter ex-wife by choice?

Had she been trying to get him back and he'd turned her down? Could she have done some digging and sent the yearbook to try to split them up? It was possible. Or maybe she wanted more than that. Maybe she'd done it for money. True, she probably didn't need it, but taking it from Jason would still give her pleasure. She'd tried to take everything when they divorced. Maybe this was her trying to clean up again? *Whoever* it was who'd sent it probably wanted money. Otherwise they'd have told other people what they'd discovered and Marcie would be in the crap right now. The thought was a relief. Everything was nearly always about money.

What was it Mama used to say? Her pearls of wisdom on the world? *Money, sex, and power are the father, the son, and the holy ghost of life, honey. Just remember that. And women can get all three if they're not stupid. So don't be stupid.*

The city looked different at dusk, the night coming to life as the day died, shadows like ghosts under each streetlamp, and she finally headed to pick up their food and take it home. Jason was in the kitchen, plates and cutlery ready, two glasses of wine poured. "Where have you been? You've been gone for nearly two hours."

"I'm sorry," she said, leaning in and kissing him. "There was a line and you know how I hate to wait so I went for a drive. Got carried away."

"I thought you weren't coming back."

He sounded so lost and lonely her heart almost melted a little. Almost.

"I'm not going anywhere." She smiled through gritted teeth. "I just needed some space." She nodded toward the cartons. "Kung Pao Shrimp. And a couple of your other favorites."

"You sure you're okay?"

"Sure," she said. "I love you." Hollow words. She found herself thinking of Keisha when she said them. Wild, free, and open Keisha. So different from this liar of a husband of hers. Her heart would recover though. It always did.

They ate as if everything were normal and then before they went to bed Marcie called the hospital to see if there had been any change. There hadn't. They hadn't heard from Virginia or Iris all day, and Marcie hadn't called them either. They were all withdrawing to process what had happened to William, and she wished she could do the same without the rest of this shit strangling them.

This evening she and Jason both undressed in the same room, Marcie dropping her clothes on top of the party dress and mask abandoned on the floor what felt like a lifetime ago. They had sex. Bodies going through the motions, enforced intimacy between sudden strangers. Finally, they fell apart, both panting. Neither of them spoke and within minutes Jason fell into a deep sleep, leaving Marcie wide awake and staring at the ceiling, wishing the man next to her and his lies were still in the guest bedroom.

At around five the thunder started, low rumblings overhead that grew into a storm, lashing the house with wind and rain and keeping the morning dark. By seven, they knew that William hadn't died in the night. He was breathing by himself and whatever life he'd been left with was refusing to give up. He was here for the long haul, living in the dark, hooked up to machines. He could afford to be. Marcie wondered if poverty would have been better for William now. At least he'd have been able to let go. To die with dignity. Instead, he'd be left to rot away in a hospital bed like some awful zombie for the next however many years they could keep him breathing.

She made coffee, the rain keeping them housebound for now, as Jason took calls from clients and the other attorneys in the firm, and for a while Marcie stood outside the study door, watching him through the narrow gap. She felt something between awe and dread at the emotion he was managing to instill in his voice without any showing in his face or manner. Who was this chameleon she'd married? He'd be at work by lunchtime, she heard him say, which was a relief. She'd have the afternoon to herself. Maybe she'd sleep. God, she needed to sleep.

48.

Keisha had found the storm comforting before the lights went on and the new day started. It was as if all the madness in her head had fled this cell and taken to the skies. She felt empty. There had been so much talking yesterday, so many questions, that her head had been left whirling. Some she'd answered and some she hadn't, depending on what her lawyer had told her to do. She'd been a good puppet as he pulled her strings and it was easier than thinking for herself.

Thunder rolled again. How loud must it have been outside if she could hear it all the way down here in the bowels of the building. It was the grumble of ghosts. *Ghosts*. Her head had been filled with ghosts. The boy—always the boy—Eleanor, Lyle, and William. Except William wasn't dead. He was somewhere in between. Did the ghosts talk to him now too? Today's nugget of treasure, a glittering jewel of a gift, had been the news that William wasn't going to die yet. Which meant that neither would she if they found her guilty. It would be attempted murder, not murder. A life in a cell for her and a life trapped unmoving in the dark for him. Buried alive in his own skin. She trembled. Guilty. Was she guilty? She hadn't wished *this* on him.

She'd expected more questions today or for this to reach what seemed the natural conclusion—they'd charge her. Even her lawyer—her attorney, as they called him—was talking about *plea deals* and *mitigating circumstances*, as if her fate was predestined to go a certain way. She should be more nervous, but it all rolled over her. She'd reached too high above her station and now she had to fall. The girls at the club would be laughing now. What would Dolly think? Had the police already talked to her? She stared at the ceiling of her cell, drifting through memories. Maybe this would be it for the rest of her life. A narrow bed. A narrow room. A narrow view. Bells and shouting and routine. No more drinking and dancing. No more aiming high. She felt suddenly, desperately tired. At least she'd escaped her family. But no more Marcie. How was she supposed to cope with that?

When her attorney returned, his fat face was smiling. It wasn't an expression she'd seen before. "I've got some good news," he said. "The game is not lost." He rubbed his hands together. A game. Her life was a game to him. "They're not charging you yet, but they have applied to keep you ninety-six hours without charge and that's been granted."

"That's the good news?" she asked. It didn't sound so good. The conclusion was still probably inevitable.

"No, that's not it." He drew himself up tall and his grin widened. "There's a fresh line of inquiry. A serious one. A new suspect. They're bringing him in now."

Keisha's head swirled as she gasped, her heart thumping, life bursting through her veins again. She'd resigned herself to this fate. She'd half-convinced herself that she'd actually done it. Now here was a glimmer of hope—a chance at freedom. It was almost too much to bear. *Him* the attorney had said. But who?

49.

Marcie knew that surreal thoughts had a tendency to fill her head when she was panicking, but that didn't stop her from being annoyed that the cleaner wasn't due until tomorrow and they were traipsing all over her house while the bathrooms weren't perfect and there were clothes on the bedroom floor.

"Do you have a personal computer in the house, Mrs. Maddox?" Detective Anderson asked. "We'll need to take it if you do."

"An iPad," Marcie said. "I think it's in the kitchen. And a MacBook in the den, where the rest of the boxes we haven't unpacked are. But I never use that." They'd already taken Jason's desktop and laptop—she'd seen them go by as the officers took them out. Her nerves jangled. He said he'd thrown the yearbook and the note in the trash. She hadn't checked. What if he hadn't? Where were they?

"Are you sure I can't get you some tea?" she asked again. She knew she was pale and trembling. At least her fear was helping her fake her shock.

She'd gotten out of the shower, a long blissfully hot affair, barely ninety minutes before to find Jason throwing clothes in a duffel bag and rummaging in a drawer for his passport. Sandy had sent him a text from the restroom telling him that the police were all over the office, locking it down. He'd snapped at Marcie to get packing. They needed to go. Immediately. Marcie hadn't moved. Wrapped in a towel, skin scrubbed pink and brain fuzzy from the heat, she'd instead sat on the bed and told him no, they couldn't run. How guilty would they look? She'd asked how obvious his *issues*— she hadn't wanted to say thefts—were in the accounts or whatever at work. He'd said they'd have to dig deep to find the start of the trail, but he didn't even understand why they were looking. There was no reason to, no one was suspicious of him at work. He was the golden boy. The king in waiting. Why would they be storming the firm as if they *knew* something?

There hadn't been any more time for discussion,

because the doorbell had rung and Marcie had quickly emptied out the bag and crammed it in the closet, while Jason answered the door, and now here they were.

Or rather here they *weren't*. Only Marcie was, in her robe with her hair still wet; her husband had been taken in for questioning, while she worried that the men searching her house were judging her cleaning standards.

"I'm fine, thank you," Anderson said, answering for both herself and the huge detective standing behind the couch where she sat. "I know this must be unsettling, but we will leave your house tidy, I assure you."

Marcie nodded. She'd already been through the *I don't understand why you're here* routine and she didn't want to lay her disbelief on too thick. They'd had a tip-off, Anderson had said, before they took Jason away, regarding his financial activities in the firm. Jason had already called Thomas Tonyer to come down and meet him. At least they didn't have to worry about representation. Attorneys always knew the best attorneys.

Marcie however, didn't have one, and she wasn't refusing to cooperate. She was a good, law-abiding Southern wife doing her best to smooth out this terrible mistake. *Oh, please God, don't let them find the yearbook.*

"On the night of the seventh of July, at William

Radford's party, your husband and Mr. Radford had an argument in his office in the house. What do you know about that?"

"Nothing really. And *argument* is a strong word. William and Jason were close friends. They didn't ever argue."

"But it was a strong disagreement then."

"As I said, I don't know. I wasn't there. I felt unwell and went home early."

"Yes, Elizabeth Glapion told my colleague that she drove you home. But she said she'd found you outside the office and you both heard raised voices. She said that you were nervous about interrupting."

So they'd been to Elizabeth before they'd come here, maybe before they'd gone to the firm, getting their ducks in a row. "I was, yes, but then I never like to interrupt Jason when he's talking to anyone about work. It's not my business."

"But there were raised voices?"

"A little, yes." She was picking her way through a minefield. She kept her hands down, resting on her knees, so Anderson couldn't see the sheen of sweat on her palms. "I think it was something to do with the system crash at the office. That was all I heard."

"So it was nothing to do with the audit that was planned? Your husband wasn't worried about that?"

"No. Why would he be? Jason was keen for the buyout to go ahead." Her heart raced. Jason had said the police would have to dig to find a trail. She had a feeling this woman intended to.

"Are you aware of any financial problems your husband might have?"

"We don't have any as far as I know."

Anderson looked around the large room. "This is a beautiful house."

"Thank you."

"You only just moved here?"

"That's right."

"Expensive though. And a big step up from your last home?"

"To be fair, that wasn't exactly small either." Marcie smiled, but not too confidently.

"It must be hard to keep up when you're close friends with someone like William Radford. A big house. Exclusive country club fees. Designer furniture." She paused. "A failed business. It must all add up."

"Do you mean my boutique?" Marcie's back stiffened. "That risk had been factored in before we started." Her face flushed again, her *tell* of anger. She hoped the detective misread it as embarrassment.

"So you never argued over money?"

"No," she answered, ignoring the memories of the

fights in this very room over her expensive choices. "Never."

"I guess it was difficult for Jason though. An older man with a much younger, beautiful wife to impress."

Marcie laughed. "I was a waitress when we met. He didn't have to do much to impress me. He fell in love with me, that was enough."

Anderson nodded, as if satisfied, before becoming thoughtful. She wasn't fooling Marcie, pretending that her questions were coming to her on the spot. This was a planned attack. Anderson was nobody's fool.

"When did your husband get home after the party?"

"I don't know. He didn't wake me." She didn't say that he'd slept in a guest bedroom. Hopefully they wouldn't notice that the sheets were used.

"Jason bought and refilled the coolant in Keisha Radford's Corvette, is that correct? You saw him?"

Marcie's eyes widened. "Well, yes, but . . ."

"And the coolant cap was loose, he said, and that had caused the leak? Is it possible, do you think, that someone could have loosened that cap on purpose? To make sure Mrs. Radford was seen learning about such a toxic substance and that it would be found in her house after the attack on her husband?"

"I don't know what you're . . . I don't understand . . ." Marcie's face was no longer flushing. It was burning.

"The grass you smoked with Keisha Radford that she'd found in Eleanor Radford's drawer—"

"I already spoke about this with the officer who talked to me after William was found. I don't make a habit of it and—"

"I can totally understand how you and Mrs. Radford ended up getting high." Anderson smiled again, all faux friendship and sisterly confidence. "Two young women together. A new friendship. That's not what I was going to ask you about. No." She leaned forward, resting her elbows on her spread knees, a masculine pose designed to intimidate. "What I wondered was if your husband knew about the other drugs Keisha found in that drawer. The morphine, needles, and syringes. Did he know about those?"

"No," she answered, her mouth drying even as she answered truthfully. "No, he didn't." She let her hands clasp together, tight and afraid. She didn't have to fake that. "Look, this is all some kind of mistake. Jason and William are best friends. Jason would never hurt William. He wouldn't. He couldn't—" She was cut off as Anderson's cell rang and the detective was on her feet, her back to Marcie. *What now?*

The call took less than a minute, and when it finished Marcie knew they were in trouble. There was a shift in the air. Her stomach turned to ice.

"We're going to need a full search," she said to her sidekick before turning back to Marcie. "Mrs. Maddox, do you have a friend you can stay with tonight?"

A friend? Keisha was her friend, but Keisha was locked up. "I think so." Her voice was quiet. "Why can't I stay here? What are you looking for? When is Jason coming home?"

"You'd better go and pack what you need. Detective Washington, go with Mrs. Maddox, please."

They didn't even trust her to get some clothes without watching her. This was bad. What had they found at the office? What were they going to find *here*?

She knew what they were looking for. The syringe. But they wouldn't find it. Jason hadn't known about the needles. Jason didn't hurt William. Still, as she threw her toiletries, a nightie, and some fresh clothes in the duffel she'd only just emptied from Jason's attempt at fleeing, she felt dizzy with fear.

It was only later, when she was in the cab, that she remembered. They'd been in the car on the way home after the first time she'd hung out with Keisha. *After the first kiss.* He'd been angry with her for getting high and she'd laughed and said it wasn't hers. She'd told him where Keisha had found the grass. She'd told him what else had been in Eleanor's drawer.

Jason very definitely *had* known about the needles.

50.

Marcie had burst into tears as soon as Iris opened the door—real, hot tears of shame and fear that made her sob loudly, surprised by her own loss of control, and she felt a rush of gratitude when the older woman wrapped an arm around her shoulder and ushered her inside to the safety of the polished wooden floor and elegant class of the old colonial mansion.

Iris had sent the housekeeper to her rooms for the evening to give them privacy, and then soothed Marcie, made her chicken soup and reassured her that it was all no doubt a terrible mistake.

Noah was out. Iris didn't say as much but he was obviously trying to manage the shitfest of William's attempted murder. The media was loving every sordid detail of it and Marcie knew that Jason would be all over the news by morning.

"I don't think it can be a mistake," she said quietly, wiping her eyes with her sweatshirt sleeve. "I don't mean that I think Jason hurt William—God, I don't believe that, I can't—but the money . . ." Tears threatened to spill again. Whatever happened now, she was pretty sure her life was in ruins. The police had found *something*. She was going to be broke again. Back in the gutter. Jason probably going to be in prison for a long time. She didn't have to fake how upset she was, and she knew it would be worse when the reality sank in. She'd be alone again.

But Iris, she thought as she sipped the homemade broth, was turning out to be a kinder person than Marcie had ever given her credit for. She wasn't the snob she'd always thought. She'd had sympathy for Keisha even when unsure whether she might have poisoned William. Would she also be sympathetic to Marcie's plight? Maybe they'd all rally around her? Make sure she wasn't left destitute? "I mean, surely they'd have let him go by now if there was nothing?"

Iris leaned across the kitchen table and squeezed her hand. "There is no point in worrying until you know if there is something to worry about. Which I know is easier said than done."

"But why would he steal from the firm? It's so . . . not Jason. Do you think maybe he has a gambling problem?"

Iris sipped her tea. "The things men do never fail to surprise me. Surprise and disappoint in equal measure. Even Noah still has his moments, old as he is. They all like to keep up, don't they? But the problem with a race is that someone is always ahead and the rest are always chasing. The *keeping up* is endless. And exhausting. The benefit of being as old as I am, my dear, is that you learn to stop giving a shit."

Marcie giggled through her tears as Iris smiled. "That's better. Nothing like an old woman swearing to make youth laugh. Now dry your eyes and finish your soup. You don't need to get any thinner. Not while I'm looking after you."

The doorbell rang and Marcie stiffened, her heart racing, as Iris went to answer it. *What now?*

Virginia. Of course it was, and Marcie heard her before she saw her, as was often the way.

"What a day, Iris. Emmett's *still* talking to the police about Jason's investments—now there's a situation that's floored me, I don't mind saying." She stopped in the doorway mid-sentence. "Oh. You didn't say Marcie was here."

"To be fair, dear, you haven't given me a chance.

Marcie's staying the night." Iris didn't add *because the police are searching her house* and neither did she look overly happy that Virginia had shown up unannounced.

"If you'd rather, I can go," Virginia said. "I only stopped by for thirty minutes or so."

"Don't be silly," Iris said. "Let's have a glass of wine. I think we all probably need it."

"What investments?" Marcie asked lightly. The email to Emmett telling him to pick up his phone. Just how much of his ill-gotten gains had Jason gambled on the markets with?

"You didn't know?" Virginia waved Iris on to fill the large glass to the top. "Although neither did I. Not my business and all, and Emmett doesn't like to talk about friends' money." She took a long sip.

"What investments?" Marcie repeated, wanting to take the glass and smash it into Virginia's too smooth, expensively plumped face.

"I don't know exactly, I'm afraid. Some big sums apparently. High risk, high yield. Some more secure but with longer investment periods. That's all I've gleaned. But now I know why Emmett was getting all those early-morning calls when we were in the islands. Jason wanted his returns or his money back. It was getting very heated apparently. Emmett couldn't get the money out as fast as Jason wanted it. I don't know how all this works, if I'm honest. But Emmett didn't know that it wasn't—" Virginia checked herself. "Might not have been—all Jason's money. He figured Jason was playing the market to raise the money to buy William out and pay the house off or whatever."

She at least had the decency to look slightly flustered and embarrassed as she spoke, but Marcie barely noticed. Her head was spinning. All those late-night and predawn calls? Were they all to Emmett? Why had Jason started panicking?

William came back from Europe early. Of course. Marcie's throat constricted as if a noose were around it. A social noose for her, and potentially a literal one for Jason. Could he have tried to kill William because the audit was going to show what he'd been doing and there was no longer enough time to put it right? He knew about the syringes—although there was no way she'd be telling the police that—he knew where the coolant was, and he knew Keisha was a bit crazy and maybe even knew that William was having second thoughts. If William had told Noah he could easily have mentioned it to Jason too.

She swallowed some wine, her fingers trembling on the glass. What was the prison time for fraud or embezzlement or whatever he'd done? It was enough for Jason's father to have killed himself rather than face it. Was it worth killing William to save himself from prison and to keep his position in this world? No, not keep. Improve it.

"We don't know anything yet," Iris said. "And Marcie's worried enough." She flashed Virginia a look. "After everything that happened with Jason's father, and how hard Jason fought to get back on track after it, I can't believe that it won't all turn out to be a mistake until someone presents me with hard evidence. And you should do the same too, Virginia."

"I was only saying," Virginia replied, archly.

"Well don't, dear."

And that was that. Iris moved the conversation to tennis and the latest tornado to hit Florida and how lucky they'd been to escape it, but maybe there was something they could do to raise money for those who'd lost their homes. Virginia didn't stay long, thankfully, a call from Emmett summoning her home like a good wife, but at least while she'd been there, Marcie had been able to zone out and sit lost in her own dire thoughts.

Would they let her see Jason tomorrow? Maybe they'd let him go. That didn't seem likely. Investing large sums with Emmett. The office being ripped apart. Their house being searched. They wouldn't do that to Jason if they didn't have some sort of evidence already. He was too well connected to want to get him pissed if they weren't pretty sure something was awry. Everyone involved in this was too well connected. Except Keisha. Had she been thrown to the wolves as a distraction?

Underlying everything, all of it, was her terrible fear for herself. Jason had said he'd thrown the yearbook away, but was it still sitting in the trash? What about her hidden box? What had he done with that? Would the police find it? Was the person who'd sent the yearbook to Jason the same one who'd tipped off the police about his fraud? And if so, why? Why try to destroy them? And why now?

"I think an early night is what you need, dear," Iris said. "I'll settle you into Eleanor's room and then bring you up a hot chocolate."

"Eleanor's room?"

"I need to stop calling it that. But it's the room she used to sleep in when she stayed over."

"Did she stay here a lot?"

Marcie's legs felt like lead as she followed Iris up the grand old staircase, her bag over her shoulder. She was dog-tired even though she was convinced she wouldn't sleep.

"Sometimes. When William would be away for work when we were a lot younger. When the kids were small they'd all play together. Lyle was smaller but such a sweet boy. And then of course, after . . ." Iris opened a door down the corridor leading to the master bedroom. "She needed somewhere she could grieve properly. So we gave her this room to have as her own. It's not the largest guest room, but the coziest I think. This house is too big. If it hadn't been in Noah's family for generations, I'd have wanted to sell and move somewhere smaller. Somewhere homier." She sighed. "I don't see why everything has to be so *big* all the time. You must feel it in that monstrosity of a house Jason just moved you into."

Marcie let the unintentional insult slide. *Monstrosity.* The house had been her choice. She'd demanded it. She'd thought it was as good as this one. Maybe Iris thought this was a monstrosity too. An albatross of history around her neck. Marcie didn't comment though, because she was too distracted by the wall of her room for the night, a room that by nobody's standards was anything other than large, at the center of which was an oversized double bed with a huge patchwork comforter on it. A thick rug lay on either side of the bed, and away from the dresser and wardrobe, against the far wall, were four bookshelves of different heights that created a quirky skyline of colored spines. Iris was right. There was something comforting about it. The wall though, the one that her eyes were drawn back to, that was something else. So many framed photographs. So many of Eleanor and Lyle. A lifetime in images.

"Wow," she said softly.

"William made it hard for her to grieve sometimes. He wanted to put it all away. Out of sight, out of mind. He couldn't cope, he said." She sighed, leaning casually against the doorframe, and in the soft yellow lighting from the bedroom lamp and the hall chandelier, there was the echo of the woman she'd been in her thirties and forties. It was hard for Marcie to imagine. But then Marcie had never imagined Eleanor as youthful and free as she appeared in some of these pictures. It took a moment before she realized that Iris was in a few too, laughing on the beach with Lyle holding her hand on one side and Eleanor's on the other, the two women having a great time. Best friends. How nice to have a friend like that, Marcie thought with a pang of envy.

"Men always think their feelings run deeper than ours when the situation is about them," Iris continued. "But it's not true. They just make more noise about theirs. And they have deep feelings so rarely compared to women that the emotions come as something of a surprise to them." She paused and then straightened up. "Anyway, there's a shower or bath and fresh towels in the bathroom, and a robe in the closet if you need it. There's also a TV tucked away in the cabinet by the window if you can't sleep. Or a book, of course. But you get settled. I'll be back up with a hot chocolate, and if you're in the bathroom, I'll just leave it by the bed. And try not to make yourself too upset. We'll know more in the morning, I'm sure. Life is always better when you know exactly what it is you have to deal with."

As she turned to go, Marcie, on impulse, called her back. "I know I've not always been too friendly," she said awkwardly. "And thank you for being very kind to me. I know a lot of people wouldn't, given everything that's going on right now."

"Oh, you'd be surprised," Iris said. "We can be funny in this town, I'll give you that. Little things matter. Surface things can become overly important. But when it comes down to it, when the big storms come, all that disappears. We take pride in our Christian values. The real ones. Not judging others too harshly. Looking for the best in people. Fairness. Kindness. I suppose that's why I ended up married to a judge." She smiled. "Plus, of course, we're all steeped in history here. Everyone has shame at some point in their family's past. You learn to be sympathetic and not judge one person for the sins of another."

"I found it hard being the second wife," Marcie said. "After the divorce and everything. I always feel—felt—that everyone thought I wasn't good enough to be part of all this. I was too coarse. Too common. Hard. Too trailer trash, I guess." The final words were out before she could stop them. No one knew about the trailer park. Not until Jason on Saturday night. But it was only a turn of phrase and Iris didn't show any curiosity.

"It's hard to come into something so established, that is true," Iris said. "But everyone worries. I remember Jacquie worrying about her Creole roots being judged. But you know what I've found in life?"

Marcie looked up at her from her seat on the side of the bed.

"Often what you worry other people might be thinking of you is most likely to be what you think of yourself. Be kinder to yourself, Marcie. Nobody's perfect."

Marcie's exhaustion took hold fast and after barely a sip of her hot chocolate, and with the bedside lamp still on, she closed her eyes for a second and was gone. She slept deep and long and dreamless, as if the dead mother and son trapped smiling on the wall had gifted her a taste of their eternal rest, and if Iris hadn't shaken her awake she'd probably have stayed lost in the darkness all day.

"What?" she muttered as she was dragged unwillingly back to consciousness. The lamplight had been eclipsed by streaks of early morning sunshine from beyond the shutters and drawn drapes. She squinted and looked up at Iris looming over her, resisting the urge to close her eyes again.

"You'd better get up."

It was the tone of Iris's voice that made Marcie suddenly alert. Gone was the tender warmth of last night. It had been replaced by something cool and suspicious. Her heart raced. "What is it?"

"The police are here." Iris paused. Her mouth was tight and her spine stiff. This was not good at all. Marcie pushed herself upright.

"You okay, Iris?"

"They say you have to get dressed. They have a warrant for your arrest."

And with that, Marcie knew her house of cards had crumbled.

Be kinder to yourself, Marcie. Nobody's perfect.

No one would be saying anything like that to her again for a long time.

51.

"You know something?" Kate Anderson looked almost entertained on the other side of the interview table from Marcie. "I don't think I've ever worked a case where my problem was having too many suspects who could all easily be guilty. The issue I have is—and don't take this personally—that you're all such truly atrocious people."

The second detective, a muscle-bound hulk of a man whose skin was so dark it shone, smiled as Anderson paused and sipped her coffee. Marcie was letting her own grow cold. She knew how it would taste from a Styrofoam cup. Plasticky, too cheap, and too strong. She'd been in a room like this before with an equally useless court-appointed lawyer beside her, just like now. The coffee was meant to amp up whatever jitters the suspect had.

"First," Anderson continued, "there's the beautiful, very young, and slightly unbalanced new foreign wife, who saw the opportunity to stick her claws into a wealthy widower far away from home. A hasty, unhappy marriage that William Radford was already regretting and planning to be free of with no financial loss." She sighed, enjoying the theater of her statement. Marcie had thought the detective was dour, but there was definite humor glinting in her eyes now. It made her look younger and happier. None of it stopped Marcie from wanting to smash her in the face. "Isn't that so often the way?" Anderson continued. "Pick something up on your vacation that looks great in its natural location and then when you get it to your house you realize it doesn't really fit with the rest of your stuff and you end up throwing it away?"

Marcie said nothing, but she got the feeling that Detective Anderson didn't much like what she knew of William any more than the people she was investigating for trying to kill him.

"Then, of course, we have your husband, Jason Maddox, Mr. Radford's colleague and close friend. We've found enough . . . *discrepancies*, for want of a better word, in the Radford and Partners accounts to be preparing to charge him with embezzlement. The way I see it is that William came back from Europe six months before he planned to and Jason didn't have time to cover all his tracks. So, both Keisha Radford and Jason Maddox had motive and opportunity to try to kill William Radford, and to be honest, I was veering very much toward Jason being the more likely candidate—he's too smooth for my taste—until he asked to speak to me at five A.M. this morning." She leaned across the table. "When he told me to go look in the air vent in your dressing room, where he'd hidden this." She pushed the old yearbook across the table, the pages open to where Marcie's young sullen face stared back. "And so here we are, Savannah Cassidy."

Her air vent. Of course that's where Jason had put it. Right back where she'd hidden everything. She stared at the old photograph. Savannah Cassidy. A name that had become her destination. With everywhere on the map to choose from, she'd moved someplace where she'd at least never forget the name she was given at birth. She looked up at Anderson.

"My name isn't Savannah Cassidy. It's Marcie Maddox. I changed it legally to Marcie Brown before I left Boise. I have the paperwork." She wasn't waiting for the poor excuse of a publicly appointed attorney beside her to interject. "Or I guess I presume you do if you have my box of private things." Any tears she may have been holding back burned dry as a flash of anger heated her.

Anderson turned the pages of the yearbook before sliding it over again. "Jonny Newham. Your high school sweetheart. So, as the mysterious note that was sent to your husband along with this asks, what happened to Jonny?"

"You know what happened to Jonny," Marcie sniped back. She wasn't going to go through all this again. Not over Jonny. That was dead and buried. The past. Screw Anderson and her shovel.

"Do we?" Anderson raised an eyebrow. "Why don't you tell us to make sure."

"Jonny died. He killed himself." Her back straightened even though she knew where this was leading. She was walking on quicksand that could drag her down at any moment. "We got married straight out of high school. He got us a trailer in the mobile home park. I worked shifts in the diner and he worked in a car shop a mile or so away. We were poor but happy and thinking of starting a family. Then there was an accident and Jonny's leg got crushed under a truck. He should have gotten compensation, but it turned out he'd been drinking on his lunch break and it was likely his fault.

He didn't fight it." She sighed. "Things got bad after that. I worked more shifts and Jonny drank all our extra money. He started on drugs. He was a different person."

"But he'd straightened out before he died."

"Yes, or so he said. Who knows really?" Her voice was soft. She hadn't spoken of this in so many years and now here she was, telling her sorry tale for the second time in a week. "But probably. He definitely seemed straighter for a month or so. He'd been doing some cash work on people's cars when he could. We were getting back on track. Talking about a baby some more. A compensation company had even come along and said they could get him some money for his accident."

"And they did, didn't they? You got that."

"I did. After he died."

"So, I repeat the question. What happened to Jonny, Marcie?"

"I don't know. I went to work. I had an eight-hour shift that evening, finishing at eleven. When I went he was watching daytime TV and there were leftovers in the fridge. He was having a bad day with his leg and he was in a real mean mood. It didn't make me want to come home. I needed a beer, so I went to the late-night place out by the freeway to meet up with Janey Spence, one of the other waitresses. I wanted to be young. Have a good time. Drink. Dance. All that stuff."

"You danced with some men that night."

"Yes, I did. Everyone knows that. It's in the files you've probably read and it was all over the local TV and radio. I danced. I got drunk. And then I went home with some guy and passed out drunk, so don't ask if I screwed him because I don't know. He said I didn't. I'll take his word for it. In the morning, I woke up hungover and feeling guilty and went back to my trailer. Jonny was cold and dead on the floor. There was a half-empty bottle of whiskey beside him." She blinked and behind her eyes in that instant she could see it all again.

His eyes were wide open and he'd fallen from the chair onto the shitty carpet with piss stains on it that they'd never been able to afford to change and that frozen expression had looked so terrified and in pain but she knew he was gone and she didn't know what to do next and then Janey came in behind her and shrieked and broke the spell and then with shaking hands Savannah had called 911 and then the circus had begun.

"It wasn't the whiskey that killed him though, was it?"

"They thought so at first," Marcie said. "I thought

so too. That he'd drunk himself stupid and his organs couldn't take it anymore. Not after a few weeks clean. But they tested the bottle and then they found it."

"Say it out loud, Marcie. For the tape. What did they find in Jonny's whiskey?"

"Coolant." The word was barely a whisper.

Anderson sat back in her chair. "Just like with William."

"Mrs. Maddox was found to be not responsible for Jonny Newham's death." The barely awake man beside Marcie finally spoke. "His death was ruled a suicide, as is clear from the records."

"Eventually it was, yes," Anderson said. "Although there was a nasty air of suspicion left hanging over you, wasn't there, Marcie? Enough that I imagine the Boise police department will be taking another look into Jonny's death now. I mean, what are the odds of two men you know being poisoned the same way? Ingesting coolant in a drink?"

Marcie's blood chilled. "You think it was me? You think I poisoned William?"

Anderson looked down at the yearbook and then back up at her wryly. "Well, it would be fair to say that you might have a prior. Even if you *didn't* kill Jonny, his suicide could have given you the idea. From his death you knew that ethylene glycol—coolant—disappears from the body quickly. If it hadn't been found in the liquor bottle then it's possible no one would have known how he really died. Same could be said for William. Another few hours and no trace may have been found in his system. So yes, it's possible."

"But why?" Marcie asked, aghast.

"Jason was in financial trouble. Maybe he'd told you about what he'd been doing and how he was close to getting caught. With your background it would be hard to give all this luxury up and live in some shitty condo, waitressing to pay the rent, visiting him in jail every couple of weeks for years. Or maybe you did it for Keisha? Maybe she was the better bet."

"Detective Anderson, this line of questioning—" Her attorney at last made a half-hearted attempt to do his due diligence in the room even though he looked exhausted and just wanted to get home rather than sit in with a murder suspect.

"I'm not asking a question," Anderson cut in. "I'm simply telling Mrs. Maddox my thoughts." She turned her attention back to Marcie. "We've seen the texts between you. Very close. Maybe too close. You two have been hanging out a lot and my colleagues in London tell me that Keisha preferred women sexually before she met William. Played for both teams at the very least. She'd been seeing one girl back home who she stayed in touch with when she got here, a Dolly Parker, but she cut off contact with her recently. Maybe she'd fallen in love with someone here? Maybe you?"

This was all crazy. "If you've seen our texts then you'll know that I was backing off from Keisha. She was too unstable. Too unhappy. Maybe you should try asking *her* about William again. She had the most to gain from his death. She was always saying she wished he was dead!" She stung with her own betrayal. It wasn't Keisha who'd put her here. It was Jason. Her supposed beloved husband had sold her out.

"I'm sure we will. But Keisha Radford commented on the coolant right after spending the morning with you. Maybe you'd had time to loosen the cap at some point. You knew about the hidden needles and syringes. You had as much motive and opportunity as either Keisha or your husband."

"Maybe I did!" Marcie finally snapped. "But even if I'd *wanted* to kill William—even if I'd known about the shit Jason had gotten himself into—why would I be so stupid as to try to murder William with coolant? After what happened with Jonny? What I went through with that?"

"Like I said, maybe you thought there would be no detectable traces left in his body by the time he was found. He was lucky he was found so early."

"I *know* how coolant kills people. Massive organ failure? There's no way that there would be no investigation into that, especially for someone so powerful and influential in this town as William. And then the carton would be found and that would be that."

"True. But the obvious suspect would be Keisha, not you."

"Except that someone out there sent that yearbook and note to Jason on the night of the party. It literally arrived a couple of hours before we left and he demanded I explain everything, which I did. And it wasn't pleasant. He wouldn't even speak to me. Why on earth would I then go to William's house and calmly try to poison him *that* night, knowing that Jason would think it was me, and more importantly *someone else* out there who knew about Jonny would think it was me? I *didn't* do it. Someone else did. Maybe whoever sent that yearbook to Jason did it. Maybe it's the same person who tipped you off to investigate him?" She sat back in her chair, breathing hard.

"And now," Marcie finished, "I think I'm done with answering your questions."

52.

Mama. Mama had been on the news cussing her out, that's what the guard had said, gleefully. As if it would hurt Marcie somehow that she couldn't even rely on the support of her own blood. As it was, Marcie wasn't surprised. Mama was still no doubt pissed that Marcie—Savannah—had disappeared into the sunset with most of Jonny's injury payout and life insurance and never looked back. It hadn't even been that much money. There was no way she'd been going to share it with Mama and her latest deadbeat boyfriend. That money had been her way out after all the crap flung her way after Jonny's death. *A cheap drunk whore, sleeping around as her crippled husband struggled to cope. Left him there to die alone in a stinking trailer, probably heartbroken. Always trouble, that Savannah Cassidy. Like mother, like daughter.*

Marcie scratched at her scalp. Her hair was greasy after a night of crying and raging and sweating against the scratchy pillowcase. How had she ended up in this position again?

She hadn't answered any more of Anderson's questions. Maybe that made her look guilty, but it seemed the detective was already convinced of that. She had too many questions of her own. Were Keisha and Jason still in custody too? Were the police playing a game of eenie, meenie to decide which of them to charge? What if they found the syringe in their house? Who would they blame then? Her or Jason? It would be her, of course. She was the trailer-trash murderess, even if she'd never been charged, and Jason was a proven thieving liar. Mud always stuck.

She was pacing the cell again, thinking of the yearbook and the tip-off about Jason, about who hated them enough to do all this, her head an exhausted mess of half-thoughts, when Anderson's sidekick, Washington, came and unlocked her cell.

"You're free to go." His drawl was deep and slow, a Mississippi-in-summer voice, and the words were so unexpected that she didn't move.

"What?"

"You're free to go," he repeated. "Come on. I'll take you to collect your things. We're finished at your house, so you can return home."

"You're not charging me?" She still hadn't moved, as if half-expecting the officer's words to be some kind of cruel joke.

"No plans to at the moment. So unless you want to start paying rent on this cell, I suggest you move."

"What's happened?" Marcie scurried after him. He took the stairs two at a time and her stiff legs struggled to keep up even as her heart soared. *Free to go.* "Have you charged someone?" *Jason or Keisha?*

"Not yet," he said. He pushed the door open and nodded at the woman behind the caged desk, who gave back her purse and cell phone, and then he led her out to the side entrance, ignoring her further questions.

"Marcie!"

She squinted in the sunlight at the call of her name. "Elizabeth?" Of all the people who might have turned up to take her home, Elizabeth was a surprise. Virginia maybe, after some gossip, or Iris out of kindness, but Elizabeth? No. "What are you doing here?" she asked.

"Turns out Ms. Glapion saved you.

"Thank you, Detective Washington," Elizabeth said. The large black man nodded in reply and gave a half-wave before turning back inside. "We should get in the car," Elizabeth said, opening the driver's-side door. "There are news people around the front."

"What did he mean, you saved me?" she asked. Elizabeth looked tired. This must have turned her world around too. Did she even have a job anymore? Probably not. The kind of assistance William was going to need was likely to be somewhat more specialized than Elizabeth could provide from now on. More bedpans than trips around the world.

"It was the coconut water," Elizabeth said as they pulled away.

"What about it?"

"I asked the police if all the cartons in the refrigerator had been injected with coolant or just the one William drank from that morning. Turns out they were all poisoned."

Marcie frowned. "How does that affect me?"

"Because it means you couldn't have done it." Elizabeth looked across at her. "At the party, you were in the corridor looking for Jason to say you wanted to go home when I found you and then we left. We spoke and then I drove you to your place. You couldn't have gone to the kitchen."

"It's been a long night, Elizabeth." Marcie's brain was still blank.

"The coconut water was fine then, because William went and got one as we were leaving. Remember? So whoever did it, it was *after* you left."

An image came back to Marcie. The last time she'd

seen William *normal* was as they drove away. He was in front of the house, and yes, he'd been drinking from a carton. Her heart thudded in relief.

"Anyway," Elizabeth continued. "Once Detective Anderson confirmed that, she wanted to make sure you couldn't have come back to the party without anyone knowing—which, given the masks and the number of people, was possible. But it turns out that your neighbors across the street had an attempted break-in a couple of weeks ago and installed security cameras. They don't catch your house, but between theirs and some on a property farther down the block they could see that you didn't go out again that night." She paused, navigating the streets while Marcie let it all sink in. "So whatever terrible things you may or may not have done in the past, Marcie or Savannah or whatever your name is, you didn't do this to William."

"Look Elizabeth . . ."

"It's not my business. I'm struggling hard enough to get my head around all of this as it is without getting caught up in things that happened in a different state to people I don't know."

"My first husband . . . ," Marcie started again. "I didn't . . ."

"I'm sorry I said anything. I'm very tired and upset. I'm sure you didn't do, well, *that* to your husband. The law decided you were innocent and I have no reason to believe any gossip to the contrary." She glanced over at Marcie. "But some people will. People who are fond of Jason. People who like to believe the worst of people for their own entertainment. Be prepared for that."

"I know, Elizabeth," Marcie said, as the tears came. "I've been here before."

53.

Once they'd parked, Elizabeth hugged Marcie as she let it all out, stroking her hair and muttering soothing words as she cried, and Elizabeth smelled good—no expensive perfumes, just clean and fresh and motherly. Mama had never smelled like that, and Marcie almost regretted when her tears dried up and there was an awkwardness between them again, the sort that came after a moment of intimacy between relative strangers. Elizabeth didn't take up the offer to come in for some coffee and by the time Marcie had gotten inside, her hard shell was locking into place and she was regretting the show of weakness.

It was strange to be back in the house knowing that probably only hours ago the police were still painstakingly going through all her things. She felt violated and dirty and headed straight to the shower. She was free. They didn't suspect her anymore. Even here, safe in her decadently large bathroom, it was hard to believe the sudden change.

She tried to keep hold of her relief, but it was overridden by other concerns. What was going to happen to her now? Even if they didn't charge Jason with William's murder, there was all the financial fallout. Had Jason gotten the money to repay what he'd stolen if his investments with Emmett paid out? What would that mean for her? Would she get to keep what money they had? This house would have to go, but it was probably mortgaged to the hilt anyway. What would she *do?*

It was an endless round of questions she had no answers for and when she finally got too hot to stay under the water and was fed up with worrying, she dried herself off and her grumbling stomach reminded her that she'd had no breakfast and it was now the middle of the afternoon.

There was very little in the fridge—there never was much and what there had been was out of date—and she couldn't face going to a restaurant alone, so she dressed in a pair of old jeans and a hoodie, dug out one of Jason's baseball caps, and put on some shades before heading to the store. Something from the sushi counter would do, and a whole cooked chicken and salad. A tub of ice cream and a bottle of wine. The rest could wait.

No one recognized her and although there was a large TV up on the wall beyond the checkouts, it wasn't showing the news, which was a relief. She had no desire to hear people tearing her and Jason apart. She'd been released, so maybe they'd ease up on her now. She wasn't holding her breath. Gossip quickly became gospel, as she'd learned in Boise, and between her past and Jason's present, they must be the talk of Savannah at the moment. Keisha, the outsider, was probably forgotten.

She waited while her items were bagged and then handed over her credit card, eager and ready to get back to the privacy of her own kitchen. The machine beeped—a little too long—and the checkout girl frowned. "Let me try again," she said. Once again there was a long beep. Marcie, flushing with embarrassment, muttered something about there being a mistake and pulled a second card from her wallet. That too failed.

"Do you have the cash?" the girl asked, studying Marcie with something close to pity. Marcie didn't. She never carried cash, not when she had Jason's credit cards. Did anyone carry cash anymore? The girl nodded her in the direction of the ATM where she tried again. With each card a message flashed up telling her to contact her bank. Her pulse throbbed in her ears as the truth dawned on her. The police must have frozen all Jason's assets while they investigated him.

She didn't return to the shame of the checkout, but instead left the store by the farthest door and rushed to her car. Surely they couldn't leave her like this? With nothing? She thought about calling Detective Anderson but decided against it. They'd only just let her go and, ridiculous as it was, she didn't want to draw any unnecessary attention to herself in case that made them change their minds. She had no choice. She was going to have to borrow some money to tide herself over until all this was sorted out. She took a deep breath, swallowed her pride, and then dialed Virginia—*let's see how far your Christian charity extends, shall we?*—as she drove, her whole body burning with shame. There was no answer. She tried again with Iris and it went straight to voice mail. Were they ignoring her? Virginia might be but that wasn't Iris's style. She was made of steel. She'd answer even if it was only to tell you she wasn't taking your call.

The club. That's where they'd be. The younger members may flout the rules of no cell phones in the clubhouse or on the course, only by the pool, but the old stalwarts were strict with themselves. Virginia's and Iris's phones would be switched off in their purses.

She felt a pang of jealousy that the four of them were no doubt having an early dinner, maybe after visiting William, observers of all the action, not participants, no stain from these events spreading to them. Her heart sank at the thought of walking into the club on her own, but she had no choice. She needed to see her friends—they were the only people likely to lend her any cash. Maybe it would be all right once she got inside and everyone saw that she was free and innocent; they might feel some pity for her.

"Ah." Catherine, as her name badge declared, one of the interchangeable women in black who took turns at the club reception desk, stared at the screen that was discreetly hidden behind the mahogany counter. "Can you wait here for a moment, Mrs. Maddox?"

"Is there a problem?" Marcie asked.

"Probably an error." Catherine kept hold of the sleek membership card between her perfectly manicured red fingernails as she glanced back at an older man working at his desk. "Sir?"

It was Ernesto, one of the day managers, and Marcie felt a flood of relief. She knew him well. He'd straighten this out. Ernesto didn't give her his usual smooth smile, however; he came around to the front of the desk before taking her to one side and keeping his voice low.

"I'm afraid your husband's membership has been suspended, Mrs. Maddox."

She stared at him, confused. Jason paid the extortionate fees annually so it couldn't have to do with the accounts being frozen. "I don't understand."

Ernesto coughed quietly behind his hand as if it were hard to get the words out before saying, "We have a policy regarding members who become involved in activities that may bring the club into disrepute. Until this current situation is . . . resolved . . . the committee has made the decision to suspend Mr. Maddox's membership. I hope you understand."

"As you can imagine, this is a very difficult time for me," she said. "But I have done nothing wrong and—"

"Sadly at this present time only men hold full memberships. Therefore, while your husband is suspended, your associate membership is not valid." He shrugged, as if it were all out of his hands.

Marcie bit her lip to stop herself from screaming obscenities she might regret at the aloof man and forced herself to smile. "I understand. But if you could ask Iris Cartwright or Virginia Habersham if they could come speak to me I'd be grateful."

"Of course, of course." Ernesto retreated behind the counter and picked up a phone.

"I'll wait out front," Marcie mumbled. So this was

it, she thought as she headed back out into the heat. She'd been ostracized already.

Both Iris *and* Virginia came, their expressions dropping as they took in her clothes, as if her scruffy look was the worst crime committed by their friendship set this week.

"Oh good lord, Marcie." Virginia clapped her hands together. "So it's true. They have let you go."

"I didn't do anything. I didn't know about anything."

"Oh, of course not, honey." Her words were a flurry of excitement. "I mean, it was quite a surprise to find out about your *first* husband—but I'm so shocked about Jason. I hear that's true. And now they think he could be responsible for *all* of it?"

"Let the girl breathe, Virginia. I told you to stay inside. Why don't you go back to the table, your shrimp will be getting cold." Virginia wasn't happy but she did as she was told. Iris waited until she'd gone. "That woman loves to *know* everything." She paused. "Would you like to come in, Marcie?"

"No." She shook her head, noting Iris's relief. The Cartwrights did not like gossip and scandal, and now they were surrounded by it. There would be no more Magnolia invites for Marcie. "I just need some . . . some help." Her eyes blurred again. "They've frozen our accounts. I couldn't pay for my groceries."

"Of course. Here, take this for now . . ." Iris rummaged in her purse and handed over $150. "Go home and let me speak to Noah. I'll come to your place in an hour or so with more."

"Thank you," Marcie said. "Thank you so much." Cash. Of course Iris carried cash and thank God for it. At least she could eat today.

Iris nodded and turned away. She wasn't filled with the sympathy she'd had for Marcie before she'd been arrested, but she wasn't icy and at least she was going to help.

Alone again, Marcie took a deep shaky breath and headed for her car. She was halfway across the lot when she heard laughter behind her. Several women had emerged, still in tennis skirts, unnecessary pastel sweaters tied around their shoulders, tanned faces Botox-smooth, looking like an ad for a Tybee Island resort.

She stared as one face looked her way. Dark hair and feline features. Their eyes met and the woman's smile grew broader. Victorious. And then the moment was gone, the woman's attention back on the gaggle of friends slipping into convertibles, no doubt heading for a cocktail somewhere on their way home.

Still, Marcie's whole body smarted.

Jacquie.

54.

Iris brought her five thousand dollars. It didn't seem very much at all, but Marcie accepted it gratefully as they stood in the vast entry hall of her mausoleum of a house.

"I'm sorry for the awkwardness at the club earlier," Iris said, her hands clasped in front of her. She was beautifully dressed, her hair swept up in a chignon. She and Noah, who was waiting in the car outside, obviously had dinner plans. Life moved on, despite William being hooked to machines and Jason and Keisha locked up. Marcie understood. Iris and Noah were smoothing out the wrinkles that had appeared in their perfect lives by continuing as normal.

"But in this town, dear," she continued, "murder is considered classier than embezzlement. Several of William's clients are club members. So, you can imagine." She looked around at the marble stairs and the expensive decor, no doubt mentally totting up the cost that came out of other people's money. "You won't remember this, but there was a lot of sympathy and help for Jason after his father got himself into trouble. This is not how people like to be repaid for their kindnesses. And sadly, although it's understandable why you would have liked to keep your past private, that has added another layer of deception that will take some time to forgive. But we have big hearts in this city, and Jason's sins aren't yours. Things will settle down."

Until things settled down, Marcie decided later, she was going to have to liquidate some assets. Once, five grand would have seemed like a fortune to her, but she was now capable of spending that during a half-hearted boutique browse. Maybe she'd have to get a job—a thought that filled her with dread, the ghost of the stench of diner fat rearing up in front of her, ready to sink into her skin.

She couldn't sleep. She'd lain awake staring at the ceiling in the dark, the sheets beneath her cool, no longer tangled and warm with passion from either Jason or Keisha. The bed was like an abandoned wasteland of love with only one survivor. A grave not yet filled.

When they'd bought the house, she'd loved its vastness, but now the size made her nervous. She found she was listening for unusual noises, afraid of any hint of an intruder somewhere inside. Someone was out there, someone who was determined to destroy Jason and Marcie and seemed prepared to kill to do so. Would they come here and try to kill her? Now that she was so alone?

She got up, going to the window and looking out at the street. The house opposite, the house that had saved her, was silent and the sidewalks were empty, as they always were after midnight. She half-expected to see Jacquie looking up at her. Everything had started going wrong when Jacquie resurfaced. Could Jacquie really be behind it all? If so, what did she want? Surely she wouldn't have gone as far as to poison William to get her revenge on Jason for being rejected? But then, history was littered with stories of the revenge of women scorned.

But Jacquie couldn't have poisoned William. How would she have known where to find the needles Eleanor had hidden away? Could someone have told her? But why? Too many unanswered questions and for now she had more immediate concerns. Her mind turned to money again, and she headed to her dressing room. They couldn't take her jewelry. Not if she'd sold it.

And the same went for Jason's cuff links and watches and some of her more expensive one-off dresses.

As she started stacking the tiny beautiful boxes that summed up their affair and a marriage's worth of gifts, she calmed down. Even if she sold it at cut-rate prices she'd have plenty left over after paying Iris back. She reached into the next drawer for her Versace scarves, suddenly feeling a sense of liberation. With Jason she thought she'd built herself a wall of protective wealth. What good had it done her? It hadn't been her money. Next time, when she married another rich man, she'd make sure she had bank accounts of her own and cash secreted away in case of emergencies. If anyone would marry her.

From Jason's drawers she took out his four watches—two of which had been gifts from her, albeit paid for by him, so she felt no qualms in selling those—and then piled up his cuff link collection—three pairs were diamond studded and none of the others were cheap.

When she was done she got back into bed and stared at the cool spare pillow—Jason's pillow—beside her. She thought of all the times in the early days that she'd lain beside Jason, breathless from sex, watching him sleep, just wanting to run her fingers down the firm muscles of his arms and chest. How obsessed she'd been with her handsome man. Then there was Keisha, dark skin against white sheets, who'd lain right here with her, warm flesh, hot wet mouth, a new ocean of sexuality to dive into.

Jason and Keisha. Keisha and Jason. One all masculinity, the other the opposite. Yin and yang. As the memories assailed her, echoes of sensation, she felt her body stir. Had Keisha killed William for *her* maybe? Marcie had kept telling her she wouldn't be poor again—was this Keisha's way of trying to secure both their futures so they could run away together with a fortune? Or maybe she had just been the scapegoat and Jason had poisoned William to free himself of his debts and save himself from prison? These two people she'd had sex with. Terrible people. The sheet brushed against her nipple and she shivered.

Jason and Keisha. Their wickedness began to drive her fantasy, the complete disregard for conformity, and then, as her hand slid down her own body, in her imagination all three of them were in the bed together, a twisting panting mess of limbs, each body eager for its own satisfaction.

Once she was done, gasping in delight as the orgasm ripped through her, she rolled over and finally fell asleep, and didn't wake up until nine the next morning, when Detective Anderson rang the doorbell.

55.

Marcie was pretty sure Kate Anderson didn't sleep. When she'd woken Marcie at nine, her skin was disgustingly fresh, even clear of makeup, and she had the energy of someone who'd been up for hours. Still, once she started speaking, Marcie woke up pretty fast herself. First, she told Marcie that they now had reason to believe the computer crash at the partnership had been caused by a remotely planted virus. She'd wanted to know how proficient Jason was at computer hacking or if he had any friends or connections who he might have turned to. All their usual leads for tech crime were staying unsurprisingly quiet. It had made Marcie laugh out loud. Jason? A hacker? No, that wasn't possible— his passwords were too easy to guess for him to be that IT savvy. She'd almost asked why on earth he'd want the crash, but then, as she started to wake up herself, the answer became obvious. To delay the audit. To buy himself time to put money back or at least make more mess to hide his crimes. No, even as she pleaded ignorance, Marcie knew that Jason might not have hacked the system himself, but that didn't mean he hadn't organized it. That day when he'd lied about where he was—had he been getting the virus removed?

Anderson's second blow was her suspicion that perhaps Jason and Keisha were in it together. Jason had been to London the previous year. He'd told William the best places to go. Perhaps this had all been a long and elaborate plan. Could he have known Keisha *before* she arrived in Savannah?

Marcie had played her usual distraught Southern wife until Anderson left, with the final bombshell that Jason had been charged with several counts of financial fraud and embezzlement and had a bail hearing due, but given that he was also being investigated for attempted murder, getting bail was unlikely.

As soon as she'd closed the front door, her head spinning, Marcie had burst into action. Jason still had influence. Therefore as his wife, so did she. And what was the point of being married to a lawyer if you didn't use your connections to pull a few strings? She needed to ask questions for herself. She needed to *know* for herself. Could Keisha and Jason be in it together?

And so now here she was, at the police station, about to have a visit with her husband, and then with Keisha, the weight of Savannah's legal power having forced Anderson's hand. Marcie wiped her palms on the thighs of her pants, suddenly nervous. *Tread carefully,* her eyes said to Jason as a guard let him into the room. *They'll all be listening.*

"I didn't do it. Poison William. You have to believe me." Jason's eyes were wide and scared, and Marcie thought he'd dropped some pounds as he sat down opposite her. Not even so much as a *How are you honey?* before going straight to his denials.

It was just the two of them in the interview room.

"Well, neither did I, but that didn't stop you from telling the police about the yearbook and Jonny."

"Someone told them that they thought I'd been embezzling money."

"What?" Marcie stared at him. "You thought that was *me?*"

He shrugged.

"God, Jason, whether you did it or not, it's wrecked my life. They've frozen the accounts. I've had to borrow money from Iris and I'm never going to be able to pay for the house. Not even one payment. Even if I'd *known* there was anything wrong"—she knew as well as he did not to admit to any wrongdoing in a visiting room—"why would I have told them?"

"Because you don't love me anymore."

It was another slap in the face, even if there was an element of truth in it. He sounded like a petulant boy. "Me not love you?" she snapped. "You're the one who's been salivating all over Keisha since she arrived." Marcie knew the best way to get the truth out of Jason was always to be aggressive. Put him on the back foot. "You know the police think that maybe you two are in it together? Tried to make me look guilty so you could run away into the sunset together. Maybe you met her in London when you were there."

"Jesus, Marcie." Jason leaned back in his chair. "She's a cheap money-grubber. I flirted with her to make *you* jealous. Nothing was good enough for you anymore. I could see you growing colder to me. I wanted our fire back! Our passion! When you got so testy about her it made me unhappy. Sure, it was an unhealthy way to get your attention, but it worked. Also, if I was going to conspire to murder someone—which I didn't—it wouldn't be with someone as flaky as her. You've seen what she's like!"

"But what about the money?"

"That wasn't me. It's all a misunderstanding." He

stared at her, a reminder, as if she needed one, that there was no way he was going down without a fight or at least a plea deal.

"But what if it was you? That's what the police think. If William found out and reported it, you'd be sent to jail for God knows how many years. Were you just going to sit back and let him? I can't see that." She sighed. "But neither can I get my head around the idea of you trying to kill him."

"Even if it *was* true—which it's not—William would never have gotten the police involved, don't you see that?" Jason leaned forward, taking one of her hands and gripping it tight. "He wouldn't let the company get damaged like that. He'd have made me resign, claim some ill health or something, but he would never have let what I'd done come to light. It would have wrecked the partnership and ruined his reputation. People would have thought he was a fool. He was already feeling stupid for marrying Keisha so quickly. He would never have allowed me to make a fool of him publicly as well. Yes, we'd probably have had to sell and move, but we wouldn't be poor and it wouldn't have been worth killing him over. Someone trying to kill him has actually made my potential situation worse. You have to believe me, Marcie." He stared hard at her. "You *know* me."

He was right. She *did* know him, and odious as he could be, he was right. He'd have taken his chances with William's wrath rather than kill him and face a possible death sentence. That was too *real* for Jason.

Whereas Jason had been immediately on the defensive, Keisha was the opposite. Even now, when she'd been locked up for nearly the maximum four days and was more than likely about to be charged with attempted murder rather than released, her first words were concern for Marcie.

"Are you okay?" she said, as she took Marcie's hand. "I've been worried about you. About Jason being charged with all that money stuff. What will you do?"

"Survive, I guess. What else can I do?" It was strange being here with her again. Beautiful Keisha, a blend of such fragility and strength, who still, if her racing heart was to be believed, held a tight grip on her. "I'm so sorry I snapped at you at the party. Jason had just gotten my high school yearbook. I guess your attorney told you about that?"

Keisha nodded. "He told me. It's so weird. Billy got an envelope that night too. It was a photo. From that voodoo rave thing we went to. The first time we . . . well, you know what we did. In the picture I was asleep on the grass and I only had my knickers on. Don't look so worried, you weren't in it. Your arm is but that's it. No one would know you were pretty much naked beside me."

Marcie flinched at what Keisha was revealing but if perky Kate Anderson quizzed her on it, they'd danced at a party and gotten a little wild. So what? What was more important was that someone *had* been watching them. Taking photos.

"William lost his shit," Keisha continued. "The final straw for me with him I think. But what's so odd . . ." She leaned forward and Marcie thought that even here, her breath was sweet and warm and fresh, and she wanted to dip her tongue into that mouth.

"What's so odd," Keisha continued, "is that the police haven't mentioned it. It's gone. Someone must have taken it that night. But who?"

"Zelda? You thought you saw her."

"Yeah, but she would have left it so the police would find it. And she wouldn't do anything to William."

"Maybe William destroyed it?"

"He wouldn't have done that. It was evidence against me. That I was a bad wife."

Marcie half-smiled, once again irreverent in Keisha's company. "To be fair, you weren't a great one."

"I know I wasn't. But I didn't hurt him. Honestly. They think I did the conjure ball and the juju dolls myself, but I didn't. I know I wished him dead, I know, but I didn't *do* it." Her eyes welled up. "It's all so confused in my head. It's dark magic, I know it is. I kept seeing that old woman with the orange hair. She's something to do with all this. Her and Zelda together maybe. Remember when we first saw her in the square? She called us *ghosts*." She shivered. "I'm so tired of ghosts. I think she knew I was cursed. From the boy. Could sense it maybe. Maybe I've tainted you all with it."

Seeing how Keisha was drifting, Marcie switched topics. She didn't give a shit about juju dolls, whatever they were. "That day you came around and I gave you the Xanax. Where did you go after that? William came to the house looking for you."

"I went out to that place where the party was," Keisha said. "The Truman Parkway. I figured I could score something down there to keep me going. The stuff you gave me wasn't touching the sides and I knew I needed more. I did manage to buy a few pills, Oxy supposedly, but it didn't really work. I should have taken the scrip you offered."

When Jason had gripped Marcie's hand, it was as if he were a drowning man determined to be saved or to make her drown too. With Keisha there was just warmth in it. Care. Love maybe. For all her tears and craziness, Keisha was tougher than Jason. She squeezed her hand back. If Keisha had been scoring drugs that day then she hadn't spent it with Jason.

"God, no wonder they think I'm guilty," Keisha finished. "I'm such a mess."

"Anderson seems to believe maybe you and Jason did it together. Maybe you knew each other in London before you came here."

"I know." Keisha half-laughed. "How ridiculous. Like I could ever fall in love with Jason." Her face dropped back into sadness. "I'm in love with you." Despite everything, the words made Marcie's heart soar.

Her spirits were still lifted when she saw Anderson and Washington waiting for her in the corridor. Kate Anderson was still riled at being coerced into allowing Marcie to visit, but there was also an amused glint in her eyes.

"So you *were* getting naked with the second Mrs. Radford. Now that would be quite the Savannah scandal, don't you think? Your fancy legal connections might not have been so keen to do you any favors if they knew about that."

"We took off a few clothes while dancing," Marcie said, not pausing as she walked past them. "It's nothing."

"The first time we . . . well, you know what we did.

Sounds pretty straightforward to me. How about to you, Washington?"

The big man grinned. "I'd watch the movie."

"You're disgusting." Marcie couldn't wait to get out of the station.

"Hey, not me." Anderson held her hands up. "I'm a sucker for a beautiful woman and she's a beautiful woman. I can see why you would."

A dyke, Marcie thought. *Of course she is.* No doubt thinking Marcie was just a straight bored housewife wondering what it was like to act like a lesbian.

"So," Kate Anderson said, as she held open the door, the sunlight making Marcie flinch, "it seems to me you had plenty to gain by William Radford's death. A lover who'd be a rich widow or getting your thieving husband off the hook and keeping your life of luxury."

"But I wasn't there, was I?" Marcie said, her tone like sharp lemons on teeth. "I couldn't have poisoned him."

Anderson said nothing but raised an eyebrow as if to suggest that this wasn't over yet.

"Have a good day, Mrs. Maddox," Washington said.

"Screw you," Marcie muttered under her breath in reply. "Screw both of you."

56.

In Keisha's dream, she was a marionette. She danced and danced, endlessly, her arms and legs pulled this way and that by wires that grew directly out of her skin. She was on a podium under a spotlight in a circus tent, and as she cried out to stop, exhaustion overwhelming her, the audience clapped and called out for more.

Uncle Yahuba, the ringmaster, cracked his whip, and overhead in the vast darkness her strings were pulled harder, the movement threatening to tear her flesh. A face lunged out of the crowd—Billy—laughing and applauding, cut wires dangling from his wrists. "Bravo! Bravo!" he called out. Beside him Auntie Ayo was on her feet, her whole body shaking as she yelped her delight. But they weren't cheering for Keisha. Their shining eyes were turned upward. To whoever was making her dance.

She woke in a sweat, her heart racing, scratching at her arms to free herself, crying out for Marcie. She still hadn't shaken the dregs of the dream away properly when her attorney arrived and told her the English police were flying an officer over. They had some questions of their own to ask.

When she got back to her cell, she scratched at her arms until they were nearly raw, and yet still she was sure she could feel wires tugging at her skin.

57.

Marcie had barely slept all night, a knot of fear in her stomach, her mind going over everything with a fine-tooth comb. Poor Jason, now charged and locked up and likely to stay that way until he was old. It made her feel strange, and despite her anger with him and her lust for Keisha, she had an awful ache of grief inside for him. So handsome. So charming. So youthful still. All that would be gone by the time he next saw freedom, if Anderson had her way. Love didn't end overnight, she was realizing. She was still grieving for her marriage, for the man she'd fallen in love with, even if he wasn't that person anymore. Maybe he never had been and she was mourning someone she'd invented.

She hadn't poisoned William and she hadn't embezzled any money, so that should have left her calm, but she wasn't so sure that innocence was a guarantee of safety in this investigation. What if neither Keisha nor Jason had tried to kill William? Keisha *wasn't* that calculating and Jason might be a lying thief but he wasn't brave. This kind of murder required an element of bravery. And she figured he was right that William wouldn't have wanted the scandal if he'd found out what Jason was up to. They'd both been so earnest when they'd spoken to her. No eyes sliding to one side, hiding truths. She'd bet money—if she had any—that they were telling the truth. But if she wasn't guilty and *they* weren't guilty, then who was?

She came out of her final jewelry stop—the diamond specialist—and as she tucked the envelope of cash in with the rest she'd gathered over the morning, the same name flashed in neon over and over in her head. *Jacquie.* It could only be Jacquie. The divorce had been bitter and now she wanted her revenge on Jason and Marcie for what they'd done.

In the car, she counted out five thousand dollars from her healthy bundle of bills and wrapped a band around it to take to Iris at the hospital before starting to reverse the car out of the tight space. She frowned as she looked in the rearview mirror. Something was stuck under the wiper on the back window. Irritated, she pulled the car level and got out to see what it was.

When she got close and realized what was trapped under the plastic, her skin crawled with horror. A coarsely made juju doll. She pulled it free, despite her revulsion, the fabric familiar under her fingertips— silk—a red slash of a mouth stitched in. Was this meant to be *her*?

She looked frantically around the parking lot for anyone familiar who might have left it, but all she saw were strangers going about their business, paying her no attention at all. Suddenly vulnerable, she scrambled back into the car and threw the doll onto the floor by the passenger seat, before locking the doors and turning the air-conditioning up high so the cool air would calm her down. She grabbed her cell to call Detective Anderson and then stopped. They'd probably think she made it herself to cast suspicion away from Jason or Keisha. She needed more than just this doll before she faced the police again.

Jacquie, Jacquie, Jacquie. The name rang like a death knell in her head. Jacquie had Creole roots, isn't that what Iris had said? Did Jacquie believe in all this shit too? William and Keisha had dolls made in their likenesses and now William was half-dead and Keisha was locked up. Marcie didn't believe in the magic but she did believe in the symbolism. That there was a *message* being sent in this doll. Was it a threat? A warning? What fate did the doll maker have in store for Marcie? Death or prison or what? And if this doll was telling her anything it was that the clock was ticking. She needed evidence against Jacquie. And fast.

Marcie raced through the hospital so fast she was breathless by the time she reached William's room.

Elizabeth was in what Marcie was coming to think of as her "vigil chair," a carpetbag on the floor beside her, *Moby-Dick* resting on top of a sweater and whatever else, perhaps toiletries, she'd brought with her. Emmett was standing behind her, one hand on Elizabeth's shoulder, a gesture of support, as they both watched the shell of a man in the bed. Emmett immediately began babbling some apology for not telling Marcie about Jason's investments, presuming that she'd known—which she didn't believe for a second, he just hadn't cared in that boys' club way—and she wanted to change the subject and save them both the embarrassment.

"Isn't Virginia with you?" she asked. It was odd seeing William still the center of attention but so passive. What conversations had they had around him? Could he hear them talking as if he weren't there or were dead already, or discussing the twenty-four-hour care he was going to need even if they did ever let him out of here? How awful that must be. Did William even like *Moby-Dick*? She tried to imagine Elizabeth attempting to do characters' voices and reading loudly when maybe all William wanted to do was rage at her to shut up and leave him in peace to sleep. But maybe not. Maybe he cherished every word of company. He should, she thought. People moved on. If he didn't die quickly he'd be spending a lot of time alone in the dark with his thoughts.

"She was here earlier," Emmett said. "She's at the church helping prepare for tomorrow's special service to pray for William's recovery." He looked back at the body in the bed, instilling his nasally voice with false good cheer. "A lot of people will be sending prayers to the big guy on your behalf in the morning, buddy. I fully expect you to be up and tap-dancing by lunchtime."

Buddy. How William would hate the lack of respect wrapped up in that word, and she couldn't imagine Emmett's ever having used that mildly patronizing tone around William when he was his normal self. But then William's power was gone now. Washed away. He'd been reduced to something less than a child. He would never be William as they knew him again, and whatever he was hearing or thinking there was nothing he could do about it anymore. It was a horrific thought and she couldn't bear to stay in the room. "I was hoping to find Iris here. I needed to see her."

"She's getting us coffee. Just down the hall," Elizabeth said. "In the family room."

"Thank you."

Marcie hadn't realized she'd been breathing shallowly until she was scurrying back around the corner near the reception desk, as if what was wrong with William was infectious, and she sucked in three deep breaths before going to join Iris, who looked up as she poured cream into china mugs. "Oh, Marcie. I didn't realize you were coming in today."

The coffee smelled strong and rich. Nothing about this place was cheap. "I called your house earlier and Noah said you'd be here," Marcie said. She pulled out the bundle of cash from her purse and held it out. "Your money back. Thank you so much for lending it to me."

"That was quick. Are you sure you don't need it?" Iris looked surprised, as if she'd never expected to see her cash again.

"I sold a few pieces of jewelry. I'm okay for now." Marcie smiled, as sweetly as she could muster. "But it was so lovely of you to help out. I know it can't be easy after what Jason has done. I feel awful."

Iris softened and squeezed her hand. "You haven't done anything, Marcie. And you really didn't have to sell anything to get me that money back. No one is judging you for what Jason has done."

Marcie thought the sentiment was sweet but found it hard to believe, especially with her own past now in the mix.

"Why don't you give me a hand with these cups," Iris continued. "My arthritis is playing up and if I'm honest, I don't trust myself to carry them all without causing an accident."

Marcie took two coffees in one hand and went to hold open the door. "I saw Jacquie's name in the visitors' register," she said casually, as Iris led the way into the hall. "It was nice of her to come see William. I didn't think they were close. I've not heard him mention her much."

"They weren't overly close, no. Jacquie was more Eleanor's friend. You know how it is, the boys play golf and the girls play tennis. But she would come down from Atlanta when Eleanor was sick. Especially toward the end. They would sit and play cards. Have dinner. She'd stay over in a guest bedroom, perhaps catch lunch with Virginia and Emmett and then head home. Toward the end, when Eleanor was sleeping most of the time and a lot of people began to stay away, she'd just sit in the quiet with her. It was a kindness. Especially in those last few weeks when Jacquie had the passing of her own husband to cope with. She can be very sweet sometimes."

So Jacquie *had* been in the house a lot when Eleanor was sick. It felt odd that no one had mentioned it—had Jason known at the time? Had William told him? Had they all kept it a secret from Marcie because they thought she'd make a fuss? To be fair, they would have had a point. Even though she'd won Jason, Marcie still felt strangely jealous of Jacquie, so hearing that her rival was visiting from Atlanta and behaving like a modern-day Florence Nightingale wouldn't have gone down a storm. Right now, though, that didn't matter. What *did* matter was that if Jacquie had spent time with Eleanor in those final weeks, then she very definitely could have known about the needles and syringes with the vial of morphine. Jacquie *could* have poisoned William's coconut water herself.

She'd also met up for lunch with Virginia and Emmett—something they'd never mentioned either—so Jacquie could potentially have known about Jason's investments and thought they were suspicious. Doors were opening in Marcie's mind and behind each one she saw her husband's first wife.

58.

Marcie felt the shift in atmosphere as she walked into the church, but even amid the quiet gasps the roof didn't cave in, and after a flurry of whispers and sideways glances, the natural politeness of the congregation settled back down to the odd word murmured behind hands. Marcie didn't care. She hadn't come to get anyone's approval or even to pray for William's return to full health. She was here for information.

Many of the guests who'd been at the party were likely to be here and no doubt Virginia, down at the front, was taking a mental roll call that all the right people had shown their faces. Marcie didn't listen much to the sermon, only occasionally fighting a smirk or a smile at some glowing recommendation of William's character, his kindness, his sweetness. No mention of his entitlement and bombastic behavior. Making Eleanor hide her grief at the loss of their only son. Marrying a much younger woman when his wife was barely cool in the ground and then trying to break her, and the way he'd always kept Jason dangling on a promise of elevation to the point that Jason resorted to theft to make it happen. Having Elizabeth at his beck and call every minute of the day. Not exactly a saint. Still, whatever he was, William probably hadn't deserved this fate of hanging in limbo between life and death, but then most people didn't deserve what life threw at them, good or bad.

The church was standing room only but over the hour of gushing words, Marcie had plenty of time to study the congregation. There were the true churchgoers, all in the front rows with Virginia and Emmett, eyes shining and singing loud as they cast their good wishes heavenward. Everyone else simply whined out the hymns under their breath, unsure of the melodies, while making token nods to the prayers. Marcie almost envied that inner circle. The power of their religion. The solidarity it gave them with their fellow believers, to automatically *belong* somewhere. The sense of community, of invisible bonds. She'd seen it with the women who helped at the Mission. United by worship and the need to serve their God in all they did, to help each other. It was anathema to Marcie. She figured religion had to get you when you were young, before cynicism set in. With her upbringing, if Mama's efforts at dragging her through childhood could be called that, cynicism had set in way before Marcie could even spell the word.

Once she'd spotted her, it was hard not to just stare at Jacquie. The brunette, hair in an elegant bun, was standing over to the right, about halfway back, *not* part of that religious inner circle. Jacquie and her bitterness. Jacquie and her revenge. *Jacquie the crazy bitch.* She hadn't glanced back, but she wasn't fooling Marcie. She knew Marcie was there. Jacquie might think she was playing with Marcie, but Marcie was on to her now.

After seeing Iris the previous day, Marcie had gone home and called her old high school, asking the secretary if they kept copies of past yearbooks. They'd put her through to the librarian, who'd laughed, surprised, when she'd said she was interested in spare copies of the 2004 edition. Apparently a woman emailed a while back asking for the same. She remembered because she never got requests for that far back, not often. People move on, don't they? Marcie's stomach had been in her throat when she'd asked if the librarian had a copy of the email, but she hadn't. The woman must have come and collected one though, because there was one fewer than there had been in the storage room. She must have come in, maybe during the vacation when there were only office staff in. The librarian promised to ask her colleagues, but wasn't sure she'd get an answer. It was several months ago and in high schools everything was always such a blur wasn't it? All that youth racing around.

Once she'd gotten rid of the wittering woman, Marcie had almost called Anderson right away to share her theories but stopped herself. She needed more.

"Hey!" she called out, as the doors opened and the crowd spilled free. "Julian!" The party planners were hurrying off toward their car, heads down and faces like thunder. "Julian! Pierre! Wait!"

Pierre stopped, peering over his sunglasses, and waited for her to catch up. "Well," he said. "I didn't expect to see you here."

"I thought I should show my face," she said. "I don't want people thinking I'm hiding. Do you want to get some brunch? My treat. I'm not going to lie, I'm in need of friends." She might be deep in the shit long term, but for now she was cash rich. "And obviously"—she winked irreverently at Pierre, knowing how to play him—"I have *all* the gossip."

"Alessi's," Pierre said, after a moment. "I could murder one of their martinis."

"Let's steer clear of the M word, shall we?"

"Deal. As long as you tell us everything about what it's like in the real world of *Orange Is the New Black*."

"Oh, you're funny," Marcie said

"Come on," Julian said, unsmiling. "Let's get out of here."

She didn't wait for a showdown with Jacquie or to chat with Virginia or Iris or any of the women who kept glancing her way as if she were radioactive, but got in her car and followed the boys out of the lot. If anyone knew about people's movements that night, it would be these two. For all their flamboyance, they were professionals and would have been sober and observant all night.

The martinis were already on the table when she slid in to join them at the booth.

"You said *she'd* be there," Julian was saying. "What a waste of a morning. You know I can't stand churches. They hate us in there."

"That's not true. They all love us. And hate is a strong word. They're confused by the gays they *don't* know. Which means they probably don't hate them at all."

"You thought who'd be there?" Marcie said.

"Elizabeth," Julian said. "We're still owed a lot of money from the fiasco of a party. The balance."

"Although to be fair," Pierre added, "the scandal

has got *everyone* trying to book us. Who would have thought attempted murder would be so profitable?"

"Elizabeth seems to have set up camp at the hospital," Marcie said. "Like a loyal dog dying with its master." She smirked. Julian and Pierre—well, mainly Pierre—unleashed the bitch in her. "But I guess you may have to wait awhile until things have settled down. I have no idea who can access William's money at the moment, if anyone can. Must be a bit of a mess." *I sure can't access mine,* she wanted to add. "Are you guys broke?"

"Oh, hell no." Pierre looked aghast. "Don't even say that word."

"That's not the point." Julian drank half his martini in one swallow. "I didn't want to do another of William's parties in the first place. Not for a second wife, however nice she might be. He always made us feel second rate and like we owed him."

Pierre leaned across the table. "In case you missed it, here's the recap. Eleanor *gave* us some money when we were starting out because she loved Julian. He was her link to Lyle."

"And William hated that," Julian cut in. "But he could never say anything about it, because then he'd have to face the truth all over again."

Marcie frowned, puzzled. "What are you talking about?"

"Lyle of course," Pierre said. "He was *gay*. He was Julian's first love. Why do you think he joined the army? To try to impress his daddy. To be a *man* in his eyes."

"Eleanor didn't want him to go. She knew he was only joining because William was so ashamed and disappointed in him and he wanted his father's approval again."

"And as if there are no gays in the army." Pierre rolled his eyes. "I mean seriously. They all work out, and they all wear uniforms. The army is basically the goddamn Village People."

Marcie sat, stunned.

"Eleanor didn't care about his sexuality, she just wanted him to be happy. But William—as we all know—isn't someone to be argued with."

"So Lyle went off to the army to make his daddy proud, and then he died and the heartbreak very nearly killed Eleanor."

"Just because William couldn't stand the thought of a gay son."

"Wow." It was all Marcie could muster. So much family history she didn't know from back when the ghosts were breathing.

"And you wondered why I have no real desire to organize parties for William Radford the Fourth," Julian said.

Parties. This was her in.

"Well, I don't think you have to worry about organizing another one for him, do you?" She smiled, trying to lighten the mood. "I left early. Thankfully for my freedom as it transpires."

"You little two-name jailbird."

"You're so funny. But thank God for that headache. Although I almost came back when I saw Jacquie turning up as I left. I thought she might be making a play for Jason, now that she's a widow. Stupid, I know. And actually, given everything that's happened since, I should let her have him."

"Straight men are such dogs," Pierre said. "But you shouldn't have worried about that. I saw them briefly talking but he didn't look very pleased about it."

"And I saw her later," Julian said. "Mask off and face like thunder. She'd gone upstairs. Said the bathrooms were all in use downstairs, although I'm not sure they were. Plus, we'd arranged those rather gorgeous temporary restrooms outside that looked like safari yurts, across the garden from the catering truck."

She'd gone upstairs. Had she been in Eleanor's bedroom stealing a needle? Then done what needed to be done?

"Now, let's get back to the important stuff," Pierre said, ignoring the brunch menu but waving the waiter over for another round of martinis. "We need to know *all* about this first husband of yours and what happened there. You're like a phoenix"—his grin was razor sharp as he waved his hands dramatically skyward—"risen from death in a trailer park to these dizzying heights."

And it was a long way to fall back down again, Marcie thought, as she resigned herself to another hour or so of grilling. But at least she'd found out what she needed. And no more martinis if she was going to speak to Detective Anderson this afternoon.

"**Can you** get her to call me?" Marcie said into the hands-free as she put the car into drive. "Marcie Maddox. It's urgent. I have some information on the attempted murder of William Radford." Kate Anderson was out at the airport apparently but would be back in thirty minutes. Marcie hung up. Maybe that wasn't so bad. It would give her time to get home and make coffee before presenting her case. Despite her resolve to not drink more, brunch had been entirely liquid, and the heavy storm clouds gathering overhead weren't helping shake the two martinis away, but her adrenaline was firing her onward as she mentally listed all the evidence—circumstantial though much of it was—she had against Jacquie.

Jacquie had been ridiculously bitter all through the

divorce. She didn't like William and had visited Eleanor plenty when she was sick so could easily have known about the needles and syringes in her drawer. She'd wanted Jason back and he rejected her. A woman had emailed and asked for a copy of her old high school yearbook. That could have been her. If Jacquie had been following Marcie, she could easily have taken the photo that Keisha said William received the night of the party. But what for? Maybe to make him pissed and snappy at people. Cause him to argue with Jason and make him look guilty? She knew Emmett and Virginia and could have known about Jason's heavy investments and guessed at money problems. Finally, Jacquie had been upstairs on the night of the party to go to the bathroom and could have taken the syringe then before poisoning the coconut waters.

Marcie sat back in the seat, her heart racing. There was definitely a case there. Jacquie hated Jason and Marcie, everyone knew that. Hell hath no fury like a woman scorned. If they arrested her would they let Jason and Keisha go? Would Jason get bail? Maybe they'd wonder if *Jacquie* and Jason were in it together. Her stomach tangled in knots at the thought of both her lovers being freed. Who did she want to see the most? Jason was a lying bastard, but he was her husband and maybe there was a way they could wriggle out of this financial mess if he wasn't under suspicion of murder—maybe she at least could keep this life while he did whatever time they gave him. Perhaps the status quo could be maintained.

But what about Keisha? She was wild and unbalanced but she did something to Marcie's insides. She made Marcie crazy in the way Jason used to, but could she stand the scandal of *coming out* with Keisha and starting again somewhere? Did she really want to live the kind of life Keisha would now she was in her mid-thirties?

She was still turning over her limited options when a flash of umber on the sidewalk ahead distracted her. She stared as she drove by. The tall old black woman, cane in hand, was shuffling along the street around the corner from Alessi's. Marcie had passed her in a nanosecond but she was sure, when she looked in the rearview mirror, that as her car drove by, the old woman had paused and beaten the ground with her stick three times, her head thrown back in laughter. Was this another of Jacquie's games? Was she trying to send Marcie as mad as she'd driven Keisha with all this voodoo stuff so that when the police finally came for Marcie—which she was pretty sure was the plan—she wouldn't be thinking clearly?

Not me, Marcie thought.

I'm ahead of you, Jacquie. You won't beat me.

59.

"Jacquie?" Marcie almost dropped the champagne glass she was holding. She'd still been a little squiffy from the martinis, but the phone call with Detective Anderson had gone so well, she was sure she had something to celebrate. But now, with Jason's ex-wife standing on her doorstep, she realized she'd been premature.

"You thought I set up Jason because I wanted him back and he rejected me?" Jacquie rested one hand on her hip, exasperated. "Jesus. Not in a million years. You'd better let me in." She nodded at Marcie's glass. "And we're going to need something stronger than that for what I have to tell you."

Marcie didn't move. "Detective Anderson told you about our call? After everything you've done?"

"I haven't *done* anything, Marcie, except up front

tell her to look at Jason's finances—but not because I wanted him back. Trust me, I'm not your enemy. Now let me in. We don't want to do this on your doorstep."

Marcie stepped aside, nodding Jacquie through to the kitchen while noting how effortlessly elegant she looked, even in jeans and a sweater. Born to this life. Marcie felt dowdy beside her, even though she had a ten-year youth advantage over Jason's first wife. Marcie couldn't help it. She hated her. And Jacquie had been the tip-off about Jason. What else had she done?

"So what is it you've got to tell me?" Marcie poured her rival a glass of champagne, ignoring the earlier request for something stronger. She didn't want Jacquie in the house any longer than she had to be. It had to be Jacquie behind all this. It *had* to be.

"Let me ask you something." Jacquie perched on a stool at the kitchen island and studied Marcie, thoughtful and cool as a cucumber. "When you found out he was stealing from client accounts did he say he'd done it for you? He was trying to keep you in love with him? Trying to give you everything you wanted?"

Marcie opened and closed her mouth as she looked for words of denial that she couldn't find. "How do you know that?" The world was spinning again, turning events once again on their head. She knew the answer before Jacquie spoke. *Because he'd said it before.*

"How do you think I know? He used all that bullshit on me. A long time ago." Jacquie sipped her champagne. "When I was young and stupid and should have seen through it." She shook her head, annoyed at her younger self.

"When I came back for Eleanor's funeral, she was buried in those beautiful South Sea pearls of hers. Elizabeth told me how she'd gotten so confused she'd lost them and then Jason found them somewhere. That was the first warning light in my head—hugely expensive pearls going missing around my darling ex-husband. I *know* Jason. He probably stole them on a whim and then realized he wouldn't be able to sell them in town so put them back. When I heard about this big new house and his plans for buying William out, and Emmett told me he'd been making some high-risk investments, I knew it. I knew he was doing it all over again."

"Doing what?" Marcie pulled up a stool of her own. *What now?*

"Everyone in town is saying *like father, like son* about what Jason's done. Bet you've even thought it."

Marcie couldn't argue that, so she stayed quiet.

"But it's not like his father at all. Michael Maddox was a good man. A kind man." She smiled wryly. "The kind of man William might have called weak. He certainly called him weak in the aftermath. When he wasn't around to defend himself."

"But Michael stole money from his client accounts," Marcie said. "Jason told me all about it. He was going to prison," she insisted. "And so he killed himself."

"Michael didn't steal anything." Jacquie looked up. "Jason did."

"But he couldn't have—he didn't—" Marcie couldn't process it. It couldn't be true. *Could it?* "Jason's always so upset when he talks about his father's death. The loss. How he had to build himself back up and get everyone's respect again."

Jacquie shook her head. "Jason was the only child. The *golden* child. Michael blamed himself for spoiling him, for the whole County Day lifestyle that can be great for those kids with drive, but for the few like Jason who are mainly arrogance and no substance, it can make them greedy. Jason was greedy, but it wasn't Michael's fault. It was just his nature."

"So why . . . I mean, he *killed* himself. Surely he wouldn't have done that if he wasn't guilty?"

"He took the blame for Jason. His wife moved back to Jacksonville and wanted nothing to do with him. She died in a car crash shortly after. Drunk at the wheel. Her family said it was the shame of it all. Michael was alone and I think when he realized the enormity of what was going to happen to him, he couldn't face the jail time and wasn't sure he could maintain his story without buckling and telling the truth. Or getting caught out in lies and accidentally revealing his innocence. I think he came to believe that suicide was the only way to really protect Jason."

"Oh God," Marcie said.

"It gets worse," Jacquie said. "Jason knew he was going to do it. He *told* me his father was talking about it. The day he hanged himself? He rang Jason, drunk, to say he loved him and would always protect him. It was a goodbye phone call. I knew it. Jason knew it. I told him to go around right away, to make sure his dad was okay, but he didn't. He finished his coffee. Let another half an hour go by before he went. I think on some level he was *happy* his dad had taken his own life. He didn't have to worry anymore."

The creaking rope. Moments too late.

"And nobody suspected Jason at all?" Could this still be part of some twisted plan of Jacquie's? Marcie wanted to cling to that idea, but somewhere inside everything she said felt true. The dead look on Jason's face sometimes. The way he lied so smoothly. *Sociopath* sprang to mind. She felt a sudden, mildly hysterical urge to laugh.

"Eleanor maybe. She'd known Michael since they were young and she liked his gentleness. I don't think she ever trusted Jason after Michael's suicide. Eleanor was perceptive. Maybe Michael had even said something to her about it. They had been close. I think she saw Jason's relief when his father died. It stank of guilt." She looked up at Marcie, suddenly seeming a lot younger than her years. Vulnerable. "I told you we were going to need something stronger."

"And you knew all this? And never told anyone?"

"I thought I could get past it. I couldn't. Why do you think I was so bitter during the divorce? I'd carried this shit around with me for years. So much guilt. He didn't feel it at all. He sailed through life while I couldn't ever sleep, trying to run away from it all at night gyms. So yeah, when he decided to trade me in for you I was angry. I wasn't jealous—I didn't love him anymore—but I hated that he thought he could end it so easily, as if what I knew didn't matter. And I guess it didn't, because I never told anyone. I was too scared of implicating myself. But now"—she smiled, momentarily joyful—"he was arrogant enough to do it again and now he's going to get his comeuppance. He's finally going to pay in some way for what happened to Michael."

"So you had nothing to do with what happened to William?" Marcie was still struggling to get her head around the wider picture.

"God no!" Jacquie said. "I mean, I didn't like William very much and Eleanor deserved better, but then don't most women? I had already been planning to talk to the police, or at least William, about my suspicions that Jason might be stealing, but then when William was poisoned I obviously suspected Jason of that too. That's why I went to the hospital. To fish for information. That's where I heard there'd been some tension and then I knew I had to say something."

Marcie had to admit that after hearing all this, she'd suspect him too if she hadn't spoken to him face-to-face. Sociopathic liar or not, she still thought he'd told her the truth. "I don't think he poisoned William," Marcie said.

"I don't actually care," Jacquie countered. "I'd still be happy for him to go to jail for it. Karma and comeuppance and all that shit. But I'll settle for the embezzlement charges. Who knows, maybe they'll look back at what happened with Michael and reinvestigate."

The ghosts will always come for you. Marcie was learning that. "So you didn't send the yearbook to Jason?"

"Your crazy past? No." Jacquie smiled. "I never liked you much, but you also didn't interest me enough to want to *know* about you. My hate was directed at Jason. Have you considered that maybe he sent that to himself? To keep you quiet? Or to keep you as a backup plan? If the police started suspecting him, he could throw your past at them, they'd see the coincidences in the deaths, and then no death penalty for Jason?"

"That would only work if he was guilty," Marcie said. "And, as I said, I don't think he is."

"And my jury is still out on that one."

They finished their champagne in silence.

"Why did you come back?" Marcie asked, as she finally led Jacquie back to the front door.

"I was alone again and I have good friends here. Good people. Coming up when Eleanor was sick reminded me of that. I'd gotten so caught up in hating Jason I'd forgotten that most people weren't like that. Most people in this town were more like Michael and Eleanor. Kind. Sweet. Caring." She stepped out into the humid gray afternoon. Overhead the heavy blanket of cloud was turning black but the air was oven roasting. "And of course I wanted to haunt Jason. To wait for him to slip up in some way. Watch him. Find some way to pass his guilt back to him and maybe get a good night's sleep again."

"I guess that worked," Marcie said as Jacquie headed back to her car.

"Hey," she called out after the woman she'd so long considered an enemy and now didn't know quite how to feel about. "One more thing."

Jacquie turned. "What?"

"Who do you know in Savannah who's into voodoo maybe? Something like that?"

Jacquie laughed. "We're in the South, Marcie. Most people have some belief in it. Why do you ask?"

"It's probably nothing." She wasn't going to share all that stuff with Jacquie. She still didn't like her. She raised a hand to wave her off. "And thank you. For telling me about Jason."

Marcie felt hollow. Turned inside out. She'd married a monster and not even noticed. Worse than that, there was still someone out there coming after her, who she figured wanted Marcie in as much trouble as Jason was, and it wasn't Jacquie. So who?

She had one more lead to follow. She threw the rest of her champagne away and made a strong coffee. Despite her fear, she wasn't done yet.

60.

The doll was on the passenger seat beside her, now filled with ominous portent like a ventriloquist's dummy in a horror film. Her thoughts kept coming back to church. That inner congregation she'd watched at William's service. That *passion*. Wars were fought over religion all over the world so it wasn't such a leap that a congregation would follow a minister's wishes, or act for fellow worshippers. Puppets having their strings pulled. Was the voodoo church any different? She thought about the strange open-air celebration she and Keisha had gone to.

How they'd ended up there had been contrived too. The way that girl had knocked into their drinks and started chatting. If they hadn't met those two girls, they'd never have gone, danced, made wishes, and gotten naked. She'd called Tiger Court at Savannah State University and asked to speak to Jade or Daria but the woman at the other end was adamant that there were no students with those names staying there. Had the girls been tasked with getting Keisha and Marcie to the rave and under the gaze of the old black woman with the orange hair? But why? To add to Keisha's belief she was cursed? Or to actually curse them? But if someone was after Jason and Marcie, what did Keisha have to do with it? Keisha *believed*, that much was true. It was in her blood, that's what she'd said. In her family.

Marcie glanced across at the doll again. Well, it wasn't in Marcie's and she refused to get freaked out about it. Outside, the sky rumbled, portentous, and Marcie pressed her foot to the pedal harder. She knew where she had to go.

"You think just because I'm black, I secretly practice voodoo?" Zelda burst into laughter, something Marcie, standing in the doorway getting wet, realized she'd never seen before. "I'm a *Christian*. A Baptist just like Mr. William." Zelda looked down at the doll Marcie was still holding, which she'd thrust out at Zelda in a dramatic gesture but Zelda had refused to take. "I don't know what that is, or what it's for. I didn't make it."

"But Keisha *saw* you. St. John's Eve. You were at the party we went to. Down by the Truman Parkway. Where the old black lady with the orange hair did some crazy song and dance. I need to know where to find her." *Dansé Calinda! We call on them to dance with us! The spirits! The ghosts! Li Grande Zombi!* Marcie could still feel the earth pounding under her.

Zelda was still chuckling. "Oh my, oh my. I'm too old to go to parties. And that Keisha is crazy. She drinks too much to believe anything she says. Maybe she did see someone she knew, but it wasn't me. I don't like her much, she can be rude." She paused and her face grew flinty. "But I like her better than I like you, Mrs. Maddox. And if you don't mind, I want you to leave now. I have to go and open up the big house for Miss Iris shortly and I have some chores to finish first."

"Iris?" Marcie asked. She didn't even know the police had finished with the house.

"She's coming to go through Mrs. Radford's things. The *first* Mrs. Radford."

Lightning shattered the gloom of the afternoon and for a moment Marcie got a glimpse into Zelda's apartment beyond the small woman. It was perfectly ordinary. No signs of anything remotely weird. But then what had she expected?

"So who made this?" Marcie asked, exasperated.

"How the hell would I know?" Zelda's laugh was filled with disgust. "You should be ashamed of yourself. Maybe go ask some white ladies."

She slammed the door in Marcie's face, leaving her alone with the rain, her unanswered questions, and the creepy doll.

The emptying clouds were so thick that although it was still afternoon the sky was almost black, lit up with crackles and flashes of lightning. Zelda had only opened the side gate for her and by the time Marcie ran back to her car, parked around the corner, she was soaked to the skin. Inside, she locked the doors, shivering against the seat and glancing around, paranoid that there were people watching her.

The sidewalks under the heavy canopies of trees were silent. Somehow that made her nervousness worse. *It's just bullshit, Savannah,* she told herself, her old name clawing up from where she'd buried it. *There are no such things as voodoo curses and magic. Whatever's being done to you, there's a flesh-and-blood person doing it, for flesh-and-blood reasons.*

Still, she jumped when her cell phone rang.

It was Detective Anderson.

"So," the officer started, in that laconic drawl that made Marcie want to carve her eyes out with a spoon.

"Seems we've got some news on your mysterious year-book. Guess who the email requesting it came from?"

"You're the detective," Marcie said, her jaw tight, in no mood for any more games. "You tell me."

"Well, here's the thing. It came from you."

"What?" Marcie sat up straighter. That couldn't be right. "It didn't. I didn't email them."

"The request came from a Gmail account in the name of Savannah Cassidy."

"I don't care where it came from, I didn't send it."

"I'm sure. But we'll soon know. We're checking the computers taken from your house and Jason's office to see if there's a history of any of them accessing that account. You know a funny thing though?"

Marcie was sure it was going to be hysterical. "What?"

"The office secretary remembers a woman coming in to collect it. A couple of months back. A blond woman, not too tall. That's what she remembers."

Marcie thought of Jason's father, and as her own lungs constricted in fear, she figured she knew how he'd felt, dangling on the rope, his life being taken from him.

"If it was me then why would I have even told you about the email to the school? That a woman had asked for the yearbook? Why would I draw attention to myself that way? Why would I report it?" With her free hand she tugged at the roots of her hair, something she hadn't done in years. Her life was unraveling again. No—someone was unraveling it. For a long moment all she could hear was the rain on the car roof and Anderson breathing in her ear.

"You tell me, Marcie," Anderson said eventually. "You tell me." And then she hung up.

"Shit! Shit! Shit!" Marcie banged the phone hard against the steering wheel as she cursed loudly in the empty car as rain slashed against her windshield. The email would trace back to her somehow, she knew it. She beat the phone against the wheel again, three times more, and as she did, lightning blew up the sky, and a tall figure appeared from nowhere in front of her car.

It was her.

Marcie shrieked, shocked. The old black woman with hair the color of autumn fire. In the flash of light, she beat her cane against the metal hood three times, and even though the storm was starting to rage outside and the woman's lips didn't move, Marcie was sure she heard her call *"Faith! Hope! Charity!"*

Marcie flinched, and when she looked up again, the street ahead was empty. Breathless, she spun around in her seat. Where was she? Where? More lightning cut the sky and in the bright beam, the woman was standing behind the trunk, cane raised. She brought it down three times again. *"Dansé Calinda!"* she shouted to the skies, her voice filled with joy. She beat the trunk again, *"You hear me in there! Make them dance! Li Grande Zombi!"*

"Hey!" Marcie shouted, her frantic fingers struggling to lift the lock on her door. She was here, the woman was here, and now that Marcie's heart had stopped racing in panic she just wanted some answers. "Hey wait!" Finally she got the door open and stumbled out into the storm. The old woman was walking away, immune to the elements as if out strolling on a summer's day.

"Hey!" Marcie called out again. She picked up her pace, the fat woman ahead somehow moving fast, although she seemed to be only shuffling. "Wait!" Marcie repeated. In reply, the woman raised her cane to the sky and shook it, shouting words Marcie couldn't hear, and then lightning cracked like a gunshot into a tree behind Marcie and she couldn't help but duck and spin around, huddling behind her car, as a splinter of tree shot across the pavement. When she turned again, the rain suddenly easing as if even the storm was shocked by the lightning's attack, the old woman was gone.

Marcie got to her feet and leaned against the car trunk, watching the smoke from the burned tree drifting into the rain. She was frustrated and angry and more than a little afraid. Where had the old woman come from? How did she know where Marcie was going to be? Was someone following her? What did she mean with her sayings and her chants? Marcie looked down, the black-gray of the clouds above letting cracks of calm blue in as the storm marched relentlessly onward. The old woman had been shouting at something in the trunk. *"You hear me in there? Make them dance!"* Marcie's fingers trembled as she reached for the catch and the sleek metal lifted silently. Flies, hundreds of them, buzzed loudly as they rushed past in a swarm, and she swatted around her head, disgusted, until the air was clear. She looked down, half-expecting to see a rotting corpse tied up against the carpet, a gift to Anderson and a final nail in Marcie's coffin, but there was no such body, and at first the trunk seemed empty.

It was only as she peered more closely, to brush away a few lingering sickly flies, that she saw it, dark against dark. She picked it up. A ball. Black and lumpy as if made of mud dredged up from the bed of a stagnant river filled with rot. Not mud, she thought, rolling it around in her hands in horror. Earth and dirt and something *else*. What was that? She got back in the car and flicked on the light before recoiling in horror. Was that fur? Black fur? She rubbed the surface harder and looked at her fingers. A deep dark red. Blood and earth and fur bound together. There was something more, catching her eye. At first she thought it was strands of cotton bound around the revolting sphere, but as she picked one free she saw it was hair. Blond hair. *Her hair.*

Maybe Keisha was right. Maybe they *were* cursed.

61.

"Tell us about the boy."

Keisha stared at the man across the table, her heart fluttering like a leaf caught in the storm outside.

"Auntie Ayo said I was cursed. She said there was no boy. She said I was seeing a ghost and I'd upset the spirits because I was a wicked little girl. She said I had to stop talking about him, otherwise the curse would never go. I had to forget about him."

"You didn't forget about him though, did you?"

"No," she said quietly. "And look where I am now."

"I don't think you're cursed, Keisha," he said, and she wondered what someone like him could possibly know about it. He was a heavy-set man, old enough that the skin of his jaw hung in jowls, dragging him downward toward his grave. His aftershave was *clean,* not suffocating and floral like Billy's. His accent was gruff and London, the words clipped and hard next to the sweet Savannah drawl, but oh, how she'd missed it. He was steady and sturdy and she doubted he dreamed. His name was Detective Sergeant Dexter.

"Tell us when you first saw him," he said.

"He was a ghost in the night," she said quietly, withdrawing back into her past, growing smaller as she remembered, the room around her fading. "I had just turned six. I remember because I didn't have a birthday party. Uncle Yahuba's cousin had come to visit and Auntie Ayo said I had to stay in my room and be quiet. I didn't mind. I didn't like him. He never smiled and he and Uncle Yahuba would get drunk on rum and talk until late. They sounded like tigers to me. One night I woke up upset. I'd been dreaming about my mother and it was the first time her face had been blurred and half-forgotten, and when I woke up I couldn't picture her at all. It was the worst thing. I wanted to go to the sitting room and look at one of the old photos taken when they were all young that Auntie Ayo had on the wall. It wasn't my mother's face as I knew it, but it would be at least an image of her."

It was strange how the memory she'd tried to repress for all these years came back so vividly. The damp smell of the house from having no central heating, only storage heaters that didn't work well. The feel of the flock wallpaper under her fingers. The carpet beneath her bare feet swirling in garish patterns. "I was nervous—Auntie Ayo said I wasn't allowed out of my room at night—she worked her best juju in the dark she said, and clients often came at midnight or later and wanted their privacy—and if I needed to pee there was a bucket in the corner of the room." A black bucket that had stayed in Keisha's room until she was thirteen and got her period. But by then, she would be fetching rum for the late-night visitors and taking their money while they waited; the bucket was no longer needed. She remembered how she'd felt when that had gone. *Trusted.* At last part of the family, even if there was no real love there.

"The house was silent and dark so I crept out, holding my breath until I was past the bedrooms and at the top of the stairs. I could hear Uncle Yahuba's cousin snoring as I passed his door, but still I didn't relax. I knew they'd beat me if I broke the rules. Uncle Yahuba liked to beat the devil out of me when I was wicked. Especially after the boy. I was halfway down the stairs when it happened." Her breath caught with the clarity of the memory. The release of it.

"He just appeared in the corner of the downstairs

hallway, stepping out of the deep shadows there. As if he'd walked through the wall. I nearly screamed but clutched my hand to my mouth and dropped to a crouch. He was small, I guess maybe my age, but not so tall as me, and he was so pale he glowed in the darkness. A ghost. He was a ghost, a spirit like Auntie Ayo would talk about. His skin was like a dead white man's and even his tight curly hair was a snowy frosting on his head. He wore a white T-shirt and shorts even though it wasn't warm and he had a burn scar up one arm. I stared at him, and he stared at me, and then he turned around and disappeared into the wall again."

Dexter was scribbling notes down, although Keisha couldn't see why any of it was important. "So this was the year 2004?" he asked, and Keisha nodded. "I guess so, if I was six."

"And when is your birthday?"

"April fourth."

Dexter paused. Another scribble. "How many times did you see the boy?"

"Seven. Over about a month, I guess. Not every night. Just now and then. I started to creep out to look for him when everyone was asleep. He never spoke and he never came up close, but we would just look at each other for a few moments before I'd run back to my room. The ghost boy in the walls, that's what I thought of him as. I wondered why he always looked so sad. Sadder than me." She paused. "I promised myself that I'd speak to him next time, but I never did. There was never a next time. And when I finally asked Auntie Ayo if she'd ever seen the ghost, she told me I was cursed."

It made her want to cry. Cursed. Forever. And all because she saw a ghost.

62.

Marcie had put the ball back in the trunk, not knowing what else to do with it, and as she stared out at the hospital entrance through the pouring rain, she was sure that under the steady thrum of the purring engine she could hear it thumping against the trunk, demanding its release. It was a stupid thought. The ball was nothing, and she didn't believe in voodoo, but still she shivered, remembering the feel of matted fur and blood and God only knew what else. It was disgusting.

She felt desolate and alone. She didn't know why she'd come here. William couldn't give her answers. William was simply another piece of the puzzle. Her, Keisha, Jason, and him, locked together in someone else's game. Who was this actually about? All of them equally, or were some just disposable pawns around one main target? William, Keisha, and Jason were in some kind of torturous limbo, and Marcie was pretty sure that she was soon to join them. Someone had laid a bread-crumb trail for Anderson that led to her and she had no idea where the next blow would come from. Maybe she should run. She'd told Jason not to, and that hadn't worked out so well for him. But how far would she get?

She was about to turn the car around and head home when a figure emerged through the hospital doors, head down against the steady rain. Marcie frowned as the person lifted her face for a second to see where she was going. She *recognized* that girl. But who was— Suddenly she had it. *Of course!* She leapt out of the car and ran, her drying clothes getting soaked again as she raced to catch up to the woman.

"Michelle!" She grabbed the young woman's arm as she panted her name. *Michelle from Michigan.* The waitress at the club that William had taken a shine to and who'd then moved away. "I thought it was you."

The girl's eyes narrowed and she frowned for a moment before recognition dawned on her too. "Are you going to tell me I'm not allowed in too?"

"What? No, I was just surprised to see you. I didn't know you were still close with William."

"I'm not. She took care of that. But I heard what happened. I wanted to see him." Her mouth tightened. "But apparently I can't."

"Who said you can't?" *And who took care of what?*

"The nurse on reception wouldn't let me in. She had *instructions* apparently. God, you'd think they'd have all gotten over our little fling now she's dead."

Marcie pulled the young woman into the shadow of the building, protecting them slightly from the rain. "What are you talking about? Now who's dead?"

"The wife. The one who made me end it." She stared at Marcie. "Wow, you really thought I went back to Michigan of my own accord? When I had a rich old guy who was sweet to me on a hook? *Eleanor* paid me to leave. She didn't give me much choice, it was that or get fired from the club and be unemployable in the city." Michelle shook her head.

"Eleanor knew about you and William?"

"She *summoned* me to the Browning room in the club to tell me she knew everything and she wouldn't have me making a fool of her husband. Like some dying queen in her wheelchair, all powdered and perfect. She looked dead already. No wonder William was so repulsed by her."

"Did William know she'd paid you off?" Marcie was starting to think that Michelle from Michigan and

William would have made a delightful couple, each as mean as the other.

"Of course not. That was the other condition. I couldn't say anything." Michelle reached in her bag for a cigarette, taking three attempts to light it in the wet air. "I pitied her, so I took her money and went."

No doubt planning to come back after Eleanor had died and pick up where she'd left off, Marcie thought. But William headed off to Europe, probably because he'd forgotten Michelle already, and then came back married.

"But it seems you people bear grudges. All I wanted was to know he was okay."

And to get your foot back in that door. "Well, he's not," Marcie said. "He's blind and locked in and his organs have massively failed. So even if you'd snuck into his room you wouldn't have gotten any conversation out of him."

"I'm done with all of you," Michelle said, smoking hard, barely listening. "Y'all think you're so much better than everyone else."

"Sounds like in your case, most people are." Marcie turned and walked away, ignoring the muttered *bitch* that followed her. She didn't care what the girl thought of her. She didn't care that the rain was soaking her to her skin again. Things were finally slotting into place.

Eleanor.

Everything came back to Eleanor. William had cheated on her when she was dying, and now he was half-dead. Jason had tried to steal from her, and she'd suspected that he'd been involved in the death of his father, Eleanor's friend. Now he was going to prison for one crime and might be charged with murder yet. Keisha was William's new wife. Married him for money, and now she was in a cell with nothing. But what about Marcie herself? Where did she fit in?

One thought overrode all her questions as she raced her car back out onto the street. Eleanor was dead and buried. She couldn't be doing this. Someone else was doing it on her behalf. But who?

Eleanor. Sweet, elegant Eleanor. Ghosts would always have their vengeance.

63.

The main gates had been left open this time and Marcie parked beside Iris's Mercedes before getting out and darting up the front steps before the rain could fully soak her all over again. Her heart was racing. Once again she was back at William Radford's house. This time she wanted answers.

"I wondered if you might need some food," Marcie said, holding up the deli bag as Iris opened the door. "I brought a bottle of wine too."

"How thoughtful of you, dear." After a moment Iris's surprise faded and she stepped aside and let Marcie in. There was no sign of Zelda. The main lights were off, only two table lamps glowing in the vast hallway, and Marcie shivered as she glanced up at the portrait of Eleanor still up on the wall, watching them in the gloom. "Must be strange being here alone," she said.

"Actually I find it quite comforting. And Eleanor's things are a treasure trove of memories to me. So much old history half-forgotten." She gave Marcie an odd smile and started up the stairs. "Why don't you go put that food in the kitchen and come and see if you'd like." She didn't look back as she glided up the sweeping staircase, and with a racing heart, Marcie did as she was told. She put the bag of cold cuts and cheese in the fridge—no coconut waters in there now—and left the French bread on the side.

She poured two glasses of wine and took a sip from one to steady her nerves. Iris was Eleanor's oldest friend, everyone knew that. She'd cared for her throughout her illness. They'd been side by side since childhood. If anyone was taking revenge for Eleanor it *had* to be Iris.

Marcie crept up the stairs, as if afraid of waking the ghosts, and followed the pale-yellow beam that led to Eleanor's bedroom. Iris was sitting on the bed, a small valise tipped out empty beside her—a collection of old photos.

"Thank you," she said, taking the glass.

"You should put more lights on," Marcie said. "Don't you think it's creepy?"

"I'm not afraid of the dark," Iris said. "As you get older you have to make your peace with it."

Marcie thought of the disgusting black ball in the trunk of the car. "I meant to ask." She perched on the mattress. "Did Midge ever show up?" Iris's missing cat, all black fur and yellow eyes.

"No," Iris said, distracted, sifting through pictures. "Sadly not. He was old. Noah says he probably crawled away to die somewhere."

Marcie could still feel the cold rough fur under her fingertips, matted in the earth and blood. Had Iris strangled Midge before skinning him? Marcie shivered. Here in the house, it felt as if she and Iris were the last people alive. Anything could happen and no one would hear them.

"Look at this." Iris held up a photo. "How young we were. I must have been maybe sixteen and Eleanor thirteen. Those three years made such a difference back then." She laughed gently. "Now three years is simply the bat of an eyelid."

"She must have been like a sister to you."

"I suppose yes, she was."

Marcie scanned the photos. Iris had been organizing them into groups according to age: childhood to glorious youth, and then family and friends, and then just family. The last two sections weren't spread out but stacked up. They weren't such *treasure,* too recent to hold any surprises.

"I miss her every day," Iris continued. "Getting old is no fun, Marcie. Whatever your problems now, at least you have youth."

Iris was still looking at the pictures. *Whatever her problems?* What was happening here? Was Iris playing innocent and waiting for the police to follow whatever trail she'd laid to Marcie? Didn't she *want* her to know she was responsible for it all?

"Oh my, look at these short trousers," Iris said, passing one old photo over. It was from the childhood spread. "Emmett was such a funny-looking boy."

"Emmett?" Marcie took the photo and looked more closely. Even as a boy, he was wearing glasses, perched high up on his nose.

"He grew up with us as well. You know how close this community is. It was a lot tighter back then. Our parents were far more conservative than we are. Society mattered more to them. Your name. Your money. Your history."

Marcie frowned, moving through several of the pictures. The same faces came up in all of them. History rewriting itself in her head. Ghosts of people they used to be. Eleanor, Iris, Emmett, and another girl. Marcie looked more closely. She was stocky with mad dark curls. Not quite filled with the confidence the others had and her clothes didn't quite fit right. Marcie knew that look from her own childhood. Hand-me-downs.

Sometimes the girl was playing with Eleanor, in one she was laughing on a swing with Emmett. All of them aging through the glossy paper, from children to awkward teens, Eleanor blossoming into a beauty, each taking turns in front of the camera. In each image, somewhere in the background, a tall black woman was watching over them. A very tall black woman. Marcie's breath caught.

"Who's that?" she asked, pointing at her.

Iris's face broke into a grin. "Oh, that was Eleanor's nanny. Well, nanny and maid, really. Mama L we called her." She smiled. "Elizabeth's mother. That's why Elizabeth was always with us. She lived there, with Mama L. My, we all loved Mama L. She came from New Orleans and seemed so fascinating. Dyed her hair orange once and, well, Eleanor's mother nearly *died* at the shock of it. She'd teach us girls love spells and charms. Told us that she was a voodoo queen." Iris laughed softly as if it had been a fairy tale. "My, how we missed her when they had to leave. I do believe that Eleanor loved Mama L more than her own mother."

"Mama L was Elizabeth's mother?" Marcie's throat

had dried. The little girl in the hand-me-downs. Elizabeth.

"Now, Elizabeth really *was* like Eleanor's little sister. They adored each other. And poor Emmett of course, well, he was the reason Elizabeth and her mother had to leave."

"What do you mean?"

"He was very taken with Elizabeth. To be fair, she was very taken with him too. They were only children really, and it was harmless, but they were inseparable and it was enough to worry his parents. Not only because she had colored blood in her, although that would have been reason enough—as I said they were different times—but his parents already had their eyes on Virginia for Emmett and they shared their concerns with Eleanor's father, and so Mama L was let go. She moved back to New Orleans, I believe. But Eleanor refused to be separated from Elizabeth for long, and as soon as she could, she called Elizabeth back and hired her as her assistant. I'm pretty sure she sent money to Mama L from time to time too." She sighed. "They were such halcyon days when we were young and free."

Marcie's head was spinning and the world once again flipped and presented itself from a new angle. She pulled out her cell phone and tapped at the screen as if there were a message there. "Oh shoot," she said.

"I have to run. Something's come up." Iris already forgotten, she hurried out of the house and back to the car.

She sat inside for a moment, before googling for the last pieces of the puzzle, and then after collecting her thoughts, she started to drive. Her phone rang as she turned toward the hospital. Anderson. She canceled the call and turned off her cell. That could wait. If she was going to prison, she wanted to understand why.

64.

Keisha was so tired. They'd been talking all day and all she wanted to do was sleep.

"I don't understand why you came all the way here to ask me about a ghost I saw as a child. A boy who was never there," she said. Billy was half-dead, the American police thought she was part of it, and yet here they were still talking about something that was just her madness, asking for detail after detail until she was exhausted. As if she could remember it all, when she'd spent so long trying to forget. The questions about Auntie Ayo and Uncle Yahuba and his cousin were easier and she'd answered them as well as she could, but they'd been talking all day and she just wanted to sleep.

She'd been back in her cell for only an hour and now

Dexter was here again. More questions no doubt. She didn't care. She was too tired to be afraid anymore.

"I think the boy *was* there, Keisha." Dexter reached down into his battered briefcase and pulled out a file. "In May of 2004, a boy's torso was pulled from the Thames. Approximately six years of age, he'd been mutilated and his organs were missing. A day later an arm was also recovered. That arm had a burn scar running up it." He opened the file and pushed a photograph across the table. It was a close-up, and Keisha almost gasped. It was the same scar, she knew it.

"You think I saw his ghost?" she asked, her voice trembling.

Dexter shook her head. "I think you saw him when he was alive. My colleagues in London have been searching your aunt and uncle's home. They've found a doorway in the hallway wall by the corner. Leads to an old cellar. You have to look closely for the catch but it's there. There is evidence that at least one child was kept there at some point. We think your aunt and uncle kept this boy in the cellar until they killed him. Perhaps others too."

"No." Keisha shook her head. "No. He was a ghost. He was so white, he was a ghost."

"No." Dexter's rough voice was surprisingly gentle. "He just looked like a ghost to a little girl."

He took another photo from his file and passed it over. "His name was Oliver Okimbe. His family had just moved from Nigeria to Yorkshire when he went missing." He paused as Keisha, with shaking hands, took the picture from him. "They moved to England to keep him safe from witch doctors in Nigeria who wanted to kill him for his body parts. Sadly, your uncle's cousin followed him and brought him to your auntie. Oliver wasn't a ghost. He was an albino."

Keisha looked down at the picture, and even as the image blurred with her tears, she knew it was him. The boy who wasn't there. The tears fell heavy after that. Oliver Okimbe. A real live boy.

She'd never been cursed at all.

PART FOUR

65.

"I wondered if you'd find your way here," Elizabeth said, not moving from her chair by William's hospital bed. "I did hope you would. You're a smart woman. And I would have hated all my planning to have gone to waste. I've been so looking forward to sharing everything with you." She smiled, contained; a still, calm figure compared to Marcie's fizzing energy. "Scratch the surface and history always wills out, isn't that true?" she finished. "And history makes us who we are. As you've discovered."

The room was quiet, only the hum of the machines feeding life to William. Marcie tossed the black ball from her trunk onto William's bed, and she was sure she saw a maggot wriggle away as it landed on William's legs. He didn't seem to mind. "Iris's cat?"

"He was dying. I didn't hurt him. A conjure ball should be made with care and I'd been fond of Midge." She shrugged. "Plus, Iris was a little too friendly to Keisha too soon. That would have hurt Eleanor's feelings. So an eye for an eye, a hurt for a hurt."

"Mama Laveau was an old voodoo queen of New Orleans at the end of the nineteenth century," Marcie said. "Her daughter took her name and kept on practicing as the original Laveau. One daughter married a white man, by the name of Glapion. Was he your daddy, Elizabeth Glapion? Is your mother the current Mama Laveau? The old woman with the crazy umber hair?"

"Bloodlines," Elizabeth said wryly. "The rich think only theirs matter, but the poor have history too. Our blood runs deep. Do you know what they call me? The *real* people of Savannah?" Marcie said nothing, and so Elizabeth continued. "They call me the White Voodoo. My pale skin hides my blood. But yes, Mama Laveau was my grandmother. Her blood is mine. Mama Laveau and Dr. John, old John Bayou? Well, they ran New Orleans back in the old days. Rivals. Mama Laveau, she had voodoo in her soul. She could do it all. Just like my mama. But Dr. John—do you know what power he had?" Marcie stayed silent and she continued. "He understood the power of information. He had servants in his pay all over New Orleans and they told him everything about the people who lived in the big houses—all the secrets only servants knew, so when his rich clients came knocking for his help and he already knew their business, they thought he was the most powerful voodoo doctor. I have some of my mother's magic. I can curse with a spit if I so wish, but I prefer Dr. John's methods. Times don't really change. To William, I was simply an assistant. But he trusted me with everything. Funny, isn't it? I know all his business. Most of his friends' business. Most of his *clients'* business. Some of them have actually become mine and Mama's clients. So, Mama takes care of the voodoo and I take care of the information and between us we have made a little fortune of our own. Eleanor knew. Eleanor loved and respected us. Eleanor believed in the power of our magic."

Marcie looked at the half-dead figure in the bed. "You did this for Eleanor, didn't you?"

Elizabeth sighed and squeezed William's hand. "Eleanor was going to murder William herself. That's why she had the morphine and the needles hidden away. She'd put them to one side and she was going to kill him in his sleep."

"Why? Because of the waitress?" Surely Eleanor wouldn't have resorted to murder over someone as obviously trashy as Michelle from Michigan?

"No, of course not. Because of what the waitress *represented*. His lack of respect. His lack of love or care. You weren't there. You didn't see how much it had taken from Eleanor to forgive him for Lyle. Lyle was her heart. Oh, he was such a beautiful boy. He deserved a long and happy life. If it wasn't for William, he might have had one. His death nearly destroyed Eleanor. It broke my heart, but that was nothing next to watching her pain. But she was a good person and she wanted to forgive William, not only for Lyle's death but for making him join up in the first place, for something so opposite to his nature. She *made* herself forgive him. She locked Lyle away in a box so William wouldn't feel guilty and she strived to make the marriage work. And I guess on some level it did."

"But then Eleanor got sick," Marcie said.

"Yes. And it became clear very quickly that William wasn't good with illness. He hid from it, barely spending time with Eleanor, sleeping in a guest bedroom. And then, when Eleanor was diagnosed as terminal, and not even Mama or I could do anything to stop it, he started his fling with that girl. As if Eleanor wasn't suffering enough. I didn't blame Eleanor for wanting to kill him, but I couldn't let her do it." She looked up at Marcie and smiled. "She was a beautiful woman inside and out. I wouldn't let her ruin herself—her *soul*—for William.

I stopped her. I had planned to retire and go back to New Orleans with Mama once Eleanor had passed. I'd made enough money through our private services to the wealthy of Savannah. Tarot readings. Love spells. Advice. Curses. When you can get that stuff right, people will pay you anything you want. Plus, Eleanor hadn't left me forgotten in her will. We were like sisters after all." She smiled again, softly but sadly this time, remembering her friend.

"So yes, I was looking forward to relaxing into a quiet comfortable luxury of my own, but although I wouldn't let her kill William, neither could I let her die without peace of mind. So I promised her on her deathbed that I'd take care of all of it. I'd kill William for her. It was her dying wish." She paused. "There's a lot of power in a dying wish."

"Maybe not so much," Marcie said. "He's not dead."

"I'm not as kind as Eleanor." Elizabeth laughed. "There are some fates worse than death. William's alive on a whim. Watching him when Eleanor was dying I learned a lot about that fat old man. Dying terrified him. The weakness of it. The becoming *irrelevant* as life moved on. He wanted a quick death, which, to be fair, is what Eleanor was planning to give him. But he didn't deserve that. Why should he get a clean death while Eleanor had to rot slowly? No." She shook her head. "Eleanor and Lyle deserved more than that after so many years of having him controlling them. But look at him now—trapped here, locked in the dark of his own mind, no power at all. The visitors will stop coming. All he has is me, sitting here, whispering to him about Lyle and Eleanor and how he failed them and how this whole situation is his own fault. He'll live awhile but eventually, if his organs don't fail entirely, the machine will be turned off. *Then* he'll be dead. That will be the moment of mercy."

"But what about the rest of us? Me and Keisha and Jason?" She paused. Quiet subservient Elizabeth had done all this to them. It would be laughable if it wasn't so terrifying. Elizabeth and her crazy mother. Voodoo queens.

"Ah, the replacement wife—mentally unstable and from a juju background full of secrets. The liar—hiding her colorful past in a box in the ceiling. And finally, the thief—who didn't even learn his lesson after his father's death. A perfect cast of characters for Eleanor's revenge. All shackled to ghosts of the dead: a boy, a husband, a father."

"You think you know so much about us," Marcie sneered, angry. "But you don't."

"Oh, but I *do*. As I said, information is my business. I had Keisha's life investigated for William, and when you arrived on the scene I did the same. I research everyone who comes into my circles. You always find something useful." She stared at Marcie, and despite the warmth in her eyes, Marcie shivered. "And my, was your past useful."

"You're going to let them go to prison for a murder they didn't commit. And what about me? Why the stupid doll and the disgusting ball?"

"Why does everyone presume voodoo is curses and devils?" Elizabeth said. "So wrong. Some spells curse and bind, and some protect. Good or bad. It's all karma."

"Which was mine? Or Keisha's?"

Elizabeth didn't answer, but stood up and went to the window. "The police are here," she said. "They'll have traced the email to your old high school back to Jason's office computer. They still don't know who sent it, but they may well now be thinking that you were a ménage à trois. You *were* sleeping with both of them after all, and Jason could well have met Keisha when he went to London. He didn't, by the way. Like I said, information is my magic. But I digress. Now, here's where you come in. I'm not going to send anyone to jail. *You* are."

"What do you mean?" Marcie was so over this shit.

"I'm going to give you a choice. Jason or Keisha?"

Elizabeth turned and smiled. "I can make it so that one of them goes free and one goes to jail for William's attempted murder."

"What?"

"Keisha or Jason. Which do you want to save? The errant husband or the flighty girlfriend? Time's ticking on."

Marcie looked down at the barely living body in the bed. She felt sick. She felt relieved. She felt like she was stuck in a fever dream. "But what if William dies? That could be the death penalty." There was noise behind them in the corridor. Detective Anderson and her sidekick arriving.

"Yes," Elizabeth said pleasantly. "It will be. But it won't be *you* facing it." She winked, and Marcie, just before answering, decided Elizabeth was mad.

66.

As Elizabeth had said they would, the police had taken Marcie in for further questioning after discovering the email to the high school came from Jason's work computer—a computer that Marcie had plenty of access to.

Marcie hadn't answered any of their questions this time, as Kate Anderson quizzed her, trying to find out if all three of them, Marcie, Keisha, and Jason, were in it together. It all was just as Elizabeth had said it would be. Marcie hadn't bothered to try to defend herself. It felt odd putting her faith in Elizabeth that she wouldn't be charged, but she found that she did. After all, Elizabeth had been pulling their strings for long enough. Instead, as Anderson had talked at her, she'd zoned out while putting the pieces of Elizabeth's plan together in her head. Thankfully, finally, the detectives were called out, leaving her alone in the room with her thoughts.

It was almost to be respected, how intricate Elizabeth's plan had been. She'd known all about Keisha before she even arrived in the city. Emmett had been in love with Elizabeth and so no doubt made sure that Jason's investments weren't going to pay out in time. Maybe he even encouraged Jason—at Elizabeth's behest—to invest money he didn't have. The figure she'd half recognized at the rave—not Zelda but Elizabeth standing behind her mother, serpent in her arms. She must have arranged for their drinks to be drugged to make Keisha more susceptible to the voodoo. The more unstable she was the more unhappy William would be. Also, the drugs made them looser, *hotter* for each other, and that was how they got the photo. Enough to make William angry that night and want to keep away from the party and tell Noah he wanted a divorce.

Marcie thought about the coolant. Elizabeth had done all the organizing for the new car and no doubt had a spare key. The light came on after she and Keisha had gone to see Julian and Pierre—*when they fucked in the car*—and Elizabeth had met them there. She could easily have loosened the cap to make it leak. Elizabeth could have been in the kitchen and injected the cartons at any point after she returned to the party. Julian and Pierre had brought their own catering Winnebago for the canapés and parked it around the back.

"Sorry to keep you waiting." Detectives Anderson and Washington came back into the room, and only then did Marcie realize that her hands were cold and legs numb from sitting still. How long had they been gone? "There's been a development, which means that you're free to go."

Marcie got to her feet, despite the pins and needles running through her calves. "What do you mean?"

"We've found the syringe used to inject the coconut water cartons and a small water bottle containing coolant."

Marcie's eyes widened. *What have you done now, Elizabeth?* "I don't understand."

"Behind the cutlery drawer in the Radford house kitchen. There's an odd gap there at the back that can only be accessed if you pull the drawer out at a certain angle. Did you know about it?"

Marcie nodded. "Yes, but—"

"If you were involved in the attempted murder and hid them there, or knew they were there, you've since had opportunity to remove them." Marcie's blank face prompted further explanation.

"You were at the Radford house earlier this evening

and Iris Cartwright tells us you were left alone in the kitchen." She paused. "Lucky for you."

"So I can go?"

"Yes, we won't be charging you."

Marcie wanted to laugh out loud. *Oh, Elizabeth. How you played us.*

She was free, and if she wasn't mistaken, if Elizabeth had stood by the choice she'd given Marcie, the future was looking pretty bright.

67.

It was a decadently hot night in the Bahamas, but a slight breeze blew in through the fluttering curtains and was delicious on Marcie's naked skin. It had been a long few months and she—*they*—deserved this holiday away from everything.

Everything had played out as Elizabeth predicted. The syringe and bottle had only Jason's fingerprints on them. The conclusion drawn was that he must have planned William's death alone and had to quickly ditch the murder equipment in the broken drawer space after being interrupted by Elizabeth on the night of the party when Keisha had started shouting at Zelda. Both Marcie and Keisha had the opportunity to retrieve and dispose of them and they hadn't. If either had been involved in any way they would have.

Poor Jason. He'd vehemently denied his guilt throughout the trial, which hadn't exactly helped his case, and Marcie had felt the hatred coming off him in waves as she played her own part, weeping quietly on the stand, giving evidence against him. So that was it. Jason had gotten life for attempted murder and the trial for his financial wrongdoings was upcoming.

She wondered what evidence Elizabeth would have produced if Marcie had chosen differently. Something equally compelling against Keisha no doubt. But she *hadn't* chosen differently. Why would she? She'd been getting bored with Jason before any of this happened and she'd never bought into that *stand by your man* philosophy.

"Can I ask you something?" Keisha murmured. "And you won't get mad?" She was curled on her side, one hand protecting her growing belly, Billy having left her with more than money after all. Was it going to be another request for reassurance? Keisha, although still glorious in bed and now fabulously wealthy, was turning out to be quite needy.

"Sure," Marcie whispered in reply.

"It's really stupid, but I just need to hear it from you. You didn't have anything to do with what happened to Jonny, did you?"

"No, of course not!" Marcie looked down at her. "You really have to ask that?"

"I'm sorry, I'm sorry," Keisha said, reaching up to kiss her. "I didn't mean it, it's just all been so crazy with Auntie Ayo and Uncle Yahuba having murdered that poor boy and maybe others, and then what Jason did, it's just all such madness it's making me question everything. Ignore me. I'm being stupid. I'm sorry."

"You don't need to be sorry." Marcie leaned down and kissed her. "But you can trust me. I love you."

They kissed more deeply and for a while Marcie let Keisha's glorious body do the apologizing.

Afterward, as Keisha slept, satiated, Marcie stared into the night, at last alone with her thoughts.

You can't cage a wild thing.

Marcie was a wild thing, always had been, and nothing could change that.

Jonny.

She sank back into the memories. How her heart had raced walking back into the trailer, not knowing whether he'd be dead or alive or if he'd even drunk the laced whiskey at all. The contrived argument the day before and then storming out to go to work. The shot of clean whiskey she'd secretly slipped in his coffee to give him a taste for liquor again. Staying out all night drinking and dancing with Janey, turned on by not knowing if her plan was working or not.

Oh yes, how her heart had raced when she walked into the trailer and saw him there on the floor, eyes wide, frozen in terror. Dead. And it had been so *easy*. Jonny always had stuff for the cars in the trailer. Oil, batteries, coolant. And sure, Jonny had straightened out for a while, but alcoholics relapse, and there was enough doubt to get her off scot-free.

So what if an air of suspicion hung over her? She'd had no intention of staying in Boise. God, she'd been banking on Jonny drinking himself to death and then she'd swan off with his payout, but no, he had to decide to get himself together. To start talking about a baby again. *Trapping* her in that life. She couldn't have that. She'd rather die. Or, as it turned out, she'd rather *he* died.

Sociopath.

That was the word the police had used about her back in Boise, even if they couldn't prove it. Same word they all used about Jason now. Like attracts like, she guessed. If she'd known what Jason was up to with the client accounts she'd have probably killed him too—but perhaps more imaginatively than she had Jonny. She'd grown as a person since then. Maybe even without the money troubles she'd have ended up getting rid of husband number two. She'd been getting bored and he'd been getting tiring with his sudden need to reproduce. She'd never wanted a child. What if it turned out to be like her?

Keisha murmured in her sleep. Ah, the irony. Marcie had never wanted kids and here she was, soon to be saddled with coparenting a screaming brat. But it would be worth it for the final financial result. Keisha, for all her charm, was fragile and needy and like a child herself. For now, Marcie found it quite sweet, especially given all of poor William's money Keisha had to spend on her, constantly trying to impress her and prove she loved her, but she was pretty sure that within a couple of years, it would get cloying. But still—they'd be married by then.

One thing all this had taught Marcie about herself was that she found love to be fleeting. She obsessed about a person and then she got bored. That was how love was for her. She'd gotten bored with Jonny, and she'd gotten bored with Jason. One day, she'd get bored with Keisha too. But Keisha had a history of mental health issues. She may have weaned herself off the Valium because of the pregnancy but it wouldn't be *that* hard to get her back on them and then to arrange an overdose or an accident. Send the kid to boarding school and live a life of luxury.

Yes, she thought, kissing the top of Keisha's head. The future was turning out very nicely indeed.

Epilogue

"Don't be so angry. Some would call it poetic justice that you're in here," Elizabeth said across the visiting room table. On the other side, Jason looked as if he could murder her. "Life with no possibility of parole." She shrugged. "Although I can see how it might not feel that way to you. Especially as it could—and will—get so much worse."

"How could it get any worse?" Jason's bitterness dripped from him. The guilty were so often bitter she found. Despite their own crimes, any small injustice stung them hard. One of life's ironies. He hadn't taken her confession well, it had to be said. He was going to take this snippet of information worse, although he really should have thought it through earlier. She was starting to think that Jason Maddox wasn't too bright.

"When William dies," she said simply. "Which he will, in the next few days. I'm tired of whispering to him what a shit he is. I think he's gotten the message now. He's giving up and shutting down. His organs are becoming more unstable. Even the doctors think that turning the machines off is for the best and after I leave here, I shall be persuading his legal representatives that death is the kindest route for him."

"What are you talking about?" The first hint of fear cracking through his anger. "What has that got to do with me?"

"It's obvious, isn't it? If William dies, then you're guilty of first-degree murder. And that's the death penalty." She smiled at him cheerfully. "And that *will* happen. Your appeal will fail. Admittedly you may spend some years on death row, but trust me, you will get the injection."

"Bullshit. You can't know that."

"But I can. I do. I *see* it. The great Mama Laveau's blood runs in mine. You can believe in it or not, but that doesn't change mine or my mama's powers. What will be will be."

"Why the fuck are you here, Elizabeth?" His words were spat nails, but his face was pale.

"I wondered if you knew why *you* were here. Why I put you behind these bars."

"Because you're a psycho bitch?"

"Oh Jason, really. No need for insults. Actually, no, you're here because I gave your wife a choice. I told her I could arrange for one of you to go free and one of you to go to jail. A choice between you and Keisha. She chose to set Keisha free and leave you to face all this. You, her husband. I guess *till death do us part* means something different to Marcie. But yes, she chose the money over saving your life."

His eyes widened. "Marcie did this?"

"In her own way, yes."

They sat in silence for a few moments while the truth of it all soaked into Jason's skin, settling inside him like a strange acceptance.

"Keisha might be a dumb bitch, but she never did anything wrong," Jason said eventually. "What if Marcie had chosen her to be guilty? You'd have let her face the death penalty?"

"Keisha was never going to end up in your position," Elizabeth said. "I knew how Marcie would choose. She would always save the rich woman over her criminal husband. And anyway, Keisha was *protected*. As I told Marcie, not everything is a curse. Voodoo is a healing practice, that's what most people don't understand. And it works in balance. To do what I've done for Eleanor, to take this revenge for her, there had to be a balance of good. Keisha was the balance. A poor girl haunted throughout her life by someone else's crimes. I have put her through the fire but she is now set *free*. She has money. She has no grasping family or domineering husband. She can finally be herself. No harm will come to her.

"I told Marcie that conjure balls and dolls can protect or curse," she continued. "Keisha's were to protect her always. Marcie couldn't harm her. It had to be you. Karma for your father, don't you think?"

The steely cold look on Jason's face made it clear that he had no time for karma.

"Anyway," she continued. "Giving people a choice is like a magic trick. You should always know what their answer will be in advance. With Marcie that was easy. She already killed one husband—I doubted she'd have any qualms about making a choice to kill another."

"You think she killed Jonny?" Jason asked.

"I spent time in her hometown. I talked to her old friends. The woman she was out drinking with that night, the night Jonny died, she said she'd seen it in her face when they came back into the trailer. A moment of victory. She said Marcie hated being married. She'd hoped he'd die. And then he did. How rare that the terrible things we hope for actually happen. Yes, I think she killed Jonny." She leaned across the table conspiratorially. "And more than that, my mama says she *knows* she did. It's in the air around her. Bad juju."

"But she's out there walking around without a care in the world?" Jason said. "With Keisha and all William's money? And you can't do anything for me? To help me?" He couldn't keep the pleading desperation out of his voice. "Nothing?"

"I'm afraid not," Elizabeth said, with a sigh, as she leaned back in her chair. "There was a third choice for Marcie, you know."

"What do you mean?"

"She could have refused to choose. She could have let justice run its course. That's what a decent person would have done, don't you think? A *good* person? She could have told Detective Anderson everything I'd said and added another suspect to the pot. But no, Marcie didn't even consider that option. She only considered what was best for her."

Elizabeth studied Jason thoughtfully, before leaning back in close to the glass. "I can't save you. No one can do that. But I granted the wish of a dying woman and now I can grant the wish of a dying man. There's power in a dying man's wish."

Jason's eyes narrowed, confused. "What do you mean?"

"I'll give you a choice, just like I gave your wife.

Would you like me to leave Marcie be? To let her live her life regardless of the harm she causes others? Regardless of her slow murder of you in here? Do you love her enough for that? Or"—she smiled—"would you like me to take her own life from her when she's least expecting it? A fitting punishment for a murderess, perhaps? As I did with William for Eleanor?" She paused. "The choice is yours."

Jason smiled, and as her eyes burned, Elizabeth knew he could see the serpents shining in them.

"I know what I choose," he said.

Acknowledgments

F irstly, a big thank-you and apology to the people of Savannah, Georgia. I visited your city about three years ago for SIBA (Southern Independent Booksellers Alliance), and along with meeting so many wonderful independent booksellers there, I also fell in love with the town and knew I would have to make it a book's home at some point. I had intended to spend a month or two in an Airbnb getting to know the place last year, but sadly my wonderful father was diagnosed with terminal cancer and all travel plans were off the table so I could stay close to home. So, while I've tried my best to get things right, please forgive any inaccuracies that may be in the pages of this book; I had hoped to know the city better!

As well as the obvious thanks to my fabulous agents, Veronique Baxter at David Higham and Grainne Fox at Fletcher & Company, and exceptional editors, Natasha Bardon and David Highfill and ALL their teams who work so hard to make any book a reality, and who have me forever in their debt, there are several other people who need a mention with regard to *Dead to Her* in particular.

Big thanks to Lynn Radford, who was very generous in her bidding for charity to win naming a character in this book—I hope Keisha likes her namesake!

Kevin Wignall and Simon Kernick for always being there and being guaranteed to make me laugh even when it feels like the world is crumbling. I couldn't ask for better friends. Likewise, the Stony Stratford dog-walking posse, who keep me and Ted grounded and sane in the early mornings.

A massive thanks to Amanda Palmer for letting me use the lyrics from her brilliant "Runs in the Family," and also thanks to Neil Gaiman for making sure my request didn't get lost in the ether.

Thanks of course to Mark for putting up with me in the madness of deadline chasing and book angst and all the other self-absorbed activities authors get so wound up about. Welcome to the world of living with a writer ;-).

Yes, we are going to go on holiday now . . . well, once I've finished the next one.

And finally, thanks to all you readers, without whom this whole business would be pointless. You're super-stars.